In Lieu of You

Keith A Pearson

Inchgate Publishing

For more information about the author and to receive updates on his new releases, visit:

www.keithapearson.co.uk

This novel is dedicated to those who've wasted time in a relationship with the wrong person. We've all been there — some of us, more than once.

Keith A Pearson

Chapter 1

Over the years, I've read countless books on personal development. Some were inspiring, some were humdrum, but one sticks in my mind solely because of the title: *Don't Sweat The Small Stuff* by Dr Richard Carlson.

I read seven chapters. Five of them annoyed me immensely.

Whilst I could understand the core philosophy of not letting the trivialities of life get under your skin, I just couldn't buy into it. In fact, that book had the opposite effect on me, and I doubled down on my own philosophy. The small stuff *does* matter. It matters a lot.

Case in point this morning: the dishwasher.

Staring down at the plate and the coffee mug, I inwardly seethe. I've asked my wife, Clare, a hundred times to load the dishwasher trays from the back and to put mugs in the top tray. Her plate and coffee mug are at the front of the bottom tray, side by side. It's happened so many times that I can only draw one conclusion, that my wife does it just to wind me up.

On cue, she breezes into the kitchen, fresh from her morning shower and dressed for a day at work. I'm still standing in front of the dishwasher, my own coffee mug and plate in hand.

"Before you say anything," Clare remarks. "I'm in a hurry."

"It would have taken one extra second to put your mug and plate at the back of the tray. One bloody second."

"If it bothers you that much, move them yourself."

"Why should I? My time is a damn sight more valuable than yours."

"Really?" she snorts. "I wish you'd mentioned that before — I had no idea."

"I'm just making a point. I don't like wasting time."

"Then, why waste it on such a petty obsession? The world won't stop turning just because my dishwasher loading technique doesn't meet Gary Kirk's precise standards, will it?"

Point made, Clare checks the contents of her handbag and snatches her car keys from the side.

"I'll see you tonight," she says, hurrying back across the tiled floor without another glance in my direction.

I wait until I hear the front door close before puffing a sigh and then rearranging the dishwasher drawer.

We're set to celebrate our twenty-fifth wedding anniversary six months from now; although it seems highly unlikely we'll host a party, jet off to some foreign clime, or even mark the occasion with ten minutes of unfulfilling anniversary sex. Neither of us has said it, and we're both guilty of ignoring it, but our marriage is in trouble. At some point, possibly before our landmark anniversary, there's a good chance one of us will finally make a decision and bring an end to this charade. Mind you, I thought the same in the months running up to our twentieth wedding anniversary, and yet, here we are, still together.

Yep, it's fair to say that marriage is no longer an institution for Gary and Clare Kirk — it's that comfortable but threadbare pair of pants that I can't quite force myself to throw out. One more wear, and then I'll bin them. Just one more wear.

I shove the dishwasher drawer shut and file away the problems with my marriage for later. I've got a busy day ahead, and I need to be focused.

"Get your head in the game, Gary."

At seven-thirty on the dot, I open the front door to a bright spring morning. There's a slight chill in the air but not a single cloud in the sky, and our avian neighbours are in fine voice.

The journey to the other side of Elderton only takes fifteen minutes, yet the difference in the scenery is stark. Our home is situated in a select development of detached houses in the leafy southwest corner of the town, whereas Kirkwood Motors occupies a one-acre site in the industrialised area on the northern fringes of Elderton.

Ironically, though, I've spent many more hours of my life at the urban site than in the cosy confines of my suburban home. Clare has accused me of being a workaholic, but what she's never really understood is that if you've experienced life with nothing, you'll do almost anything to avoid having nothing again. I do work bloody hard, but it's who I am, and I make no apology for wanting to better myself.

One of the perks of being my own boss is that I get a prime parking spot next to the office building at the rear of the site. Money was tight when I first acquired the land, so the architect's brief was simple — design a two-storey building that could be constructed quickly and cheaply. He did exactly as I asked, as he did four years later when we added another building to the site. That building became home to a service centre and a body shop. It was a huge investment at the time, but it paid off as the additional services boosted profits. It also made our core business of selling used cars so much easier as we could service, repair, and tidy up the bodywork of the cars we brought into stock without the hassle and cost of using a third party.

I unlock the door at the side of the building and deactivate the alarm. Being the only one on site, for now, it's down to me to put the kettle on. Soon enough, though, I'll be joined by fourteen members of staff. Eight of those staff work in the office, including two salesmen, and the other six work in the service centre and body shop. It's a lot of pay cheques to cut every month, but I don't suffer quite as many sleepless nights about the responsibility as I used to.

Once I've made a cup of strong coffee, I head to my office. It benefits from windows facing both north and east, so I can view almost the entirety of my automotive empire. Some might consider it small fry but to Gary Kirk — a kid who grew up on a council estate and left school with barely a qualification to his name — it's a source of great pride. Yes, the business has experienced some challenging periods over the last twenty years, but ultimately, it's provided us with a decent quality of life.

One day, when the time is right, I'm hoping it'll fund the next chapter of that life.

Chapter 2

I've never had any preconceived ideas regarding the gender of my employees. If a female mechanic applied for a position and she was suitably qualified, she'd stand the same chance of success as any male applicant. However, in the twelve years since I opened the service centre, we've never received an application from a female mechanic. Equally, whenever I've advertised for admin staff, the vast majority of applicants were female.

Despite my open mind when it comes to gender roles, all six of the staff working in the service centre and body shop are men, and the six who work in the main office in admin roles, are women. My mum, who tends to see life in simple terms, once offered her opinion on the subject: women prefer organising, and men prefer fixing. The only two male employees who don't get their hands dirty on a daily basis are Mo and Justin, the two sales consultants tasked with helping our customers find the right car at the right price.

We are like a family in every sense — we get along most of the time, but occasionally, we fall out. On the whole, though, it's a happy ship.

"Morning, Gary," Janine says, poking her head around my office door. "Coffee?"

"I'm good, thanks."

"I'm not — I'm desperate! Do you mind if I grab one before the morning meeting?"

"Go for it."

Janine is the office manager and a single mum with two school-age boys. She secured the office manager's role four years ago after her youngest started school. The epitome of organised, I'm often in awe of her boundless energy levels, and I couldn't run Kirkwood Motors without her now.

I'm still trying to organise my diary when Janine returns with a mug of coffee in one hand and a folder in the other. She takes a seat in front of my desk.

"How was your weekend?" she asks before blowing across her coffee.

"Not bad. Yours?"

"I've had better if I'm honest. Stuart was supposed to take the boys out on Saturday, but he called ten minutes before he was due to arrive, saying he didn't feel well."

"That's a shitty thing to do."

"Par for the course with my ex, but it's not fair on the boys. They deserve better."

"Well, at least they have a superhero for a mum."

Janine finds a wan smile. "Thanks."

The sudden change in her body language signifies Janine's switch to business mode. She's not one to bring her woes to work, and now she's aired her grievance, it's time to put on her management hat.

"Anyway," she says brightly. "Want to know what today has in store for you?"

"Go for it."

We hold a ten-minute meeting every morning so we can assess what each of the three departments is up to. The service centre and body shop are expected to run at ninety per cent capacity, so any trends up or down signify we either need to hire additional staff or spend more on marketing. Both are booked close to target today.

"How many cars have we got going out?" I ask.

"Just the four today, but there's nine booked for tomorrow."

This is pretty typical as we sell more cars at the weekend, but it takes a couple of days to get them ready before the customer can collect their new motor. Each of those cars represents a not-insignificant chunk of profit, so it's critical I keep a close eye on the stock going out, as well as what's coming in.

Janine hands me a sheet of paper, providing a raft of information on the four cars heading out. I cast a brief eye over the document and I'm about to put it aside when I notice a vaguely familiar name in the bottom row of the spreadsheet. Elderton is a relatively small town, so it's not uncommon for me to spot a familiar name, but some stick out for the wrong reason.

"Darren Slade," I mumble to myself.

"Sorry?"

I look up from the sheet of paper. "Darren Slade. I see he's collecting a BMW X5 this morning."

"Yes, Mo sold it on Thursday. Why the interest?"

"It might not be the same guy, but there was a kid at my junior school called Darren Slade."

"He'll be here at eleven if you want to say hello."

"I might just do that," I reply, sliding the sheet of paper onto my desk. "But for now, anything else on the agenda for today?"

"Kate Palfrey from the Elderton Herald wants to interview you at three this afternoon."

"Err, why?"

"About Friday?"

I stare back at Janine, perplexed.

"The awards dinner at the town hall? I did remind you last week."

"Ohh, right. Yes."

A few months back, Janine entered Kirkwood Motors into the Elderton Business of The Year Awards, and the winner will be announced at an event on Friday evening. I don't rate our chances, so I'd put it to the back of my mind.

"Even if we don't win, we'll still get a ton of free publicity," Janine continues. "Which is why it's important you make a good impression with the reporter from the Herald."

"Okay. Noted."

Janine then moves the conversation on to more mundane matters, like last month's management accounts. I only half listen as my mind is still lingering on the possibility of being crowned Business of The Year and the interview this afternoon. I've never been interviewed by a newspaper reporter before, and although it's only the local rag, it's still another notch on my list of accomplishments.

We finish up the meeting, and Janine gets to her feet. I clear my throat.

"I know I don't say it enough, but I do appreciate everything you do. We might not win on Friday, but we wouldn't even be in with a chance if it wasn't for you, so thank you."

"I remember all the times you've cut me slack when I've been late or had to take a day off when one of the boys has been ill, so the appreciation is mutual."

We swap smiles, and Janine turns on her heels. I watch her all the way to the door, which she pulls half-shut behind her. Alone again, I return my attention to the computer monitor.

An hour later, having completed every task that requires my attention, I leave my office and head downstairs to the sales floor. Roughly the size of a tennis court and enclosed on two sides by floor-to-ceiling windows, it's my favourite part of the entire site because it's where I feel most at home.

I sold my first car at the age of seventeen: a 1982 Austin Maxi. I paid two-hundred quid for an untidy example of British motor manufacturing, but I didn't care how ugly or temperamental it was because I knew I could sell it for a modest profit. The thrill of doubling my money on that deal remains one of my career highlights because it set me on the path to where I am today. It was the genesis of Kirkwood Motors.

The sales floor is large enough that we're able to display four prestige motors, which we rotate on a fortnightly basis. The four cars currently on display are worth over £150,000 retail and include a gleaming black Tesla Model 3, barely a year old.

I make my way past the cars to the area where our two sales staff live. Each has a desk, and there's an informal seating area with a coffee machine that cost more than some of the cheaper cars we sell. It was supposed to be for the benefit of our customers, but Mo and Justin seem to get more use out of it than anyone.

"Alright, Boss," Mo chirps once he notices me.

"Not bad. Where's Justin?"

"Outside with a customer. Not often we see someone car hunting at this time on a Monday morning."

"They must be keen. I hear you've got a customer of your own due in soon. Darren Slade?"

Mo glances at his monitor momentarily.

"Yeah, he's collecting an X5."

I perch on the edge of Mo's desk and double-check the exact details of the car Mr Slade is due to collect.

"That colour and spec level is rare."

"I know. The customer said he's been looking for the best part of two months."

"He must be delighted."

"Put it this way — he didn't haggle over the price or take much convincing to pay a holding deposit."

I ponder Mo's reply for a moment before asking a final question.

"What was he like?"

"Not sure what you mean, Boss."

"Was he polite?"

"Civilised, but he was, um …"

Mo appears reluctant to confirm his exact thoughts.

"Just be honest, Mo. I'm interested in your opinion."

"He was a bit standoffish, arrogant even. You know what some blokes are like when they're paying top money for a car; they think they're something special."

I glance up at the clock on the wall behind Mo's desk. Fifteen minutes until Darren Slade is due.

"I'll do the handover to Mr Slade," I confirm.

"Err, okay. Do you mind if I ask why?"

"I'm almost certain we were at junior school together. I think it'll be a nice surprise to catch up with him after almost thirty-five years."

"Right, no problem."

Mo confirms the car is waiting outside in the collection area, and then he hands over an envelope containing all the documentation the customer needs to read and sign. That done, I suggest he goes on a break while I use his desk.

Once Mo has scooted off, I sit down and wait. This isn't how I expected to spend part of my morning, but I can't deny I'm looking forward to catching up with Darren Slade.

Chapter 3

My dad, Dave Kirk, has a life motto he's always willing to share with anyone who'll listen — *use it or lose it.* The *it* he's referring to is the human body.

At sixty-eight years of age, he's as fit as a flea and puts his good health down to the fact he exercises every single day, although he doesn't maintain his fitness in the kind of swanky gym I joined a few years back. No, Dad prefers to get his exercise in the great outdoors, either on his allotment or by regularly rambling across every hill and dale in Hampshire.

Because I respect my dad and I'm also on the vintage side of forty, I've willingly adopted his motto. I'm almost the perfect weight for my six-foot frame, and I like to think my regular gym visits have helped delay the ageing process by a few years at least.

The same cannot be said of the man waddling across the sales floor in my direction.

Maybe an inch or two shorter than me and at least six stone heavier, I'm no longer sure this is the same Darren Slade who attended West End Junior School. I remember that kid being much taller and thinner. More surprising, however, is that he can afford a forty-grand motor, considering his wayward attendance at school. I heard he was expelled from the secondary school he eventually attended — fortunately, not the same one as me.

"Mr Slade?" I ask as the man approaches.

"Yeah, that's right," he replies. "I'm here to collect a BMW X5."

I offer my hand. He appears reluctant to shake it but eventually does, probably because his hand is as clammy as it is chubby.

"Please. Take a seat."

"Where's the Asian kid?" he asks in a disparaging tone while carefully lowering his fat arse towards an unfortunate chair.

"Mo? He's tied up with another customer at the moment, so you'll have to put up with me. I'm Gary, by the way."

It's clear from his lack of interest that Darren Slade certainly doesn't recognise me. I need to check I'm talking to the right man.

"Excuse me for asking," I say in as polite a tone as possible. "Did you ever attend West End Junior School?"

"I did. A long time ago."

Now he's confirmed what I suspected, I don't know how much longer I'll be able to maintain my plastic smile. I'd all but cast Darren Slade from my mind, but the moment I spotted his name in print, the memories flooded back.

"I went to West End, too, which is why your name sounded familiar."

He takes an exaggerated look at his watch. "Can we cut the small talk? I've got a meeting in an hour."

"Of course. My apologies."

I open the envelope and pull out the documents relating to the sale.

"Right, I see you paid a £500 holding deposit, which means there's a balance to pay of ..."

I slide my finger down the page until I reach the bottom of the invoice, confirming a balance of £39,500.

"A balance of £79,500. How would you like to pay, Mr Slade?"

"Jesus wept," he huffs. "The balance is £39,500."

"It was, but unfortunately, the price of that particular car doubled this morning."

"Don't piss me around," he barks, his face reddening. "Someone has cocked up the paperwork, obviously. I paid a deposit last week, and the screen price of that motor was £40,000."

"You also signed a pre-contract agreement, which states that until the balance of the invoice is paid, Kirkwood Motors reserve the right to withdraw from the agreement at the discretion of the business owner."

"You'd better bloody fetch him, then, 'cos I ain't got time for this shit."

Sitting back in my chair, I summon a thin smile. "I'm the owner. Gary Kirk."

I wait to see if my name rings any bells. Judging by his frown, I'd guess not.

"You don't recognise me, which is understandable, but I thought you'd recognise my name, Darren. I was in the year below you at West End Junior School."

"Why the hell should I remember some kid from school? It was decades ago."

"I remember quite a lot from my time at West End, Darren. In fact, I can vividly recall a three-month period in the autumn term, almost as if it happened yesterday. I'm surprised you can't."

If his body language is any barometer, Darren Slade is close to losing his cool. He leans his arm on the desk and fixes me with a baleful glare. "I ain't got time to listen to your trip down Memory Lane. Sort out your admin cock-up so I can be on my way."

"There is no cock-up, Darren, and as I've already explained, the price of that car is now £80,000. Do you want it or not?"

"You can't do this."

"I can, and I have. Call it penance for what you put me through at school."

"What?"

"I doubt you knew it at the time, but my family didn't have much, which is why Mum bought my school shoes from the market. Granted, they were clumpy and cheap looking, but for some reason, you and your mate, Lee, decided to seek me out every break time just to take the piss out of my shoes. You did it for weeks and weeks."

"For fuck's sake," Slade groans. "You're stiffing me on a deal just because of some childish banter at junior school?"

"No, I'm stiffing you on a deal because of what you did one day *after* school. Do you remember?"

His reply comes in the form of a grunt and a shrug.

"You and Lee cornered me in the underpass as I walked home. After more verbals and a bit of pushing and shoving, Lee held me down while you pulled my shoes off. Remember throwing them in the canal?"

"Eh? No."

"You say no, Darren, but I've worked in the used-car trade since I was seventeen, and you know what they say: you can't bullshit a bullshitter. You must remember what you did because you took so much glee from taunting me about it for the rest of the school term."

"I was just a dumb kid, alright. If it's an apology you want, fine — I'm sorry."

"No, I don't want an apology. I want you to remove your fat arse from that chair and get the fuck out of my showroom."

To emphasise my point, I stand up and fix Slade with a suitably aggressive glare.

"What about my deposit?" he replies after swallowing hard and clambering to his feet.

"It'll be refunded within seven working days, minus £50 to cover the cost of those shoes, plus thirty-five years of interest."

I step around the desk and stand toe-to-toe with my childhood Nemesis.

"And if you think about complaining to anyone, or posting a negative review about my business online, don't forget I've got your address on file. Nothing would give me greater pleasure than dropping by and smacking you in the mouth a few times."

Like most bullies, when confronted, Slade cowers into his shell and avoids eye contact. Shoulders slumped, and without saying another word, he turns and shuffles back towards the main doors.

"Have a nice day," I call after him.

Once Slade has skulked away, I leave a note on Mo's desk to confirm the sale fell through, but he'll still get his commission. That done, and with good fortune seemingly on my side today, I head back up to my office to take full advantage.

My good luck seems to hold as an hour later I end a call with a potential new stock supplier — one I've been chasing for months — having booked a meeting next week. Securing reliable suppliers of reasonably priced, good-quality cars is a never-ending challenge in this game, so the possibility of working with a large leasing company could be a real boon for Kirkwood Motors.

I'm about to celebrate my constructive morning with a panini and a Danish pastry when my phone beeps to signify a text message. It's from Clare — *I'll be late tonight. X*

The kiss at the end is how Clare signs off every message, rather than a small sign of affection. The lack of detail is also a sign of how little we communicate these days. A few years ago, she would at least offer a cursory explanation why she wouldn't be home in time for dinner, and apologise. Now, I wonder why she bothers at all.

I don't resent Clare working late, but I do resent how I'm expected to change my plans without question. As annoyed as I am, there's no point in complaining because we've been there so many times in the past. My wife sees her vocation as a calling, and it takes priority. I see it as utter claptrap.

When I first set up Kirkwood Motors, I couldn't afford staff so Clare would come in once a week to help out with the admin. Like all young couples trying to forge their way in the world, we endured some tough times, financially. However, after a year or so, I was able to afford a full-time administrator, much to Clare's relief.

A few months later, Clare's younger sister, Mandy, invited my wife to a Shamanic retreat in the New Forest. It sounded like a new-age cult to me, but Mandy was into spirituality and pseudo-therapies, and I presumed my wife was only going along to keep her sister company. Little did I know how much that weekend would change our lives.

Clare returned from the retreat a different woman. Over the ensuing weeks and months, she trained to become a Shamanic healer, and even though I couldn't see the point, I wanted to support my wife as much as she'd supported me while I was building my career. Not that I ever shared my scepticism with Clare, but I thought it was a fad that would pass in time. Then, she came home one day and revealed her plans for setting up a Shamanic healing centre here in Elderton.

If Clare had set up her new venture as a business, I might have been more enthusiastic, but she didn't want to charge for her so-called treatments and intended to run it as a charity. The entire enterprise would operate solely from donations and fundraising, and my wife would earn next to nothing. Despite my continued scepticism, I tried to remain supportive.

Clare eventually managed to persuade the local council to lease her the small building that once housed the children's library before it was amalgamated into the main library. Because of the charitable status, the rent was heavily subsidised, but Clare would have to find the money to cover the cost of internally refurbishing the building. And so began a frenetic period of fundraising.

Eight months later, Clare finally realised her ambition as she stood with a host of local dignitaries to watch the town's mayor officially open Tungus Lodge — the name my wife decided to bestow on the former children's library building.

Ironically, Clare's sister eventually lost all interest in Shamanic healing after she met a new man, Dean. They married, and then the first of their two kids arrived. As Mandy settled down into her traditional but contented life, my wife took a journey in the opposite direction.

At the time, it was clear how much Tungus Lodge meant to Clare, but her enthusiasm became an obsession as the years rolled by. To this day, she continues to run her charity on a shoestring budget, not once admitting to herself that perhaps the good people of Elderton prefer conventional fixes to their ills rather than obscure treatments like soul retrieval, ancestral healing, and energy-balancing workshops.

Looking back over the last decade, it's now obvious that our marriage has long been a secondary concern to both of us. I've focused all my attention on Kirkwood Motors while Clare has fully committed herself to Tungus Lodge. On my part, I'm glad that Clare had her own obsession because it meant she had little time to question mine.

One husband, one wife, two separate lives. It's a minor miracle we've stayed together as long as we have.

Chapter 4

I went to bed just after ten last night. Clare was still at Tungus Lodge, presumably. Some of her workshops don't begin until eight o'clock in the evening, and they can run for two or three hours, depending on the energy levels in the room, apparently. Personally, I much prefer the energy levels in the pub, but each to their own.

Such is the difference in our nocturnal routines and our individual needs for sleep, we decided some years ago it would be beneficial if we slept in separate bedrooms. Initially, it was just a convenient way to ensure we both got a decent night's sleep but over time, our respective bedrooms have evolved into our own personal domains to furnish, decorate, and occupy as we see fit.

It's been both an interesting and perhaps alarming experiment, highlighted whenever I have reason to step foot in Clare's bedroom.

"What time did you get back?" I ask while standing in the doorway, grimacing at the clutter strewn across every flat surface.

"Just before midnight," she replies from the vanity table, her back to me as she brushes her hair in the mirror.

"Right. Everything okay?"

"I was working on the plans for Tungus Lodge … when we get the funding."

I've no idea what funding she's referring to, but the 'we' in question is her charity's only other employee, Angie. Clare hired her as a part-time therapist a few years back, although Angie seems to spend almost as much time at Tungus Lodge as my wife. I've met her a few times, and on the first occasion, Angie offered to cleanse the toxic energy from my aura. I declined, and every time I've met her since, my initial view has not changed — she's batshit crazy.

"Sorry, what funding?"

"I thought I told you."

"No."

"We desperately need more space which means building an extension. I applied for a grant a few months ago, and we're expecting a decision any day now. I want to be prepared to get on with the building work without delay."

"Oh, okay."

"We'll probably need a bit more money over and above the grant if you're interested in making a donation."

"Hasn't my business donated enough to Tungus Lodge in one way or another?"

"You have, but I wouldn't say no to another cheque."

Despite Clare only taking the minimum wage the law allows, Tungus Lodge remains perpetually underfunded, according to my wife. Via my business, I've donated sizeable sums over the years, but there are limits. Like most charities, no matter how much money they receive through donations, it's never enough.

"What happens if you don't get the funding?" I ask.

"That should be a moot point because an inside source at Elderton Council tells me we're odds-on favourite to get what we asked for."

"I'll keep my fingers crossed for you."

Clare doesn't respond, and I'm temporarily distracted when I catch sight of a pile of dirty laundry on the floor next to the wash basket.

"We should hire a cleaner," I remark.

"Why?"

"To clean."

"I'll do the washing later. I'm not paying someone to wash my smalls."

"And hoovering?"

Clare's reflection in the mirror glares back at me. "Shouldn't you be on your way to work by now?"

"I'm just going, but I wanted to remind you about the awards dinner on Friday evening and double-check you're still coming."

"I'm not going to lie, Gary — it did slip my mind."

"You don't have to come. It's entirely up to you."

"No, I'll come along. Who will be there?"

"The usual freeloaders from the council, I expect, and our local MP, apparently. The Herald are sending a photographer and a reporter."

"I'd better think about what to wear," she replies. "Presuming you don't want me turning up in jeans and a sweater?"

"A dress would be good. Maybe that dark-blue one you wore to the Christmas party last year."

"I didn't make the Christmas party last year."

"Oh, right. Maybe the year before?"

"It was four years ago, Gary, and I'm not sure it'll still fit me."

"Was it really four years ago? Christ, where does the time go?"

It was a rhetorical question, but Clare answers it with a slight shake of her head and a sigh.

"Anyway," I remark, checking my watch. "I'll see you tonight."

"Yeah, bye," she replies, returning her attention to the mirror.

Ten minutes later, I'm sitting in a slow-moving queue of traffic. The cause, some hundred yards ahead, is a set of temporary traffic lights. It's an opportunity to ponder what I should do about my marriage. I've asked myself a thousand times if I truly love Clare, and I still don't know the answer. I care about her deeply, but that's not enough to sustain a marriage, is it?

As for physical attraction, it's telling that I can still remember a dress Clare last wore four years ago. She looked stunning that evening, but it was a rare one-off. Clare dresses for comfort these days and seems to take less and less pride in her appearance with every passing year. I'm not a superficial man, but anyone who says that physical attraction plays no part in a relationship is a liar. For that reason I sometimes wonder if my wife dresses as she does to avoid my attention. Our sex life is virtually non-existent, and I can count on one hand how many times we've shared a bed over the last five years. I'm almost certain we haven't had sex in a year, and before that, the sex we had was more an act of need rather than desire — we both needed a release, and all that was missing was a handshake and a polite thank you afterwards.

The traffic lights finally change.

An hour later, I'm about to wrap up the morning meeting with Janine when she throws me a question.

"Do you want me to organise some flowers for your parents?"

"Err, I'm not with you."

"It's their anniversary today."

"Shit. Thank you for reminding me."

"You could put it in your own diary, you know."

"I did, I think."

I click the mouse to bring up my online diary. There is indeed a note about Mum and Dad's anniversary, but no reminder set. Thankfully, I have a highly efficient office manager to cover my arse.

"So? Flowers?"

"No, don't worry, thanks. Seeing that there's not a lot in my schedule this morning, I might pop over and see them."

"Don't forget you've got a meeting with Adrian at one."

"How could I possibly forget the prospect of listening to our accountant for an hour? It's the highlight of my month."

"You're being sarcastic?"

"Yes, I am. And don't worry, I'm painfully aware of how much Adrian charges, so I won't be late."

We finish our meeting, and the second Janine leaves my office, I pick up the phone. My call is answered on the fourth ring, Mum announcing the phone number forever etched in my memory. Much like my parents, it hasn't changed in decades.

"It's only me," I reply. "Happy anniversary."

"Morning, Sweetheart, and thank you."

"I was just checking if you're likely to be home later this morning. I was hoping to pop over for a quick cup of tea and a natter."

"That'd be nice. Let me just check with your dad."

Mum then covers the receiver, so all I get to hear is a muffled conversation. It doesn't last long.

"We'll be here."

"Great. I'll see you in an hour or two."

I end the call and turn my attention back to the list of tasks I have to complete before I can leave. Some might argue that being able to skive off whenever I fancy is a perk of being boss, but it's not really a perk at all. Everything on my to-do list will remain on my to-do list because there's no one else to complete it. I can delegate certain jobs, but ultimately, there are some jobs and some decisions that are mine and mine alone.

Time passes quickly when you're busy, and before I know it, it's eleven o'clock. I confirm with Janine that I'm heading out for an hour and then hurry down to my car. The journey itself is relatively short, and I've time to pick up a bunch of flowers and a card on the way.

Number 16 Denby Place is a two-bedroom ground-floor maisonette in a block of six identical maisonettes. It's one of eight blocks that make up the small estate where my parents have lived for almost their entire adult lives. It's also the same estate I spent the first nineteen years of my life, although it's changed beyond recognition since then. Growing up in the eighties, every one of the maisonettes was owned by the council, but now I think they're all privately owned after Thatcher's 'Right to Buy' scheme gifted tenants the option to buy their homes. My parents bought number 16 in the early nineties, and after twenty-five years of diligently paying their mortgage every month, they now own every brick and tile.

I ring the doorbell, and Mum opens the front door.

"I thought you'd forgotten where we live," she jokes. "Come in."

I step into the hallway and give Mum a peck on the cheek before kicking off my shoes. My mother is house proud to the point of obsessive, and woe betide anyone who dares enter her home with their shoes on.

"Come on through," she beckons.

Dad is sitting in his armchair in the lounge and drops a magazine on his lap when I enter.

"Morning, Son," he beams. "How's tricks?"

"Not bad. You?"

"Mustn't grumble."

If there was ever a phrase that sums up Dave and Sue Kirk's outlook on life, it just passed Dad's lips. Anyone who lived through the early eighties in Britain would tell you how tough times were, but my parents did their damnedest to protect me from the harsh economic realities of the time. And, they did it with good grace, never complaining about their lot in life.

"What brings you over here on a weekday morning, then?" Dad asks as Mum bustles off to put the kettle on.

"Your wedding anniversary. I hope you haven't forgotten."

"Course I haven't."

"I wanted to see if you fancied doing anything later. Dinner, maybe — my treat."

"That's a nice thought, but your mum and I have plans. It's quiz night at The Rose & Crown, so we thought we'd have fish and chips for our dinner and wander up there."

"You'd rather have a chippy tea and a few pints at The Rose & Crown than spend the evening at a nice restaurant?"

"Yes, we would," Mum replies, returning to the lounge. "It's lovely of you to suggest a fancy restaurant, but we like our pleasures simple, don't we, Dave?"

"Absolutely."

"Fair enough. Is there anything you'd like as a present?"

"Seeing as the chance of a grandchild is now long gone," Mum replies with a wry smile "I don't think there's anything else we want."

Mum's remark is one she throws in my direction every now and then, and even though there's no malice intended, it never quite loses its sting.

"Would a puppy help fill that grandchild-sized hole in your life?" I respond, tongue in cheek.

"The last thing I want is a puppy running around the place, doing its business behind the sofa, thank you very much."

"That's a no, then?"

Mum comes over and sits on the sofa next to me. "You know I'm only kidding about the grandchild, Sweetheart. I shouldn't say it."

"It's alright, but you know you're not the only one who's lost out. I might have wanted kids, too."

"Too busy at work, I'd imagine," Dad interjects. "Children are a job in themselves."

"Besides," Mum continues. "It's silly of me to gripe about what we haven't got when we've been so blessed. We have our health, a lovely home, and a son we couldn't be more proud of."

Mum cements her statement with a squeeze of my hand.

Perhaps because of their aversion to grumbling my parents are possibly the most grateful people I've ever met. It might be argued that life hasn't given them a lot, not in terms of material possessions, but what they have is seemingly enough for a happy life.

"That's lovely of you to say, Mum, but I can't let your anniversary pass without buying you a present. There must be something you'd like."

"Save your money for our fiftieth," Dad replies. "We quite fancy one of those European river cruises we saw on TV."

"Shame about the cost," Mum adds. "But we've got two years to save."

"No, you haven't. You choose the holiday of your dreams, and I'll pay for it — no arguments."

"But, Sweetheart, those cruises cost thousands."

"I don't care what the cost is. Besides, I'm planning to sell Kirkwood Motors within the next two years, so money won't be a problem when your fiftieth wedding anniversary rolls around."

"You've made your mind up, then?" Dad asks. "You're definitely selling up?"

"Yep, and I've got a meeting with my accountant later to go over the figures."

"What does Clare think?" Mum asks.

"Um, she doesn't have any strong opinion."

"Doesn't she?"

Mum's arched eyebrows are a clear sign that she doesn't quite believe me. I'd never want to play poker with my mum because there's no point bluffing when she's at the table.

"We haven't discussed it," I admit.

"Why not?"

"Because ... because I'm not sure we'll still be married by the time I sell the business."

If my revelation comes as a shock to my parents, it doesn't show in either of their expressions.

"You're not happy, are you?" Mum says.

"Not really, Mum, no. I don't think either of us is happy, truth be told."

"In which case, do what you have to do — you'll always have our support."

"You're not disappointed?"

"Of course we're disappointed because we always hoped you might have what we've got."

"I've got piles the size of plums," Dad interjects. "He wouldn't want those."

Mum tries to stifle a chuckle. "David Kirk," she chides. "I'm trying to have a serious conversation with our son."

"Sorry. Carry on."

"Listen, Sweetheart," Mum continues. "You're still a relatively young man, and there's plenty of time for you to meet someone else. It'll be painful, as all divorces are, but there's no sense in living a lie. If you're not happy, you've got to move on."

"I just hope Clare feels the same way."

"I think we all know that your wife isn't happy unless she's playing with crystals or summoning spirits. Don't get me wrong — everyone needs a passion in life — but Clare chose Tungus Lodge over her marriage long ago."

It's fair to say that Clare has made as little effort with my parents as she has with our marriage. I can't blame her because, deep down, I think she's always been a little jealous of my relationship with Mum and Dad. Clare's mum passed away the year after we married, and she's never had any kind of relationship with her dad.

"You'll see her alright, money-wise?" Dad then asks, ever the pragmatist.

"Of course. I've already paid up the mortgage on the house, and she'll get half of whatever we sell it for, plus there's a tidy sum in our savings account. She'll walk away with more than enough to start again."

Satisfied with my answer, Dad jokingly asks Mum what happened to the cup of tea she promised. I then swap small talk with my parents for another half hour before making my excuses.

"Are you sure there's nothing you want for your anniversary?" I confirm while putting my shoes back on.

"I've already got everything I need," she replies, and I believe her.

"Alright. Maybe we can go out for lunch on Sunday if you can find time in your busy social calendar."

"We'll see," Mum says with a smile. "It's hard work, being retired, you know."

"Clearly."

I depart with a goodbye hug and head back to work. Now I have my parents' blessing regarding a divorce, I just need to work on the practicalities. Hopefully, the man I'm due to meet shortly will help on that front because he knows the factors that will determine my timescale.

It might still be a year or two away, but 'Project Single' is slowly coming together.

Chapter 5

Adrian Griffin is a similar age to me and we both own successful businesses. However, we've followed very different paths through life to reach the same point. Adrian went to a private school and studied accountancy at university before working in the City for ten years. He then returned to Elderton and set up Griffin & Co. We met at a networking event where he approached me, intent on pitching the benefits of his business over the accountancy firm I was using at the time.

Adrian might be a great accountant, but he's no salesman, as our first meeting proved. He turned up to sell the benefits of his business and left an hour later, having agreed to buy a Jaguar XE for twenty grand. I'm not sure he really wanted a new car, but he got one, and I eventually agreed to use Griffin & Co to manage our company accounts.

"Good to see you again, Adrian," I say, shaking his hand. "Grab a seat."

He smiles warmly and places his briefcase on my desk.

"Can I get you a tea or coffee before we start?"

"I'm good, thank you, Gary. I overindulged at lunch."

The other area where we're different is our aesthetics. Adrian is stocky, round-faced and dresses like a country squire, always bedecked in a tweed suit and matching waistcoat.

We chat for a few minutes about nothing in particular before I glance at my watch. Adrian notices.

"Don't panic, old boy," he chuckles. "This is a fixed-fee consultation, so no need to clock watch."

"In which case, maybe you could valet a few cars when we're done in here. I like to get my money's worth."

"I don't think your customers would be too pleased with my woeful cleaning skills, as Mrs Griffin will gladly attest."

Adrian laughs at his own quip and then unlocks his briefcase.

"So, Gary," he begins. "You wanted an assessment of the current state of play regarding assets and liabilities, correct?"

"That about sums it up."

"Not that I would discourage you from spending money with my firm, but you could have waited until your annual accounts are prepared. The end of the financial year is only weeks away."

"True, but I know it usually takes a couple of months to compile the accounts, and I need the information sooner."

"Tell me to mind my own business, but why the rush?"

I glance over Adrian's shoulder just to double-check that my office door is shut.

"Whatever I tell you, it's treated in the strictest confidence, right?"

"That goes without saying. Anything you tell me will remain between the two of us ... unless you're planning on setting up a money-laundering scheme, in which case I'm duty-bound to tell the authorities."

"No, it's nothing nefarious. I'm planning to sell up."

"Oh," Adrian responds, seemingly surprised. "When?"

"That very much depends on what you tell me over the next fifteen minutes, but I had hoped to be out of here within two years."

"I see. We'd better get on with it then."

He plucks a folder from his briefcase, together with a pair of tortoiseshell reading glasses.

"What exactly is it you want to know, Gary? Specifically?"

"When the mortgage on the site ends, and the loan I took out for the service centre and body shop building."

"Understood. Give me a few seconds to find the relevant information."

Adrian returns to the folder and flicks through a thick wad of papers. He eventually finds what he's looking for and extracts a spreadsheet.

"The good news is that the final mortgage payment on the site is due in December this year."

"That's just about the best Christmas present I could ask for."

"Indeed, but I seem to recall you took out the loan a few years after you purchased the site, correct?"

"Correct."

Adrian runs a sausage-like finger across the page and then down to the bottom.

"From today, you've still got twenty-two monthly repayments to make."

"What if I wanted to pay off the loans early?"

"You can, but according to my documentation, you'd incur financial penalties for early settlement. Depending on when you settled, you could be looking at a penalty of £25,000."

"Ouch."

"Not what you were hoping to hear?"

"Yes, and no. I wasn't planning on selling up tomorrow, but I'm keen to sell up as soon as the debts are cleared. There's no way I want to be running this business with my fiftieth birthday approaching."

"In which case, you don't have a problem. You're forty-five at the moment, aren't you?"

"I am."

"So, you'll only be forty-seven once the loans are settled. Even if it takes you a year to sell the business, you'll be a free man long before your fiftieth."

"That's what I wanted to hear, but there is one other question I'm hoping you can answer. How much do you think the business is worth?"

"Well, I'll need to go away and crunch the numbers, but I can probably get an answer to you within a week."

"If you could, that'd be great. It's hard to plan ahead without knowing how much I'll have to fund the next phase of my life."

"What are your plans once you sell the business?" Adrian then asks.

"I'm still fine-tuning my plans, but I intend to go travelling for a couple of months."

"Isn't travelling usually the remit of uni students on a gap year?"

"I'm not travelling for pleasure or to find myself. There's a growing market in importing and exporting classic cars, so my travels will be for research purposes. A month in America and a few weeks in Australia, hopefully."

"You want to start a new business?"

The slight inflexion at the end of Adrian's question suggests he's surprised.

"Not just a new business — a bigger, better business."

"It's a bold move if I might say. You already have a successful business here in Elderton."

"I guess that depends on your definition of successful. There's a limit to how much I can earn with Kirkwood Motors, but there's no limit on what I might earn with an import and export business."

"Sounds like you've made your mind up."

"There's still a lot of planning and research to do before the real work begins, but yes, I think my mind is made up."

I like Adrian, but we're not close friends, so I'd never admit to him that I don't have every aspect of my future mapped out — there's the small matter of my marriage.

We finish the meeting and my accountant departs with a promise to get back to me with a valuation figure as soon as possible.

The rest of the afternoon is routine, and once I've cleared my to-do list, I turn my thoughts to a question Adrian asked. Specifically, the way he asked it. As good an accountant as he is, I wouldn't expect him to understand my motivation for starting a new business.

Adrian has slipped into a life of easy hours and long lunches. He's enjoyed a comfortable life from childhood, and he seems content continuing that comfortable life until the day he retires. I've never asked, but I'd imagine his comfort is born from never having faced the alternative. I, on the other hand, have, and if there's one surefire way to experience it again, it's allowing complacency to take hold.

I've got to keep pushing on, planning, plotting, and growing. Yes, I've built a successful business, but our industry is changing fast, and I'm paranoid that one day it'll move at such a pace that small used-car dealerships like Kirkwood Motors will become obsolete. Some might call me paranoid, but over the years, I've met plenty of business owners who no longer attend networking events on account they're no longer in business.

However, of all the business owners I've met over the years, there's one in particular that sticks in my mind, although I never met him at a networking event.

When I was a teenager, maybe fourteen or fifteen, there was a video rental store a few streets away from where we lived. The guy who owned it, Jonny Collins, had spent a decade building his business to the point he had two branches in Elderton and three more in neighbouring towns. One reason Jonny sticks in my mind is that he owned a bright-red Porsche 911. Apart from in magazines, I'd never seen a Porsche until the day I left the video store, just as Jonny pulled up outside. To a kid from a council estate, it was like being in the presence of a movie star or professional footballer, such was my awe.

Jonny didn't spark my interest in cars, but he did spark my interest in business and making money. I desperately wanted what he had.

I don't remember exactly when, but some years later, I spotted Jonny in a supermarket car park. He'd traded the bright-red Porsche for a rusty Ford Escort, and his designer suit for an ill-fitting staff uniform. I didn't want to embarrass the guy by asking what happened to his business empire, but I did make a few enquiries later that day.

Even with the benefit of hindsight, Jonny Collins should have noticed the shift away from video and DVD rental long before the bailiffs turned up to change the locks at all five of his stores. Unsurprisingly, personal bankruptcy soon followed for Jonny.

It's funny, but I can pick and choose almost any car I want these days, but even though I lusted after a Porsche 911 as a kid, I will never own one. To me, that model of car is now cursed, and every time I see one on the road, it reminds me of how quickly the complacent can fall.

I don't intend to be one of them.

Chapter 6

Three days after my meeting with Adrian, I'm still eagerly awaiting his call with the business valuation figure. Last night, I binge-watched a TV series featuring an auction house that specialises in selling classic cars. I don't believe in fate, but it certainly fuelled my determination, and I couldn't stop thinking about it as I sipped coffee at the breakfast table this morning.

For now, though, I'm having issues with another table and who'll be sharing it with me this evening.

"None of them?" I repeat to Janine, currently sitting on the opposite side of my desk.

"Wayne is going away for the weekend, Jimmy has an important darts match, Connor is attending his mate's birthday party, Shay has to babysit because his wife is going out, and Addy has a family function he can't get out of."

"What about Steve?"

"He said, and I quote, I'd rather spend the evening trying to lick my own arsehole."

"That's a no from Steve, then?"

"I'd say so."

I flop back in my chair and sigh. "How many of the admin staff are coming?"

"Me, obviously, and Alice, Julie, and Ayisha, plus partners."

"That's nine of us, assuming my wife doesn't cancel at the last minute."

"What about Mo and Justin?"

"Mo is working tomorrow and claims he likes to be in bed by nine on a Friday."

It's Mo's turn to work tomorrow, alongside our weekend sales staff, Jeff and Andrea.

"Do you believe him?" Janine asks.

"He's a used-car salesman — of course he's lying. I'm not going to force him to come."

"And Justin?"

"He said he'll try to make it, but he's picking up his sister from the airport at seven. Jeff and Andrea both have prior commitments."

"So, nine definite and one maybe?"

"Looks like it," I huff. "That's a poor show considering I booked a table for twenty."

"It's their loss, Gary," Janine replies in a consolatory tone. "We'll still have a great evening; especially if we win."

"I suppose so, but it would be even sweeter to have the whole team there."

"If you're looking for a silver lining, the garage staff were always most likely to get drunk and make tits of themselves. It could be a blessing in disguise that none of them wants to come."

"That's true. I still have nightmares about the Christmas party."

"Exactly."

Janine then glances at her watch. "If there's nothing else, do you mind if I get going?"

"Go for it, and I'll see you circa seven o'clock."

"Yes, you will," she replies with a grin.

Once Janine hurries off to pick up her boys from school, I check my own schedule for the rest of the afternoon. For once, my to-do list is relatively short, so I take a rare moment to sit back in my seat and breathe. My thoughts turn to Janine and what she's got on her plate between now and seven o'clock this evening. I once overheard a conversation between Janine and Alice, in which the latter asked the former how she managed to be so organised. Janine then explained that, as a single parent, her life would quickly descend into chaos if she didn't methodically plan every minute of her day. Personally, I don't know how she does it. I guess every parent just finds a way, but I never got the chance to find out.

There came a point, maybe five or six years ago, when Mum stopped asking when we were going to give her a grandchild. Perhaps she tired of hearing the same excuse, or maybe she just woke up one day, resigned to the fact that no one would ever call her grandma, so what was the point in asking?

The truth is, Clare and I never had the conversation about kids. My wife was thirty-one when she took on a full-time role at Tungus Lodge, and I had my own problems with Kirkwood Motors to contend with at the time. After the banking crisis, the economy took a nosedive and flatlined for several years, and I had to make a couple of staff redundant just to keep our heads above water. I worked sixty to seventy hours a week, every week, and it nearly killed me. Eventually, the economy improved, and people started buying cars again, but I was so paranoid that another slump might be on the horizon I only eased off the throttle a fraction.

Then, one day, I woke up on my fortieth birthday with no idea where the previous decade had gone. Maybe that was the moment, the final opportunity, for Clare and me to sit down and talk about kids, but it just never happened. I took the view that if Clare cared about motherhood, she would have raised the question, but she never did, and neither did I. Now, it's too late, although we've still never discussed what might have been.

Too late for regrets. I need to look forward.

Two hours later, the office is silent, and everyone has departed for the day except Justin, who is finishing with a customer in the showroom. I head outside to find the service centre and body shop are locked up. Wayne is in charge of both, and whilst he's great at what he does, he's a dyed-in-the-wool clock-watcher. If the sign on the wall says we close at 5.00 pm, he'll ensure the doors are locked, and he's on his way home by 5.01 pm. Maybe he's got the right idea, but then he doesn't have to fret about paying everyone's wages at the end of the month.

I return to the showroom to find Justin putting on his jacket.

"How'd you get on?" I ask, referring to the now-departed couple he was dealing with.

"Wasters, Boss."

"How so?"

"They want a Tesla, but they've barely got the budget for a Toyota."

"Cars and houses, Justin," I chuckle. "Everyone wants the one they can't quite afford."

"Very true."

My colleague then glances at his watch.

"I guess you'd better be going."

"Yep, busy evening."

"I don't envy you. The roads to the airport will be rammed this evening."

"I know, but I don't need to be there for almost three hours."

"Janine said you were picking your sister up at seven o'clock. I know maths isn't your forte, but that's less than two hours from now."

"Oh ... err, yeah. Seven."

Something tells me that Justin might be telling fibs about his airport run, but I won't embarrass him by testing his lie.

"I'll see you Monday, then."

"Yeah. Night, Boss."

Justin scuttles away, clearly forgetting that he said he'll try and attend the awards event later.

After ensuring the security system and cameras are all operational, I lock up and climb into my car. One day closer to a new owner going through this tired routine.

I arrive home to an empty house which I hadn't anticipated. Knowing my wife as I do, and how long it takes her to get ready, I assumed she'd be home by now. I ping her a quick text, asking where she is.

I'm halfway through making a sandwich when Clare replies: *I'm in the middle of a crisis. I'll go straight to the town hall. x*

I inwardly seethe. Although the invitation states there's no dress code, everyone representing Kirkwood Motors this evening is on strict instructions to make an effort. I'm not expecting ball gowns and black ties, but Clare left the house this morning wearing jeans and a shabby, oversized jumper.

Trying to focus on the bright side, that at least my wife still intends to turn up, I reply to her message with a thumbs-up emoji.

I gobble down my sandwich and then head up to the bathroom. Once I've shaved and showered, I splash on my favourite cologne before getting dressed: a crisp white shirt, silk tie, and a black, Tom Ford suit I rarely wear because it cost an absurd amount of money. Admittedly, that absurd amount of money does reflect in the fit, perfectly balanced between contemporary and classic.

Five minutes before the taxi is due, I double-check my appearance in the hallway mirror.

The last time I dressed up to go out with Clare, probably that Christmas party four years ago, she caught me checking my reflection in the same mirror and accused me of being vain. I'm not a vain man, but I do care about the way the world sees me, judges me.

A horn beeps from the driveway. I take a final check in the mirror and head outside.

The taxi driver doesn't have a lot to say on the journey into town, only speaking to confirm the fare once he pulls up outside the town hall. I pay the man, plus a few quid as a tip, and get out. I then glance at my phone to see if anyone else has messaged with a last-minute excuse and, seeing a blank screen, I hurry up the steps to the main doors of the town hall.

There's not a soul in the foyer, but I'm early. I'm always early. There is, however, a large noticeboard by a set of double doors, confirming tonight's Business of The Year Awards, hosted by Elderton Borough Council. I push open the right-hand door and enter the main hall. I'm greeted on the other side by two women behind a table, just inside the door. Both look surprised to see me.

"Sorry, you've caught us on the hop," the older of the two comments. "We weren't expecting an early bird."

"No problem," I say. "Do you want me to wait outside until you're ready?"

"No, no. I presume you're here for the awards?"

"Yes. I'm Gary Kirk of Kirkwood Motors. We've been nominated."

"Congratulations," the woman replies with slightly too much enthusiasm. "I'm Linda, by the way. Let me show you to your table."

If I'm looking for a good omen, our allocated table is at the front of the hall, close to the stage. Linda wishes me good luck, points out where the bar is, and then bustles away. Wishing I'd booked the cab twenty minutes later, I amble across the room to the far corner, where a young guy is arranging bottles behind the bar.

"Are you open for business yet, mate?" I ask.

"Just about. What can I get you?"

I scan the limited choice from the four pumps. I request a pint of Heineken, and the barman duly obliges.

Drink acquired, I return to the table and choose a seat that affords a view of both the main doors and the stage. The table itself is dressed with a white linen tablecloth and each of the twenty places is set with silver cutlery and two glasses. There's an arrangement of dried flowers in the centre and a laminated card in a holder, listing this evening's order of awards. I take a closer look and my heart sinks when I realise there are twelve awards in total, with the one we're nominated for being last on the list. Winners or not, it looks like we're here for the duration.

At ten to seven, a rotund guy in an ill-fitting suit strides onto the stage and approaches the podium. He tests the microphone and Linda gives him a thumbs-up before opening the double doors. Classical music then leaks from the speakers dotted around the hall. It appears the event is underway.

The first gaggle of guests eventually filter in, and head to a table on the far side of the hall. They're soon followed by a smaller group and then a handful of couples. Slowly but surely, the tables begin to fill, and I grow increasingly self-conscious that I'm the only occupant of a table for twenty. Then, a lone female guest breezes in and exchanges words with Linda. When she turns around and looks across to our table, I have to blink twice to confirm I'm looking at my office manager.

I get to my feet as Janine makes her way over.

When I asked the staff to make an effort with their attire this evening, I knew I could rely on at least one of them to set a good example.

"Thank God you're here," I remark as Janine reaches the table. "People were growing suspicious I was just a waiter taking a break."

"I don't think many waiters wear designer suits at work," she shoots back with a grin.

Her comment is followed by a moment of awkwardness because I don't know the correct greeting protocol. We're not in the office and it's not the start of a work day. This is a social event, and if it were anyone other than a colleague pitching up, I'd greet them with a kiss on the cheek.

Assuming it'd be rude to do nothing, I lean in and risk a quick peck to Janine's cheek.

"You look great, by the way," I remark. "If I'm allowed to say that kind of thing in this day and age."

"We're not in the office so don't worry, I won't sue you for being inappropriate."

"That's reassuring."

"Besides, I'm flattered. I can't remember the last time anyone paid me a compliment."

"Hey, I compliment you all the time."

"Yes, on my organisational skills. Regardless of what you might read on Twitter, some women do still appreciate being told they look good."

"Duly noted."

Not that I'd ever dream of sharing my thoughts with her, but if I had to tell Janine every time she looked good, it'd be a daily occurrence. Neither would I dare tell her that I love the way she giggles at my naff jokes, or the way she subconsciously places a hand on my arm whenever we're chatting in the staff room.

"Fancy a drink?" I ask.

"I thought you'd never ask. Large glass of Chardonnay, please."

"Grab a seat. I'll be back in a sec."

I reach the bar area, now much busier with small groups milling around and others waiting to be served. As I line up at the end of the bar, my phone beeps. It's another message from Clare: *I'll be an hour. Sorry. X*

I'm less bothered than I should be, and I wonder how much of that is because of the woman who did make an effort to get here on time.

I put my phone back in my pocket, not entirely sure if I should message my wife back and tell her not to bother coming at all.

Chapter 7

Although the menu was limited in options, the food was surprisingly good. Saying that, I couldn't face dessert. Janine, fortified by several glasses of wine from the dozen bottles on our table, insists I sample hers.

"Come on, Gary," she urges, holding a spoon laden with Eton Mess inches from my face. "Just one mouthful."

"I don't like meringue. It makes my teeth itch."

Equally buoyed by free Sauvignon Blanc, everyone else at the table adds their encouragement.

"One mouthful," Janine repeats with a mischievous grin. "I promise you'll love it."

For a quiet life I open my mouth. Janine guides the spoon towards my tongue, her eyes flicking between mine and the target. The spoon lands, and I close my mouth.

"Oops," Janine then sniggers. "You've got a bit on your chin."

Without warning, she leans forward and uses her thumb to wipe cream from the edge of my mouth.

"You're a mucky pup, aren't you?"

Maybe it's the wine or our close proximity or the enticing scent of Janine's perfume, but her cheeky remark sets off the butterflies in my chest, just as they once fluttered in Clare's company. I can't help but hold her gaze.

"Having fun, are we?"

Snapping out of the moment, I look up, knowing exactly who will be standing at the table. I push my chair back and scramble to my feet.

"Oh, hi. You made it then."

"Just in time, by the looks of it," Clare replies flatly. "I quite like Eton Mess."

Without telling me she saw Janine spoon-feeding her husband, Clare just confirmed she witnessed Janine spoon-feeding her husband.

"Yeah," I laugh nervously. "I told them I hate meringue, but they insisted I try some. Anyway, grab a seat, and I'll pour you a glass of wine."

"Make it a large one," she replies. "The bigger, the better."

With Clare at the table there's a noticeable shift in the atmosphere. Conversations are toned down, and there's distinctly less laughter. It's not because any of my team have an issue with Clare; it's because they barely know her. I can count on one hand how many times my wife has popped in to see me at work over the last decade. It might also be down to the fact Clare patently didn't read my memo about making an effort this evening. It's not necessarily her workday clothes but her sallow complexion, tired eyes, and greasy hair tied into a ponytail. A sudden pang of guilt arrives.

"Listen, Clare," I say. "You look exhausted. I'm glad you're here, but don't feel you've got to stay just for my sake."

"No, I'm fine. The wine is doing what it needs to do."

To prove her point, she empties her glass and reaches for the nearest bottle.

"I take it you're not driving home?"

"No, I'll leave the car on the street and collect it in the morning. I need a drink tonight."

"Okay, if you're sure. I'll keep the wine flowing, but to warn you, there are twelve awards tonight, and our category is up last."

"Let's hope it's worth the wait, eh."

Clare raises her freshly filled glass and chinks it against mine. "Cheers."

It's the most unenthusiastic cheers I've ever heard.

With the conversation strained, it's a relief when a female voice squawks from the PA system, asking everyone to take their seats as the first award is about to be announced. A few minutes later, the classical music is replaced with an up-tempo instrumental tune. The PA announcer then asks everyone to put their hands together for this evening's compère, Paul Hart.

According to Janine, Mr Hart used to be an actor in a moderately popular daytime soap before the writers killed off his character. Apparently, he now earns a living as a compère, host, and after-dinner speaker in the corporate world.

"Good evening, ladies and gentlemen," our compère booms in a broad Mancunian accent. "Welcome to the annual Elderton Business Awards, organised and sponsored by Elderton Borough Council."

As I study the man on the stage, I wonder if anyone else has noticed that Paul Hart bears a passing resemblance to former US President Bill Clinton. Like the man himself, I suspect Mr Hart's career highlights are now well and truly behind him.

To warm up the audience, he begins with a couple of anecdotes from his acting career, slipping in a handful of lame jokes that barely prompt a polite chuckle. After ten minutes or so, he finally senses that the crowd want to get on with the awards, and he duly obliges.

"Without further ado," he announces. "I'm delighted to confirm the nominees for our first award of the evening: the award for environmental sustainability."

There are six nominees, and after reading out the name of each company, he pauses to allow for applause. Perhaps he's trying to raise the tension, but this is not the Oscars, and it only serves to stretch out the tedium.

Eventually, Paul Hart announces the winner, and a group of seemingly pleased individuals gather on the stage to collect their award. One of them — a man with a severely receding hairline and blotchy cheeks — approaches the microphone and delivers a speech so long and so dull it physically hurts.

As the group return to the table to yet more applause, I check my watch. From the second Paul Hart confirmed which award he was about to present to the moment the recipients departed the stage, ten minutes elapsed. At this rate, it'll be at least two hours before he gets to our category.

I turn to the faces around my table. "Shall I order another dozen bottles of wine?"

They reply unanimously and enthusiastically in the affirmative — even Clare manages a faint smile. Only alcohol can now save us from two hours of abject boredom.

Unable to hold any kind of meaningful conversation as our compère slowly works through the awards, my team takes turns in disappearing to the toilet or outside for a cigarette. I visit the gents twice and, despite the health risks, consider taking up smoking for the evening just to kill time. Thankfully, we're granted a fifteen-minute interlude after the sixth award. En-masse, everyone around the table shoots off to stretch their legs or, quite possibly, throw themselves under a passing bus to alleviate the boredom. In the end, it's just me and Clare left at the table.

"You okay?" I ask. "You're very quiet."

"I'm fine."

"I know this isn't much fun, and my suggestion still stands if you want to shoot off. I wouldn't blame you."

"Nope, I'm here until the end."

"Okay."

We both reach for our glasses, and I then take another stab at conversation.

"What was the crisis at work?"

"You don't want to know."

"Clearly I do, otherwise I wouldn't have asked."

"We received confirmation about our funding this afternoon or, more specifically, confirmation that there won't be any funding."

"Oh dear," I groan. "I thought it was in the bag. You implied it was just a formality."

"I thought it was, but the committee changed their minds at the last minute."

"Shit, I'm so sorry, Clare. I don't know what to say."

"Nothing to say," she shrugs. "I failed to convince the committee so we can't build the extension to Tungus Lodge. The net result is that all our plans are now in tatters."

Judging by the bitterness of my wife's tone, I don't think it's in either of our best interests to dwell on the negativity.

"It's just a setback, a blip," I say, placing a consolatory hand on her shoulder. "You can apply again next year, and there's every reason to believe they'll give you the funding second time around."

"You think?" she scoffs. "Unless they change the ratio so there's more than two women on the committee, I don't fancy our chance next year ... or any year."

I don't know what else to say, and truth be told, there's usually no talking to Clare when she's in such a doleful mood. When my wife's spirits are high, they're high, but when she gets a bee in her bonnet about something, she isn't shy in letting me know.

The strained silence is thankfully short-lived when our sales administrator, Alice, and her husband, Danny, return to the table. I don't know Danny that well, but I know he's a football fan, so I pose a few questions about the recent England match. I'm not that interested, but it's telling that I'd rather hold a conversation with a virtual stranger than my own wife.

Paul Hart eventually returns to the stage and tries to liven things up with another anecdote. It flops miserably, and he moves swiftly on to the seventh award.

Over the ensuing hour, I rotate through half-hearted rounds of applause, refilling my wine glass and occasionally glancing at the women either side of me. Janine catches my eye on one occasion and pulls a face to indicate how bored she is before giggling to herself. Whilst my office manager is no doubt tipsy, my stoney-faced wife appears hell-bent on drinking her own body weight in wine. As she reaches for yet another bottle, I consider suggesting she slows down a bit. I don't get the chance.

"And now, ladies and gentlemen," Paul Hart shouts into the microphone. "The moment you've all been waiting for."

"You to bugger off," someone heckles from the back of the hall. It raises the largest laugh of the evening.

"Very funny," Hart responds, rolling his eyes. "But, no. Here are the nominees for Elderton's Business of The Year."

Everyone at our table sits up straight and focuses on the failed actor at the podium. To my surprise, Kirkwood Motors is the very first nomination, and Janine responds with enough hand clapping and enthusiastic whooping for everyone. There's far less applause for our competitors as Hart reads out the list of nominees.

Finally, the moment arrives, and our compère makes a big deal of opening a gold-coloured envelope. He then slowly pulls out a piece of card and clears his throat.

"I'm delighted to announce that the winner of Elderton Business of The Year is ..."

Chapter 8

There's a fine line between tension and tedium. Paul Hart has just crossed it. After clearing his throat for a second time, he takes a slow sip of water and repeats himself.

"I'm delighted to announce that the winner of Elderton Business of The Year is ..."

I'm tempted to run on stage, snatch the bloody card from his hand, and announce the winner myself.

"Kirkwood Motors!"

It's just as well this isn't the Oscars because if there were a camera trained on my face, it would have caught me blurting a less-than-inspired line.

"Fuck me sideways!"

Everyone around me is on their feet, but my legs are slow to react. Stunned, I finally stand up and, with back slaps and high fives, lead my team from the table to the stage. It's a surreal moment but intoxicating. I've only ever won one award in my life, and that was at school for coming second in our annual spelling bee.

I climb the steps to the stage, and Paul Hart strides towards me, hand outstretched.

"Congratulations," he says while enthusiastically shaking my hand.

He then offers me a rather underwhelming wood and brass shield before guiding me towards the podium. Only then does it dawn on me that I'm expected to make a speech. The applause dies down, and my mouth immediately dries up. With the room silent, I've no choice but to say something.

"Um, I ... err ... I know it's a line that every winner of every award trots out, but I didn't write a speech because I didn't think we'd win. I'm genuinely gobsmacked to be standing here and ... err ..."

Dredging my mind for something worth saying, all I can do is take our compère's lead and recite a business-related anecdote.

"It's funny, but whenever I tell people I run a used-car business, they always make the same joke about honesty ... or the lack of it in my industry. Everyone's got a joke about a used car salesman, right?"

My question prompts a few chuckles from the audience.

"Whenever I hear those jokes, I think back to the days when I first opened Kirkwood Motors and a young lad who popped in, hoping to buy his first car. As it happens, he'd celebrated his twenty-first birthday and passed his driving test in the same week, so when he decided to buy a little Ford Fiesta, I knocked off a few hundred quid for no other reason than to sweeten the deal for him. He went away, pleased as punch, and I'm proud to say he came back three years later to buy his next car, and the next, and the next."

I take a moment to sip from Paul Hart's glass of water.

"That same customer returned last month with his seventeen-year-old daughter after she passed her driving test. He thought it was only right that she should buy her first car from the same trusted, reliable dealer that looked after him all those years earlier."

I pause for a second, unsure what to say next.

"I guess what I'm saying is that some stereotypes are wrong. We've been in business for twenty years, and the main reason we've survived that long is because we look after our customers. I can't thank them, or my fantastic colleagues, enough."

I turn to my right, where every member of my team is standing shoulder to shoulder, beaming out to the audience.

"That's about all I've got to say, apart from offering my thanks to Elderton Borough Council for this evening, and the award, obviously. It genuinely means the world to me, and I'll head home tonight as the proudest man in town."

To my surprise, the mayor and all the council dignitaries at the front table get to their feet and applaud. The example set, everyone else follows suit. It'd be lovely to drink in the feeling all night, but I suspect most are keen to get home. I raise the award in the air and mouth a thank you before stepping away from the podium. My team then follow behind as I cross the stage and head down the steps towards our table. The applause continues until I reach my seat, the lump in my throat too large to swallow.

I sit down and take a huge gulp of wine.

"I'm so proud of you, Boss," Janine says as she takes her seat next to me. "That was a lovely speech."

"Thank you."

She suddenly leans across and plants a kiss on my cheek. My already warm skin burns red.

"If anyone deserves applause, it's you," Janine adds.

I reply with a smile, unable to find the words, but then Janine's expression suddenly changes to one of confusion as her gaze drifts past my shoulder towards the stage. Instinctively, I turn to see what she's looking at. I then adopt the same confused look because my wife is still on the stage, standing at the podium. Clare then leans towards the microphone and taps it a few times.

"Hello. Hello."

As her voice echoes around the hall, the now-seated audience all look towards the stage. My confusion then becomes inertia, as I've no more an idea of what Clare is about to say than anyone else in the hall.

"My name is Clare Kirk, and I'm the founder and manager of The Tungus Lodge Shamanic Centre."

Her voice travels far enough for all to hear, but I wonder if they can also hear the slight slurring of her words.

"I hope you're all enjoying your free dinner ... courtesy of Elderton's taxpayers," she snorts. "But I'm not here to talk about how much money your council has spunked on this pointless charade. I'm here to tell you that ..."

Paul Hart, realising that Clare is not at the podium in any official capacity, steps over and tries to guide her away. The moment his hand touches her elbow, she reacts aggressively.

"Don't you touch me, you fucking has-been," she snarls.

Paul Hart raises his hands in surrender and backs away. I don't blame him. The woman at the podium might be my wife, but I don't recognise this frothing version of her.

"I just wanted you all to know," Clare slurs into the microphone. "That, the bunch of freeloading wankstains sitting at the top table are the same people who ... who, today, decided that they'd rather spend your money on ... on a bloody five-a-side football pitch when they could have used it to gift wellness to every Elderton resident."

I'm so stunned by my wife's outburst I don't know what to do. Stopping her from humiliating herself any further is the obvious call, but I think that ship has sailed. I get to my feet and edge around the table. Clare spots my advance and doubles down.

"You'll also notice," she rages. "That Elderton Council is run by middle-aged misogynists, and ... and they're only interested in doing favours for their mates. Fuck the rest of us, especially the women."

Clare takes a second to belch and then staggers back from the microphone. It's a brief pause, but long enough for me to hurry up the steps and approach her.

"Enough," I hiss through gritted teeth. "Get off the stage."

My wife turns and fixes me with a demented sneer. She then steps back to the microphone and glares down at the table of council dignitaries.

"Enjoy the rest of your evening, tossers!"

I reach the end of my tether and attempt to wrap an arm around Clare's waist, intent on frogmarching her away from the microphone. She reacts badly and throws out an arm, missing my chin by a fraction of an inch. Fortunately, she appears to have said all she wanted to say and staggers across to the steps on the opposite side of the stage.

Unsure what else to do, I turn to the microphone and blurt an apology before hurrying after my wife. Drunk as she might be, Clare has already made good progress and is tottering down the left-hand side of the hall towards the exit. As I pass each table, I'm greeted by tuts, scowls, and snorts of laughter, adding to my humiliation.

I reach the double doors just as the right-hand door swings shut. Barging through it, I catch up with Clare as she's about to exit the building.

"Wait!" I snarl, coming to a stop. "What the hell was that all about?"

My wife stops and slowly turns around.

"Oh, I'm so sorry," she replies mockingly. "Did I ruin your evening?"

"Yes, you bloody well did."

"Never mind," she grunts, trying to suppress a burp. "There's always next year."

It dawns on me that there's precious little point trying to hold a conversation with Clare while she's so intoxicated. For now, I just want her as far away from this building as possible.

"You need to go home."

"Don't you dare tell me what I need to do," she hisses, jabbing her index finger in my direction. "I don't take orders from any man."

I stare back at the woman I've been married to for almost twenty-five years, but tonight, she might as well be a stranger.

"What happened to you, Clare?" I ask, my voice level. "Where has all this bitterness come from?"

"It's called life, Gary ... but what would you know?"

With that, she turns around and continues on towards the main doors. After a moment of indecision, I follow.

"Where are you going? I call out as she hurries down the steps outside the town hall.

"Where I'm needed," she replies without looking back. "Tungus Lodge."

My concern for her well-being eases a fraction. Tungus Lodge is only a five-minute walk away, and even if some mugger is lurking in the darkness, I wouldn't fancy his chances against Clare in her current mood. Nevertheless, I stand at the top of the steps and watch her all the way to the end of the street.

Once my wife is out of sight, I consider my own options. A significant part of me wants to leave, but it wouldn't be fair on my colleagues, and I have a lot of apologies to make back in the hall if I'm to limit the damage to Kirkwood's reputation.

Resigned to my fate, I turn around. To my surprise, there's a painfully thin woman standing directly in front of the double doors. Dressed in a smart navy jacket and skirt, the collar of her white blouse is so loose, it gapes around her tortoise-like neck.

"Hello, there," she says crisply. "Going back to face the music, are we?"

I don't recall seeing the stranger in the hall, but her officious tone suggests she might be a council employee.

"Looks like it," I huff.

"Is your wife okay?" the woman then asks. "That was quite a performance she put on."

"I'm sure she'll be just fine now she's pissed off and left me to clear up her mess."

"Yes, it is a mess. I don't envy you, Gary."

"Wait," I reply, my eyes narrowing. "How do you know my name?"

"Doesn't everyone know Gary Kirk of Kirkwood Motors? You're an award-winning businessman in Elderton, are you not?"

"Err, I suppose."

The woman then strides forward, thrusting out her hand. "I'm Edith Stimp, although you didn't see fit to ask."

"Sorry, I'm ... nice to meet you, but you'll have to excuse me as I've got a lot of grovelling to do."

"May I ask you a question?"

"If it's a quick one."

"Do you and Mrs Kirk have children?"

"Um, no. Why do you ask?"

"Because I cannot help couples with children, but that's obviously not a concern in your case."

"My case?"

"I'll get straight to the point. I'm what you might call a relationship resolution advisor."

"Right, and what makes you think we need advising?"

"Anyone with eyes can see you and your wife have ... unresolvable issues."

"That might be so, but I think we're almost past the point of marriage guidance."

"I'm not a marriage guidance counsellor, Gary. I offer, shall we say, effective but unorthodox solutions to marital problems."

"Well, I'll bear you in mind if we get to that point."

"Please do. My premises are at the end of Dent's Passage, just off the High Street. Do you know it?"

I've lived in the town all my life, but I haven't the foggiest idea where Dent's Passage is.

"Um, I'm sure I'll find it," I reply. "If I need to."

"You won't regret it."

Edith Stimp then flashes me a strange smile before making her way towards the exit.

"Toodle-pip, for now," she calls over her shoulder.

The distraction over, I turn and puff a long sigh. What should be one of the proudest nights of my life is now anything but, and I dread to think what kind of reception is waiting for me beyond the double doors.

Sadly, there's only one way to find out.

Chapter 9

Unsurprisingly, very few of the council officials at the Elderton Business Awards wanted to hear my apologies last night. So, not only do I have a mild hangover this morning, but the embarrassment is still raw. If only the person responsible were at home, I'd have the opportunity to vent.

I can only assume Clare either spent the night at Tungus Lodge, or on Angie's sofa. I've yet to hear from her this morning, but I hope she's suffering the mother of all hangovers and sufficient levels of shame. It's the least she deserves.

Sitting on the sofa with a strong coffee for company, I try not to let my mind drift back to last night. It's a pointless task because every minute of it will remain etched in my memory for a long time. It's hard to imagine any situation that would produce a similar emotional swing. One minute I'm glowing with pride; the next, I'm red-faced with humiliation. How could Clare do that to me?

My phone beeps. Presuming it's my wife, I'm in no hurry to check, but I'm curious how she intends to explain her actions. The message isn't from Clare but from Janine: *Hope you're okay this morning. If you want to talk, I'm around all day. X*

Most of my team skulked away last night, probably because they wanted to disassociate themselves from Gary Kirk and his demented wife. Janine, however, stayed by my side as I grovelled at the table of council dignitaries. As angry as I was at Clare, I couldn't have been more grateful for Janine's support.

I send a message back: *I'm okay, thanks, and I owe you one for sticking around last night when no one else did. I think I'll spend a few hours in the gym to burn off the negativity, but I appreciate the offer of a chat. X*

Her reply comes back within a minute: *No worries. How is Clare this morning? X*

My response doesn't take long to compose: *Absent, fortunately for her. X*

I then send another message, thanking Janine again and telling her to enjoy her weekend. She replies with a series of emojis I'm in no fit state to decipher.

I'm about to get up and get changed for the gym when the front door opens and closes. My wife has returned. I gulp back the remains of the coffee for a much-needed caffeine boost and then hurry out to the hallway.

"Made it home, then," I say flatly.

After hanging up her coat and bag, Clare turns to face me. "Looks like it."

"Now you've sobered up, perhaps we can talk about what you did last night."

"I don't want to talk about it."

"Tough! I do. You humiliated me."

"I'm sure you'll get over it."

Clare then kicks off her shoes and strides straight past me towards the kitchen. I wasn't expecting her to sob a heartfelt apology, but I thought she'd show some measure of remorse for her drunken outburst. I follow after her.

"Aren't you even going to apologise?" I ask as Clare stands at the sink with her back to me.

The sound of running water fills the silence for a few seconds until my wife turns around, holding a full glass in her hand. She takes several gulps before placing the glass on the side.

"I can't apologise for something I don't regret," she says. "If I could turn back time, I'd do it again."

"You don't regret humiliating me?"

"That was unfortunate, but I couldn't let the opportunity pass."

"The opportunity?" I snort. "To make a show of yourself."

"No, to highlight the scandalous way Elderton Council allocate funding — it's corrupt."

"You've got proof of that, have you?"

"I know what I know, Gary, and the fact there were reporters from the local paper there last night means their corruption is out in the open. I might have made a show of myself, but those reporters are now bound to investigate my allegations."

I'm tempted to scoff at her suggestion because she sounds like a demented conspiracy theorist, but I've got a more pressing point to make.

"And you couldn't make your case any other way? You had to sabotage what should have been one of my proudest moments?"

"Fuck's sake," Clare spits. "The world doesn't revolve around you and your poxy business, Gary."

"No, but it sure as hell revolves around Tungus Lodge, doesn't it? That place is the only thing you care about, and I mean the *only* thing."

The tension in the room is palpable. Now we've both said our piece, one of us has to break the silence and if my wife has any intention of de-escalating our conflict, now would be the ideal opportunity to backtrack.

"It's not the only thing, no. I do care about you."

It's not quite the white flag I expected because her tone implies there's a caveat coming.

"But?"

She takes another gulp of water and then suggests we sit down at the table. Without saying a word, I comply. Maybe I'm reading too much into Clare's body language, but is this the moment she confirms what we both already know?

Sitting across from me, my wife closes her eyes for a moment before screwing up her face. It could be that she's suffering from a hangover headache, or it could be preparation for a difficult conversation.

"I'm going to stay with Angie for a while," she finally says in a low voice.

"Okay. Can I ask why?"

"Two reasons. Firstly, I need to work out what I can do about the proposed extension to Tungus Lodge now that the council won't fund it."

"They might have given you funding in the future, but your antics last night will have changed a few minds."

"Those minds were already made up, and they've cut their funding back to almost nothing since the first year. I'm past the point of relying on the council. I need to come up with a different funding strategy, and Angie is the only person who really understands the challenge."

"Alright. What's the second reason?"

"I think you and I need some time apart so we can ... so we can decide how we move forward."

"If there's something you're trying to say, Clare, just spit it out."

"Alright, the truth is that I'm really struggling to see a future for us."

Her bombshell dropped, my wife puffs a tired sigh. I remain mute, not because I don't understand what's going on but because I want to think carefully about what I say next.

"Are you going to say anything?" Clare asks.

"I'm thinking."

"Surely this can't come as a shock, Gary. We've been treading water for years, and I can't believe you're happy with how things are."

"No, I'm not."

"But you've never said anything."

"Life just drifts on, but seeing as we're being honest with one another, I was waiting for the right time to confront the problem. I guess the right time is now."

"We're in agreement then? We need time and space to decide if ..."

Clare seems unable or unwilling to say the dreaded word.

"If we divorce?" I say.

She nods solemnly. "Yes. That."

After almost twenty-five years of marriage and one strangely emotionless chat across the kitchen table, we're now at a cliff edge. All that remains is for one of us to jump.

"How much time do you need?" I ask, unsure what else to say.

"A few days, a few weeks ... this is uncharted territory, so I can't say for sure."

I nod, partly in acknowledgement and partly in agreement.

"Is there anything else you want to say?" Clare then asks.

"Yes, no ... I don't know. I'm not really in the right headspace to say anything worthwhile."

"Which is why we need time apart. Whatever we decide, we both need to be certain and living under the same roof won't help with that."

"You're right, I guess."

"One thing I will say, though, is that I hope that whatever happens with us, we'll at least remain civil to one another."

"Not friends, then?" I reply with a limp smile.

"You'll always be my friend, and not that I want to influence your decision one way or another, but I'll always love you."

"Ahh, is this the moment you deliver that immortal line? You love me, but you're not in love with me."

"I'd never be so clichéd, but there's some semblance of truth in it. I've loved you since I first clapped eyes on you as a teenager, but ... but love isn't always enough, is it?"

"No," I sigh. "Not always."

We swap sympathetic half-smiles and then Clare looks up at the clock. "I'll ... um, I should pack some clothes."

"Do you need a hand?"

"Can't wait to get rid of me, eh?"

"No, I—"

"I'm joking, Gary, and thanks for the offer, but I'll be fine."

"Will you? Be fine, I mean?"

"Are we talking about packing clothes or in a broader sense?"

"You know what I mean."

"I do, and I believe the Universe will guide me along the right path."

She pushes her chair away and steps around the table. To my surprise, she stops and plants a delicate kiss on my cheek. I don't ask why, and she doesn't volunteer a reason.

Left alone with my thoughts, the most unlikely feeling descends. Before Clare returned home, I half-expected a heated row about last night, but whatever I felt fifteen minutes ago, those emotions are now usurped by a potent newcomer: relief.

I'm surprised but not shocked because this has been on the cards for a long time. However, shouldn't I feel sadness or at least disappointed? It says a lot about the state of our marriage that my initial reaction to the beginning of the end is no different to the feeling I get after paying our quarterly VAT return on time.

Maybe my feelings will change in time, but for now, a good session at the gym feels appropriate. I head upstairs to my bedroom and change into my kit. On the return journey, I stop at Clare's bedroom where she's in the process of transferring clothes from her wardrobe to a suitcase.

"I'm off to the gym," I confirm. "Will you still be here when I get back?"

"Probably not."

"Right ... well, um ... I guess I'll see you when I see you."

Clare steps around the bed and pulls me into a hug. I can still distinctly recall the first time she wrapped her arms around me, and how much I never wanted that feeling to end. Now, it feels awkward, almost forced.

Once we separate, there are no tears, no fond farewell. I don't know when I'll see my wife again, and vice versa, but our goodbye is no more emotional than if I were popping to the shop for a loaf of bread.

I step through the front door and stop on the driveway to look back at the house. It's been our home for over eighteen years, and in many ways, it represents everything I wanted to achieve when I first set out in business. I amassed the moderate trappings of success and hard work, but to what end? Later, I'll be returning to our detached, mock-Georgian house with its four bedrooms, two bathrooms, double garage, and high-end kitchen with every mod-con, but I'll be alone.

As I get into the car, I can't help but wonder if the prospect of being alone in my mid-forties was one of the reasons why I never addressed the problems in our marriage sooner. It's academic now because whatever Clare and I tell ourselves, deep down we both know our brief separation is only a precursor to a permanent one.

"This is it now, Gary," I whisper to myself. "Time to move on."

Chapter 10

A renowned doctor once said that if it were possible to encapsulate all the benefits of exercise into a pill, it would be considered a miracle cure for many of life's ills. I'd never consider myself an exercise evangelist or, God forbid, a hardcore gym prick, but I tend to agree with that notion. However, what the good doctor failed to mention is the trade-off. To enjoy all those benefits, you must endure a lot of pain and discomfort. On Saturday, I pushed my middle-aged body to its limit for more than two hours, and I could barely walk by the time I left the gym.

The pain I usually endure during my gym sessions is always worthwhile, though, because of how I feel for the ensuing twenty-four hours. The flood of endorphins helps to wash away negative thoughts, and I always sleep like a baby. Considering what happened before my gym visit, I had reason to expect a sleepless night on Saturday, but I was out for the count as soon as my head hit the pillow. With nothing else to do with my Sunday, I returned to the gym again, and although the session wasn't as intense as the day before, it helped while away a couple of hours.

As I drive into work this morning, the faces of many of my fellow motorists all reflect the fact it's a Monday. I, on the other hand, feel ready to face the day. Maybe it's down to the weekend gym sessions, or maybe it's because, now that I've come to terms with Clare leaving, I can finally start planning my new future. But I feel good. I feel *really* good. The only slight chink in my good mood is the fallout from Friday's awards ceremony. I've no idea what to expect, but fuck it — we won the award, and no one can take that away from me.

Whilst I can't control what the general population see or say about Clare's outburst, I can at least control the narrative at Kirkwood Motors. For that reason, I sent a message to every employee yesterday, telling them to convene in the showroom at 8.45 am for a brief staff meeting.

I pull up in my parking bay and unlock the building. One by one, my colleagues filter in over the next twenty minutes until they're all congregated in the sales area, cups of coffee in hand. Some of their faces mirror those of the Monday morning motorists, but that's because they've no idea why they've been summoned.

"Morning, all," I announce. "Before I get started, I just want to reassure you that there's nothing sinister at play, and I haven't ordered you in to deliver bad news."

There's a collective sigh of relief, particularly amongst the mechanics.

"Now, some of you were at Friday's awards dinner, and for those of you who weren't, I'm guessing you probably heard what happened, right?"

A few glances are swapped, and there's a general reluctance to admit what I already know.

"Yeah, Boss," Wayne eventually acknowledges. "We heard your missus lost the plot."

"Actually, I was referring to the fact that we won Elderton Business of The Year, but seeing as you mentioned my wife's ... my wife's protest to the council, I need to apologise to those of you who were there. For those who weren't, you missed out on a half-decent meal and a good piss-up. Nevertheless, we bloody won, and that's down to all of you."

I clap my colleagues and one by one, they all join in. It's too early for a more enthusiastic celebration.

"So, as a mark of my gratitude, there'll be an extra hundred quid in your pay packets this month, and I'd like to arrange a night out so we can all celebrate together ... without any distractions."

Wayne raises his hand.

"Yes?"

"This night out. Where will it be?"

"Probably just a pub or bar, so don't worry, there won't be a dress code or formal dinner. If you've got any suggestions, let me or Janine know."

"Nice one."

"Okay, on that note, I'll let you all get on ... and thanks again for all your hard work. Remember, we're an award-winning team now, and that's down to each and every one of you."

As they all head off, there are enough smiles for me to feel confident they'll now be talking about their bonus and the night out rather than gossiping about Friday evening. I learned early in my management career that idle gossip quickly leads to idle hands. And, considering the subject of the gossip, it made sense to talk about what happened and then create a distraction.

With the working day underway, I head up to my office and wait for Janine to join me for the morning meeting. She doesn't keep me waiting long.

"Morning, again," she chirps. "Are we all set?"

"Ready when you are."

Janine closes the door and sits down.

"Thank you so much for the bonus," she says before I've even opened my diary. "You've no idea how much that extra cash will come in handy."

"Yes, about that. You're not getting the hundred-pound bonus."

My office manager's smile dissolves in an instant.

"Eh?" she gulps. "Why not?"

"Because you deserve more than anyone else. It was you who orchestrated our involvement in the business awards, and to show you how grateful I am, expect an extra five-hundred quid in your wages at the end of the month."

"Oh, my God," she gushes. "I don't know what to say ... thank you!"

"You're welcome."

"But I was only doing my job. I don't think I deserve five-hundred."

"You bloody well do, but to be honest with you, Janine, it's also partly to offset my guilt."

"Guilt? For what?"

"My wife ruining what should have been a brilliant evening. We never even got the chance to celebrate properly, and I feel bad after all the effort you went to."

"I did it because I love working here, and at least it was a memorable evening, I suppose."

"That it was," I chuckle. "For all the wrong reasons."

Janine's smile loses its brilliance, and I know what's coming next.

"How was Clare at the weekend?"

I stare at the desk and weigh up the pros and cons of sharing the truth. I haven't even told my parents yet, but Janine has always had a sympathetic ear.

"We've decided to separate," I eventually admit.

"Oh, dear. I'm so sorry, Gary."

"Don't be," I shrug. "It's been on the cards for a long while, and Friday was really just the final straw. It's for the best."

"How long is a while … if you don't mind me asking?"

"A few years at least. I've been so obsessed with this place and Clare with Tungus Lodge; we just neglected our marriage."

"So, is the separation temporary, or …"

Her question hangs in the air, and for the first time since Saturday, I'm faced with verbalising an answer that's as good as set in my mind.

"It's almost certainly permanent. I don't know about Clare, but we're just going through the motions now. It doesn't matter if we spend a few days apart, or a few weeks or even months; it's too late to go back to what we once had."

"Are you sad?"

"That's the strange thing — I don't feel sad at all. It feels like a release."

"I'm not surprised."

"Oh? Why do you say that?"

Janine shuffles in her seat.

"You won't be offended if I tell you what I really think?"

"Of course not."

"I think it's obvious that you haven't been happy at home for a long time."

"How did you fathom that out?"

"Everyone talks in the office about their life outside work. We all discuss our social lives, holidays, what we did at the weekend … that kind of thing. I don't think I've ever heard you mention doing anything with Clare."

Her observation is valid and rooted in the truth.

"We're very different people to those two lovestruck kids who met and married young. Different values, different interests, different … different everything, really."

Janine taps the tip of her biro against a notepad for a few beats.

"If it's any consolation, at least you've both achieved something in your lives, despite the marriage failing. I wish I could say the same for Stuart."

I don't know the full story behind Janine's failed relationship, but I'm aware of the lowlights. Stuart was the lead vocalist in a band, and they met at one of his gigs when they were both in their mid-twenties. After a whirlwind romance, they married in Las Vegas, and six months later, Janine fell pregnant with their first child, Louis. A year later, she was pregnant again and along came Felix.

You'd think that marriage and fatherhood would force a man to grow up and accept his responsibilities, but not Stuart, by all accounts. He continued to gig with his band in the hope that fame and fortune would call. Neither did call, but that didn't stop Stuart from indulging in drink, drugs, and one too many women. The couple eventually divorced, their marriage only lasting four years. To this day, Stuart still remains as feckless and irresponsible as he always was, according to Janine.

"If only we could go back in time and do it all again, eh?" I remark wistfully. "I'd certainly do things a bit differently."

"I do wonder what would have happened if I never met Stuart, but for all the crap he's put me through over the years, I wouldn't be without my boys."

"Some mistakes are worth making, eh?"

"They are, although I might have answered differently if you'd asked me earlier when the little shits wouldn't get out of bed."

As always, Janine manages to lighten the mood with her devilish brand of humour.

Souls bared, we get back to business and run through the list of today's tasks, targets, and appointments. I've already got a few tasks on my to-do list, but they're not business-related. Now that Clare has moved out, I think it would be prudent to focus on the practicalities of the inevitable. Disentangling one long-term relationship into two separate lives is going to take some time, so it makes sense to get the groundwork underway sooner rather than later.

Once Janine has returned to her desk, I get on with what I need to do, and by mid-morning, I've made enough progress to warrant a large coffee. When I return to my office, I turn my attention to my personal to-do list and call a business acquaintance, Aaron Brooks. He answers my call by announcing his name.

"Aaron, it's Gary Kirk."

"Hello, Gary. Long time no speak."

Aaron manages an estate agency in Elderton and although we didn't deal with him at the time, we bought the house through his company. I occasionally bump into him around town and the odd networking event.

"I know you're probably busy, but can I pick your brains for two minutes?"

"Pick away."

"I don't want this going any further, but I might need to put our house on the market soon. Can you give me a ballpark valuation figure so that I can work out my finances?"

My question is met with a silence so prolonged I have to check Aaron is still on the line.

"Hello? You still there, Aaron?"

"Err, yeah. Sorry."

"Something the matter?"

"It's kind of awkward."

"What is?"

"Your wife called me an hour ago, asking the same question."

"Oh."

Barely forty-eight hours after suggesting we need space, Clare is already researching the value of our marital home. Rather than considering her future, it seems my wife is already working out how to fund that future on her own. I'd be miffed if I wasn't already making similar plans myself.

"You've probably worked it out by now," I continue. "Clare and I have separated."

"Ahh, I'm sorry to hear that. Gary."

"Thanks. Did Clare not mention it?"

"Not directly, but I've been doing this long enough to read between the lines when it comes to a seller's motives."

"Right, well, I guess I need to know what number you came up with."

"Yeah, of course. Let me just pull up the details on our system again."

Being that we bought the house through Aaron's agency, he already knows what we paid for it and the scale of the accommodation.

"Have you done anything to the place since you moved in?" he asks.

"Nothing significant, apart from a kitchen refit seven or eight years ago."

"In which case, I'd suggest an asking price of £550,000, and if the market is still as buoyant as it is today, you should receive offers within ten grand of that price."

"That's more than I estimated, which is good news. Thanks, Aaron."

With a promise I'll let him know once we've reached a decision, I end the call. I then open up a fresh spreadsheet on my computer and enter the number Aaron quoted minus costs. My plan is to add the value of our combined marital assets to this list so we can carve everything up fairly when the time comes.

Seeing as Clare has already begun a list of her own, that time might come sooner than I expected.

Chapter 11

I wake up in an empty house for the fourth morning in a row. As I stand in the shower, I think back over the last twenty-five years, trying to remember if Clare and I have ever had such a prolonged period of separation. I quickly conclude we haven't, but then the clue is in the name — separation. We are now separated, pending divorce, as seems likely.

After discovering Clare's call to Aaron yesterday, my mind dwelt on her reasoning and the hurried timing. It did cross my mind that maybe she's met someone else. I don't know the stats, but I'd bet that the majority of marriages end due to infidelity over any other reason. The more I thought about it, the more it made sense that my own marriage could be another of those statistics, although my wife is perhaps trying to paint a different picture.

Now I've had the chance to sleep on my theory, I'm more inclined to believe there's some substance to it. Clare is not a vindictive woman, and I'm sure she'd go out of her way to avoid hurting me. I reckon she only suggested the separation to soften the blow and avoid conflict. I don't know how I'd feel if it does transpire that she's seeing someone else, but I'd be lying if I said it wouldn't sting to some degree. That's not because I have any appetite to fix our marriage but because no one likes being lied to or deceived.

The question is: do I confront her with my suspicions, or just let it ride? Does it really matter one way or the other, as we'll end up at the same place eventually? Divorce is divorce, whatever route you take to get there.

Thoughts of new relationships — new or imagined — aren't far from my mind on the drive to work. Although I'm excited by the prospect of starting a new business, I've had no reason to consider a new relationship. I suppose that I might meet someone down the line, but it's not a priority because I'll need to commit myself wholeheartedly to the new venture. However, now I've had cause to think of Clare with someone else, it's forced me to think a bit harder about who I might want to share my life with when the time is right. On a more practical level, though, how the hell do people my age find a partner?

I know most singletons use websites and apps to find a date, but neither holds much appeal. It's been a long time since I went on a date, but those dates were always the result of a chance encounter.

I met my first girlfriend, Alison, at a mate's party, and we went to the cinema the following week. We got to know one another organically, although knowing Alison's favourite band and her dream holiday destination were of no help when we finally shared a bed. Both virgins, memories of that awkwardly brief encounter still make me cringe to this day.

We broke up a few months later after I discovered Alison had been secretly honing her bedroom skills with another kid from school, Steve Barker. He got a punch in the face for his troubles, but I was the one who went home and cried.

After Alison, I went through a phase of being a thoughtless little prick. I had several one-night stands and cheated on both the girls I dated. I wasn't proud of my behaviour, but looking back, I lacked the emotional maturity to deal with rejection and subsequent heartbreak from my first proper relationship.

In the end, I thought it was best to remain single until that fateful evening when I bumped into Clare Wood. I'd just turned eighteen, and Clare was a few months younger.

The rest, as they say, is history, but it won't be the future. Certainly not for Clare, anyway, because I suspect her future now involves a different man.

The start of my working day is nothing if not routine. The business has now reached the point where everyone knows their role inside out, and, on the whole, it ticks over without any real drama. After all the challenges and stresses over the years, I should welcome this long phase of stability, but some days are longer than others because there's no variation. Still, if I have a quiet day today, I can continue working on my other plans.

Two hours into my morning, I receive a call from Adrian Griffin.

"You're the talk of the town, old boy," he chortles. "I wish I'd popped along to the awards ceremony now, but they're usually such a drab affair."

I should probably be offended by Adrian's casual mocking, but I've known him long enough to realise how dry his sense of humour is.

"Thanks for that," I groan. "I've spent the last five days trying to forget what happened."

"You know I'm only joshing — we've all been there. My better half once threw up over the former mayor after she downed one glass of Prosecco too many at a civic dinner."

"You're joking?"

"I wish I was. Do you have any idea how much it costs to dry clean ceremonial robes? A small bloody fortune, I can tell you."

Spousal nightmares shared, Adrian gets to the point of his call.

"Sorry it's taken slightly longer than anticipated, but I have a valuation figure for you."

"Great. I'm all ears."

"Before I give it to you, bear in mind that when it comes to selling a business, the price you achieve depends on the market at the time, so I've erred on the conservative side. I estimate your business to be worth approximately £700,000."

"That's a little less than I estimated but good to know."

After thanking Adrian, I end the call and open up the year planner on my computer. From there, I start piecing together a timeline for how events might unfold over the next couple of years. At some point, whether it's next week or next month, Clare and I will likely have a conversation about our separation, and if my theory holds true, she'll want to move on with the divorce. I've no idea how long that process takes, but I'd guess no more than six months. That means I'll likely be a single man again come the autumn, and living somewhere else because we'll have to sell the marital home. By then, I might only have to wait another twelve months before I can put Kirkwood Motors up for sale and get on with the next instalment of my life.

I sit back in my chair and take a moment.

Circumstances seem to be nudging me in a certain direction, and maybe that's no bad thing. For now, though, I need to keep the business ticking over for at least two years. Whatever happens then, I'll be a free man. I just need to be patient.

As the day progresses, I'm busy enough not to think too hard about the future. Janine leaves at three, and I head down to the showroom to cover for Mo while he's at the dentist getting an emergency filling. In the hour Mo is away, I see two customers and take a deposit on a twenty-grand Lexus from the second of those customers. Once I've completed the paperwork and bid a very happy gentleman goodbye, Justin pipes up from his desk.

"I've been trying to sell that bloody Lexus for three weeks. What's your secret, Boss?"

"There's no secret. People trust me, so they're more likely to buy from me."

"I wish more punters trusted me."

"Maybe you should do a little less talking and a bit more listening. That's the key to gaining a customer's trust."

Justin slowly nods as if he's digesting my advice. He won't take it because he's young and brash — the archetypal used-car salesman. In fairness to Justin, he has improved a lot since I hired him eighteen months ago, but he's still a work in progress.

Mo returns just as I'm in the process of handing the paperwork to our sales administrator, Alice. I check he's recovered from his dental intervention and then reluctantly return to my office. Given the choice, I'd much prefer to spend most of my time in the showroom because I love selling cars, but the business won't run itself.

I spend the next hour dealing with the unrewarding elements of being the boss, and just as I'm about to wind down for the day, my mobile rings. Clare's name is on the screen.

"Hi," I say casually. "How are you?"

"I'm good. You?"

"I'm fine, thanks."

"Good. Good."

The conversation is so stilted that anyone eavesdropping would think we're casual acquaintances, not a married couple.

"Are you doing anything later?" Clare asks after a moment of uncomfortable silence.

"I've nothing in my diary. Why?"

"Can we meet up?"

"Sure, but can I ask why? Four days ago, you wanted space."

"I've had time to think since then, and I'm ready to talk now."

"Okay. Do you want to come over about sevenish?"

"No, let's meet at The Cherry Tree. I'll be there at seven."

Unsure why she wants to meet at a pub rather than the house, I agree and confirm I'll be there. Clare then says she has to go before I can ask specifically what she wants to talk about.

I put my phone down, and my earlier thoughts begin to circle again. Four days after saying she wants space, Clare is now ready to talk. It's a shame I can't place a bet on the subject of our conversation because I'd wager a large sum that in two hours' time, my wife will confirm that she's met someone new.

Unless I'm mistaken, tonight will mark the beginning of the end.

Chapter 12

I cooked a Spanish omelette for dinner, but I struggled to finish it because of the knot in my stomach. There's no reason I should feel apprehensive about meeting Clare, but for some reason, I do. Maybe, in part, it's because I'm fairly certain I know what she's going to say, and there's a world of difference between guessing that your wife has met someone new, and her confirming it in person.

Although not the nearest pub to our home, The Cherry Tree has always been our local. However, it must be well over a year since our last visit together, and that wasn't the greatest night out because Clare kept complaining about the bad energy in the room. She never confirmed it, but I suspected that most of the bad energy emanated from our table.

The pub is a good twenty-minute walk away but the weather is pleasant enough, so I decide to leave the car at home. There's also a strong likelihood I'll need one or two stiff drinks during and after my chat with Clare.

I push open the main door to The Cherry Tree ten minutes before seven. Being a Tuesday evening, it's relatively quiet. The main reason we prefer this place over the nearer pub is the food, which is always top-notch, and people travel from all four corners of Elderton to eat here. Even though the public bar is near empty, I'm pretty sure the car park and dining room are not.

A member of staff I've never met before pours my gin and tonic, and I take it to a table in the bay window where Clare and I can hold a conversation with some degree of privacy.

Seven o'clock comes and goes, as does my gin and tonic. Just as I'm about to return to the bar, Clare finally breezes in. As I'm one of only five customers, it doesn't take her long to spot me as I cross the room. We greet one another with a kiss on the cheek, but there's little to no affection on either side.

"Drink?" I ask.

"I'll just have a Coke, thanks."

"Still suffering after Friday's session?"

She doesn't reply or explain why she's on soft drinks. I order her Coke and another gin and tonic.

"I've got a table in the window," I then confirm. "Not that it's exactly packed in here tonight, but I thought we might need some privacy."

"Good idea."

We take our seats opposite one another, and Clare sips from her glass.

"How have you been?" she then asks.

"I'm okay. How's life at Angie's?"

"It's fine, although her spare bedroom isn't much more than a cupboard."

"Not quite what you had in mind when you said you needed space, eh?"

Clare's reply comes in the form of a tepid smile. She then looks out of the window at the near-dark street. I wouldn't say the suspense is killing me, but I'm keen we get on with whatever it is she wants to discuss.

"So?" I say. "You wanted to talk."

Clare turns back to face me and then sighs. "Yes."

"I'm here, so let's talk."

She takes another sip of Coke.

"I know four days isn't a long time, but it's allowed me to reach a decision."

"About?"

"Well, about a lot of things, actually, but I suppose our marriage is top of the agenda."

"And what decision have you reached?"

"I've spent all day trying to think of a way to say it that doesn't sound so brutally frank, but I can't, so I might as well just spit it out — I think we should divorce."

I draw in a deep breath as Clare studies my face for a clue to my feelings.

"Are you going to say anything?" she asks.

"Have you met someone else?"

"What?" she snorts. "Don't be ridiculous."

"Would you tell me if you had?"

"Of course. What would be the point of lying to you?"

"I don't know, but partners who cheat aren't renowned for their honesty, are they?"

"If you want me to swear on my life, I will. There's no one else."

Based on Clare's tone of voice and body language, I'm inclined to believe her.

"What made you think I was seeing someone else, anyway?" she asks.

"An overactive imagination and ... and the fact you called an estate agent yesterday, enquiring about the value of our house."

My wife's frown deepens. "How do you know I called an estate agent?"

"Cards on the table. By pure chance, I called the same estate agent an hour later and asked him the same question."

"Great minds, eh?" Clare responds as the tension in her features eases.

"Yep, and you know I'm nothing if not a pragmatist."

"I take it that you were thinking along the same lines as me, then?"

"About the possibility of divorce?"

"Yes."

"It obviously crossed my mind, and deep down, I can't deny that it's probably in our best interests. Much as it pains me to say it, we're now so far away from that couple who met as teenagers, it's hard to believe we're the same people."

"It's what happens, Gary. Sometimes, couples just drift apart."

"I know, but I never thought we'd be that couple."

"It is what it is, and there's no point trying to work out how we got here or who's to blame. All that matters now is that we move forward."

"Agreed."

"And that brings me to the other decision I've made."

Clare reaches into her handbag and withdraws a piece of paper. She then unfolds it and flattens it out on the table in front of me. It's a set of estate agent's sales particulars featuring a photo of a rather sorry-looking detached house.

"It's a former guest house," Clare confirms. "It's been empty for over a year, and it does need a lot of work, but it's got seven ensuite bedrooms, three reception rooms, a car park, and a garden at the back."

"Okay. And?"

My wife sits forward and straightens her shoulders. "I want to buy it."

"Oh."

"Is that all you've got to say?"

"Err, I don't know what to say apart from the obvious. Why?"

"Because Tungus Lodge no longer meets our ambitions as we're unable to extend it. This house, however, is an opportunity for us to branch out, and because it has so much space, I'll have somewhere to live, and we can run residential retreats. Plus, I'm sick of being beholden to Elderton Borough Council and every stupid rule they want to enforce on us."

"You want to buy a house for the charity?"

"No, it'll be my house in my name, and rather than paying rent to the council, the charity can pay me instead. It's an ideal solution."

Clare's rationale might be sound, but when my eyes return to the page, a six-figure number printed below the photograph raises another question.

"It's five-hundred grand."

"The estate agent is confident they'll come down ten per cent for a quick sale."

"I bet he's confident," I scoff. "On the photo alone, it's a right state."

"We've done some fag packet sums, and I reckon another sixty grand will cover all the essential works."

"That's a serious amount of fundraising, so I hope the seller is willing to be patient."

"It's been on the market for months, so I don't think it'll sell tomorrow, but we are keen to put in an offer as soon as possible."

I might have jumped to a hasty conclusion about Clare seeing another man, but her haste in seeking a valuation of our home and organising this chat now makes perfect sense. I'm not going to make the same mistake twice, though. I want Clare to tell me.

"I admire your ambition," I say casually. "But what has this got to do with our divorce?"

"Not to put too fine a point on it, money."

"I'm listening."

"Look, I know it sounds cold and calculating, but if we're both in agreement that our marriage is finished, surely it makes sense to get the divorce sorted quickly?"

"By divorce, you mean the financial side of it?"

Clare adopts a pained smile. "Yes, but I'd like to think we can deal with it amicably, and it'd obviously be in both our best interests not to let the process linger on too long. I'm sure you want to get on with your life, right?"

"I do, yes."

"Good, so we're in agreement? You're happy to split everything fifty-fifty?"

Even though I'd reached the same conclusion, Clare's assumption does prickle a bit. Because she earns so little, she's never contributed a penny to our mortgage payments or our savings account.

"I'm not sure happy is the word I'd use, but I'm willing to split our marital assets fifty-fifty."

"Thank you for being so reasonable. It's a real weight off my mind."

And just like that, we've settled the terms of our divorce. No fighting, no bitterness, and most importantly, no bloody lawyers. We'll probably need one to draw up the formal agreement, but the cost will be negligible.

"I guess champagne would be inappropriate?" I say in jest, just to fill the silence.

"I'd take a glass with you if I didn't have the car, but I'll put a bottle on ice for when we complete on the guest house."

"You do realise that we have to sell the house, and it'll take time, right?"

"When I spoke to Aaron, he was confident he could line up a buyer within a month. He said there's a real shortage of detached family homes at the moment, and spring is traditionally a good time to sell."

"Okay, but I'm not willing to let it go for peanuts just to get a quick sale."

"I don't want to give it away either."

"In which case, I'll call Aaron tomorrow and get the ball rolling."

"That would be great. And what about our joint savings account?"

"I'll transfer fifty per cent over once we're ready to sign the divorce papers. Fair enough?"

"That should work."

Clare reaches across the table and squeezes my hand. "I know this must feel so rushed, but it's for a good cause. The sooner I can relocate the charity to larger premises, the more people we'll be able to help."

"You don't need to remind me of your cause, but how do you intend to fund the rest of the purchase price and the refurbishment costs?"

Clare withdraws her hand and sits back in her seat.

"What do you mean?" she asks, seemingly puzzled by my question.

"If you tot-up your share of the house and our savings account, you're still a few hundred grand short. Where's the rest of the money coming from?"

"Err, you said we'd split everything fifty-fifty."

"Yes, I did."

"But you've overlooked one significant asset, Gary."

"No, I haven't."

"Yes, you have — Kirkwood Motors."

Utterly dumbstruck, I can only stare back at Clare, open-mouthed.

"I know roughly what the business is worth," she continues, oblivious to my shock. "So, whilst my fifty per cent share is worth roughly three or four-hundred thousand, I'm willing to walk away with two-hundred as long as you transfer the funds to my account within six weeks."

My mind is so scrambled that forming a cohesive response is suddenly beyond me. Long seconds pass before I manage to spit out a few words.

"No. Fucking. Way."

"Sorry?"

"You heard me. Kirkwood Motors is mine, and mine alone."

"I'm not denying it's your business, Gary. I'm saying that I'm entitled to half of it."

"That's utter bullshit," I snort. "I don't know where you got that idea from, but you can forget it."

"I can see you're angry, but you did agree to split our marital assets fifty-fifty."

"The business is not a marital asset, and no court in the land would say otherwise."

"Oh dear," Clare sighs. "I'm sorry for the confusion, but you're wrong."

"That's your opinion. I disagree."

"It's not my opinion. It's my lawyer's opinion."

"What? Since when did you have a lawyer?"

"Technically, he's not my lawyer yet, but Angie's older brother runs a successful law practice in Winchester, and he's very kindly offered his services for free."

Clare's revelation is yet another unforeseen blow. Ironically, it does feel like I've taken a solid punch to the guts. I need to regroup.

"If your fancy lawyer wants to waste their time fighting a lost cause, fine. Even if you are entitled to half of my business, which I strongly reject, how does that help you get your hands on two-hundred grand before someone else buys your stupid guest house?"

"You've been talking about selling the business for a few years, so why not now?"

"I'm not ready to sell it, and when I do decide the time is right, it'll likely take months to find a buyer."

"I thought you'd say that, but there's an obvious alternative if you don't want to sell the business now. We sell the house, and rather than split the equity fifty-fifty, I'll take it all. It's less than I'm entitled to, but I'm willing to make that concession so I can buy the guest house."

Breathing heavily through my nose, I close my eyes for a moment to regain some level of composure.

"You're willing to make a concession? By taking every penny from the sale of a house that *I* paid for?"

"I'm being more than fair, Gary. If I lose the opportunity to buy the guest house, my motivation to accept a lower payoff goes with it. If that happens, I won't settle for a penny less than fifty per cent of Kirkwood Motors."

I'm taken aback by my wife's cold indifference. It only stokes my indignation, and I can now see why she was keen to have our chat in a public space. If we were at home, I'd be yelling obscenities across the table.

"What even gives you the moral right to do this?" I snarl. "I built that business from nothing, and you contributed nothing. I paid for the house, and I put money in our savings account. In fact, apart from groceries and your own clothes, what the hell have you ever paid for? Shit, I even paid for the car you drove here in."

"That's irrelevant, but to say I contributed nothing to the business is inaccurate."

"Is it? I must have been asleep at my desk when you worked all those hours."

"Who helped you with the admin when you first started?"

"You did one day a week for twelve months."

"I still helped you get the business up and running. And who came up with the company name?"

"Jesus wept," I groan. "You tagged your maiden name to my surname — hardly the work of Saatchi & Saatchi."

"Alright. Who did you talk to when you came home from work? Who listened to all your problems and tried to help you find solutions?"

"You might have listened to me moan a lot, but when it came to significant decisions, you were nothing more than an occasional sounding board."

"I still gave you my opinions, and you acted on those opinions more than once."

"Big deal. You had no active role in the business."

"So you say, but outside of the business, who did all the housework when you were working long hours? Who cooked? Who did all the washing and ironing? Who mowed the lawn, and who managed all the household bills?"

"You did, which is why I'm willing to split the value of the house fifty-fifty. You had fuck-all influence over my business, though, and don't pretend otherwise."

Clare snatches up the sales particulars and returns them to her handbag. She then stands up.

"You're obviously angry, and I'm not prepared to sit here all evening going around in circles. I've made you a more-than-fair offer but if you're not prepared to be reasonable, I'd suggest you seek legal advice."

She then pulls a business card from her pocket and flicks it across the table towards me.

"My lawyer's details are on there," Clare snaps. "Hopefully, once you've slept on my offer, you'll see sense, and we can get on with the divorce. Fair warning, though — if you want to be bloody-minded, it'll cost you."

Without saying goodbye, my so-called wife then strides towards the door and barges straight through it without so much as a glance back.

Chapter 13

I barely slept a wink. It didn't help that I was still awake at two in the morning, scouring countless websites in the hope I'd find evidence supporting my cause. I stayed in The Cherry Tree for another hour after Clare left, downing two double whiskies and a pint of strong lager. The alcohol only fuelled my indignation.

I'm stone-cold sober this morning, but my views are just as entrenched as they were yesterday. I've been more than fair in giving Clare half the value of our house and our savings account, and she's not getting a penny more. How dare she even suggest it? Unfortunately, I couldn't find any information online to back up my assertion one way or another, so whilst I might be rigid in my stance, it looks like I will have to seek legal advice.

One thing I am sure of is that I'm going to play Clare at her own game. She's not the only one who can deliver an ultimatum. I'm hoping I can find a lawyer who'll tell my wife that if she doesn't sign the divorce papers within thirty days, I'll argue that she hasn't paid a penny towards the house and, therefore, she's not entitled to a single brick.

My only problem is that I don't know a lawyer with sufficiently sharp teeth. I do, however, know a man who might.

I arrive at work and hurry up to my office. I've no idea what time Adrian Griffin begins his working day, so I call his mobile number rather than his office. When he finally answers, it sounds like he's in the car.

"Adrian, it's Gary Kirk."

"Morning, old boy. What can I do for you at this ungodly hour?"

"A favour, possibly."

"Go ahead, but I'll warn you — I've not had my second coffee of the day yet."

"It's about my situation."

"Specifically?"

"I mentioned on the phone yesterday that my circumstances have changed, and last night I realised how abruptly. In short, I'm getting divorced."

"Oh, I'm sorry to hear that."

"I suspect I'll hear that a lot over the coming months, but anyway, I could really do with the help of a divorce lawyer. As you're the most connected man I know, I wondered if you knew of anyone?"

"What's wrong with the firm of solicitors you use for Kirkwood?"

"They're okay for employment law and business contracts, but they're not specialists in divorce. I want someone who knows what they're doing."

"I do have an old university chum, Lucas Mayhew, but he's based up in London and charges London rates. Mind you, he's one of the best divorce lawyers in the country, and I wouldn't want anyone else in my corner if Mrs Griffin decided she'd had enough of me."

"He sounds ideal. Could you text me his number when you get a moment?"

"I'll do it the second I arrive in the office."

"And is it okay to mention your name when I call him?"

"Of course, but don't expect Lucas to do you any favours on his fees. He might be more inclined to take on your case if he knows we're connected, but that's as far as my influence will stretch."

"That's great. Thanks so much, Adrian."

"You're welcome, and hopefully, a mere letter from Adrian's firm will prove enough of a deterrent if your wife's lawyer is pushing their luck. In battle, many cower at the mere sight of their opponent and flee before a single shot is fired."

"I really hope you're right."

I end the call and flop back in my chair. Fingers crossed, Adrian gets to the office soon because there's no way I'll be able to focus on work until I've spoken to a legal expert. My mind is all over the place, and I need some assurance that what Clare is asking is unreasonable. Then, we'll see how much time her own lawyer is prepared to give up for free. Not much, I suspect.

Over the ensuing half hour, my team arrive one by one, but my phone remains silent. It isn't until Janine pops her head around the door to say good morning that Adrian's text finally arrives.

"Err, yeah," I mumble back, my attention on the phone. "Morning."

"Are you okay?"

"Slight crisis on my hands. Can you come back in fifteen minutes?"

"Sure."

Janine closes the door while I plug Lucas Mayhew's number into my contact list. It's just gone nine, so perhaps now is the ideal time to call before he gets too stuck into his day. I tap the phone screen to dial the number. It's answered almost immediately.

"Lucas Mayhew."

"Mr Mayhew, my name is Gary Kirk, and I'm told you're the man to speak to regarding a divorce settlement."

"How did you get my number?" he asks, somewhat defensively.

"Adrian Griffin. He's my accountant."

"Ahh, okay," Lucas replies in a slightly warmer tone. "How is the old dog?"

"He's good."

"Glad to hear it. So, what can I do for you, Gary?"

"In short, my wife and I have literally just agreed to divorce, and she wants half my business. As you can imagine, I strongly disagree with her demand."

"Understandable, which is where a divorce lawyer comes in, I presume?"

"Exactly. Can you help?"

"Possibly, but my diary is rammed for the next three weeks, and then I'm away on holiday for a fortnight. If you can wait until mid-May, I'd be happy to meet with you then."

My heart sinks.

"Unfortunately, Lucas, time is not on my side. My wife has set an ultimatum, and I need to establish if she has grounds or if it's just a bluff. If she does have grounds, which I don't think she has, missing her deadline could cost me an additional six-figure sum in any settlement."

"Sounds like she's got you running scared."

"I've spent twenty-odd years building my business, and the thought of her taking half of it makes me feel physically sick. I've offered her half the house and our savings, but that's not enough, apparently."

"Do you have children?"

"No."

"Any other joint dependants?"

"None."

The line falls silent until I hear the repeated click of a mouse.

"I'll tell you what I can do," Lucas finally says. "Email me with a brief overview of your financials, plus some background info on your marriage. I'll have a look once I get ten minutes free, and from there, I can give you an idea of whether your wife's claim is legally sound or not."

"That would be fantastic. Thank you, Lucas."

"Any friend of Adrian's is a friend of mine. Send me that email as soon as you can."

"Yes, will do."

We quickly swap email addresses before Lucas has to rush off to a meeting.

I drop my phone on the desk and puff a long sigh of relief. If a lawyer as successful as Lucas Mayhew thinks it's worth looking into my case, I must have good grounds. He doesn't strike me as the kind of man with time to waste on hopeless cases.

With a few minutes to spare before Janine returns, I do what I should have done before I called Lucas and google his name. At the top of the results page is a link to his company: Morgan, Mayhew & Partners. I click through to a slick website and check the location of their office. It's situated in Belgravia — one of London's most exclusive and expensive areas. That alone should scare the shit out of Clare's lawyer.

Research over, I rush through the morning meeting with Janine and then spend an hour carefully composing an email to Lucas with all the facts relating to my marriage and financial circumstances. I end it with a summary of what Clare is demanding and how stringently I refute that demand.

Once I click the send button, I try to get on with my morning. However, the spectre of Clare's claim haunts my every thought and action. When lunchtime comes, I eat a sandwich at my desk while browsing Rightmove for possible apartments I might buy when the marital house sells. I have absolutely no intention of renting somewhere because it's dead money, and that thought alone helps to reinforce my resolve. Clare cannot and will not get what she demands.

Through some mystic sense of understanding, Janine goes out of her way to avoid disturbing me for the next few hours. At three o'clock, she pokes her head around the door to confirm she's finished for the day.

"Are you okay, Gary?" she asks, her voice tinged with concern. "You look exhausted."

"I'm fine, but thanks for asking."

"Don't work too late, eh."

"No, I won't. Scout's honour."

Janine throws me the look she probably reserves for her boys when they claim they've tidied their bedrooms. It implies she's not convinced.

"I'll see you tomorrow."

"Yeah. Bye, Janine."

For the next two hours, I split my time between staring at my phone, checking my email inbox, and wearing out the office carpet. Lucas didn't say when he'd get back to me, but it could be days. The waiting is torturous because I know Clare is already several steps ahead of me. I need to catch up, and quickly, but until I hear from Lucas, I've no choice but to loiter impatiently on the start line.

As half-five comes and goes, so too have all my team. I'm left alone in an empty building, waiting for a call that's unlikely to come. Lucas is doing me a huge favour, so I can't complain, but I hate feeling so helpless, so vulnerable.

I shut my computer down and turn off the lights.

Wearily, I lock my office door and trudge along the corridor to the stairs. Just as I reach the end, my phone trills from my pocket. I snatch it out, almost dropping it in the process, and jab the screen to accept the call.

"Gary Kirk," I bluster.

"Gary, it's Lucas Mayhew. Have I caught you at a good moment?"

"Definitely," I pant. "I'm still in the office."

"Right, well, I'll get straight to the point — if you were my client, I'd recommend you agree to your wife's proposal."

My heart stops beating momentarily, but that can't be the only part of my body malfunctioning. I must have misheard Lucas.

"Sorry? You're suggesting I give her the house?"

"Based on the little information you provided, I do."

"But ... but why?"

"You strike me as a solid, no-nonsense kind of chap, Gary, so I won't sugarcoat your predicament. If you went the distance with this, there's a fifty-fifty chance you'd win. The problem is that there are no guarantees in court, apart from one."

"Namely?"

"The high cost of getting that far."

"I've got money to fight this."

"I'm sure you have, but why would you spend tens of thousands of pounds on legal fees when your chances of winning are only fifty per cent?"

"It's a matter of principle."

"It probably won't come as a surprise to you, but I hear that a lot. The difference is, many of my clients are so wealthy that the legal fees are pocket change to them. In all good conscience, I'd never let a client in your situation get as far as court."

"Are you seriously saying I should just roll over and let her have what she wants?"

"Because you're not officially my client, Gary, I'll let you into a little secret — the only winners in a divorce are firms like mine. Our clients want us to limit their payout or get the maximum payout. In both cases, they're usually unhappy with the result because we have to reach a fair settlement. No one wins, but no one goes home feeling like they're a loser."

"That's easy to say when it's not your business on the line."

"Your business is only on the line if you decide to contest your wife's claim and lose. Not only could your wife take half your business, but you'll also have a five-figure legal bill to settle. Think about that."

"I ... I ..."

I'm incensed, but there's no point aiming my anger at Lucas Mayhew.

"It's just so unfair," I huff.

"If it's any comfort," Lucas continues. "At least you don't have kids. Money can be earned, but when your kids are unjustly taken from you, that's a whole different level of unfair."

"If we'd had kids, I doubt I'd be talking to you now."

"Who knows, but it's not really the point. I need to be somewhere else, but if you want my advice, get drunk tonight, be angry, and then once you've slept on it, I hope you make the right decision."

His point made, Lucas wishes me well and terminates the call. It takes every ounce of resolve not to hurl my phone against the nearest wall.

I am angry, and I might go home and drink myself into a stupor, but that's as far as I'm willing to run with Lucas's advice. There has to be another way.

Chapter 14

I don't have the tidiest handwriting at the best of times. Last night, after seven cans of strong lager, the slip of paper currently sitting on the kitchen table is barely legible. That's not to say I don't know what numbers I scrawled because they are now permanently etched in my mind. I stare at the slip of paper while sipping a strong coffee.

House (after selling costs) — £530,000
50% of savings account — £51,700
TOTAL = £581,700

When I offered Clare half the house and half of everything in our savings account, I thought I was being generous. It's more than enough for her to buy a nice home of her own without a mortgage, something she'd never have been able to do if we hadn't walked down the aisle almost twenty-five years ago. Not only did I fund every meaningful aspect of our lives, but I also supported Clare so she could indulge her obsession with pseudo-therapies and that ridiculous charity.

And what thanks do I get? A threat to take half my business if I don't give her the house I paid for. Even if I overlook Clare's completely unjust claim, just thinking about the consequences boils my blood. She'd end up with an asset worth half a million quid while I'd be left to plug a huge hole in my finances.

It's not fair, and it's not right, and despite Lucas Mayhew's advice, I'm just as wound up this morning as I was yesterday. In fact, I'm so infuriated that my first task upon waking up was to email our company solicitor, Ian Burke, asking to see him on a matter of some urgency. Lucas might be one of the best divorce lawyers in the country, allegedly, but even the best make mistakes. I need a second opinion, and I won't rest until I've got one.

An hour later, I flop down in my office chair and switch on the computer. As I wait for it to boot up, a message alert pings on my phone. I grab it from the desk and, upon seeing Clare's name, the hackles rise. *You haven't contacted Aaron to put the house up for sale yet. Why not?*

My first instinct is to reply with a few choice words and a reminder that I paid for the bloody house, but I need to tread carefully. From this moment on, Clare and I are at war, and I don't want to reveal my strategy or let her know she's got under my skin. I reply with a short, succinct message: *It's in hand.*

I place my phone back on the desk and stare at it, waiting for Clare to reply. A minute passes, and the phone remains silent, suggesting my message did what I intended. Turning my attention back to the computer monitor, I open my email program and watch on as dozens of messages cascade in. At the top is a reply from Ian Burke, sent only five minutes ago. I open the email, and I'm relieved to see Ian has managed to squeeze in an appointment for me at 11.00 am. Considering how much money I've paid his firm over the last twenty years, it's the least I expected, and I hope Ian's eagerness to please his clients continues after we've met.

To distract my thoughts from divorce-related matters, I sift through the rest of my emails until Janine arrives.

"Good morning," she trills. "Coffee?"

"Morning. Yes, I'd love a coffee, please."

"You look like you need it. What time did you leave the office last night?"

"Err, not late, but I had an appalling night's sleep."

Janine replies with a sympathetic smile and then scoots off to make us both a coffee. She returns a few minutes later, and we get started.

"You've got a Zoom meeting with John Douglas from Apex Finance at ten," she confirms. "And then Nina Williams from Trading Standards is coming in at eleven."

"Cancel her."

"Why? We've been waiting to begin the accreditation process since January."

"Because I'm going to see Ian Burke at eleven."

"It's not in my diary."

"I only booked the appointment ten minutes ago, but it's kind of important I see him urgently."

"Oh. Anything I need to worry about?"

"Why do you ask that?"

"Arranging an urgent meeting with the company solicitor sounds a bit ominous."

Janine's expression matches the slight apprehension in her voice. In an ideal world, I'd keep my private life private, but I don't want her to worry.

"If I tell you something, I need your word it won't go any further."

"How long have you known me, Gary?"

"Err, a number of years."

"Long enough to know that I'd never betray your trust, wouldn't you say?"

"Yes, I would."

"So, what's the problem?"

"I told you that Clare and I have separated, but the situation has escalated in recent days, and we're getting a divorce. I need to see Ian because Clare is making ridiculous demands."

"That's ... I don't know what to say other than sorry."

"Thank you."

"Dare I ask what she's demanding?"

"I'll spare you the whole story, but she wants our house plus half our savings. It comes close to six-hundred grand in total."

"Shit," Janine gasps. "No wonder you've looked so stressed in recent days. I knew something wasn't right."

"As always, you read me like a book."

"It's because I care about you, Gary. You're not just a good boss but a good man."

"That's kind of you to say, but, unfortunately, my initial research suggests that even good men get stiffed in the divorce courts. Whatever the outcome, I know it'll cost me a small fortune."

"You'll hate me for saying this, but at the end of the day, it's only money."

"That's taken two decades of hard graft to amass."

"I know, but if I've learned anything over the last few years, it's that you can still be happy even if money is tight."

"Are you happy, then?"

"I am," she replies with a broad smile. "I've got two beautiful kids, a small but lovely home, and a supportive family ... oh, and a job I love. My life is almost perfect."

"Almost?"

"Yes," she chuckles. "I'm still waiting for Mr Right to make a move, and then life will be perfect."

If the gossip I've overheard is to be trusted, Mr Right is a sales rep called Gavin. He pops in and flirts with Janine at every given opportunity.

"Well, whoever he is, I hope he doesn't keep you waiting too long."

"He's worth waiting for," Janine replies with a strangely forlorn frown. "But, it's complicated."

Neither of us says anything for a moment, but then Janine snaps back into business mode. She confirms she'll rearrange my eleven o'clock meeting, and then we plough through the rest of the day's agenda. That done, my office manager hurries back to her desk, but the scent of her perfume lingers around for a while longer. I like it. I like it a lot.

All too soon, I'm stuck on a Zoom call with John Douglas from Apex Finance. Kirkwood Motors makes a tidy commission whenever a customer uses finance to buy a car, which is the only reason I'm willing to tolerate John's monotone voice and painfully dull conversation. Twenty minutes into it, I cut the meeting short and promise to catch up with John at a later date. If I can avoid that date for two or three years, it'll still be too soon.

I check I've got my car keys and phone, then confirm with Janine that I'm heading out and I'll be gone for at least an hour.

The offices of Burke & Co are located on Elderton High Street, just over two miles away. It's a journey that usually only takes ten minutes, but the route has been blighted by roadworks all month, and I'm not willing to risk being late. My prudence is proven justified after I cross a roundabout and enter the top end of the High Street. The road is blocked with barriers, and a yellow sign states that all diverted traffic should turn right.

Five frustrating minutes later, the detour ends at the opposite end of the High Street. Only then do I realise that both ends are closed to traffic.

"Bollocks," I groan.

With no other option, I continue on until I find a parking space. I still have to walk the entire length of the High Street to get to Ian's office, but fortunately, time is on my side.

I seldom have reason to visit Elderton's town centre, but the last time I wandered up the High Street, I was taken aback by the number of empty shops. Maybe it's just my memory playing tricks, but I could swear there are even fewer businesses still trading on this occasion. It's a sorry sight and a far cry from the bustling town centre I remember from my youth. It's a timely reminder of what happens to businesses when consumers change their buying habits. The reason there are no travel agents on the High Street is that hardly anyone pops into town to book a holiday these days. Who's to say that used-car dealers won't suffer the same fate in the not-too-distant future?

With five minutes to spare, I reach the offices of Burke & Co and push open the door. After confirming my appointment with the receptionist, she leads me through to Ian Burke's office. As I enter, the man himself stands up behind his desk and greets me warmly.

"Morning, Gary," he beams. "Lovely to see you."

Ian is closing in on retirement age, but despite the craggy face and white hair, there's still a distinct twinkle in his pale eyes.

"You too, and thanks for seeing me at such short notice."

We sit down, and Ian poses a few polite questions about the fortunes of Kirkwood Motors before getting down to business.

"Might I assume you're here because of an urgent legal matter?" he asks.

"Yes, but it's not business-related. I want a divorce."

If Ian is taken aback by my forthright reply, he doesn't let it show.

"The end of any marriage is always a shame," he sighs. "But, sadly, a higher percentage seem to fail with every passing year."

"Good for business, though?"

"I never wanted to add divorce litigation to our services, but you're right — it now accounts for a quarter of our income."

"That suggests you've had plenty of practise, helping your clients reach a fair settlement?"

"Indeed," Ian replies. "Which brings us nicely to your situation. Have you got as far as discussing the broader terms of your settlement with Mrs Kirk?"

"We've discussed it, but we're miles apart on what we think is fair, I'm afraid."

"Right, you'd better give me the details, then."

I explain every bitter detail of Clare's demands and my refusal to accept those demands. Ian listens patiently, scribbling the occasional note but remaining unreadable.

"You can understand why I wanted to see you so urgently," I say in conclusion.

"Yes, I can."

Ian then sits forward, resting his arms on the desk.

"And, are you willing to fight my corner?"

"Of course, but I must be honest about our odds of success, Gary."

"Which are?"

"Put it this way. If I were representing Mrs Kirk, I'd feel a lot more confident about winning."

I swear under my breath.

"I'm sorry," Ian continues. "I know it's not what you want to hear, but I'd advise you to let her have the house."

"The house I paid for."

"I understand your frustration, Gary, and I'm on your side. But as your legal advisor, I'd grab that deal while it's on offer. If your wife goes after the business, the financial ramifications could be catastrophic."

"You don't have to tell me, but ... but the thought of giving away so much money sickens me to the pit of my stomach."

"I'm sure it does," he replies in a slightly patronising tone. "No one likes losing money."

"With respect, you don't get it, Ian — it's not just numbers on a spreadsheet."

"Isn't it?"

"No, that house represents a significant milestone in my life, and to just give it to Clare feels like … I don't know … the only way I can explain it is like a man serving a long-term sentence in prison, knowing that he's wasted so many years he'll never get back. I worked so bloody hard to buy that house, and then I worked even harder to keep it. If Clare has her way, it's like she's taking all those years from me."

Frustrated, I sit forward and pinch the bridge of my nose. I know I'm wasting my breath because Ian Burke is a man of the law, and there's no room for emotion or sentiment in law.

"What do you want me to do?" he asks.

"I don't know."

"I could write to Mrs Kirk's solicitor and put forward a counter-proposal, but it's not without risk. From what you've told me, her sole motivation is to buy that property, and if she doesn't fulfil that ambition, she'll have nothing to lose by going for the business."

"No, just … I need to think about it."

"Understood."

Having made his position clear, Ian offers a few platitudes and then suggests I call him once I've decided on my next move. With two legal experts telling me I should give up the house and walk away, my options appear limited.

I thank Ian for his time and leave.

Chapter 15

As I traipse back along the High Street, my mood is as dark as the clouds overhead. It'd be just my luck if the heavens open before I make it back to the car. I pass a coffee shop and consider nipping in to console myself with a double espresso, but what I really want, in truth, is a double scotch.

Christ, I never thought I'd say it, but I fucking hate my wife.

A couple of years ago, I watched a crime documentary on Netflix about a business tycoon in America who was having an affair with his secretary. His wife found out and, unsurprisingly, began divorce proceedings. Her lawyer demanded a $100 million settlement, but a month later, Mrs Tycoon's bloated corpse washed up on a local beach. It took over two years to prove the case, but in the end, the husband received an eighty-year sentence for murder.

At the time, I remember thinking the tycoon was an absolute twat. Even if he'd given his wife $100 million, he'd still have $100 million in the bank — more money than anyone could ever need. It made no sense, even when they interviewed him in jail, and he claimed it wasn't just about the money; it was about winning.

No matter how much I hate what Clare is doing, I'd never wish harm on her, but now I understand how that murderous tycoon felt. It's not so much about losing money but losing. There's also the issue of funding my new venture. I've not got as far as drafting a business plan, but having significantly less capital to invest would curtail my ambitions right from the outset.

I trudge on with my hands in my pockets, trying to think of another way to undermine Clare's demand, ideally without resorting to murder. I'm so lost in my thoughts I almost bump into a woman stepping across my path.

"Sorry," I mumble, even though the minor brushing of shoulders wasn't my fault.

"Hello again, Gary," the woman replies.

I reply with a puzzled frown. Her gaunt features and clipped tone ring a bell somewhere in the back of my memory, but I've met a lot of people over the years, including thousands of customers. I can't possibly remember everyone's name.

"Um, hello," I reply. "How are you?"

"Alive, still. You?"

"I'm fine, thanks."

"And how are things on the marital front?"

I'm confused by her question, and I think it shows on my face. The woman tilts her head slightly, her semi-smile unwavering.

"You don't remember me, do you, Gary?"

I reply with a grimace. "Sorry. I'm terrible with names and faces."

"We met at the town hall last week. Edith Stimp."

I've tried hard to forget last Friday, which is probably why I've not given a moment's thought to the woman now standing in front of me.

"Oh, yes. My apologies."

"I'm sure you've had a lot on your mind, so no apology required."

"I have, yes, but sorry, anyway."

"Would I be right in assuming you're still having issues?"

"With my marriage?"

"Yes."

"Yeah," I snort. "You could say that."

"I'm sorry to hear that, but my offer still stands."

"Your offer?"

"I suggested we talk about your options."

"It's been a hectic time, so to be honest with you, Edith, I'd forgotten."

"Never mind. Would you like to have a conversation about the state of your marriage?"

She turns and points over her shoulder towards the opening of an alleyway.

"My premises are at the end," she says. "I can spare ten minutes if you can."

The time is neither here nor there — it's the motivation I can't spare.

"Thanks, but my marriage is past the point of saving."

"I wasn't offering to save your marriage, Gary. My expertise lies elsewhere."

"But didn't you say you're a relationship counsellor or something along those lines?"

"No, I said I'm a relationship resolution advisor. I can help you fix your current difficulties at the very source."

"I'm not sure I understand."

"If you have ten minutes, I can explain. I promise you won't regret it."

The prospect of trading ten minutes of my time for almost six-hundred grand is too tempting. Besides, now I've had my legal rights confirmed for a second time, I really don't have anything to lose.

"Okay. I can spare ten minutes."

"Splendid," she beams. "This way."

Edith Stimp then guides me towards the cobbled alleyway she appeared from. I follow a step behind and happen to glance up at the road sign fixed to a decaying brick wall: *Dent's Passage*. I must have walked past this alleyway hundreds of times over the years, but I've never had reason to investigate what's down here. It's no wonder the name didn't ring any bells.

Hemmed in on both sides by brick walls, the alleyway is the last place anyone suffering from claustrophobia would wish to wander. The cobbles are worn down in the centre of the narrow path, and their very existence implies this must be one of the original parts of Elderton, back when it was just a village.

We reach the end and a solid wooden door recessed into another wall with moss-tainted bricks and crumbling mortar. Edith Stimp gives the door handle a firm twist and leans her left shoulder up against the wood.

"It's a bit stiff," she remarks. "One shove should do it."

She thumps against the door, and it creaks open.

"Come in, Gary," she urges.

Tentatively, I step through the doorway, wondering if maybe I should have popped into the coffee shop after all.

"Welcome to my humble abode," Edith announces somewhat theatrically.

It isn't what I expected. Roughly the size of a double garage, the walls are exposed brick with thick oak beams running left to right above my head and slabs of solid stone beneath my feet. It's also crowded with period furniture and, although I'm no expert, I'd guess each piece is from a different period.

"Do you like it?"

The vibe is more antique warehouse than therapist's office, but I nod politely.

"Yes, it's ... interesting."

"The collection is a little eclectic, and I've far too many pieces, but I just adore each and every stick of it."

She runs her fingers across the top of a mahogany trunk-like box decorated with intricate gold patterns. I couldn't even begin to guess its provenance or purpose.

"Come and take a seat," Edith then says.

We zigzag through the maze of furniture to the back of the room, where two wingback armchairs are separated by a coffee table that looks too old to be called a coffee table. She's yet to reveal anything about her supposed solution to my marital issues, and with every passing second, I'm beginning to suspect Edith Stimp might be as full of shit as she is eccentric.

"I must apologise for the temperature," she then remarks. "Would you like me to take your jacket?"

Her apology is well-founded because it is uncomfortably warm. Edith Stimp's energy bills must be eye-watering.

"It's important to keep the building at eighty degrees Fahrenheit, or approximately twenty-seven degrees centigrade if you prefer metric."

"Thanks," I reply, slipping off my jacket, which Edith transfers to a coat stand in the corner.

Without explaining why the building needs to be so warm, my host gestures for me to sit. She then slowly lowers herself into the other armchair and crosses her legs. Like the first time we met, she's dressed conservatively, the hem of her dark-grey skirt resting midway between her knee and her ankle.

"Have you lived in Elderton long, Gary?" Edith Stimp then asks.

"All my life."

"And how long is that life, thus far?"

"Forty-five years."

"The years have treated you well. You could easily pass as forty, possibly even late thirties."

"That's, err ... thanks."

Even if I were so inclined to return the compliment, which I'm not, I couldn't begin to guess Edith Stimp's age. The edges of her green eyes are beginning to show the slightest sign of crow's feet, and her skin is so pale it's almost opaque. Her attire, though, is that of a much older woman, as is her hairstyle; a tightly wound bun of chestnut hair sitting atop her head. She could be in her mid-forties, but I wouldn't be shocked if she claimed to be in her late-fifties.

"As a lifelong Elderton resident, it might interest you to know that you're currently sitting in one of the town's oldest buildings. It dates back to 1812."

"Is it listed?" I ask out of politeness rather than curiosity.

"I couldn't possibly say, but I do know it was originally a servant's lodge for the Manor House. Unfortunately, the main house burned to the ground just before The Great War. Almost every building in the town centre is built upon the grounds of the original Manor House."

"Oh, I didn't know that."

"The past is a fascinating place to spend time, Gary, and a source of incredible knowledge."

"I'm sure it is, but—"

"My husband acquired this building some years back because he wanted a place to tinker. Sadly, he passed, so I repurposed the old place ... well, most of it."

Edith Stimp looks up toward the oak beams and exhales a heavy sigh. Now she's mentioned her dead husband, it would be rude to get up and leave without at least offering a token platitude.

"I'm sorry for your loss."

"So am I, Gary, but I was so blessed to have spent thirty-six years married to Allan. In fact, the very reason I do what I now do is partly as a tribute to my own relationship."

"About that. Can we get to the part where you tell me what it is you actually do because I really need to get back to work?"

"Yes, of course, but let me explain my motivation because you need to understand why I'm about to offer you the chance of a lifetime."

"Whenever I've heard that phrase, it's usually just before someone asks for a large sum of money."

"You're concerned about the cost of my solution?"

"No, because I'm not a mug, but if you're about to sell me an overpriced course on healing relationships, forget it."

"I'm not about to sell you an overpriced anything, Gary. The cost of my solution is one British pound."

"A quid?" I scoff.

"Yes, but I don't much like that word. It's a coarse description of the monarch's currency."

"A quid, a pound ... whatever. You can't buy anything for a pound these days, and I don't even know what it is you're selling."

"I'm not selling anything, but I am conscious you're in a hurry, so I'll try to explain what I'm offering you and why. You can owe me the pound – I trust you."

"Thank you," I reply, resisting the urge to roll my eyes.

Edith sits upright, locking her hands together and resting them in her lap.

"Your marriage is in crisis, yes?"

"It's past the point of saving if that's what you're asking."

"How long have you and Mrs Kirk been together?"

"We met in 1996 and married two and a half years later. All told, we've been a couple for twenty-seven years."

"How would you describe those twenty-seven years? Have they been happy?"

"We were certainly happy for the first decade, but, in all honesty, we haven't been happy for a long time."

"As sad as that is, Gary, it's all too common a situation. So many couples remain together for decades, settling for apathy and self-delusion over happiness."

"That's a pretty good summary of my marriage."

"Does that make you sad?"

"Of course it does. Everyone wants to meet their soul mate, fall in love, and enjoy their happily ever after, don't they?"

"They do, and some of us are fortunate enough to experience exactly what you just described. Allan was my soul mate, my best friend, and I couldn't imagine loving any man more than I loved my husband."

"You were lucky, Edith. I wasn't."

"I'm not sure how much of a part luck played, but yes, I was fortunate. You, on the other hand, were clearly not."

"Not on the marital front, no."

"I understand, and that brings me to an important question: if you were gifted the opportunity to go back and do it all again, would you meet and marry the same woman?"

"Christ, no," I snort. "Not in a million years."

"Your reply sounds grounded in negative emotion. Can I ask you to take a moment to think a little deeper and then answer the question again?"

"You want me to consider if I'd knowingly make the same mistake?"

"I never said it was a mistake — you did. But, yes, I'd like you to consider the implications thoroughly. Would your life be better today if you'd never met? Would your wife's?"

"In the last few weeks alone, I've lost count of how many times I've daydreamed about what might have been if I hadn't met Clare."

"My question doesn't relate to an abstract idea, Gary — I'm talking about a literal proposal. If you could go back in time and avoid meeting your wife, would you?"

"In a heartbeat," I reply without hesitation.

"You genuinely mean that?"

"Yes, and I also genuinely think I'm wasting my time if all you've got to offer is ridiculous hypothetical questions."

I place my hands on the arms of the chair, ready to push myself up.

"Who said it was hypothetical?" Edith eventually replies.

"Pardon?"

"My question. Who said it was hypothetical?"

Chapter 16

My hands are still on the arms of the chair, but my backside remains pressed to the cracked leather seat. Edith Stimp is staring at me, her thin eyebrows arched in anticipation of a response.

"Do you understand the meaning of the word hypothetical?" I ask.

"Of course."

"Are you sure, because there's no context for your question other than the hypothetical?"

"There are a handful of people who would beg to differ, Gary, and I include myself amongst that blessed handful."

My thoughts scattered, I know for sure that the opposite of up is down, and the opposite of left is right, but for the life of me, I can't determine what word is the opposite of hypothetical. Real? Actual? Neither sounds right, but my brain isn't willing to dig any deeper.

"Let me get this straight," I say with an appropriate level of scorn. "You're asking me if I want to what? Travel back in time and somehow prevent my younger self from meeting Clare?"

"Do you remember where you met your wife?"

"We met at a pub here in Elderton called The Black Prince. Developers bulldozed it two years later and built a block of flats in its place."

"And what about the date?"

"I know exactly when we met."

"How can you be so sure?"

"Because it was the 6th of April — my dad's birthday. I was supposed to meet him for a drink in The Black Prince, but for reasons I really don't want to get into, he didn't make it. So, yes, I'm sure of the date."

"That's splendid," Edith says brightly. "Then, yes, I am asking you if you'd like to travel back in time and prevent your younger self from meeting the future Mrs Kirk."

"Is this a prank?"

I turn in my chair and look up towards the oak beams, hoping to spot a hidden camera. There isn't one, but I suppose the whole point of a hidden camera is that it's hidden.

"No, it's not a prank, Gary."

"A bet, then?"

"A bet?"

"Have you made a bet that you can convince some random sucker that you've achieved what no scientist has ever been able to prove is possible, let alone achieve?"

"I don't approve of gambling. It's such an uncouth pursuit."

"So, if it's not a prank or a bet, there's only one remaining conclusion to draw, and I'm too well-mannered to share that conclusion with you."

"You think I'm insane?"

"Not quite the word I had in mind, but close."

"But, what if I'm not? What if I really have just offered you the chance of a lifetime?"

"Time travel is impossible."

"No, it is not."

"Yes, it is."

"We could sit here all day and argue about it, so would a practical demonstration change your view?"

"Sure," I snort. "You've got a DeLorean parked out back, right?"

"What's a DeLorean?"

"It's a car they used in the time-travel film, *Back to The Future*."

"I've never seen it."

"You should. It's a great film."

"I'll be sure to look it up if I'm ever at a loose end."

I take an exaggerated glance at my watch and stand up. "Gosh, is that the time? I'd better be going."

"You don't want to see a practical demonstration of time travel?"

"I would, but I've got a niggly feeling that I'm unlikely to see one here this afternoon."

Edith gets to her feet and takes a couple of steps towards me.

"I understand your scepticism but only a fool would turn his back on such an opportunity without making even the slightest effort to determine if it's genuine. Are you a fool, Gary? Have I misjudged you?"

"I'm no one's fool, which is why I'm leaving now."

"Fair enough," Edith sighs. "But I hope you come to terms with the question."

"What question?"

"The question that has plagued every single human at one point in their life."

"Namely?"

"What might have been?"

"Guess I'll have to live with not knowing."

"Yes, it seems so, but for your sake, I really hope you are able to live without knowing who you might have married if you hadn't met your wife. Or what kind of father you might have been."

Rather than depart, I stare back at Edith Stimp. "What makes you think I wanted children?"

"Did you?"

"Maybe."

"But you didn't have any. Why not?"

"I don't know. The timing was never right."

"The timing wasn't right ... or the prospective mother?"

"Both, I guess."

"And you regret not having children?"

"Some days I do, but I've never much seen the point of regret. You can't change ..."

"The past?"

"No."

"If you genuinely believe that with every fibre of your being, you'd better be on your way."

"I do."

"With every fibre? There's not even the smallest voice in the back of your head, whispering those quiet questions you can't answer. Would you have had a daughter, a son, or both? What names might you have chosen? Could you see them taking their first steps or waving a tearful goodbye on their first day at school?"

I'm not about to admit it, but I've asked every question and so many more. Countless times I've imagined every milestone moment of a child who was never meant to be.

"Last chance, Gary. This is a one-time, never-to-be-repeated offer."

I rock forward on the balls of my feet, but it's almost as if there's an invisible thread tethering me to the stone floor. It wouldn't take much to pull away, but it's strong enough to halt my progress for another second.

"This is ridiculous," I mumble. "I've got a thousand things I should be doing."

"Five minutes is all it'll take. Those thousand tasks can wait five minutes, I'm sure."

"I don't know what's crazier — your claim or my willingness to indulge it."

"The worst that can happen is you'll leave here five minutes from now, slightly miffed that you wasted the time it takes to hard boil an egg. Compared to what you might gain, I'd say that's a risk worth taking, wouldn't you?"

"Fine," I huff. "Show me whatever you want to show me, but make it quick, okay."

If Edith Stimp is pleased with her powers of persuasion, she doesn't let the satisfaction reach her face.

"Very well," she says crisply. "Come this way."

She turns and strides towards a large mahogany armoire near the right-hand wall, beckoning me to follow. For a moment, I question why we're heading towards a brick wall but, as we skirt past the armoire, the reason becomes evident — a door.

Edith Stimp opens the door and flicks a switch just inside. A weak bulb illuminates a wooden staircase leading up to, I presume, another floor. If that staircase had led in the opposite direction, down to a basement, I'd be far less inclined to follow. I've seen enough creepy films to know that only bad things happen in basements.

I follow a few steps behind as we climb the stairs, each tread squealing a creak as if surprised by the sudden call to do its job. As I approach the last stair but one, Edith stops on a small featureless landing lit by another weak bulb. To her right is a door, distinctly different to the one at the bottom of the stairs. Faced in stainless steel, it appears to be a fire door but with a levered handle rather than the traditional horizontal bar.

"It's just through here," Edith Stimp confirms as she pushes down on the door handle.

The door opens with a mournful groan, much lower in pitch to the squeal of the stair treads. Edith passes through the doorway and disappears from view. With some hesitation, I climb the last two stairs and come to a stop on the landing. I want to see what's in the room before committing. The answer is more of a surprise than a shock.

"Come on in," Edith urges from the other side. "And please excuse the décor. It's not what you'd call homely, I grant you."

From my vantage point, I can see the room is roughly the size of the average lounge in the average home, but that's where the room stops being average. Every surface is crudely covered by a patchwork of steel sheets: the ceiling, the floor, and the three walls I can see from the doorway. It is, to all intents and purposes, a windowless metal box, but with one prominent feature in the centre.

"Is that a barber's chair?"

Edith turns around and stands to the side of said chair. My question was partly rhetorical because the chair obviously is a barber's chair, albeit a vintage model judging by the flaking paint on the base.

"Yes, it is."

"I've seen it all now," I snort. "You can travel back in time while getting a short back and sides."

"It's just a chair, Gary. I presume Allan chose it because of its sturdy construction."

"Your husband is responsible for ... this?"

Edith rotates the barber's chair around and leans up against the backrest.

"Yes, although I had no idea until a few months after he passed. When I first discovered this room, I couldn't begin to fathom what purpose it served."

"Was your husband a scientist or just an unqualified ..."

I stop myself from saying the word nutjob because although it might be true of Edith's late husband, it would be disrespectful to say it out loud.

"He was a man of science, yes, but he left his place of employment shortly after his fiftieth birthday. From that day onwards, he spent most of his free time here."

"Let me guess — developing a time machine?"

"I know you're deeply sceptical of my claim, Gary, but I'd be grateful if you dropped your mocking tone. Even though Allan is long gone, this is his life's work, and a little respect would be appreciated."

"Sorry," I mumble.

"Apology accepted. Now, would you like me to explain what I know about this room and the wonders within?"

"Fire away, but please bear in mind your audience is already close to incredulous."

"As was I when Rupert suggested what Allan might have been up to."

"Who's Rupert?"

"One of Allan's oldest friends and one-time colleague at the institute. After I discovered the room, I asked him to pop over because I wanted to know what on earth my husband had created."

Edith nods towards my left shoulder, and I instinctively spin around. Behind me, to the right of the door, are two shelving units. Each of the six shelves is crammed with electronic paraphernalia, but I couldn't begin to guess what any of it is. To the side, in the corner, sits an old-fashioned safe the size of a washing machine but likely weighing five times as much.

"I'm no electronics expert," I reply. "But to me, it looks like your husband liked hoarding junk."

"That was my first thought, too, until Rupert found the operating switch and activated the machine."

"And then, what happened?"

"Nothing."

"Nothing?"

"Not nothing, exactly. The equipment on the shelf hummed, and an array of lights began flashing, but that was that. Rupert spent over an hour trying to fathom the machine's purpose but to no avail. He left, and I poured myself a large glass of brandy, but I might have accidentally ..."

Edith stops mid-sentence and looks at her watch.

"I'm conscious that you have neither the time nor the belief for me to explain in detail, so why don't we cut to the chase? Do you want to go back in time and prevent your younger self from meeting your current wife?"

"This is ridiculous. I don't—"

"Yes, or no, Gary."

"Okay, I'll humour you. Yes, I do."

"Splendid," she replies. "Take a seat, and I'll explain the rules."

"What rules?"

"If you sit down, I'll tell you."

I shrug my shoulders, step over to the chair, and sit down. As crazy as this is, part of me is curious how far Edith Stimp is prepared to go with her delusion.

"Rule one," she begins. "It varies slightly from trip to trip but do whatever you need to do within two hours."

"Why two hours?"

"You'd have to ask an expert in quantum physics for the actual answer. All I can tell you is that around the two-hour mark, you'll begin to feel light-headed and mildly nauseous. That feeling quickly escalates but don't be alarmed — it's all part of the process."

"What do you mean by escalate?"

"You'll develop a migraine-like headache, and then you'll pass out. When you wake up, you'll be back in the chair."

"Alright."

"Rule two. You cannot under any circumstances interact with your younger self or with family members or friends. In fact, you should avoid interacting with anyone you know."

"Why?"

"Because the ramifications are as dire as they are complex. Any interaction, no matter how insignificant, could change their future beyond all comprehension."

"If that's the case, how the hell do I change what happened when I met Clare?"

"Use your imagination," Edith frowns. "Did you seriously think you could just stroll up to your teenage self and tell him what to do?"

"Yes."

"Well, you can't."

"Then, how do I stop us from meeting?"

"One of my previous clients knew his future wife was on a train in the minutes before they met. When he travelled back, he journeyed on that same train, but in a different carriage, and pulled the emergency cord. The driver had no choice but to slow the train to a standstill while the guard checked the carriage. The delay ensured my client never did bump into his future wife in a sandwich shop at King's Cross."

"Oh. Clever."

"Yes, it was, and I must re-emphasise that you cannot make any form of contact with your younger self. It might be tempting, but it won't end well."

"Okay. Understood."

"Rule three. There are no second chances, so don't mess up."

"That doesn't make any sense. If you own a time travel machine, surely you can go back as many times as you like and make as many changes as you like."

"I thought exactly that too, until I realised that every journey subjects the participant to a not-insignificant dose of gamma radiation."

"Gamma?" I cough. "As in deadly gamma rays?"

"Don't panic, Gary," Edith says calmly. "One trip is no more likely to cause harm than an X-ray but take it from me — you do not want to risk a second trip, never mind a third, fourth, or fifth."

"That's reassuring," I lie.

"Good. Now, can you repeat the three rules for me, just to be sure you understand them all?"

"First rule, I've only got two hours."

"Correct."

"Second, I can't interact with anyone I know, including myself."

"That's very important. Next?"

"Third, don't mess up because I'll only have one chance."

"Excellent," she says, clapping her hands together. "All I need now is the exact date and time of your first meeting with your future wife, and we can proceed."

Edith steps over to the bank of electronics and taps away at a keyboard as I, still bemused by the whole charade, casually quote the date and approximate time I first met Clare. That done, Edith turns around.

"Are we all set?"

"To travel back in time," I reply with a hint of sarcasm in my voice. "Yep, I'm all set."

She nods and then turns to a switch on the wall that wouldn't look out of place next to an electric chair. She pulls the switch down, and a low hum builds from the bank of electronics.

"There's a one-minute timer before the chair activates," Edith then confirms. "Because of the radiation, I need to wait outside.

Don't be alarmed if you suddenly feel a little unwell — it's perfectly normal."

Before I can question what she means by unwell, Edith bustles over to the door and promptly closes it behind her. Only then does it dawn on me that this might not be such a great idea. Panic mounts as the hum from the electronics intensifies.

"Stay in the chair," Edith's voice then booms from a speaker above my head. "If you're not in the chair at the point of departure, you risk injuring yourself when you arrive at the other end."

"Eh? No. I've changed my mind."

"It's too late," comes the reply. "Once the system is activated, I can't unlock the door — it's a safety mechanism."

I jump up and grab the door handle. No matter how hard I push down, the damn thing won't budge.

"Sit down, Gary," Edith demands. "Now!"

The lights begin to flicker, and it suddenly feels like I'm locked in a giant microwave oven with a swarm of electronic wasps. Pressure begins to build in my skull like a head cold, not helped by the swell of an acidic tide that threatens to breach my oesophagus.

"Ten seconds! Sit down!"

I push the door handle again but to no avail. Left with no choice, and my legs growing weaker by the second, I stumble back across the room and fall into the barber's chair.

"Five seconds, Gary."

"Stop! I don't like this!"

"Three ... two ... one!"

Chapter 17

I awake with a jolt and blink at the harsh light. Three initial thoughts crash in. Firstly, I'm not dead, which is a relief. Secondly, I'm still in Edith Stimp's metal-clad shrine to period electronics. Thirdly, there's an awful smell in the air, like burnt hair. Instinctively, I reach up and check it's not mine. It's not.

Despite a slight wooziness and a raging thirst, I'm no worse for my ordeal, but I could kick myself for playing along with Edith's fantasy. Jesus, she could have killed me or kept me imprisoned as a sex slave, although I don't currently have the mental capacity to consider which would be the worse of those two fates.

I clamber out of the chair and stand for a moment to check all my faculties are functioning. Physically, I'm okay, but when I look towards the door, my mind goes into panic mode again — am I still locked in? I stagger forward and grab the door handle, keenly aware that if it's still locked, I'm in deep shit. I offer a silent prayer and push the handle down.

"Thank you, God," I whisper as the thick metal door creaks open.

Halfway down the stairs, I happen to glance at my watch, which I'm relieved to see is still on my wrist. The stainless-steel Rolex was a fortieth-birthday present to myself, and although it's one of the brand's less expensive models, it's still worth the best part of five grand. However, whilst Edith Stimp didn't steal my watch while I was unconscious, I can't yet say she hasn't taken my wallet or phone — both in the pocket of my jacket.

I reach the bottom of the stairs and open the door to the warehouse-like room I first entered.

"What the …"

My jacket isn't on the coat stand because there is no coat stand. In fact, the room is completely empty — Edith Stimp's entire collection of antique furniture; gone. I take a couple of faltering steps forward, turn a full three-sixty degrees, and blink three times. My eyes, it seems, are not deceiving me.

How long was I unconscious? Patently long enough for a team of porters to whisk away dozens of items of furniture. I take another glance at my watch, but on this occasion, I actually check the time: 11:44 am. That can't be right.

The obvious conclusion is that I've lost an entire day because I left Ian Burke's office at roughly 11.25 am, but then I notice a troubling issue with my watch. The second hand that's gracefully swept around the dial every second of every minute since I first slipped the Rolex onto my wrist over five years ago, is now stationary.

I tap the glass twice, but unsurprisingly, the second hand resolutely refuses to turn. Rolex is famous for the reliability of its watches, so I can't understand why mine has stopped. For now, though, I have more significant concerns, namely my missing jacket, phone, and wallet.

I've still got a number of questions I'd like answered, but they'll have to wait because I want to check my car is where I left it. If it is, I'll need to plead with a random stranger in the hope they might let me borrow a phone so I can call Janine. She'll be able to bring me the spare key from my desk drawer, but there isn't much I can do about my missing phone.

"Bloody Edith Stimp," I grumble as I cross the stone floor towards the exit.

The main door isn't as stiff as it was when I followed my host into the building, swinging open with relative ease. What is stiff, though, is the breeze that greets me on the other side. It's markedly chillier than when I entered Edith Stimp's lair, and I again rue the decision to hand her my jacket.

I hurry back up Dent's Passage towards the High Street, still not feeling one-hundred per cent. The air might be chilly, but hopefully, it'll help clear the fog in my head. What it won't solve is my thirst, though. I'd kill for a can of Pepsi, but without my wallet or phone, I'll have to wait until I'm back in the office.

I reach the end of Dent's Passage and turn left, increasing my pace to ward off the cold. I've barely covered a dozen paving slabs when an old Transit van passes me by. Judging by the engine rattle and the clouds of black fumes it leaves in its wake, it shouldn't even be on the road.

Seeing the van on the High Street suddenly prompts a question. So sudden that I come to a standstill. When did they re-open the High Street? I'm sure the sign I saw earlier stated that it'd be closed for five days. I can't have been unconscious that long, surely?

"Excuse me, mate," a guy says gruffly as he tries to step past me.

"Er, sorry."

He continues on his way, ignoring my apology, and I watch him stride ahead until my eyes fall on a sign jutting out from the wall. Still standing in the middle of the pavement, I stare up at the sign in disbelief. I squeeze my eyes shut and open them again, but the sign is still there.

"No way," I gasp.

I blink again and again, but it makes no difference. The sign is definitely there, but it sure as hell shouldn't be. Elderton's branch of Woolworths closed down in 2009 following the financial crisis, along with every other branch across the country. I distinctly remember it because I nipped into town one day to buy a CD for Clare's birthday, only to find the doors locked and a sign in the window confirming the permanent closure. The premises remained empty for a number of years until it became another pound shop.

This has got to be a prank. An elaborate one, granted, but there is no way I'm staring up at the sign of a long-since-closed Woolworths store. I take a few tentative steps forward, checking every doorway and vehicle just in case Ant and Dec leap out. But, as I look closely at every vehicle, my attention quickly shifts away from the diminutive TV duo.

I would never proclaim to be an expert on anything bar one subject — British motorcars of the last thirty years. I've bought and sold just about every make and model of car, from Bugattis to Bentleys, from Rovers to Renaults. For the more mainstream cars, I can pin down the production period just by the shape and the year it was first registered from the number plate prefix. The M-reg VW Golf I'm looking at is a Mark III from 1994. Behind it is a G-reg Ford Escort Mark IV, from 1989. And behind that is a Mark III H-reg Vauxhall Cavalier from 1990. What connects all three, besides the remarkable condition of cars that are roughly thirty years old, is that each one has a tax disc in the window. The DVLA phased out tax discs almost a decade ago.

If this is a prank, and I cannot see any other logical explanation, the attention to detail is astounding.

I continue on until I'm standing outside a branch of Woolworths that shouldn't be there. A young woman in a uniform is loitering at the door, bidding goodbye to each customer as they leave. She notices me.

"We close in ten minutes, Sir," she says.

"Uh?"

"I said we're closing in ten minutes, so you'll have to be quick."

"Right," I reply, trying to spot a tell-tale sign of deception in the young woman's eyes. All I see is tiredness and poorly applied mascara.

No matter how elaborate a prank, it would be virtually impossible to recreate a branch of Woolworths from 1996. All I have to do is step inside the store, and I'll know for sure within a minute or two.

I hurry in.

Like most people of my generation, Woolworths is probably the one store we remember more than any other because it catered for every stage of childhood and adolescence. As a kid, I spent ages drooling over the selection of Pick 'n' Mix sweets that Mum couldn't afford. I probably spent even longer in the toy section, although I never much cared for the annual trip to buy school shirts and trousers. As a twelve-year-old, I bought my first single in Woolworths — *Ice Ice Baby* by Vanilla Ice, to my eternal shame — plus countless albums on cassette and CD throughout my teenage years.

Fond memories, but that's what they are: memories. What I'm staring at now, though, is a perfect recreation of those memories. Directly in front of me is the Pick 'n' Mix display I remember so vividly, containing the same selection of sweets I seldom got to taste: fizzy cola bottles, strawberry bon bons, white mice, pineapple cubes, and chocolate éclairs.

Bewildered, I shuffle towards the display, and after a quick scan to check no one is watching, I snatch a fizzy cola bottle from the nearest tub and pop it in my mouth. The extreme sourness brings some much-needed moisture back to my mouth, along with a raft of memories. Because Clare and I never had kids, sweets really haven't featured in my life, so I can't even remember the last time I tasted a fizzy cola bottle.

I swallow the sweet and move further into the store. It's nice to reminisce, but it doesn't help in my quest to understand what's happening here.

The next hit of nostalgia comes when I reach the music section, and for the second time in as many minutes, I'm drawn back to my younger days. The layout is exactly as I remember it, including a section displaying the top-forty albums of the week.

"You've got to be kidding me," I murmur while scanning the stacks of CDs.

I've had a Spotify account for close to a decade, so I can't recall the last time I purchased a physical CD. For that reason, I couldn't even guess what albums occupy the charts at the moment, but I'm pretty sure the likes of Take That, M People, Alanis Morrissette, Pulp, and Garbage aren't all in the top ten.

"Is there anything in particular you're looking for?"

I spin around. A twenty-something lad with floppy blond hair is smiling at me.

"Um, just browsing, thanks."

"No worries, but we're closing soon."

"Right. Sure."

As he turns to walk away, an opportunity presents itself. If this is a prank, surely whoever organised it wouldn't be able to prime a young lad with the requisite knowledge of nineties music.

"Can I ask a question?"

"Of course."

"What's the current number one single?"

"*Firestarter* by The Prodigy."

"And last week?"

"The same record."

"And the week before that?"

"Take That. *How Deep is Your Love*."

"What's your favourite single of the year so far?"

"Hmm, that's a tricky one," he muses.

Rather than question why a middle-aged man is testing his pop music knowledge a few minutes before closing time, the young lad takes a moment to consider his answer.

"Do you want the cool answer or the honest answer?" he eventually replies.

"Both."

"If a mate asked that question, I'd say *Gangster's Paradise* by Coolio, but between you and me, I adore Bjork's *It's Oh So Quiet*. Do you know it?"

"I've heard it once or twice, yes. It's a great song."

"It's not very cool to admit it, though ... not at my age."

"How old are you?"

"Twenty-two."

"So, you were born in ..."

"1974."

I do the maths. Either the forty-nine-year-old guy standing in front of me has discovered the fountain of eternal youth, or he's lying. For the sake of my sanity, I need to prove it's the latter.

"Excuse the barrage of questions, but what's today's date?"

"It's the 6th of April."

"You're sure?"

"Positive. I'm off to see The Power Station with a friend this evening, so the date has been etched in my diary for weeks."

"Power Station? That's the group with Robert Palmer, right?"

"He's lead vocals, yes."

"But he's dead."

The young lad stares back at me, open-mouthed.

"He died twenty years ago," I add with perhaps a little too much glee in my voice.

"He didn't sound very dead when I heard him on Radio 1 earlier today. Or when he was on *Top of The Pops* a few years back."

"*Top of The Pops*?"

"I know it's a bit lame, but I occasionally still watch it."

"But ... they cancelled it."

"Who's they?"

"The BBC."

"When?"

"I don't know. Sometime in the mid-noughties."

"The what?"

Before I can answer, an older woman with glasses and limp hair interrupts. As she's also wearing a Woolworths uniform, I'd guess she's the young lad's supervisor.

"Are you nearly done, Brian?" she asks.

"I think so, yes."

"Can you empty the bins before you leave, please?"

Brian throws a peculiar look in my direction before darting away. His supervisor makes a show of looking at her watch before reminding me that the store is about to close.

"I'm just leaving," I reply. "Brian was just telling me about his gig tonight."

The woman rolls her eyes. "He's been on about it all week. Not my cup of tea."

"No? Who do you like?"

"None of the modern rubbish — can't stand it, particularly those two thuggish brothers. What's their band called? Oasis?"

"Modern? Oasis split up years ago."

"You're obviously talking about a different band because my nephew went to see them play in Cardiff only last month. Waste of money if you ask me."

Before I can interrogate the woman any further, a voice echoes from the store's PA system, asking all customers to finish their shopping as the branch is about to close.

"What is the time?" I ask the woman.

She holds her wrist up so I can see the time on her digital watch.

"Five-thirty," she then confirms. "Closing time, thank heavens."

I don't respond to her remark because I'm still staring at her watch. It confirms the time is five-thirty, but that's not what's holding my attention. That would be the six digits below the time: 06-04-96.

"The date on your watch is wrong," I remark as the woman lowers her arm.

"Really?" she replies, checking it herself. "No, it's not. Today is the sixth of April."

"1996?"

"Yes, 1996."

"But ... it can't be."

"I know, time flies, eh ... except when you work in retail."

After pointing me back towards the doors, the woman bustles away. I amble back the way I came, every step leading me closer to a truth I'm struggling to accept. Is it possible that Edith Stimp isn't as crazy as I thought?

Chapter 18

Back on the pavement, I lean up against a lamppost, close my eyes, and pull a few sharp breaths. When I open my eyes again, nothing has changed. Still unwilling to believe the impossible, I spend a few minutes studying the flow of traffic along the High Street. Scores of vehicles pass by — cars, vans, motorbikes, and a couple of buses — not one of them registered after 1996.

"Holy shit," I gasp as it finally dawns on me that this isn't a prank.

And, if this isn't a prank, that only leaves one explanation, albeit totally implausible — I did travel back in time. I am actually standing on Elderton High Street in 1996.

It's ridiculous. Ridiculous and impossible.

Still unconvinced, despite the already overwhelming evidence, I push away from the lamppost and make my way up the High Street towards the side road where I left my car. My attention remains split between the passing vehicles and the shops, most of which are in the process of closing up for the day. It can't be more than an hour ago that I walked in the opposite direction towards Ian Burke's office, and yet, the scene couldn't be more different.

Premises that were empty are now occupied by businesses that ceased trading years ago: Tie Rack, Barratts Shoes, Athena Cards, and Thomas Cook travel agency. To add further proof, I then pass a DVD rental store, pausing to study a poster in the window. Splashed across the top are the words *New Release*, with a picture of Mel Gibson's face in the centre. I couldn't say for sure when *Braveheart* was released, but to label it a new release is laughable. My parents went to watch it at the cinema while I was still a teenager living at home.

I reach the end of the High Street and turn left. Struggling to find the fortitude, I steel myself and look up the road to where I parked my car. Not only is the car not there, but neither is the bay where I left it. It's now just a stretch of tarmac with a steel railing running some thirty feet towards a pedestrian crossing.

The vehicles, the shops, and now, the streets themselves — all as they were back in 1996.

Pinching myself would be too much of a cliché, and it wouldn't alter the clear evidence of my own eyes. This *is* real. This is what Edith Stimp promised me. Today *is* the day I met Clare.

"No bloody way," I mutter. "This can't be real."

But I'm here.

It strikes me that I could spend the rest of my life trying to understand how this happened, but I'm more likely to fry my mind than come to terms with it. Perhaps it would be better to embrace this insanity for a moment. I need to stop wondering how and focus on the why.

Clare.

Today is the day I met my future wife, but only if I consider it in the past tense. Here, now, I'm yet to meet her, or at least my eighteen-year-old self is yet to meet her.

The realisation proves a much-needed jolt to my system. If this is real, I need to do what I came here to do, and the clock is ticking. Edith Stimp claimed I only have two hours, and I've already lost maybe twenty minutes trying to undermine the evidence — this actually is a once-in-a-lifetime opportunity.

I begin with a pledge: I am not a tourist, I'm here for a purpose, so I need to think calmly and rationally. There's a problem to be solved, and I have very little time and even fewer resources at my disposal to solve it. I've no means of transport, money, or phone, and as it stands, no idea how I'll prevent Clare and me from meeting later.

What I need is a plan, and for that, I need to sit down for five minutes.

I turn around and head back to the High Street and a bench outside the Post Office. Given the circumstances, rational thought might be tricky, but I suppose I should be grateful this is 1996 and not 1946 — it's not as though I'm likely to witness anything I've not seen before, and society hasn't changed that much over the last few decades. I've already noticed one or two people using mobile phones, but in an era before smartphones, no one is snapping a quick selfie, playing Candy Crush, or sharing memes in a WhatsApp group.

Trying to ignore my thirst, I focus on recalling the fuzzy memories of what is set to happen later. The obvious place to start is with the facts I can be sure of.

I arranged to meet Dad at The Black Prince at seven o'clock. I was still living at home, but I'd spent the afternoon at a car show where I managed to flog a customised Mini I'd purchased a few weeks earlier. The reason I remember that car so well is the lesson it taught me. The previous owner had a custom paint job in lime-green and purple, and I loved it. However, the mass market didn't, and I struggled to find a buyer through my usual channels. The car show crowd were a little more enthusiastic about it, but not the price I asked. I was desperate by late afternoon and ended up accepting an offer of fifty quid less than I paid for the bloody car. I also had to walk two miles back to the town centre, which is why I agreed to meet Dad at The Black Prince.

I got to the pub just before seven and waited at the bar. Twenty minutes passed, and I began to worry because Dad was, and still is, a stickler for punctuality. I didn't have a mobile at the time, so I used the pub's payphone to call home. The ensuing conversation with my dad is one I've tried hard to forget. With the house to themselves and a birthday to celebrate, my parents decided to indulge in a little late-afternoon delight, as Dad called it. Their exertions must have taken a toll because they fell asleep afterwards and were still in the land of post-coital nod when I called.

I told Dad not to bother dragging himself into town, and we agreed to go out for a pint the following day. I then put the phone down and trudged back to the bar to finish my pint. With my last gulp of lager, I was about to leave when a girl pitched up at the bar, looking a little sheepish. I'm not sure how I knew, but something about her body language suggested she was nervous. Only later did I discover she was nervous about testing her fake ID because she was only seventeen.

Being a gallant young man, I stepped forward and offered to buy her a drink. Clare, faced with the choice of taking a drink from a stranger or being asked to leave the pub if her ID wasn't up to scratch, accepted my offer.

We sat at a table and talked for half an hour before her friend, Julie, eventually turned up. It was long enough for me to realise how much I fancied Clare, and before I left, I nervously asked for her number. She obliged with a smile, scribbling her home phone number on a beer mat using an eye-liner pencil.

The rest, as they say, is history, although, at this precise moment, it's actually the future.

If I had a quid for every time I've thought about the moment I first met Clare, I wouldn't now be stressing about the financial consequences of divorcing her. If Dad hadn't taken so long to answer the phone, I'd probably have left the pub before Clare arrived. If I'd forsaken two gulps of tepid lager and left straight after that call, I wouldn't have witnessed a cute but nervous girl approach the bar.

To think, almost twenty-five years of marriage would never have happened if it wasn't for a single minute in a pub in 1996. Sixty bloody seconds that altered the path of our lives to where we are today.

I can't let that happen again.

The problem, on one level at least, is straightforward. I simply need to think of a way to delay Clare's journey to the pub by one solitary minute. However, if I'm to adhere to Edith Stimp's rules, I can't just stop Clare in the street and ask for directions, nor can I wander into The Black Prince and tell my teenage self to leave.

My thoughts then turn to Clare's journey from her home to The Black Prince. Did she ever tell me how she got to the pub? Maybe, but with no reason to retain such an inconsequential snippet of information, I can't recall. It doesn't get dark until half-seven, so maybe she walked? Her house is just over a mile away, so it's possible, but she was wearing heels, so maybe not. It seems unlikely she booked a taxi because she was a college student, and her only income came from working in a pet shop on Saturdays. No, she wouldn't have wasted money on a cab.

Thinking back, up until she passed her driving test, Clare usually got from A-to-B on the bus or by cadging a lift from her mum. Considering how chilly it is and how much Clare hates the cold, my money would be on the lift. I can't imagine her mum allowing her to stand at the bus stop, shivering.

It's not ideal, but my best guess will have to do. Now, I need to fathom how I delay Clare's departure by at least a minute without making any form of direct contact with her.

My thoughts switch from Clare to her mum. What if I call their home phone number just before they leave? I'm sure I can conjure up some bullshit name and reason for calling and keep her on the phone for a few minutes. I let the idea percolate, but a significant flaw kills it dead — I can't remember their phone number. Even if I did, I don't have coins for a phone box.

Being as I can't influence Clare or her mum, I'm left with their mode of transport. Can I somehow sabotage the car? From memory, the house once had a small front garden, but Clare told me her granddad tarmacked it to provide a parking space. With the car parked right outside the house, there's a risk I might be spotted from a window, so I won't have long to implement my plan. There's really only one option, and that's to deflate a tyre.

Again, I let the idea percolate. This time, I can't think of any reason not to try it, but it's not without its risks. The worst-case scenario is that either Clare or her mum spot me, but what are they going to do? If I run off, they're unlikely to give chase, and if they call the police, I'll be long gone before they turn up. Either way, it'll delay Clare's departure by the required minute, if not longer.

I'm about to get up and start walking towards Edward Street when a slight chink in my plan becomes apparent. If I instigate my act of sabotage too early, and either Clare or her mum notice, they'll have ample time to pump up the deflated tyres and leave as they originally planned. Timing will be crucial.

I look down at my very expensive and now completely useless Rolex. There's something quite disorientating about not knowing the time, but in this situation, it's also problematic. As luck would have it, a passing couple confirm it's 5.45 pm.

Clare's house is only a twenty-minute walk away, and I'd estimate she and her mum will probably set off for The Black Prince just after seven. Ideally, I don't want to instigate my act of sabotage until they're close to leaving, which means I've got just over an hour to kill.

I get to my feet and ready myself for the slowest of slow walks.

Chapter 19

As I amble down the High Street, I gaze in a few shop windows and snort at the mid-nineties products and prices, but the glow of nostalgia is short-lived. Alongside the nervous apprehension about my impending challenge, the enormity of my situation begins to bite.

There aren't many shoppers on the street, but there are still a surprising number of people around. Many, I guess, have just left work and are heading home to sit in front of the TV and watch whatever constitutes Saturday evening entertainment in 1996. I'm sure they all have their day-to-day problems, but not one of them knows what their future holds. Neither do I, but I do know what fate has in store for certain individuals.

I know that sixteen months from now, Diana, Princess of Wales, will meet her maker in a Parisian road tunnel. In five years and five months, thousands will fall prey to terrorists on 9/11. I know that on Boxing Day in 2004, 228,000 people will die in the Indian Ocean tsunami. So many lives, so much pain and suffering, but with only two hours at my disposal, there's not a single thing I can do to prevent fate from playing out.

Edith Stimp warned that my fantastical visit to the past would only last two hours, and I wonder if there's a reason behind that. Two hours is too short a time to do anything other than affect small changes. Even if I wanted to avert some of the disasters I know are coming down the line, it would take months of planning, and God knows how much trouble convincing those in charge to plan for those disasters. I mean, how do you convince the US administration that a group of terrorists will one day fly planes into the Twin Towers and The Pentagon? And that's before the tricky part — telling them the exact date it will happen.

With just two hours, the best anyone could do would be to write a letter to the President, confirming what will happen, and then send copies to a bunch of newspaper editors as a safeguard. It's hardly foolproof, but it might be enough to shift the US Government's attention an inch in the right direction.

The more I think about it, the more I consider penning such a letter. Then, the futility strikes. I don't have a pen, never mind a ream of paper, envelopes, and stamps. Nor do I have any money, and even if I did, the shops are now shut. The alternative is just too ridiculous to contemplate. If I approached a random stranger and told them what I know, who'd believe me? They'd more likely assume I've been in the pub all afternoon, or I've escaped from an asylum.

As I approach the final hundred yards of the High Street, I have to concede that despite my knowledge of the future, I'm as good as impotent when it comes to doing anything to change it. That is, apart from one minor detail relating to a young woman currently getting ready for a night on the town.

I reach the end of the street and turn right, almost bumping into a guy my age coming the other way. Whilst I was distracted by thoughts of averting global disasters, he was distracted by a phone call.

"Sorry, mate," he blusters, temporarily moving the phone from his ear.

"No worries."

I happen to glance at the antiquated device in his hand — a block of black plastic with a small LCD screen and a stubby aerial.

"Just got it today," the guy remarks proudly. "It's the latest Nokia."

If memory serves, I'm still in an era where owning a mobile phone is an expensive novelty, and most folk don't. I think I bought my first phone later this year.

"Cool," I remark out of politeness.

"You got one?"

"Yeah."

"Nokia?"

I can't help myself. "No, an iPhone."

The guy returns a blank stare.

"It's American," I confirm.

"Oh. Explains it."

The guy continues on his way, as do I, and cross the road. The conversation with a random stranger, brief as it was, helps to shift my thoughts away from all the future horrors I can't do anything about. It also serves as a reminder that no one today has the first clue how much their lives will change over the next two decades due to the internet and companies like Apple. The internet does exist at the moment, but it's not in widespread use. As for Apple, they haven't even launched their iconic iMac computers yet, let alone the first iPhone.

For sure, 1996 was a simpler year, an arguably better time before the influence of smartphones and social media. Actually, if someone asked me to name the best year of my life, 1996 would be a strong contender. The fact I turned eighteen and could legally drink in pubs and clubs might be a reason, but there were many others. Those first few months dating Clare were amazing, and despite a few hiccups along the way, I was making a half-decent living buying and selling second-hand cars. It was also the year that football came home, as England hosted the Euro Championships during the early summer. Britpop was in full force, and although I wasn't that interested in politics or the economy at the time, I don't recall any significant turbulence.

All in all, it was a great time to be young, and I don't think I've enjoyed any summer quite as much as that of 1996. Sadly, all I get to relive is two hours of an overcast day in early April. I guess that makes me the world's only ungrateful time traveller, but hey.

The novelty of spotting retro cars soon loses its appeal, as does the slow plod through suburbia. To kill minutes, I take a detour to view parts of the town as they once were; fields destined to become housing developments, tranquil lanes that will become busy byways clogged with traffic, and perhaps the saddest sight, the old Gale & Powell Printworks.

The vast Victorian building once housed a significant workforce, and the company was the largest employer in Elderton — my own mum worked there for a while, cleaning the offices. It shut down in the early nineties, and three-hundred people lost their jobs. The building itself lasted another six years before the first bulldozer arrived on site. Within a fortnight, the demolition crew had razed it to the ground, wiping away over a century of local history.

My colleague, Justin, recently purchased one of the hundred flats that now occupy the site, although he did gripe about the price when he discovered how much his new home sold for when it originally hit the market in 1997 — £50,000. He paid £175,000. Justin and his generation are certainly paying the price for property inflation, and he has my sympathy. I've definitely benefited from that inflation, but not to the same degree as those who invested in the nineties. It's a shame I wasn't one of them, but how was I to know that properties would prove to be such a strong investment?

If only I knew then what I know now. Ironically, there wouldn't be the need for this miraculous trip if I'd invested in property because even if Clare deemed to take half my assets, I'd still have more than enough for a comfortable life. Saying that, I didn't have the money to invest in property in the nineties, so there's precious little point in ruing my lack of forethought.

I continue on past the old Gale & Powell Printworks and cross the street, heading back towards Clare's house. My mind is still a firestorm of thoughts and emotions and a surreal sense of detachment. Perhaps understandable, given the circumstances.

I feel so out of sorts I increase my pace to a brisk stride. Much like when I'm on the treadmill in the gym, the slight elevation of my heart rate goes some way to settling my mind. I might arrive in Clare's street ahead of schedule, but I can always take a walk around the block to kill time.

Barely one minute and a few hundred yards of pavement later, I develop a mental itch. I coined the term for occasions when the seed of a good idea germinates in the subconscious part of my brain. Some of my best ideas and innovations for the business have evolved this way, usually when I'm in the gym.

This feels different, though, because the usual flush of dopamine is more of a torrent. In an effort to remove distractions and increase focus, I stop walking and stare down at the pavement. A series of recent thoughts, words, and phrases tumble through my mind: *internet, letters, Apple, investments, Euro Championships, social media.*

"Ohh."

My mind goes into overdrive, forging connections and imagining outcomes. Seconds turn to a minute, and as I continue to stare down at the pavement, I'm struck by an overwhelming buzz of excitement. It proves short-lived, though, as my mind continues to process practicalities.

Notwithstanding those practicalities, I'm incensed that I've been so dumb. How has it taken me over an hour to see the obvious? My teenage self can't buy properties because he only has a limited amount of money, but I have knowledge that could multiply that kid's modest bank account balance a hundred-fold, possibly a thousand-fold in time.

I take a seat on a low brick wall and put my head in my hands — not as an act of despair, but to concentrate.

Edith Stimp made it clear I cannot, under any circumstances, interact with my younger self, but she didn't say I couldn't send him an anonymous letter. The thought alone is beyond tantalising, as are the possibilities of what information I might share. I could tell my younger self the result of every England game in the Euro Championships this summer, including the score for the final. And I could do the same for the World Cup in 1998. I can't begin to calculate the odds of predicting France beating Brazil 3-0 in the final, but if my younger self placed a bet on that result before the start of the tournament, he'd likely multiply his stake fifty times over. And then there's the year Leicester City won the Premier League, back in 2016. It was such an unlikely achievement, bookmakers were offering odds of 5000-1 at the start of the season. The newspapers went crazy with stories of fans who'd placed smallish bets and won six-figure sums.

I could also add a shortlist of stocks to buy with the money won through betting: Apple, obviously, Google, Amazon, and Facebook. Not that long ago, I read an article on a business blog about shares in American tech companies and how they've rocketed in value over a relatively short space of time. The author of the article cited Amazon's shares as the most remarkable because up until the early noughties, they consistently struggled to hit 30¢. On the day of the article, those same shares were trading at $150. Even in recent years, shares in companies like Tesla and Netflix have soared.

Christ, when I think about the amount of money I could make with just a single page of betting and investment tips, it'd make the value of Kirkwood Motors look like loose change. And I wouldn't have to spend twenty years working my arse off or endure all that stress and worry along the way.

However, knowing what to write in a letter and getting it to my younger self is a problem I'm not confident I can solve in the time available.

Much like when I'm faced with a challenge at work, the only hope I have is to break it down into individual problems.

Problem one: how do I get my hands on a pen and paper?

Problem two: how do I send a letter without money to buy a stamp?

Problem three: how do I solve the first two problems in less than an hour?

My initial excitement quickly turns to panic. I can imagine it's like knowing you've purchased a winning lottery ticket, but you can't remember where you put the ticket.

"Think, Gary. Think."

The first problem is getting my hands on a pen and paper. The shops are shut, and I've no money, but as I look up and down the street I'm currently on, an obvious alternative comes to mind. In every drawer in every house in view, there's bound to be countless pens and enough paper to write a novel. If I can concoct a plausible excuse, all I have to do is knock on a door and ask to borrow a pen and a slip of paper.

Now, why would someone wandering up a random street suddenly and urgently need a pen and paper, and why would any homeowner feel obliged to give that random stranger what they're asking for? Fortuitously, a source of inspiration is sitting on the street, just across the road — a dilapidated Ford Cortina from the early eighties, minus an offside wing mirror.

I leap up from the wall and stride up the pavement, checking the cars on the driveways as I pass. I'm looking for a clue to the homeowner's age as I'm hopeful an older couple would be more likely to offer what I desperately need. Then, I spot an immaculate ten-year-old Austin Maestro on the driveway of an equally immaculate semi-detached house.

If I had time, I'd invest ten minutes honing my story, but time is of the essence, so I've no choice but to wing it. I hurry up the path and knock on the front door. Long seconds pass before it's opened by a silver-haired man in a fetching beige cardigan. He looks every bit the kind of man who drives a ten-year-old Austin Maestro.

"Sorry to trouble you," I say in my politest tone of voice. "I'm wondering if you have a pen I might borrow for a minute ... and a slip of paper?"

The man eyes me suspiciously.

"For what purpose?"

"I was walking along when a Ford XR3i came hurtling up the street, clipping the wing mirror of a parked car. I got the registration plate, and I was hoping to leave a note for the owner of the damaged car."

"I'm not surprised," the homeowner replies, his taut expression easing a touch. "Some people treat this road like a bloody racetrack. I've complained to my local councillor, but he's as much use as a cheese tambourine."

I'm not sure his metaphor makes sense, but I daren't question it.

"So, Sir, are you able to help out a Good Samaritan?"

To my relief, he nods. "Wait here."

The man closes the door but returns within a minute. He then hands me a disposable biro and a single sheet of lined paper, likely torn from a jotter pad.

"That's very kind of you," I smile back. "I'm sure your neighbour will be grateful."

"I'm sure," he replies. "Just post the pen back through the letterbox when you're done with it. We're about to sit down for dinner."

"Sure. No problem."

The man puts his hand on the edge of the door and begins to close it.

"Sorry, do you know what the time is?" I ask. "My watch isn't working, and it'd be useful to note the approximate time of the accident."

"6.24 pm," he confirms before closing the door.

I turn around and hurry back up the path. I've solved one problem, but I've still got two more to overcome. I can now write a letter to my younger self, but how do I get it to him? With no time to think too long or too hard, I quickly conclude there's only one way — I have to deliver it by hand.

My solution is far from perfect, but I know for sure that my parents are currently sleeping off their late afternoon tryst, and my younger self is walking back from the car show, so there's no risk of bumping into either, but how do I ensure the young Gary Kirk picks up the letter, rather than his parents? More importantly, can I get across town in time? I know from experience that it's a good twenty-five-minute walk from Clare's house to my former home, so there's no chance of delivering the letter before I sabotage Mrs Wood's car.

"Priorities, Gary," I whisper.

I'm sure the curmudgeonly pensioner is already tucking into his dinner, but I don't want to risk him coming out of his house and asking questions, so I jog up the road until I reach a phone box at the end. There, I place the sheet of paper up against one of the flat glass panels and begin writing the most improbable of letters.

I begin with a hard-hitting statement: *Keep this letter safe and DO NOT share it with anyone. This information will make you a multi-millionaire by the time you're 30.*

I begin by listing the dead-cert bets for the Euro Championships, adding as much detail as I can remember. Then, every result I can recall from the World Cup in 1998, and the Leicester City miracle. With time running out, I quickly list the tech investment opportunities, plus a note at the end about the 2008 global financial crash. I don't know if my younger self will be able to capitalise on that knowledge, but those who predicted it certainly did.

Satisfied with my work, I fold up the sheet of paper and tuck it into my back pocket. At a guess, I've got roughly forty minutes to get to Clare's house, sabotage her mum's car, and then make the two mile dash to my parents' place.

Who knew that time travel would be so stressful?

Chapter 20

As I turn into Jubilee Road, it dawns on me that it's the first time I've been here in years. The last time was when I helped Clare and her sister to clear their late mother's home — twenty-three years ago, or thereabouts. Here and now, that mother is still very much alive.

The familiarity is strange because it mirrors my memories exactly, but if I wandered up Jubilee Road tomorrow, back in reality, it's unlikely it'll look quite so familiar. For now, though, it's the same street with red-brick terraced houses on one side overlooking an expanse of scrubby grass, and a play park frequented more often by glue-sniffing adolescents than young children.

I slow my pace and check for potential witnesses as I approach number nineteen. Being a chilly evening in early April, and close to the time most families are sitting down to eat dinner or watch TV, the street is quiet. That doesn't help my nerves, though, as I approach a tatty old Ford Fiesta parked on a patch of tarmac. Thankfully, Lady Luck appears to be on my side as Clare's mum reversed the car into the parking space, meaning the front offside wheel is only a few feet from the pavement.

I come to a stop and quickly check the three windows facing the road. There's no sign of activity in the upstairs windows but the one of most concern is the lounge as it's directly behind the Fiesta. I can just about make out the TV in the corner of the room, and if memory serves, the sofa is on the wall opposite. Assuming Clare is up in her room getting ready and her mum and sister are watching TV on the sofa, I'm good to go.

I step closer to the front wheel of the Fiesta and squat down as if I'm tying my shoelace. It only takes a few seconds to remove the dust cap, and then I press the edge of my thumbnail against the valve. The hiss of escaping air isn't loud enough to draw anyone's attention, but I know I'll have to keep my hand in place for at least a minute to deflate the tyre sufficiently.

I'm barely halfway through my task when a bolt of cramp spasms up my calf — a result of squatting in an odd position and dehydration. I grit my teeth and change position before pressing my thumbnail against the valve again. If I've learned nothing from this experience, at least I now know that it takes more than a minute to expel ten litres of musty air from a car tyre.

Somewhere up the road, an engine fires into life. The tyre still isn't as flat as I need it to be, but if that vehicle is heading in my direction, the driver is bound to see me. They might continue on their way, but it's just as likely they'll stop and ask what I'm up to, and I can't afford a confrontation with a neighbour.

"C'mon. C'mon," I urge, adjusting my position again to keep the cramp at bay.

I take another furtive glance up and down the street and then at the windows of number nineteen. I can't see anyone, but I can still hear the engine ticking over. Turning my attention back to the tyre, the rim of the steel wheel is just over an inch from the tarmac, and there's enough rubber splayed out from the edge to make driving difficult. Even if Clare's mum doesn't spot the flat before driving off, she'll know about it the moment she turns the wheel.

Mission accomplished.

I get to my feet and limp away, the pain in my calf still sharp enough to induce a wince. It's the last thing I need if I'm to get across town before I'm sucked back to the present.

I reach the end of Jubilee Road and stop by the corner shop where I used to buy popcorn and a bottle of cheap wine when Clare and I had a night at hers. I'm so thirsty I'd lick my own eyeballs if I could, and just the sight of a sign advertising ice-cold drinks is the final straw. I push open the door and move quickly to the fridge. Then, I grab the first bottle my hand touches and bolt from the shop.

A dose of adrenalin helps to mask the pain in my calf as I sprint away. I'm sure the shopkeeper is incensed that a middle-aged man just nicked a bottle of 7-Up, but I'll pop back tomorrow evening and slip a fiver through the letterbox. It's a measure of how badly I'm suffering from dehydration that I'm three streets away before I realise that my tomorrow will be twenty-seven years for the shopkeeper. Best I make it a tenner.

Unable to run any further, I come to a stop and hide behind a parked van. I don't have time to hang around, but I'm desperate for fluids. The cold, sugary liquid barely touches my lips, and I need every last calorie because now the race is really on.

Leaving the bottle on the kerb I begin a steady jog up the road. Having spent countless hours pounding a treadmill in the gym, the jog isn't a problem, but it's a challenge running in Timberland boots rather than trainers.

I've barely covered half a mile when a dull ache begins to creep across my forehead. I put it down to dehydration; the half-litre of 7-Up nowhere near enough to properly quench my thirst.

Passing my old secondary school, I'm tempted to stop and take a breather, but I'm concerned that if I stop, I won't start again. My legs feel like lead, and the headache is approaching migraine status. I've just got to keep going and focus on the new life I'll return to — one where I'm wealthy beyond my wildest dreams, and Clare is just a random Elderton resident I've never met.

I pass a road where one of my oldest mates used to live, but I can barely read the sign. Blinking helps to clear the misty haze from my eyes, only for it to return within a few seconds. Am I just suffering from acute dehydration, or are my symptoms those that Edith Stimp warned would signify the end of my travels?

Summoning every last ounce of resolve, I push through the worst of the pain, and I'm rewarded when I turn the last corner into the small estate where I grew up. There's no more than a hundred yards to go, but there's still one final hurdle to overcome when I get there. All I can do is pray that the spare key that Mum placed under a rock by the back door is still there. She got sick of me going out at night and forgetting my key, so it became a permanent fixture. Dad used it more than me if I recall.

By the time I reach the block of maisonettes, I can barely walk, let alone run. My head feels fit to explode, and the urge to throw up is overwhelming. I've had some hangovers in my day but nothing as God-awful as this.

Staggering forward, I crash into the side gate and flounder at the handle. Somehow, I manage to open the gate and stumble onto the crazy-paved path leading to the back door. Concerned my legs might give way any second, I fall to my knees and crawl.

Yards become feet, and feet become inches. I've barely enough energy to nudge the rock away, but the sight of a single brass key is a much-needed morale booster. I snatch it up and fumble as I try to slide the key into the lock. It takes four attempts before I can turn it and pull at the handle. I don't know how this process works, but I can't have more than a minute left before my opportunity is snatched away.

With only a few feet of carpet to cover, my bedroom door is within sight. All I have to do is crawl those final feet and place the sheet of paper on my bed. It should be a simple task, but not in my current state. It feels like I've run a marathon, swallowed half a bottle of hallucinogenic pills, and then fallen down a flight of concrete stairs.

Reality begins to bleed away as I drag my broken body across the carpet. I reach the door to my room and, straining every muscle, every sinew, somehow manage to flop over the threshold. I've done it — I'm in my teenage bedroom. I flap my right arm towards the back pocket of my trousers. It lands where I hoped, and I fumble to pull out the letter.

It's not there.

A sudden shot of panic momentarily distracts my mind from the prospect of my eyeballs bursting. I delve my hand into the pocket and confirm my worst fear — the letter is definitely not there. Is it in the left-hand pocket? I roll to my front and, after three attempts, manage to coax my left arm where it needs to be. All I can feel is the fabric.

This can't be happening — I've lost the letter.

I try to think back over the last twenty minutes to where I might have dropped my ticket to a life of untold wealth, but my brain is having difficulty instructing my lungs to function.

My vision blurs to almost nothing as my oxygen-starved body begins to shut down. The pain subsides, but so too does consciousness.

Then, nothing.

Chapter 21

I awake with a gasp and a familiar scent in the air: burnt hair. My eyelids flutter at the stark light as I slowly awake from what must have been the most surreal and ultimately horrifying of nightmares.

I tilt my head forward and grimace. What the hell happened to me?

As my senses reboot, I open my eyes and double-check what I'm already certain of — I'm sitting in a barber's chair in the same room Edith Stimp lured me into.

How long have I been here?

I raise my left arm to check the time, but my Rolex is no longer on my wrist. The indignation then ebbs towards confusion when I catch sight of what's on my feet. The dark-grey Timberland boots are gone, and I'm wearing a pair of cheap-looking trainers. They're not the only inconsistency with my attire. I might be confused, but I know for sure I wasn't wearing jeans when I bumped into Edith Stimp earlier, or the turd-brown coat I'm now sporting.

Where are my clothes, and more importantly, where's my Rolex?

I clamber out of the chair, but I'm still weak from my ordeal and have to grab hold of the arm to find balance. As if my physical discomfort wasn't bad enough, I'm also suffering a mental fog so dense I can't seem to separate facts from fantasy. Did I really just spend a couple of hours in 1996? Surely not.

One thing I can be certain about is my rabid thirst. I desperately need a drink.

I draw a few deep breaths and stretch, hoping to ease the stiffness in my limbs before crossing the floor to the door. As much as I want to get out of here, I'd rather avoid falling flat on my face.

Slowly, I put one foot in front of the other until I'm at the door. I grab the handle and tug it open. My next goal is to make it safely to the bottom of the stairs and get the fuck away from this place.

I descend the stairs like an arthritic octogenarian and open the door at the bottom. If I needed confirmation that I've just experienced a psychotic delusion, it comes in the form of antique furniture. I knew it was ridiculous to think a team of porters had emptied the room, and now, looking across the same collection of bookcases, armoires, desks, and trunks, I was clearly right — the room is as packed with antiques as it was when I first entered it.

"Welcome back, Gary," Edith Stimp coos as she steps into sight. "How are you feeling?"

"What ... what did you do to me?"

"Come and sit down. I've got a large glass of water waiting for you."

My need to rehydrate is greater than my need to escape, and besides, my car keys are still in my jacket. Wincing hard, I reluctantly follow Edith Stimp back to the far side of the room and the two wing-backed armchairs. As promised, there's a pint glass sitting on the coffee table.

"I'll let you drink, and then we can have a chat."

My mouth is so dry I doubt I could argue if I tried. I grab the glass and gulp down every last drop of water.

"Another?" Edith Stimp asks.

"No," I rasp. "I want my watch back ... and my jacket."

"We should talk, Gary. Please, sit down."

"I don't want to talk. I want to get back to work."

"Yes, I'm sure you do, but that's why we need to talk. You no longer work at Kirkwood Motors."

"What?"

Edith Stimp casually sits down and waves her hand towards the empty armchair opposite.

"We've got a lot to discuss, so you might as well make yourself comfortable."

I don't want to sit down, but I'm also too weak to protest. Maybe I should sit down for five minutes, just until the symptoms of dehydration pass. I shuffle over to the armchair and flop down.

"How was 1996?" Edith Stimp then asks. "Much like you remembered it?"

"I don't know what happened to me up there, but ... what did you do to me?"

"As you asked. You wanted to go back in time and erase the moment you met your future wife, and you succeeded, Gary."

"Wait. Are you saying that what I think I just experienced was real?"

"Did it feel real?"

"Yes, but it couldn't ... I mean, it's impossible."

"Even though you've just changed the future? Well, your future."

"I did?"

Edith Stimp crosses her knees and smiles back at me. "There's a lot to explain."

"I'm listening."

"You might have been away for two hours, Gary, but as far as this timeline is concerned, you were only away for less than a minute. However, once complete, the process renders the participant unconscious, so you've been asleep for almost an hour. I used that hour to research your new life. Would you like to know what you achieved?"

"I'd like to know where my Rolex is," I reply before glancing across to the coat stand. "And my jacket. Come to think of it, why am I wearing jeans and trainers?"

"You don't own a Rolex, and as for your attire, it's what Gary Kirk decided to wear this morning. The second you returned from your trip, your timeline merged with this one, so you're now back where you were earlier, minus a couple of hours."

"I'm confused. I'm not married to Clare?"

"No, you're not. You've never married."

This is not what I imagined when I set out to prevent my younger self from meeting Clare.

"I'm single?"

Edith reaches down and pulls a notepad from beneath the chair.

"Let me give you a brief synopsis of what I've learned about your life ... this life. Bear in mind I've only had an hour, so there will likely be a few holes, but I'm sure you'll fill them in time."

It's a measure of this insanity that I'm now reliant on a woman I barely know to provide an update on a life that isn't mine.

"Ready?"

"Guess so."

"I'll begin with the good news. Your life continues on a similar path after the ... intervention, and you set up a used-car business in 2003 called Kirk Motors."

This makes sense. If I never met or married Clare Wood, there would be no reason to tag her maiden name onto my company's name.

"Then, in 2009," Edith continues. "You brought a new partner into the business and expanded the operation by opening a second branch on the other side of Elderton. In 2011, you won Elderton's Businessman of The Year Award, and by 2012, company profits had quadrupled, according to the financial records I checked online."

I sit up in the chair. This is indeed good news, although whatever success I've achieved, it won't come close to the money I could have made if I hadn't lost that bloody letter. It is, however, some consolation.

"But I don't work there now?" I respond. "I presume I sold the business?"

"No, you didn't, and I'm afraid that's where the good news ends."

"I don't understand. If I didn't sell the business, why am I not still working there?"

Edith Stimp adopts what I presume is a sympathetic expression.

"Your business partner was a chap by the name of Darren Slade. I believe you both attended the same school."

My jaw drops. I can't think of a single reason why I'd take on a partner, never mind an absolute arsehole like Darren Slade — the same Darren Slade who bullied me relentlessly at junior school.

"Are you sure?"

"Positive. I've checked the records at Companies House, and the two directors of Kirk Motors are listed as Gary Kirk and Darren Slade."

"This doesn't make any sense. I despised Slade, and he'd be the last person I'd want as a business partner."

"Looking at the company accounts from 2009 I suspect you had no choice."

"The accounts were fine in 2009. I had to make a number of redundancies, but we got through the financial crisis."

"That's not what happened in this timeline, Gary. It seems you took out a significant business loan in 2008, but by late 2009, you were behind with the repayments and on the point of insolvency."

A scene forms in my mind. The kitchen of a suburban home occupied by Gary and Clare Kirk and our conversation about the impact of the financial crisis. I was torn between making redundancies or taking out a loan to weather the storm. It was Clare who tipped the scales in favour of redundancies. The same Clare I never married in this reimagined facsimile of Gary Kirk's life.

"Shit," I gasp.

"Quite."

"So, what happened with the business?"

"Fortunately or not, depending on one's viewpoint, what happened is well documented. In December 2012, the police raided both branches of Kirk Motors. You and Darren Slade were arrested and subsequently charged."

"Huh? Charged with what?"

"Money laundering and possession of class-A drugs with the intent to supply."

If Edith Stimp had leapt out of her chair, lifted up her dress, and pissed in my lap, I think I'd be in a lesser state of shock.

"What ... besides the odd spliff when I was a kid, I've never had anything to do with drugs."

"I believe you, and there is some good news."

"There is?"

"The Crown Prosecution Service were unable to prove you had any involvement with the drugs, but you were found guilty of money laundering."

"On what planet is that good news?"

"Darren Slade wasn't so fortunate. He was convicted of both charges."

"This doesn't make any sense," I whimper. "What do drugs and money laundering have to do with Kirkwood ... Kirk Motors?"

"The reason Darren Slade bailed out your business with an investment is that he identified the perfect opportunity to launder the proceeds of his illegal drug operation. I'm sorry to say, Gary, but the reason your business flourished was that Mr Slade was using drug money to buy cars from your second branch. It was how he laundered the money."

"But ... why was I found guilty if it was Slade?"

"Ignorance is no defence, which is why, in 2013, you were sentenced to six years imprisonment. You were released after serving four years, though."

Darren Slade. Drugs. Prison. It's a preposterous tale, and with no evidence to back her up, why am I taking everything Edith Stimp says at face value? Her claims are as insane as the trip back to 1996.

"You're making this up," I scoff. "I don't believe you."

"I understand that this isn't what you were hoping for, Gary, but why would I lie? Once you leave this building, you'll return to the life that occurred after you intervened in the past, and you'll be free to confirm the facts at your leisure."

I get to my feet.

"I'd like my Rolex back, please, and my jacket."

"Oh dear," Edith Stimp sighs. "You're not getting this, are you? In this timeline, you don't own a Rolex and any jacket you own is likely hanging in a wardrobe back at your flat."

"I don't own a flat."

"That's true. You're renting it."

"What?"

"You live at 14B Rochford Road, according to the electoral register."

"Rochford Road? I wouldn't live there if you paid me — it's in one of the most run-down parts of Elderton."

"That's a matter of opinion, but as you're no longer a successful businessman, it's likely the best you can afford."

"No, I don't believe you ... this can't be right."

"Check your wallet. I suspect there's a driver's licence in there confirming your address."

I instinctively pat the pockets of a coat I have no memory of owning, let alone choosing to buy. There are bulges in both the right and left-hand pockets, and a set of keys jangle on my second pat. I unzip the left-hand pocket first. There is a wallet inside.

"Well?" Edith Stimp prompts. "Are you going to check?"

I might not be willing to accept anything I've heard in the last ten minutes, but I can't pretend I'm not nervous as I flip open the cheap wallet. Inside, there's a debit card for a High Street bank and a handful of loyalty cards for various stores. Opposite, behind a transparent plastic window, is a driving licence. The photo is of me, or a version of me I barely recognise, and below my name and date of birth is an address: 14B Rochford Road, Elderton.

"Believe me now?" Edith Stimp asks.

"It could be a fake," I reply with more conviction than I truly possess. "It's not proof of anything."

"What about the mobile telephone in your other pocket?"

I reach in and pull out a budget Android phone with a hairline crack running across the bottom corner of the screen. It would be easy to claim Edith Stimp planted it in my pocket, but that theory is shot down when I place my thumb on the screen and the device unlocks.

"Modern technology is amazing, isn't it?"

"I've never seen this phone in my life."

"Not your old life, but at some point in this life, you purchased it, and you set up the fingerprint security measure. No one else but you could have done that, Gary."

I don't know what to say. The licence and the phone are compelling evidence that I changed the course of my life, but I never asked for this.

"I don't want to live in a shitty flat in Rochford Road, and I never agreed to partnering with a drug dealer. This isn't what I wanted."

"Perhaps not, but it's where you are."

"I ... no, I'm not having this. I want to go back again."

"Back where?"

"To 1996. Send me back, and I'll fix this."

Edith Stimp closes her eyes for a moment and then stands up.

"I told you the trip was a once-in-a-lifetime opportunity, didn't I?"

"Yes, but surely you can make an exception."

"If you go back again, it's likely you'll die within twelve to eighteen months."

I stare back, gobsmacked. "Sorry?"

"I warned you about the radiation. One trip is just about safe, but take it from me; a second is akin to a slow suicide. It won't matter how you influence your life because it'll be over long before you reach your fiftieth birthday."

"Right, well ... you can go back and fix it for me."

"Gary, if the circumstances were different, I'd be happy to oblige, but another trip will literally be the death of me. I'm sorry, but I can't do it."

"Someone must be able to, surely?"

"If you can convince someone to take a trip, I could organise it, but time is of the essence."

"I'll ask my parents. I'm sure my dad will do it."

"Assuming your parents are in their sixties, neither would be viable candidates. As you've discovered, the process is physically taxing, and for someone of advanced years, the risk to their life would be significant. Could you live with the consequences if one of your parents died whilst trying to undo your mistake?"

I look up at the beams and slowly shake my head. "No."

"Any candidate would need to be fifty or under and in good physical health. Do you know of anyone else who might be willing?"

"That's the problem — if this isn't an elaborate hoax and I really am stuck in this life, I don't know *who* I know."

"You know your ex-wife."

"Except you're telling me that she's not my ex-wife. She's a stranger."

"But you know her. Could you convince her?"

The suggestion is so ridiculous I'm almost tempted to laugh.

"And how do you think that conversation might pan out? 'Hi, Clare, we were married for almost twenty-five years in a parallel universe, and I really need a favour from you. Could you travel back in time and undo the moment I sabotaged our past?'"

"Granted, it's a tall order."

"It's not tall. It's preposterous."

"I don't know what else to suggest, Gary, but whatever you plan to do, don't wait too long — certainly no more than a couple of weeks."

"Why only a couple of weeks?"

"I don't have long myself, and I need to take one final trip."

"You said you can't make another trip."

"I said it would be the death of me. That's inevitable, but I've got one final task I need to perform in the past before I'm ready to shuffle off this mortal coil."

Throughout my life, I've always met every challenge head-on. I'm an optimist, and up until the moment I met Edith Stimp, my can-do attitude has served me well. Standing here now, in another man's clothes, I'm struggling to find a single thread of positivity.

"So, that's it? I'm just supposed to accept this?"

"Yes."

"And what if I don't want to?"

"That would be foolish. You have but one life, Gary, and although you've had a setback, you're a free man. You can start a new relationship and find that happiness you so craved. Remember we talked about you finding your soul mate?"

"Fat chance of that," I snort, flinging my hands in the air. "What kind of women would be interested in a middle-aged ex-con who lives in a shitty flat and wears shitty clothes?"

"There's someone for—"

"Wait. Do I even have a job?"

"Ah, yes. You do."

"Doing what?"

"You work for an engineering company."

"Oh, okay … that doesn't sound so terrible. I presume I'm in the sales department."

"Actually, you're in the packing department."

"Packing! Oh, for fuck's sake."

"Please mind your—"

Edith Stimp's response is cut short when she yawns.

"Boring you, am I?" I mutter.

"No, but I really do need a lie-down. I'm exhausted."

"And what am I supposed to do?"

"I'd suggest you go and check out this new life of yours. It might be better than you think."

"On the evidence of the last ten minutes, I'd say that's unlikely."

"It is what it is, Gary. Now, if you'll excuse me, I really need to sleep."

"Wait. What if I find someone willing to take a trip for me?"

"Bring them here but remember what I said — you don't have much time so I wouldn't spend too long sulking. Gary Kirk might not be in a position to change the past, but he can certainly change the future."

With a swoop of her right arm, Edith Stimp then ushers me towards the exit.

"Off you pop, now," she says. "And remember, Gary, the clock is ticking."

Chapter 22

I find myself standing on Elderton High Street like a child having departed an orphanage on their sixteenth birthday — bewildered and confused about the world they're suddenly expected to participate in. The only thing I'm certain about is there's a discernible lack of retro vehicles passing by, or any vehicles for that matter. The road is closed, but that's about the only similarity between this reality and the one I left behind a few hours ago.

I need a plan, and I guess the best place to start is by working out just how crappy a life this is. That means visiting Rochford Road, or home as it is now.

Reaching into my coat pocket, I pull out a set of keys: two silver door keys and the fob with the Rover logo branded on the front. This version of me really has hit rock bottom if he's driving a Rover.

My first and most pressing challenge is to find the car, but that assumes it's even parked in town. I should have clarified what the downtrodden version of me was doing before he woke up in Edith Stimp's lair. Rochford Road isn't that far away, so I suppose I just walk in the general direction and press the key fob whenever I pass a Rover. It's not an ideal solution, but when looking for a rust-encrusted shitbox of a needle in a haystack, you have to start somewhere.

I trudge up the High Street in the direction of the parking bay where I left my shiny, year-old Mercedes coupé this morning. Much like Woolworths, the travel agents, and the DVD rental store, I fear that car is long gone.

When I reach the end of the road, I mutter a silent prayer and turn left. The parking bays have returned, but they're currently occupied by a Range Rover and a Mini. The sight is enough to wash away the final remnants of denial — I meddled with a perfectly decent life, and this godforsaken existence is my reward.

What a twenty-four-carat twat I am.

I trudge on for another half mile until I pass a newsagent. I'm still unbelievably thirsty, so I hope I've got the necessary funds to purchase a drink because I'm not willing to shoplift again.

I head inside.

After grabbing a bottle of water from the chiller, I take it to the counter and then rummage through the wallet. Fortunately, there's a crumpled fiver tucked in the back.

Out on the pavement, I gulp back the water. It helps to bring clarity to my thoughts, but not necessarily in a good way. I'm suddenly overwhelmed by a sense of loss, and it cuts as deep as any bereavement. I'm in mourning for a lost life, but it's my own. The lovely house, the established business, the financial security — all gone.

I allow myself a minute of self-pity, but I cannot let it drag me down. Gary Kirk is a doer, and if I'm to escape this mess, I need to be doing, not sulking.

Shoulders back, chin up, I continue on my way.

After a few wrong turns, I eventually reach the start of Rochford Road. It's a busy thoroughfare between an industrialised part of town and a large housing estate, lined on one side with a row of post-war terraced houses split into flats and bedsits. Opposite, there's a mix of shops to meet every need of the local residents: a bookmaker, a kebab shop, an off-licence, a tattoo parlour, a tanning salon which, ironically, is likely a money laundering operation, and a vape shop.

A dozen yards on, I reach a row of parking bays, and my heart sinks at the sight of an eighteen-year-old Rover 45 in the second bay along. I pull out the fob and press the button, hoping for the best but prepared for the worst. The indicators on the Rover 45 blink, and I die a little inside — it is my car.

I remind myself I need to remain positive. At least I have a car, and once I've inspected my living quarters, there's somewhere I'm keen to go. Not that anyone is likely to steal it, but I lock the Rover and continue on until I reach the front door of number fourteen.

The first impressions are not positive. If I were a presenter on a property show, I'd say the building is severely lacking in kerb appeal. The render is blistered and cracked, the windows are rotten in places, and the front door looks like it was rescued from a skip. Even the house number is cheap and nasty; two stick-on numbers in an ugly italic font.

I try one of the silver keys in the lock, and for the first time today, strike lucky.

Things aren't much better on the opposite side of the door. What was probably once an impressive entrance hall is dark and dingy. The door to flat A is on the right, with the stairs to the two other floors directly ahead. As I climb the stairs, the distinctive smell of takeaway food and marijuana intensifies. For now, I'll skip introducing myself to the neighbours, although the alternate version of me must have already met them, I presume. I, however, haven't, which could be awkward if I bump into them.

That thought encourages me to scuttle up to the first-floor landing and the door to flat B. I quickly unlock it and hurry inside, leaning up against the closed door and breathing a heavy sigh.

The tour of my new home doesn't take long, but it's nowhere near as bad as I imagined. There's a double bedroom, a functional bathroom and kitchen, and a lounge with a large window overlooking Rochford Road. Although the place could do with a lick of paint, it's clean and tidy, and the furniture, although low-quality flat pack, is modern.

After I've tested the sofa and the bed, I return to the kitchen in need of more water. Without thinking, I open a cupboard and grab a glass from the shelf. Only when I turn on the tap does it cross my mind that I either beat eight-to-one odds in opening the right cupboard the first time or I somehow knew which cupboard the glasses are stored.

I drink two glasses of water and conclude it must have been a fluke.

Thirst sated, I return to the bedroom and open the wardrobe doors.

"Christ," I mumble.

There's no expensive Tom Ford suit, but three pairs of non-branded jeans, a couple of jumpers, and two polyester jackets. The chest of drawers by the window offers up an equally bland range of t-shirts, polo shirts, socks, and underwear. I know this version of me hasn't had the best of times, but when did he stop giving a shit about how he dresses?

A sudden trilling sound draws my attention away from the chest of drawers. I step over to the bed and retrieve the mobile phone, although I'm in two minds about answering it. The caller ID confirms who's trying to reach me: *Dave (work).*

I know more than one Dave, and in this reality, I obviously work with one. Should I answer the call? As I fumble with the unfamiliar Android phone, I inadvertently make a decision. A voice leaks from the speaker.

"Gary? You there?"

Fuck!

"Err, yeah. I'm here."

"Sorry, mate. Have I caught you at a bad moment?"

"Um, kind of. Can I call you back?"

"It's only a quick one. I know you've booked the week off, but is there any chance you could come in tomorrow?"

Not only do I not know where I work, but how do I explain that I've suddenly forgotten how to do the job I presume I've done for some time?

"I'd love to help," I reply, trying to sound appropriately unwell. "But I'm not feeling too clever at the moment."

"In what way?"

"Sorry?"

"In what way aren't you feeling too clever? You're not having … you know … problems with your noggin again?"

"My noggin? Um, no … it's just one of those forty-eight-hour bugs."

"Are you sure?"

"Positive."

"Okay, fair enough. I'll leave you in peace, but if you want to talk, you know where I am."

"Right. Thanks, Dave."

He ends the call by confirming he'll see me next week. Presuming today is still Thursday, I've got three full days to fill in the many gaps relating to my employment. It then dawns on me that I'm holding a potential goldmine of information in my hand — everyone's life history is stored on their phone.

It takes but two minutes to ascertain that my predecessor can't have owned the phone very long because the photo gallery is empty and he hasn't installed any of the most common apps, including Facebook and Twitter. There are only three people

listed in the contacts: Dave (work), Dr Graham, and Mum &
Dad. What a sad indictment of this man's life.

As the phone has proven to be next to useless, I tuck it in
my pocket and return to my original priority. I lock up and
hurry down to the street, to the car I can't believe I have to
drive. Aesthetically, the metallic silver hatchback is inoffensive,
but there's a reason why the Rover 45 was so popular with
pension-age drivers. This won't be a thrill-a-minute driving
experience.

Once I've got the measure of the clunky gearbox and woolly
steering, I switch into autopilot and barely register the journey
I've made more times than I can recall. Approaching the final
few hundred yards before my final destination, I slow to a
crawl and brace for what I suspect is going to be a significant
emotional impact.

It is.

I pull up to the kerb and kill the engine. Across the road, a
large sign that once proudly welcomed customers to Kirkwood
Motors now displays the logo and branding of Honda. At
some point after my predecessor went to prison, the site must
have been sold, and the forecourt is now lined solely with the
Japanese manufacturer's cars.

I wanted to see for myself what happened to my business, but
I underestimated how sickening a sight it'd be. I don't know
whether to vomit, cry, or punch the steering wheel. As I'm
weighing up my options, a guy in a mid-grey suit strides over to a
Civic at the end of a row and starts snapping photos. I recognise
him because I gave Justin his first job in car sales just a few years
ago.

Before I can question the logic, I jump out of the Rover and
hurry across the road.

"Justin," I call out.

He lowers his phone and stares back at me as I approach.

"Err, hi," he replies.

"How are you doing?"

"I'm good, thanks."

Standing only six feet away, there's not so much as a flicker of recognition on Justin's face.

"You don't know who I am, do you?"

"I'm really sorry," he grimaces. "I meet so many people in this job, I struggle to remember everyone. Did I sell you a car?"

It was hard enough seeing my business gone, but Justin's confirmation that he doesn't even know who I am is a knife to the heart. It's not that my life will be any better or worse without him in it, but the significance of his oblivion stretches so much further. In this reality, I lost the business around 2013, whereas in my former life, I continued trading and eventually employed Justin and more than a dozen other staff. His being here now, though, is nothing more than a coincidence, a quirk of fate.

"I didn't buy a car, no," I reply in a low voice. "But you were kind enough to take me on a test drive."

"Oh, right. I'll have to try harder next time."

"It wasn't anything to do with your sales skills. I just couldn't afford it."

"Good to know," he smiles back.

"Anyway, I'll let you get on."

"Thanks."

As he turns to continue his task, I grab the opportunity to ask after another of Kirkwood's employees.

"Sorry, Justin, but is there someone called Janine working in the office here?"

"Janine?"

"Yeah, she's about thirty-seven. Dark-brown hair and green eyes."

Justin shakes his head. "No, I'm pretty sure there isn't."

I'm not surprised by his reply, but I am saddened. Janine always said how much she loved working at Kirkwood, and I'd hate to think she's any less happy with whatever job she's doing in this reality.

I return to the Rover and sit for a while, watching the comings and goings at Elderton Honda. I don't recognise anyone, and although the buildings still remain, they've been remodelled to reflect the image of a global car company. Everything I worked so hard for; gone and forgotten by all but me.

"Not all," I then mumble as my thoughts head closer to home.

There are two people who definitely still know me, and they're the only two people who can help me understand who I am in this life.

I turn the ignition key and pull away. It might not be the most sensible of ideas, but I really want to see my parents.

Chapter 23

I stop for a second and stare at the gate. It was only a few hours ago that I staggered towards it on my quest to drop off a letter. A few hours, but it was actually twenty-seven years ago.

If I hadn't dropped that letter, would I be here now? No, I wouldn't. I'd likely be sunning myself on a yacht in the Caribbean. Instead, I'm a former criminal, living in a rented flat, driving a crap car, and I pack stuff in boxes for a living. Christ, talk about snatching the most humiliating of defeats from the jaws of victory.

I ring the doorbell.

The journey to my parents' place took longer than it should. Not because of the Rover's feeble engine but because I needed time to think about how I deal with the fact I'm not the man they remember. Ten years have passed since they witnessed their son in a dock, being sentenced to six years in prison. Whatever that did to my predecessor, it must have been unbearable for my parents.

Mum opens the door.

"Hello, Sweetheart," she says. "What are you doing here?"

"Day off, and I thought I'd pop by for a cup of tea ... if that's okay?"

"It's always okay. You know that."

Mum steps aside so I can enter the hallway. She closes the door, and I lean down to give her a hug. I've never needed one more, truth be told.

I break from my mum's arms before she becomes suspicious, but she holds on to my lower arms and looks up at me.

"You alright?" she asks.

It's not her question that steals my breath but the look in her eyes. For as long as I can remember, those eyes have conveyed pride. Now, all I see is pity.

"I'm good, honestly," I reply. "Or at least I will be once I've had a cuppa. I'm parched."

Satisfied with my response, Mum leads me through to the kitchen.

"Where's Dad?" I ask.

"Down at the allotment."

"How is he?"

"You know, bearing up."

Mum puts the kettle on and silently removes a couple of mugs from a tree on the side. She usually never stops chatting from the moment I walk in till the moment she kisses me goodbye.

"Is everything okay, Mum? You're very quiet."

"Am I? I'm just a bit tired, that's all."

"You're not sleeping well?"

"I told you last week I wasn't sleeping well. You've got a memory like a sieve these days."

"Sorry. I've been a bit distracted of late."

On the way over here, I planned how I could lure my parents into revealing more information about my life and, more importantly, who is still part of that life. I need to find a willing candidate to take a trip in Edith Stimp's fucked-up time-travel chair, and it'll be an almost impossible task convincing a friend, never mind a stranger.

"Do you need to see Dr Graham again?" Mum asks.

I don't even know who Dr Graham is, so there's no easy answer to Mum's question.

"No, it's fine. I'm ... um ... I'm good."

"You swear?"

"Cross my heart."

The kettle boils, and once Mum has made the tea, we go through to the lounge. It's not dramatically different from the last time I was here, but there are fewer photos dotted around. I don't suppose there have been too many happy family moments in recent years, what with my incarceration.

I'm about to sit down when I spot a new addition to my parents' photo collection, and it's one I definitely haven't seen before. Cased in a silver frame, it features Mum, Dad, me, and a random woman I'm positive I've never met, which is odd as my arm is draped around her shoulder.

"If I'd know you were coming around, I'd have put that in a drawer," Mum says apologetically.

"Why?"

"What do you mean, why?"

I pick the photo up and take a closer look. I must be in my early thirties, I'd guess, and if our smiles are any barometer, everyone looks blissfully happy. However, establishing who this woman is and why Mum would choose to hide this photo from me isn't going to be easy.

"I mean, we look so happy, don't we? Surely that's a good memory, right?"

"We look happy because we were, but I didn't think you wanted a reminder of what you've lost."

Mum's choice of the word 'lost' is a concern. I need to tread carefully if I'm to understand what exactly it is I no longer have.

"What did you think of her?" I ask, in as light and level a tone as I can.

"Why are you asking that?"

"I don't know, Mum. Sometimes we forget how good things were, and maybe how good things could be again."

"I liked Tara."

Tara? Whoever she is or was, I suspect Mum wasn't Tara's number one fan because she used to say she liked Clare. That feeling never evolved to fondness, let alone love.

"Happy days, eh. If only we could turn back time."

"If only, Son," Mum replies wistfully.

"Remind me: when was this photo taken?"

"Gosh, it must have been sometime in the summer of 2012. I remember the London Olympics being on at the time."

"So, the same year I was arrested?"

Mum puts her cup on the table and fixes me with an expression I've not seen since I was a child.

"What's got into you? You're acting very ... strange."

I've barely learned anything about my past, and Mum has already rumbled me. I've no option but to switch into car salesman mode and deploy some grade-A bullshit.

"I had an epiphany last night," I remark.

"What's that when it's at home?"

"It's like a moment of clarity ... like seeing a completed jigsaw puzzle rather than all the individual pieces."

"Did you now?" Mum replies with a trace of parental scepticism. "And what triggered this moment of clarity?"

"I started reading a book about self-improvement. The author said that to understand the past and the mistakes you made, it sometimes helps to hear the views of those closest to you ... a different perspective, if you like."

"I don't see what good it does, raking over the past."

"Because that's the only place I'll find answers, Mum. It's a bit like watching a film with someone else and getting their perspective — a fresh set of eyes, if you like. Does that make sense?"

"Not really, no."

"I want to understand what happened from your perspective."

"It was bloody awful. That enough for you?"

"Just humour me, Mum. I know this must sound odd, but I want to learn the lessons from what I did wrong, but there are only so many ways I can look at the past from my own perspective. I need someone else to tell me how they felt when events unfolded. It'll help me move forward."

"That sounds like a terrible idea, and I don't see what good it'll do. You've got your life back on track now, and I can't bear the thought of you slipping back to where you were."

"Do I sound like I might? Be honest?"

"Well, no. You sound more like your old self than you have in a very long time."

"That's down to the book I'm reading. I promise you; it's helping in ways I can't begin to explain."

Mum eyes her cup of tea for a long moment and then puffs out her cheeks.

"What do you want me to say?" she eventually asks.

"I'd like to pretend I'm a journalist or a reporter. Someone you can speak candidly to."

"No, I'll feel silly."

"At the start, but you'll soon see how useful it is in breaking down barriers. I need you to be completely honest with me, which is why I want you to answer my questions as if I'm not your son."

"Fine," Mum huffs. "If you think it'll help, then I'll play along. But if I'm not comfortable, we stop. Agreed?"

"I promise."

I sit forward and rest my arms on my thighs.

"From your perspective, tell me what happened in the months after the photograph was taken."

"Really?" Mum groans. "You know—"

"Please. Just talk to me as if you're telling the story to someone you've never met."

Based on her expression, Mum still isn't happy about her part in my made-up role-play experiment, but after a sip of tea, she gives me a nod to continue.

"So, what happened in the months after the photograph was taken?"

"Nothing really, apart from planning your wedding. As you want me to be honest, I will tell you that me and your Dad felt a bit overwhelmed by it all, but Tara obviously wanted a big, fancy do, so we went along with it."

Shit, I was due to marry the mysterious Tara.

"Why did you feel overwhelmed?"

"I guess we're old-fashioned, and when your dad proposed to me, we were wed within six months, and it was just a small affair. I couldn't understand why you booked a wedding two years ahead … until Tara shared her plans with us. So much money and so much extravagance on one day didn't seem right to us."

I need to ask a risky question. It's risky because I don't know what my parents said to me back then.

"Why didn't you say something?"

"You wouldn't have listened."

"What makes you think that?"

"Because I thought … we thought that she had you under her spell. A bad influence, your dad used to say."

"In what way was Tara a bad influence?"

"Listen, I don't want you to think we didn't like the girl. I'm sure she loved you, but she wasn't shy about spending your money."

"You think she was using me?"

"Not consciously, no. I think she got carried away with portraying a certain lifestyle ... you both did. That's what happens when you date a girl rather than a woman."

"Right ... err, you think I should have dated someone closer to my own age?"

"Don't you, in hindsight?"

I think for a second and, rather than answer the question, pose another risky one of my own.

"I'm interested in your view, Mum. Do you think the age gap was too big?"

"Nine years isn't that big a gap, but you were at different stages of life. When you proposed to Tara, I don't think she was ready, and the wedding had nothing to do with love and everything to do with appearance."

Conscious of not digging too deeply into my relationship with a much younger woman, I respond with a reassuring nod and a half-smile. I have to move the conversation on.

"Can we talk about what happened with the business?"

"If you want."

"Did you ever believe I was guilty?"

Based solely on Mum's scowl, I think she's genuinely offended by my question.

"What a horrible thing to ask me," she chides. "Of course we didn't."

"Sorry."

"But you were guilty of taking your eye off the ball."

"In what way?"

"If you'd spent more time at work, keeping an eye on that tosspot Slade, he wouldn't have been able to do what he did. You worked so hard to build that business, Son, but the moment you got together with Tara, your priorities changed."

"For the worse, you think?"

"Too bloody right. I dread to think how much money you spent that year: weekends away at swanky hotels, five-star foreign holidays, and too many shopping trips to London. It wasn't about the money, though; it was the time. While you were away, living the high life with Tara, Darren Slade was free to use your business to clean his dirty money."

I asked for honesty, and now Mum is in her stride, she's certainly not holding back.

"That was stupid of me," I concede, although I had no part in what occurred. "Maybe I should never have got involved with Tara."

"I don't blame Tara for what happened. She was a naive young woman who enjoyed being spoilt. You, Son, should have known better, though."

"You're right. One-hundred per cent."

Mum's frown softens at my admission as if it's the first time she's heard it.

"You asked me to be honest, so I am, but not for one minute do I think you deserved what happened. Prison all but destroyed you."

Sitting here now, I can't begin to imagine how bad life in prison was, and yet, I was there for four years. It's so detached from the life I had, it just doesn't seem feasible.

"Truth be told, Mum, I don't remember much about it," I admit. "I've tried to block it out."

"All of it?"

"Let's not dwell on what I think. I'm interested in hearing about it from your perspective."

"Seriously," Mum replies with mild incredulity. "You want to know what it was like visiting our son in prison?"

"No, I want to know your thoughts on what happened in the four years I was in prison."

"The worst four years of our lives by a country mile, particularly that final year."

"Why the final year?"

"Is that a serious question?"

"Yes, and I know you must think this is stupid, but I need to hear it."

"I'm not comfortable with that. You were doing okay up until that final year, and the last thing I want to do is remind you of what happened."

Mum appears resolute as she reaches for her tea.

"Look at me, Mum."

She takes a sip and then looks across at me.

"I'm not the same man who walked out of that prison, and I swear that this is helping me."

"God knows how," Mum sighs. "But if you want me to go over it, fine."

"It's all part of the process."

"And does that process include you remembering the day you found out that your former fiancée had married another man and she was expecting his child?"

Ouch. I can't imagine life in prison, but I can imagine what a kick in the balls that news must have been. One day you're planning your wedding to a beautiful young woman, and the next, you're in prison while some other guy is living the life you'd envisaged with that same beautiful young woman on his arm.

"People move on," I reply, trying to sound magnanimous. "That's all Tara did."

"If only you'd been so relaxed about it at the time. Trashing your cell and assaulting a guard cost you an extra ten months inside, remember."

"Not my greatest moment."

"Dr Graham pinpointed that day as the beginning of your … problems."

"Be specific, Mum. What problems?"

"Your depression."

"Oh, that."

"Oh, that?" Mum snaps. "For three years, you struggled to get out of bed most days and couldn't function without medication, and all you can say is 'Oh, that'?"

"Sorry, I didn't mean to sound trite, but … I'm trying to get past it, minimise what it did to me."

"I wish we could," Mum gulps. "We were constantly worried sick that you'd do something stupid. It was a living hell, seeing you like that day after day, week after week, for three long years."

Mum reaches into the pocket of her cardigan and pulls out a tissue which she then uses to dab her eyes. Realising I've gone too far, I leap out of the chair and kneel down in front of my mum.

"I didn't mean to upset you," I say softly. "I'm sorry, Mum."

She swallows hard and, with one final dab of her eyes, finds her stiff upper lip again.

"I didn't think I had any more tears to spill," she says. "Maybe your stupid little game isn't so stupid after all."

"You've got to purge the old to start with the new."

"You might be right, and it certainly seems to have had a positive effect on you."

"Do you think?"

She takes my hand and gives it a squeeze. "This is the first time we've had a proper chat in a long time. I've missed you, Sweetheart."

"And for that, I'm truly sorry, but that old version of Gary is gone now."

"Good, and can we stop with the questions, please?"

"Can I ask one more?"

"Just one, and then we're done."

"Promise."

I give Mum's hand another reassuring squeeze and retake my seat.

"If I had a problem and needed help with it, who would I ask?"

"Your dad and me, I'd hope."

"That goes without saying, but besides you two, who would I ask?"

After a moment's pause and a resigned sigh, I get my answer.

"Truthfully? No one."

"What about my old mates? Dave? Paul? Ian?"

"Did you bump your head on the way here?"

"No. Why do you ask?"

"Because you seem to be suffering from amnesia. You burned your bridges with your old mates when you were dating Tara. You stopped going to the pub, playing football, and Dave wasn't best pleased when you booked a holiday with Tara the same weekend he was getting married."

"That's a shitty thing to do."

"Precisely what your dad said, but you did it anyway. And let's not forget you went to prison for four years. They all moved on with their lives while you were away."

Hearing how badly I treated my old mates isn't easy. How could I have been such a dick?

"Do you know if they're okay?"

"I saw Dave's sister at the supermarket a few weeks back. He's living in Kent now with his wife and a couple of kiddies. Paul is somewhere up north, I think, working for the NHS, but Ian is still local. He's got a lot on his plate because his mum hasn't been well for a while, the poor woman."

"What about the people I worked with? Why wouldn't I ask one of them?"

"Funnily enough, Son, they weren't too happy with you when the police raided the business and closed it down. They all lost their jobs."

I'm sure it wasn't Mum's intention, but the more of my predecessor's life she reveals, the less I want to hear. Christ, no wonder he suffered from depression — he had a lot to be depressed about, and from what little I've gathered thus far, most of it was self-inflicted.

"Well," I puff. "I think it's fair to say I've made some crappy decisions, but I do appreciate you being honest with me, Mum. I needed to hear it."

"You can't change any of it, and you've already paid your dues, so don't dwell on the negatives."

"I won't."

"Did it help?"

"More than you'll ever know."

"I really hope so, Sweetheart. We all make bad choices in life, but you've got to get up, dust yourself down, and carry on. No point stewing in your own juices, is there?"

"Couldn't agree more."

I wasn't responsible for my predecessor's bad choices, but unless I can find someone to help me out of this mess, I'll be the one left stewing.

Chapter 24

I stayed with Mum for another half-hour and then made my excuses. I've no idea what she's been through over the last decade, but it's left a lasting impression. It's another reason I have to find a way to undo my tinkering with the past, not that I don't have enough reasons already.

I drive one of those reasons back to another — the flat. I refuse to call it home and, as it's rented, it's not mine. Although the hour I spent with Mum helped fill in some blanks about this life, it confirmed my fear that the shortlist of potential volunteers for a trip back in time couldn't be any shorter. I'm hoping I might find something in the flat relating to other friendships I've forged in the last few years.

Once I step through the door, I head straight to the bedroom and kick off the awful trainers. I'm no brand snob, but you get what you don't pay for with cheap footwear: blisters.

I only had a cursory nose around the flat earlier, but now I've got all time in the world, except I haven't. As Edith Stimp stressed, the clock is ticking.

The foraging for information begins in the bedroom. There's nothing of interest in the bedside table or chest of drawers, but I do unearth a filing box at the bottom of the wardrobe. I transfer it to the bed and begin sifting through the compartments. There's nothing to aid my quest, but I get a clearer picture of the financial situation I've inherited, courtesy of three months' bank statements and a copy of a tenancy agreement. The bank statements reveal that I'm left with a shade under three-hundred quid a month in disposable income before food and clothing. Now I understand why there are only a handful of cheap garments hanging in the wardrobe — I'm skint.

I return the box to the wardrobe and head for the lounge.

Standing in the doorway, I'm struck by how much the room reminds me of the first flat Clare and I rented together. Every stick of furniture screams cheap or second-hand, and the walls are painted in a similar shade of insipid magnolia. The main difference is the television set because ours was a hulking beast built in the early nineties, whereas this room features a thirty-two-inch flatscreen set, albeit an older model.

It seems unlikely I'll learn anything new about my life in here, which is why I step towards the centre of the room more in hope than expectation. I couldn't see it from the doorway, but there's a flat-pack bookcase to the left of the two-seater sofa, and every shelf is full. I've never been much of a reader because I don't have the time or attention span, but my predecessor patently had plenty of both.

There is, however, a more interesting item poking out of a magazine rack next to the sofa: a laptop.

I snatch it up and sit on the sofa. Knowing how much of our lives we store on digital devices, this has to be my best bet for information on Gary Kirk's life. Fingers crossed, it has more to offer than his mobile phone.

I hit the power button and flip open the screen.

"Ugh."

I don't know why I expected any different, but the laptop is painstakingly slow because it's running a version of Windows I've not seen for the best part of a decade. When it eventually boots up, at least I don't have to worry about modern security protocols.

To begin, I open up a web browser and head straight to Facebook, but I'm greeted by a screen prompting me to log in. On my devices, back in the reality I should still be in, I'm permanently logged in to all my social media accounts. Either this Gary doesn't have a Facebook account, or he diligently logs out after every session. I click on the field where the user is prompted to enter their email address, hoping the browser might remember it. No such luck.

I then look at the most recently viewed websites, and although there's nothing overtly useful, it does list Gmail. I click through to the home page, but once again, I'm prompted to enter an email address and password. I might be able to guess the latter, but Gary Kirk's email address could literally be anything.

With nothing else to go on, I click through various folders on the hard drive. There's precious little of anything. It's not beyond the realms of possibility that the laptop was reconditioned and wiped clean, and my predecessor picked it up on eBay for next to nothing.

One thing I have learned is that after spending four years in prison, where Gary Kirk wasn't allowed electronic devices, he suffered from severe depression for a couple of years. That would explain why he had to start from scratch, having been off grid for so long. And from what Mum told me, it's not as though he had many friends left to connect with on social media.

I sit back and try to imagine what those years must have been like. I've had a few issues with my mental health, but nothing more than the occasional bout of anxiety. Ironically, the only time I've felt weighed down by negative thoughts happened to be in the days before I bumped into Edith Stimp, prompted by Clare's demands. Now I've rewritten history, my wife won't even get the chance to get her hands on my money, not that I have any.

Thoughts of Clare then pique my curiosity. I've fucked up my life by ensuring we never met, but I wonder how this life has treated her. Did she marry and have kids? Did she still go on that stupid Shamanic retreat and then set up a clinic to treat the pathologically gullible?

I open Google on the laptop and search for Clare Wood. It's a fairly common name, so there's every chance I'll have to dig deep into the results to find the woman I once married, and that's assuming she didn't marry someone else. For all I know, Clare has used an entirely different surname for the last few decades, and I've no more chance of guessing that than I have of guessing Gary Kirk's email address.

The laptop takes forever to load the results, but when the page finally updates, I instantly dismiss the first result because it's a Wikipedia page. For an individual to have their own entry into Wikipedia, they must be considered notable: celebrities, politicians, professional athletes, academics, and the like. I cannot see how the Clare I married would ever fall into any of those categories.

I'm about to move my attention to the next item on the search results, but a familiar word snags my attention. My eyes dart to the left of the page, and I read the snippet of text in its entirety.

Clare Wood is a British spiritualist, faith healer, and philanthropist. She is also the founder and CEO of the Tungus Trust.

"No way," I gasp.

I click the link, and the Wikipedia page opens. Any doubts as to the name 'Tungus' being a coincidence are shattered when the page lists Clare Wood's birthday as the exact same date as my wife's. If that wasn't evidence enough, there's a studio-quality photo of her on the right of the page. Her hair, makeup, and attire are more befitting of a politician, but I'm unquestionably looking at the woman I married.

I read on, although there are only a few paragraphs of information. Unhelpfully, it doesn't say much about her early life, but in 2007, at the age of only twenty-nine, Clare Wood founded The Tungus Trust with a personal donation of £3 million. It goes on to say that the purpose of the trust is to facilitate the foundation and development of Shamanic and spiritual healing centres across the UK.

The rest of the information sounds a lot like marketing guff, but at the bottom of the page, there's a link to The Tungus Trust website. I click the link and then scour the page for information on the trust's founder. There's nothing directly related to Clare, but there is an 'About Us' page. Right at the top is a photo of a gleaming glass and steel building tagged as the head office for The Tungus Trust. It takes a couple more clicks to ascertain the building is in Winchester, barely twelve miles from Elderton.

I sit back and try to digest what I've just unearthed. As discoveries go, it's not as shocking as a trip back in time and a subsequent stint in prison, but it still beggars belief.

Clare Wood: multi-millionaire philanthropist and founder of a trust with branches across the UK.

If not for the compelling evidence of a photo and matching date of birth, I'd dismiss the notion entirely and assume it was a different woman.

I re-read the two paragraphs of text again and then again. The words and sentences all make perfect sense, but the information conveyed is nonsensical. The Clare I know wasn't particularly business-minded, and never in a month of Sundays could I imagine her amassing enough wealth to donate three million quid to a charitable trust before her thirtieth birthday.

Did the deletion of our relationship really change Clare's fortunes so dramatically? It seems impossible, yet the evidence is here in black and white.

My discovery is a distraction from far more pressing matters, but it's impossible to re-route my thinking around this discovery. I could, and maybe should, be pleased for Clare, so why do I feel so incredulous?

The answer promptly arrives — Clare has the wealth and success I designed for myself. I should be a multi-millionaire, not an ex-con living in a rented flat. My wife has what I was supposed to have if I hadn't lost that bloody letter.

The letter …

No …

Surely not …

Up until five seconds ago, I assumed I'd dropped the letter during the frantic dash to my parents' place. What if it fell out of my pocket while I was crouched down on a driveway, sabotaging Mrs Wood's old Fiesta? I force my eyes shut and try to recall the few minutes I spent deflating a tire. I changed position a few times because of a cramp, so it's not inconceivable that the letter slipped out of my pocket while I repositioned myself.

Did Clare find it?

My mind struggles as it tries to unfurl the possibilities. Surely, most eighteen-year-olds would look at a list of random betting and investment tips and toss it in the bin. Why would Clare give the letter a second thought, never mind act on the information it contained?

"Oh, God."

My mind catches up and answers the question. I penned a line at the top of the letter. *Keep this letter safe and DO NOT share it with anyone. This information will make you a multi-millionaire by the time you're 30.*

All Clare had to do was keep hold of the letter for a few months, and she could have tested the first bet with England's game against Switzerland in Euro 96. Maybe she placed a small bet on the result, and that bet would have doubled or possibly trebled her stake. If she bet her winnings on the next match, she'd have realised within a few matches the true value of the information I recorded.

It's pure speculation, but how else could Clare have amassed so much money before her thirtieth birthday? I must have dropped the letter on her driveway, and she must have found it. There's no other plausible explanation.

I get up and pace the tiny lounge as a gut-wrenching irony nips at my heels — I only entertained Edith Stimp's insane proposal so I could avoid paying Clare the fat end of six-hundred grand, but now she's a multi-millionaire, and I have nothing. Salt and wounds spring to mind.

The pacing soons becomes stomping, and then I realise there's someone living downstairs, and I don't want to attract the attention of a neighbour I've never met. Besides, all the indignation in the world is not going to change the situation. I need to calm down and consider how I might be able to use what I know to my advantage. I'm the only person on the planet who knows how Clare Wood funded her empire, and I also know more about her than perhaps anyone.

I sit back down on the sofa and grab the laptop. Now is not the time for tantrums. It's the time for plotting and planning.

Chapter 25

For a nanosecond everything is well with the world. I might have just suffered a terrible dream but, as I slowly awake, I can thank my lucky stars that none of it was real.

Until I open my eyes.

"Fuck's sake," I rasp.

Despite the lumpy mattress, I slept soundly — no great surprise, considering the physical and mental toll I suffered for what felt like a week but was only one day. However, I don't feel the usual rush of happy endorphins associated with a good night's sleep because there's bugger all in Gary Kirk's life to be happy about.

But there is the tiniest microbe of hope.

I spent the remainder of yesterday researching Clare Wood's life, interrupted only when I needed food or the bathroom. My predecessor had the good grace to stock the freezer with microwave meals, and although there wasn't any milk in the fridge, or alcohol, both the coffee and sugar caddies were half full.

The life Clare has led in this reality is incomparable to the one we lived together. Besides the Wikipedia entry, Google returned scores of articles, interviews, and news reports on Clare Wood and her charitable trust. I wouldn't go as far as to say she's reached celebrity status, but she definitely has a public profile. What was of greater surprise, though, was discovering that she has almost a million followers across Twitter, Facebook, and Instagram. Many seem to have bought into her preachings, and after spending half an hour scouring her posts, I concluded Clare's social media persona isn't far from that of a cult leader, and her followers seemed more like acolytes.

I also discovered that Clare never married or had kids. In an interview with a magazine six years ago, she said that her work is too important and all-consuming, so there's no room for relationships or parenthood. The reporter probed a little deeper with her next question and asked if Clare had ever fallen in love, and at that point, the interview took an unexpected turn. Clare said that loving oneself was far more important than seeking love from another, and her purity was sacrosanct. The reporter then pushed her luck by asking a question most likely to intrigue the reader: are you still a virgin? Clare didn't directly answer the question, only repeating the line about her purity being sacrosanct.

The rest of the interview was unremarkable, but that one line about Clare's virginity caught the attention of her acolytes. Much like Queen Elizabeth I was hailed as the Virgin Queen and treated with deity-like reverence, so too was Clare after the publication of the interview. Clare Wood quickly became more than just another fruitloop pedalling her pseudo-science beliefs — she was set on a path to becoming the untainted Puritan Goddess of the UK spiritual community.

I continued to sift through more interviews and articles about the divine Ms Wood, but what was interesting wasn't the amount of coverage her PR agency had achieved but the complete absence of information relating to her early life. I found the odd reference to her mum and sister and Clare's time at secondary school, but nothing about the decade of her life before she set up The Tungus Trust. No one seemed to question how a woman who grew up in a terraced house in Elderton and flunked her A-levels became so wealthy.

With that question rattling around my head, I eventually closed the laptop down, deciding to sleep on what I'd gleaned.

This morning, I'm still trying to fathom out if Clare is a distraction or a solution. Something in my gut tells me she could be both, but I've yet to work out how. Still, I've not exactly got a packed diary today, so once I've had a shower and something to eat, I'll sit down and give the matter the attention I think it might deserve.

Wandering around an unfamiliar flat in my underwear, it does feel like I've checked into a two-star hotel, albeit one where they provide guests with two-star boxer shorts. The choice of breakfast options is also decidedly budget, with just a loaf of cheap white bread and margarine in the fridge. I toast a couple of slices and sit in the lounge to eat it, not that there's anywhere else to dine.

Whilst chewing on a tasteless slice of toast, I switch the TV on and flick through to a news channel. It did cross my mind that maybe my minor tinkering in the past might have altered the future in some other unknown way — the butterfly effect, I think it's called. However, after fifteen minutes of watching the news, it's clear that science fiction films lied because nothing has changed from the reality I erased. The politicians are still self-serving, the public is still deeply divided on a host of issues, and the England men's team still haven't won a major football tournament. No one seems very happy.

Bored of the same old, same old, I change the channel. I can't remember the last time I watched daytime TV, and it doesn't take long to confirm I've not missed anything. I switch the TV off before my already-taxed brain dissolves into grey mush.

Sitting in silence, it feels like my mind is teetering on a knife edge. On the one hand, I could so easily fall prey to the same debilitating negativity that blighted my predecessor. His depression, however, was born of remorse for a succession of dreadful decisions, whereas I only made the one. I'm not depressed, but I could easily head that way if I can't think of a way to escape this hell. To do that, I've got two options and the first of those — finding someone gullible enough to take a trip back in time — seems the hardest. My last and only hope is that I'm close enough to one of my work colleagues and they're willing to help. How I establish that when I don't even know the names of my work colleagues is a problem in itself. I've got until Monday to figure that one out, but in the meantime, I need to consider another possibility. What if I can't go back and this is now my life?

This life is, without question, shit, and as it stands, it's impossible to see how it'll get any better. At forty-five, my most productive years are behind me, and I don't think I've got the fortitude or appetite to start anew. Even if I possessed both, I've no resources. It takes years, possibly decades, to create something from nothing. I'd hoped to be on my way to becoming a multi-millionaire with a second successful business by the age of fifty, but here I'll be lucky if I'm chief box-packer by then.

That thought alone is enough to spike my resolve as I recall one of my favoured business maxims — fail to prepare, prepare to fail. If returning to my previous life proves impossible, I need a backup plan.

I scour the flat until I find a notepad and a pen. Tellingly, the notepad has never been used.

I've always found it helpful to jot notes down while I'm thinking. It helps to draw out the crux of a problem, like solo brainstorming. I'm also a big fan of lists, and on one side of the page, I scribble a column header: Resources. It'll be a short list, but I need to ascertain what I've got at my disposal.

The process is frustrating until my mind suddenly latches on to a different list — the one I lost. During my brief visit to 1996, I had literally nothing besides the clothes on my back, but I did have one invaluable resource, and that was information. If that information had found its way to the person I intended it for, I wouldn't be sitting here now, but the point is still valid. Information invariably has value.

What information do I have, and how can I use it?

I know how to run a successful used-car business, and I've gained an almost encyclopaedic knowledge of mass-market cars, but so too did my predecessor, and he faced the same problem I now face. With no cash to invest in stock, it'll take forever to build a business to the same level as Kirkwood Motors, and times have changed in the industry. Even if I had the money for stock, and the industry wasn't on the verge of significant change, my predecessor couldn't have done a better job in trashing his reputation. And his reputation is now my reputation. Who'd want to buy a used car from a man who's served time for money laundering?

I might have all the knowledge and experience, but I have to face a hard truth. There is no realistic hope of me ever returning to my previous profession. It's an admission that stings more than I could have envisaged, and I can see how it might be the precursor to darker thoughts. I refuse to go there.

Returning my attention to the notepad, I draw three solid lines under the word *Information*. There's something else, I know it, but I can't seem to flush it out. What do I know that I can use to my advantage? Like every other person on the planet, I've no knowledge of the future, and Edith Stimp has already closed the door to another trip back in time, so all I've got is what I know today.

I know that I'm skint and Clare is not.

"Clare," I mumble.

I write her name in capital letters on the notepad and then draw a horizontal line across the page, connecting the words *Clare* and *Information*.

There is one thing I know that no other person on the planet knows, and that's Clare Wood's history. I know how she made her money and almost every facet of her first eighteen years of life because I was married to her for the best part of twenty-five years.

I have information, and Clare has money. How do I use the former to gain access to the latter? That is now the question I need to answer.

Turning to a fresh page, I furiously scribble down everything I know about Clare that most people don't. It's a long list that eventually leaks onto a second page and then a third. Most of it is fairly banal, and I can't see one of the national tabloids paying big bucks for an exclusive story about Clare Wood once shitting her knickers on a train journey to Portsmouth. In fact, even if I had proof that Clare once punched a barista in Starbucks, who'd care? For all her wealth, Clare Wood doesn't have the same public profile as a politician or soap star.

Ironically, I do have a story about Clare that every newspaper and news outlet in the world would pay a king's ransom for — if I could prove it, which I can't. There simply isn't a news editor insane enough to believe that Clare Wood amassed her fortune after finding a list of betting and investment tips that I left behind after a quick journey back in time.

I return to the list of facts about Clare's life and dismiss one after another. She likes dunking Weetabix in her tea. Odd, but not newsworthy. If she gets one hand wet, she has to make the other hand wet before drying them. A quirk but wholly uninteresting. She snogged another girl at a drunken house party when she was sixteen. Hardly a scandalous act. Her first holiday abroad was to Benidorm, just before her seventeenth birthday, and she ...

I drop the pen.

Something happened on that holiday, and if it were to become public knowledge, it wouldn't merely embarrass Clare, it would severely damage her reputation. And, as far as I'm aware, only one other person in Clare's life knows the truth, and that's her mum.

I sit back and consider my next move. I have information that Clare definitely wouldn't want in the public domain, but what do I do with it? At best, a desperate news editor might pay five-hundred quid to fill a few column inches on the seventh page of their paper, but that sum of money doesn't come close to what I need to rebuild this broken life. I need thousands. Tens of thousands. Maybe hundreds of thousands. What I need, and what I deserve, is the money I intended for myself when I stood on a street corner in 1996 and listed all those bets and investment tips. The same list I'm certain Clare benefited from.

It's a dirty word, blackmail, and up until this moment, I could never have envisaged a scenario where I might use information to obtain money. However, it might not even come to that if I can persuade the proposed victim that I'm entitled to a fair cut of what I helped create.

I jump up off the sofa. Today is Friday, and whilst I don't know where Clare lives, I know where she works. If I don't grab the opportunity today, I'll have no choice but to turn up for my packing job on Monday.

With little more than the crudest of plans, I put on my trainers and leave the flat. There's time enough to refine the plan on the thirty-minute drive to Winchester. When I get there, I can only hope Clare Wood shares many of the same traits as the woman I married. She is, after all, the same woman.

Chapter 26

I've driven to Winchester countless times over the years so I don't require a sat nav to guide me there. That's just as well, as the Rover isn't equipped with one. It does, however, have one feature that my top-of-the-range Mercedes coupé does not: a CD player. When I first started buying and selling cars, I traded in older, cheaper stock, so many of those cars had a cassette player. Eventually, I progressed to more modern cars with CD players, but seven or eight years ago, manufacturers began phasing them out. With the advent of streaming music and a plethora of digital radio stations available, I guess no one needs to take their music with them anymore.

I press the play button, curious if my predecessor's taste in music is any different to mine. Rather than music, a woman's voice leaks from the speakers. It only takes ten seconds of listening to ascertain it's a self-help CD.

"Jesus," I snort while pressing the stop button.

I should be focusing on what I'm going to say to Clare but, as I head out of Elderton, my thoughts drift off in a metaphysical direction. I've always believed that you create your own luck in life, and if you work hard, you'll get your just rewards. Now I'm able to directly compare two versions of the same man's life, I'm less convinced.

After the financial crisis of 2008, I took the tough decision to jettison a couple of members of staff, whereas my predecessor took out a loan. Both options were reasonable and pragmatic, but one would ensure a prosperous future for Kirkwood Motors while the other would land its founder in prison. To think, if my predecessor had taken the same decision as me, I'd have woken up to a very different reality. I'd likely be married to the infamous Tara, and we'd probably have kids, but weirdly, she wouldn't be *my* wife, and they wouldn't be *my* kids. I would, however, still have a business and a half-decent home. That, of course, assumes Tara herself wouldn't have bankrupted me.

As the miles pass by, so too do a raft of different permutations. If this, that. If that, this. The more I think about how fate can turn on even the most innocuous of decisions, the more convinced I become that life, in many ways, is a lottery.

Before I know it, I'm only a few minutes from the outskirts of Winchester. Not only am I ill-prepared for meeting Clare, but I'm also more nervous than I anticipated. On further analysis, the nerves aren't relevant to meeting a woman I know intimately, but the conversation itself. How much do I reveal about the reason I lost the list on her driveway?

Only then does it cross my mind that I could be completely wrong, and Clare might have amassed her fortune another way. I've based my assumption on the fact that she hasn't mentioned it in any of the many interviews I found online. I know she hasn't got any wealthy relatives so I can discount inheritance, and if she'd built and sold a successful business, that information would definitely be in the public domain. All I've got to go on is a feeling in my gut and an absence of a plausible alternative. It'll have to do.

I slow down and take a right turn into Bishop Park: a glorified trading estate built in the late nineties when it was suggested that Hampshire might become the UK's answer to Silicon Valley. It never quite panned out that way, and besides a telecoms company, most of the units were eventually let to decidedly low-tech businesses like paper merchants and insurance call centres. Now, the largest building in Bishop Park is home to a national charity.

On an overcast day, the headquarters of The Tungus Trust looks less impressive than it did on the website. I pull into a parking bay marked for visitors and make my way to the main entrance, grimacing at my reflection in the mirrored glass as I approach a set of automatic doors. If this meeting goes as planned, my first priority will be a trip into town and a clothes store.

The doors open and I step into a foyer that's as large as it is soulless. The only clue to the nature of the organisation that occupies the building is the new-age music piped from above. The Clare I married had hundreds of CDs of similar music, but it all sounded the same to me: finger cymbals, wind chimes, and the tuneless wail of pan pipes.

I step towards the main reception desk, where a twenty-something woman is staring at a computer monitor. She looks up when I reach the desk and flashes a tired smile.

"Welcome to The Tungus Trust."

"Morning."

"How may I be of assistance?"

"I'd like to speak to Clare Wood."

"Do you have an appointment?"

"No, but it is a matter of some urgency."

"I'm sorry, but Ms Wood only sees visitors with an appointment."

"Can I book an appointment?"

"May I ask what it's regarding?"

"As I said, it's an urgent matter ... and of a private nature."

"I'm afraid I won't be able to book an appointment for you without knowing the reason you'd like to see Ms Wood."

I had a feeling I might have to pass a gatekeeper to see Clare, but it's not the first time I've faced a jobsworth receptionist.

"I understand you're only doing your job, but if I walk away without seeing Clare — Ms Wood — I promise you that she'll be annoyed when she finds out. We go back a long way."

"You're friends?"

If she calls up to Clare's office and mentions my name, it'll be meaningless.

"Not friends as such, but our paths crossed as teenagers, and that's why I need to see her urgently."

"You might have to elaborate on that."

"All I'm asking you to do is call up to Clare's office and tell her that there's a man who'd like to discuss a letter she found outside her mum's house on Jubilee Road in 1996. She'll know what I'm referring to."

There's a moment of indecision, but the receptionist then scrawls a line of text on a pad and picks up a telephone handset.

"Can I take your name, Sir?"

"Gary. Gary Kirk."

"I can't promise Ms Wood will have time to see you," she says. "But I'll pass on the message."

"Thank you."

I take a few steps back from the desk and wait as the receptionist taps the phone's keypad.

"Hi Kate, it's Sophie down at main reception. I've got a gentleman here who says he needs to see Ms Wood as a matter of urgency."

I wait with Sophie for a reply, although the stakes are somewhat higher for me than the receptionist.

"Yes, I told him that, but he asked if I'd pass a message on to Ms Wood."

Sophie demonstrates her dictation skills by repeating my message almost word for word.

"Okay. I'll hold."

Long seconds pass, and Sophie turns her attention to the computer monitor while I shuffle nervously on the spot. Somewhere in the building, I can picture the CEO of The Tungus Trust receiving the most unexpected of messages. At best, I think there's only a fifty-fifty chance she'll want to meet the messenger.

"Right, will do," Sophie eventually says. "Thanks, Kate."

This is it. I'll know within the next five seconds whether I've blagged my way into Clare's office, or I need to come up with a plan B. Sophie looks up at me, her expression unreadable.

"If you can bear with me one moment, Mr Kirk, I'll ask someone to escort you up to Ms Wood's office."

"Oh, err ... great. Thank you."

Sophie picks up the phone again and says a few words to whoever is on the other end. Within seconds, the sound of footsteps echo from behind me.

"This is Grant," Sophie says, nodding beyond my left shoulder. "He'll escort you."

I turn around to be greeted by a guy who wouldn't look out of place in a TV drama set in an FBI field office: tall, close-cropped hair, square jaw, and a dark two-piece suit.

"Come this way," he says impassively.

I follow Agent Grant across the foyer to two lifts, one of which is waiting at ground-floor level. We step inside, and then I endure the most awkward ten-second lift journey of my life.

The doors open to another reception area, smaller but more lavishly furnished than the one I've just left. I wouldn't swear on it, but the choice of soft furnishings and wallpaper could easily be the choice of the woman I'm about to meet. Clare would call it free-spirited or even Bohemian. I'd call it messy and disorganised.

"Take a seat, Sir," Grant says. "I'll see if Ms Wood is ready to see you."

"Cheers."

He strides off towards a corridor. I'm too nervous to sit down and choose to stare out of the window. We're obviously on the top floor of the building, and the view, whilst not exactly Manhattan, is as good as you'd expect on the outskirts of Winchester, the tower and spires of the famous cathedral visible in the distance.

I'm still trying to work out my bearings when Grant returns.

"Ms Wood will see you now."

"Great."

"I'll need to frisk you first."

"What? Why?"

"Ms Wood has a huge following, but our work here occasionally draws the odd screwball out of the woodwork. I need to check you're not one of them."

"Fair enough."

If I thought sharing a silent lift for ten seconds was awkward, it pales when compared to an over-zealous FBI wannabe feeling his way around my body.

Content that I'm not concealing a meat cleaver down my pants, Grant then ushers me to follow as he turns and makes his way back up the corridor. I hurry after him and catch up just as he turns a corner and enters an open office with a desk positioned centrally and a sofa and coffee table near the floor-to-ceiling window. The woman behind the desk stands up.

"Mr Kirk?"

"Yes."

"Ms Wood only has fifteen minutes. Grant will wait outside and escort you back downstairs once you're finished."

Reading between the lines, the receptionist's statement is a thinly veiled warning that I'd better not do anything stupid. I guess Clare is no different from any other prominent woman with a public profile in that she has to err on the side of caution when it comes to her personal security.

Grant opens the door and waves me inside.

I straighten my shoulders, take a deep breath, and step forward. I've got fifteen minutes to convince a woman who's never met me that I am the man responsible for her fortune, and we were married for a long time in a parallel reality.

As good a salesman as I am, I've got my work cut out.

Chapter 27

I take three steps into the office and the door closes behind me. The room isn't much different to the one next door, just bigger, and the walls are decorated with scores of framed photographs. There's a desk directly ahead of me, but an oversized monitor is blocking the face of whoever is behind it — presumably, Clare.

"Hi," I venture.

Pushing her chair back, I finally get to see the woman I inadvertently made: Clare Wood. When she stands up and looks over the top of her glasses at me, it's enough to determine that this is not my wife. There's no hint of recognition or emotion, not even the tepid smile that used to greet me most mornings during the latter years of our marriage.

"Mr Kirk. Take a seat."

A single chair sits a safe distance away from the desk, almost in the centre of the room. I suspect Grant placed it there intentionally.

I heed the instruction and sit down. Clare doesn't return to her chair, choosing to perch on the side edge of her desk. Maybe it's a power play, a sign of dominance, that she's chosen to conduct our conversation from a higher vantage point.

Besides her cold eyes, the other marked difference between this woman and my wife is their attire. This Clare is wearing a tailored blouse, so white it's almost dazzling, and olive-green trousers. She looks like the consummate CEO, whereas my Clare considered every day a dress-down day.

"You mentioned a letter," Clare says, almost aggressively. "And my mother's house on Jubilee Road."

"That's right."

"You obviously assumed I'd know what you're talking about."

Clare might be looking down on me, but I need to maintain control of the conversation.

"Shall we cut to the chase? I know for a fact you found a letter on your driveway roughly twenty-seven years ago, and that letter provided gambling and investment information that you've used to your advantage."

"You know for a fact? How?"

"That's not important."

"What is important, then, Mr Kirk? Why are you here?"

"I'm here because that letter was mine."

"I've no idea what you're talking about."

"If that were true, why allow me up here?"

Christ knows how similar the woman in front of me is to my wife, but I do know that Clare was terrible at poker. I sit silently, waiting for her next move.

"Okay," she eventually replies. "Let's assume your letter did exist. How do you know I found it?"

"Trust me; you wouldn't believe me if I told you."

"Those who truly know me would tell you that I'm one of the most open-minded individuals they've ever met."

"Oh, I know you, Clare, better than you could possibly imagine."

"That's exactly the reply I'd expect from a stalker. Are you a stalker, Mr Kirk?"

"I'm not, and call me Gary."

"If you're not a stalker, who are you? Actually, more to the point, what do you want?"

"All I want is a slice of what should rightfully be mine."

"Money?"

"Yes."

"How predictable," she snorts.

"I don't think you're in any position to dismiss my claim. You'd be nothing without the information in that letter."

"Again, you're assuming a lot."

"No, I'm ... I've got a pretty good inkling how your life would have turned out if you hadn't found that letter, I can assure you."

"Based upon the same inkling for football results and stock investments?"

"Exactly the same."

"How did that information come into your hands?"

"As I said before, it's not important."

"In which case, I think we're done here."

She leans across the desk and reaches out for the phone.

"Wait," I interject. "What do you want to know?"

"I'd like to know exactly how that note ended up under the wheel of my mum's car."

"So, you admit you found it?"

"There's only you and I in the room, so whatever I admit is irrelevant."

"Fair enough. I dropped the note."

"And it's taken you twenty-seven years to claim ownership?"

"It's complicated."

"Then run me through the simple version."

"Give me a break, Clare," I groan. "I'd rather we discussed—"

"I beg your pardon," she snaps. "It might have escaped your attention, but you're in my office, and I don't appreciate your tone."

Too late, I realise I responded as if I was speaking to the woman I shared a house with, rather than a stranger.

"I'm sorry, but if I told you the full story of how I ended up here today, I suspect you'd laugh in my face."

"Try me."

"I'd rather not."

"It's your choice. You either tell me, or you leave."

I hadn't got as far as role-playing this meeting, but it did cross my mind that at some point, I might have to tell the truth. It'll be unbelievable at first telling, but if I have to reveal the more sensitive aspect of Clare's youthful misdemeanour, it'll sound slightly less insane.

"The letter was meant to be delivered to someone else."

"Who?"

"Me ... well, the eighteen-year-old version of me."

"I don't follow."

"This is the part that you're unlikely to believe but however crazy it sounds, it is the truth."

"I'm listening."

"A woman called Edith Stimp gave me the opportunity to travel back in time, to 1996. I only had a couple of hours, but I came up with the idea of sharing information with my younger self — information that would make him a wealthy man. Obviously, I lost the letter and you found it."

"So, let me get this straight. You travelled back in time, and you were on your way to deliver a letter to yourself when you decided to stop at our house. That's when you dropped the letter?"

"More or less."

"Did you have anything to do with the flat tyre?"

"Seeing as you asked for the truth, yes. That was me."

"Why?"

"Because I wanted to delay you leaving your house."

"For what purpose?"

"You were on your way to The Black Prince, right?"

Clare's arched eyebrows betray her poker face.

"How could you possibly know that?"

"Because that's where we first met, twenty-seven years ago."

"I have no recollection of us ever meeting before."

"That's because we haven't. When I let down the tyre on your mum's car, you arrived at The Black Prince after I left ... or the younger version of me left. You were waiting for your friend, Julie."

I warned Clare that the explanation sounded crazy, and the deep lines across her forehead imply I was right.

"I don't know how you know about The Black Prince, or Julie, but what you're suggesting is impossible."

"And yet, you found the evidence and profited from it."

"So, tell me. What would have happened if you hadn't let down that tyre?"

"We'd have bumped into one another in The Black Prince, and then ... then we'd have started dating and eventually married."

I expected dismay but Clare snorts once, and again. The dam then breaks, and the room fills with the sound of near-hysterical laughter. It continues for an uncomfortably long moment.

"Have you finished?" I huff. "I did say you wouldn't believe me."

"Oh, Gary," she replies, wiping a tear from her cheek. "I do have an open mind but ... I don't even know where to begin. The universe does work in mysterious ways, so maybe there is a way to travel in time, but to suggest I'd ever marry a man like you is beyond preposterous."

"But you did. We were married for almost twenty-five years."

"In some parallel universe, I assume?"

Her question is valid, but the tone in which it's asked is too close to mocking for my liking. To add insult, the question is followed by more laughter, although it's less raucous than the first time.

"I don't know how it happened, but it happened, okay? We were married, and I was … I managed to travel back in time for two hours. I wrote a letter intended for my younger self, but the main reason I went back was to stop you and I from meeting."

"If we were married for twenty-five years, perish the thought, why were you trying to sabotage our first meeting?"

"Because I wanted to avoid wasting all those years. Before I meddled with our past, we were about to get divorced."

"On the grounds of lunacy, perchance?"

"No, we just … the marriage fizzled out."

"I'm amazed it lasted twenty-five days, never mind twenty-five years. You are not my type, Gary … no offence."

"Scoff all you like, but it's the truth."

Shaking her head, Clare chuckles to herself. "This has been one of the more interesting meetings I've had of late, but I think we're done now."

"You owe me, Clare. All I'm asking for is a reasonable share of the money you made from my information."

"And if I say no?"

"That wouldn't be in your best interests. However, I'd rather we dealt with this quickly and amicably."

"Is that a threat?"

"No."

"Good, because I don't respond well to threats."

"But if you're not willing to do the right thing, I'll have to find another way to make money from the information I have on you."

"What information?"

"Whether you believe me or not, we were married for a very long time. And, like all married couples, we shared our secrets. I might not know anything of your life after you found my letter, but I know an awful lot about what happened before."

"If you think you can blackmail me over some trivial gossip from my teenage years, you're even more deluded than I first thought. Now, I've got more important—"

"Would you consider what happened in Benidorm trivial?"

Clare freezes and stares back at me. Whatever's going on in her head, she manages to keep it there. The onus is on me to prove how much I do know.

"You lost your virginity to a Swedish guy named Johan, remember?"

No response bar a slight twitch of her left eyelid.

"And then, four weeks later, you discovered you were pregnant. The only other person who knew was your mother because she drove you to the appointment at the abortion clinic and stayed with you right until the end of the procedure."

Clare remains silent, but her expression says everything.

"There's plenty more," I casually add, although it's a bluff. "But I've no interest in sharing what I know with anyone, providing I get a fair share of what's morally mine."

Silent seconds pass until Clare slowly returns to her chair. She clears her throat and rests her arms on the desk as if reinforcing her composure.

"You can make up stories if you like, Gary, but you don't have any evidence. Without it, who's going to believe you?"

"How do you know I don't have evidence? Do you not think the abortion clinic kept records? Maybe I know a Swedish guy named Johan who slept with an English girl at the Malabar Hotel in Benidorm in August 1995. Or maybe my original claim is actually the truth, and I only know your little secret because you told me. It doesn't really matter because once it gets out, the damage to your reputation will be done long before anyone bothers to check the facts."

I sit back and fold my arms. I've played the best hand I could with the cards at my disposal.

"How much?" Clare then spits.

"I was thinking a round million."

It's a ridiculous sum, but after years of haggling deals, I know the psychological value of an ambitious opening gambit.

"Not a chance," Clare sneers. "I'll give you £500,000 and not a penny more, but that's only if you sign a non-disclosure agreement. I won't have you coming back for more."

Unbelievably, my tactic has paid off, with Clare oblivious to the fact I'd have settled for a tenth of her offer. I feel like jumping up and punching the air, but the art of a successful haggle is not to let your opponent feel like they've lost.

"Six-hundred," I counter.

"No."

"Come on, Clare. You can do six-hundred."

"Which part of five-hundred and not a penny more didn't you understand?"

I allow my shoulders to slump and after a brief pause, I puff a sigh. "Fine. Five-hundred will have to do, I suppose."

"It's more than you deserve."

"It's a drop in the ocean compared to how much money you've made from my information. I'm only agreeing because I don't want to draw this out."

"That, we can agree on."

Clare turns to the computer monitor and places her hand on the mouse.

"I need your personal information for the contract: name, address, date of birth, and your bank details."

I open my predecessor's wallet for the bank details and postcode of the flat, and duly confirm the requested info. She types it into her computer and then sits back in her chair.

"Bearing in mind today is Friday, you'll have to wait until at least Wednesday before my lawyer can draw up the contract. They'll contact you directly to arrange a signature and once you've signed it, the money will land in your bank account within twenty-four hours."

"I'll wait until Wednesday but not a day later."

"Don't push your luck," Clare replies with a frosty glare. "Now, get the fuck out of my office."

I reply with a smile and get to my feet.

"It's been nice meeting you, Clare … again."

Chapter 28

I decided to start the day by blowing fifteen quid of my predecessor's meagre wages on a full English breakfast. The upmarket café is one I used to occasionally frequent when I fancied treating myself, and after yesterday's meeting with Clare Wood, I reckon I deserve a treat.

Half a million quid.

When I returned to the flat yesterday, I was still caught up in the elation of my victory. However, twenty minutes of sitting in a poky lounge listening to the neighbour's collection of grime music soon bought me back down to earth. I landed with a stark realisation — the money I extorted from Clare only matters if I remain here.

Unable to think, I left the flat and walked to the least awful pub in the area. There, I bought a pint and made myself comfortable in a quiet corner. I had plans to plot.

My thoughts initially turned to the windfall and what difference it would make to this miserable life. Three-hundred grand would buy me a decent apartment in a nice part of town, and I'd still have two-hundred grand left over. Initially, my pulse quickened when I thought about my original plan for importing classic cars from the US and Australia. However, a quick internet search confirmed how difficult it would be to enter either country with a criminal record.

I spent a couple of hours in the pub, pondering potential business opportunities I could invest in, but the stumbling block remained in place. It struck me that when someone commits a crime, their sentence doesn't end the day they leave prison. My predecessor served his time and paid his dues, but three years on, the punishment continues. It's not hard to see why so many who end up in prison return to crime within a few months of their release. Even if you want to move on and rebuild your life, wider society isn't so quick to forgive and forget.

This morning, I'm still unsure of my future, but at least I now have options if I'm stuck in this present.

I finish my coffee and consider how I might spend the rest of the day. My spirits are higher than they were before the meeting with Clare, but I still have to contend with this life for today and the next four days. I'd rather not spend any longer than necessary in my dismal flat, but it's not like I have a long list of friends to call upon or any kind of social life. I used to fantasise about being single and how much fun I might have at the weekend without Clare, but this reality isn't what I envisaged. Going out on the town tonight, on my own, and with only twenty quid in my pocket, holds little appeal.

Rather than dwell on my limited options for this evening, I decide to call my parents and see what their plans are today. Spending the afternoon trudging around a garden centre isn't my idea of fun, but after my chat with Mum, I feel I've still got work to do, convincing them that the door to depression is now well and truly shut.

As always, Mum answers.

"Good morning," I chirp.

"Morning, Sweetheart."

"I was wondering what you're up to today?"

"We were planning a trip down to the coast, seeing as it's a nice day."

"Oh, right. Um, I don't suppose I could tag along?"

"You're more than welcome, but we're only going for a walk along the front and maybe a game or two of bingo."

"That sounds nice, but if you'd rather just the—"

"No, of course, you can come along."

"Would you like me to drive?"

"I'm sure your dad would be pleased because his back has been giving him grief lately. I keep telling him to take it easy at the allotment, but he never listens."

"Men, eh," I chuckle. "I'll see you in an hour or so."

Plans made, I end the call and order another coffee. The waitress returns within a minute, and I sit back and consider what I've let myself in for this afternoon. A trip to the coast is marginally more interesting than a garden centre, but only from a nostalgic perspective. Whenever my parents refer to the coast, they inevitably mean Hayling Island: an eleven-square-mile nugget of land linked to the mainland by a road bridge. It's the same small island we'd spend one week every summer throughout my childhood, sometimes in a bed and breakfast and sometimes in a dilapidated caravan. Although it's only a fifty-minute drive from Elderton, I haven't had cause to visit the island in three decades. Up until five minutes ago, I wasn't sure I'd ever visit it again.

I pull up outside my parents' maisonette just after noon. Rather than beep the horn, I get out of the car and ring the doorbell. While I wait, it takes all my resolve not to look at the gate to the side of the building and those last harrowing moments of my trip to 1996.

Dad answers the door.

"Alright, Son."

"Pretty good, thanks. You?"

"Mustn't grumble."

He then looks back towards the hallway and calls out to Mum, asking if she's ready.

"One minute," comes the reply.

Rather than invite me in, Dad steps out onto the doormat and pulls the door ajar.

"Your mum said you dropped by on Thursday," he says to me in a low voice.

"That's right."

"She said you've been reading some book."

"Right again."

"And it's helping, you know … with your head?"

Men of Dad's generation, and plenty from mine, struggle to talk about mental health issues, so I can only guess how hard it's been for Dad dealing with my predecessor's depression. More than likely, he'd have suggested that all I needed was a good boot up the arse. He might have been right.

"Tell you what, Dad, why don't we enjoy the afternoon, and you can judge for yourself by the end of it. Deal?"

I can't quite decipher the look he gives me but knowing what my predecessor put him and Mum through, it's likely scepticism. It'll take more than a bullshit story about a self-help book to convince Dad I'm a changed man, even though that's exactly what I am.

Mum finally comes to the door, and the three of us wander over to my car. Dad sits in the passenger's seat while Mum makes herself comfortable in the back. Just as we're about to set off, Mum leans forward and hands me a CD case.

"Can you put this on?" she asks. "It brings back good memories."

"Sure," I reply, grabbing the CD.

I instantly regret agreeing when I read the album title on the front: *Summer Holiday* by Cliff Richard and The Shadows.

"I bet you haven't listened to that in years," Mum says.

"No," I reply, sliding the CD into the player. "Fortunately."

"You used to love it when you were little. You'd sit in the back seat of the car and sing your heart out."

"I was a naive child, Mum," I chuckle. "I knew no better."

"You're not too old for a clip around the ear, young man, which is exactly what you'll get if you disrespect my Cliff."

I glance across at Dad. He replies with a smirk and a nod towards the CD player.

"Fair enough," I sigh, jabbing the play button. "Cliff it is."

We set off, and within a few miles, my parents slip into their parts — Mum humming away merrily from the back seat and Dad gazing out of the window at the passing scenery. They both appear content, so besides the odd derogatory remark about other road users, I keep quiet.

The traffic is kind, and just over half an hour later, we cross the two-lane bridge to Hayling Island.

"You'll have to direct me from here, Dad. I'm lost without a sat-nav."

"Righto."

"I presume we're heading to the southern side of the island?"

"That's right, the car park on Southwood Road."

"Isn't Southwood Road where the caravan park was?"

"That's the one."

I follow the road for another half mile and then Dad's instructions. Eventually, we come to a junction with a car park directly ahead and a thin band of sea just about visible beyond.

"Here we are," Dad announces.

"What? This isn't where we used to stay."

"A lot has changed, Son."

We get out of the car and I head to the ticket machine whilst trying to tally the view of the street against my fuzzy memories. For all the similarities, I might as well be staring at a different street in a different town. I pay for a ticket and return to the car where my parents are both perched on the bonnet, breathing in the sea air.

"The place is unrecognisable," I remark. "Everything I remember has ... gone."

"I think they call it progress, Son," Dad replies.

"Wasn't there a pub on the corner there?" I ask, pointing to a block of flats just beyond the boundary of the car park.

"That went about ten years ago."

"And the little parade of shops? Wasn't there a cafe, a newsagent, and a shop that sold flip-flops and postcards and beachballs?"

"They demolished the entire lot a few years before the pub went."

I stare back at the street and shake my head. "What about the amusement arcade?"

"That was the last to close. Five or six years ago, maybe."

Having destroyed my own past in such a miraculous fashion, I didn't expect to feel such sadness for a past that's quietly slipped away over many years. This is not the nostalgic stroll down Memory Lane I hoped for.

"You okay, Sweetheart?" Mum asks.

"Err, yeah. I'm just a bit taken aback that it's all gone."

"They can knock the buildings down, but they can't take away our memories."

"True, but I was hoping you'd give me fifty pence to spend in the arcade, just for old time's sake."

"There's still an arcade up towards the golf club," Dad interjects. "But I don't think fifty pence will get you very far these days."

We swap smiles and then set off towards the promenade, which I presume is still intact.

The southern coast of Hayling Island is only a shade over three miles long, but we take our time. With the spring sun high above us and the gentle lapping of waves from the Solent, it's a surprisingly relaxing stroll, made all the more pleasant by the sharing of our holiday memories. At one point, we venture onto the stony beach and walk along the thin strip of virgin sand washed clean by the waves.

Eventually, we arrive at the far end of the island with its small fun fair and amusement arcade. Despite the unseasonably mild weather, very few people are around to enjoy it. As we pass the arcade, I spot a remnant of my childhood, and the urge to relive a fond holiday memory is too great.

"God, I haven't played a coin-pusher in years," I gush. "Do you mind if I have a go?"

It then strikes me that I'm forty-five years of age, but I just asked my parents' permission to play an arcade game. Maybe that's why they swap smiles and follow me inside.

After converting a pound coin into two-pence pieces, I step up to the coin-pusher and marvel at how similar it is to the one I played as a child. For all I know, it could be the same machine because, unlike its video counterparts, the coin-pusher's beauty is in its simplicity.

I feed the machine and watch my coin bounce off a series of pegs and settle on a shelf laden with two-pence pieces.

"You remember playing this as a kid, then?" Dad asks.

"I do. Fondly."

"You never played it like the other kids."

"In what way?"

"You'd come in with your bag of two-pence pieces and count them out. Then, you'd inspect all six sides of the machine, checking which had the most coins."

"Fail to prepare," I snigger. "Prepare to fail."

"You prepared alright, and then when you were ahead, you stopped playing."

"Did I?"

"Yep. While all the other kids kept going until they'd spent every penny in their pockets, you seemed to have a knack for knowing when to quit."

Still digesting Dad's words, I watch the shelf slowly nudge three coins over the edge and into the chute.

"Not today, though," I eventually reply. "I'm playing for fun, not profit."

"And that, Son, is exactly how you should live your life — play for fun, not profit."

Dad has never been much into philosophy, but when he says something profound, it always hits home. I don't really know what to say in response, but then Mum drags Dad off to play the Tuppenny Nudger fruit machine, to likely lose every coin in her purse in pursuit of a one-pound jackpot.

If there's one thing I love about my parents, it's that they always practise what they preach.

Chapter 29

Standing in my parents' kitchen, Mum plants a kiss on my cheek.

"It's been a lovely day," she says, keeping her hands on my upper arms. "Did you enjoy it?"

"You know what, Mum, I really did."

"I'm pleased, and … and I can't tell you what a relief it is to spend some time with the old Gary. I've missed him, you know."

"Me too, Mum, but I think he's here to stay now."

"You promise?"

"Cross my heart."

Mum gives me a goodbye hug, and then Dad sees me to the front door.

"Thank you for this afternoon, Son," he says while I'm putting my trainers on. "It did your mum the world of good."

"And what about you? Do you still think that self-help book was a waste of time?"

"I'd love to know who wrote it because I owe them a pint. It seems to have completely changed your outlook."

"Maybe I just needed pointing in the right direction."

"Let's hope so. We could all do with a bit more normal in our lives, don't you think?"

"Absolutely."

"On that note, how are things going at work?"

"Err, they're good."

"You looking forward to getting back there after your week off?"

"I wouldn't go that far," I chuckle. "Eight hours of packing boxes isn't anyone's idea of a dream job."

"No, I suppose not, but never underestimate the value of a good day's graft. That job got you out of a rut, so be grateful."

Now is not the time to tell him that my days of packing boxes will soon be over, one way or another. If I can persuade a colleague to sit in Edith Stimp's chair, I'll return to my reality. If I can't find a colleague willing to indulge my admittedly ridiculous request, then it's likely I'll be trapped here for good. However, Clare's hush money will ensure I no longer have to settle for a dead-end job.

"I am grateful, Dad."

He pats me on the shoulder, and we say goodbye.

As I settle back into the Rover's driving seat, I notice the time: 8:33 pm. I think it's the first time I've looked at my watch since I picked my parents up at lunchtime. I can't recall when I last had such scant concern for time, being that I built a business by maximising every hour in every day and every day in every week. Time has always mattered.

Another departure from my previous life occurred to me on the drive home from Hayling Island, albeit one I wasn't so pleased to identify — I couldn't remember the last time I'd spent so long in my parents' company. I took them out to a fancy restaurant at Christmas but looking back, I don't think they really enjoyed it. Both seemed far happier picking chips from a paper cone on the seafront than picking items from an à la carte menu. Truth be told, I preferred the chips too.

When we returned to Denby Place, Mum invited me in for a cup of tea and a doorstep of homemade fruitcake. We then sat in the lounge and watched a film together — thankfully, not *Summer Holiday*. Initially, I stayed because I didn't fancy spending my Saturday evening alone in a dingy flat, but I really stayed just because I wanted to be there.

As I navigate the streets of Elderton, I make a vow to visit Mum and Dad more often when I get back to my reality and to spend a bit more time enjoying their company. They might have missed this version of their son, but if I've learned anything from our trip to the coast, it's how much I've missed spending quality time with them. It's also proven to be the perfect distraction but, as I turn into Rochford Road and the route back to my humble abode, I'm brought crashing back to reality.

To perk myself up, I decide I'll spend the remainder of the evening browsing property websites just in case this temporary reality becomes permanent. Realistically, I know it can take several months to complete the legal process, so the sooner I find somewhere suitable, the sooner I can get the ball rolling.

I park up and trudge back along the street to the communal front door of number fourteen. I'm about to slide the key in the lock, but it seems one of my neighbours didn't bother shutting the door properly, and it's slightly ajar. Tutting under my breath, I enter the hallway, ensure the front door is properly closed, and climb the stairs.

The second I enter the flat, I kick off my trainers and slap the wall in search of the light switch. I find it on the third slap, but when I click the switch, the hallway light doesn't come on. I'm not inclined to scrabble around the flat looking for a spare lightbulb, so I nudge open the bedroom door and turn on the light switch. I remain in darkness.

"Bollocks."

Considering what I've been through in recent days, familiarising myself with the location of the flat's fuse box wasn't one of my priorities. I've no idea where it is. I pull out my mobile phone in the hope it has a torch function, but I'm distracted by a sudden and unidentifiable noise. I take a few hesitant steps forward, but the hallway remains silent.

Just as I'm about to return my attention to the phone, everything happens all at once. It begins with a flash of movement to my right, and then almost instantaneously, an unknown object smashes into my ribcage. Even before I've time to register the cause of the impact, never mind process the pain, my legs buckle. Unable to breathe or see, my face plants into the hallway carpet. Then a force begins pulling at my jacket collar, dragging me towards the lounge doorway.

When it comes, the pain of looking straight up at a bright light barely registers. Gasping for air, I squint and identify the source of the light: a bulb within a cheap lampshade. The electricity is back on, but as a figure then looms over me, I realise I've now got a problem of much graver nature than a tripped fuse.

"If you shout, scream, or even whimper," the figure says. "I'll cut your throat."

I've heard the voice before, but I can't remember where. Still squinting, I look up, and slowly the figure takes on form.

"You," I gasp. "I don't ..."

It's the FBI wannabee from Clare's office. Greg? No, Grant.

"Shut up. I'm doing the talking."

He steps back until he's no longer in my eye line. I turn my head to the side so I'm no longer staring up at the light. Only then do I realise that Grant isn't alone. Standing a few feet away and guarding the door to the hallway is a guy with a close-shaved head, dressed head-to-toe in black.

"Get up and sit on the couch," Grant then demands.

Knowing that the impact to my ribcage was likely a fist does little to lessen the pain. Wincing hard, I just about clamber to the sofa.

"What ... what do you want?" I gulp.

"I said I'd do the talking," Grant replies, stepping within kicking distance of the sofa.

I assess my options and quickly determine they're limited to sitting where I am. If the pain in my ribcage wasn't so acute, I might stand a chance of jumping up and barrelling past Clare's henchman, but the so-far silent door guardian has the build of a cage fighter. I couldn't currently fight my way out of a paper bag, never mind a cage.

"My employer does not appreciate you making threats or attempting to blackmail her," Grant snarls. "And for that reason, I'm here to inform you that if you follow through on your threat, the consequences will be grave."

Despite my pain and the further threat of violence, I'm incensed that Clare has backtracked on our agreement.

"I won't follow through if Clare sticks to our deal. Tell her that."

"You don't get it, do you? We know who you are and every sordid detail of your criminal past, so there is no deal."

"I want Clare to come here and tell me that."

"You won't be seeing her again; of that you can be certain."

"Whatever," I snort.

"I'm serious. If you attempt to make contact with Ms Wood again or spread your malicious lies, my associate and I will drive over to Denby Place one night and have a stern word with your parents. At their age, I can't guarantee how that will pan out … if you catch my drift."

Grant folds his arms and smirks down at me. I've never wanted to punch someone in the face so badly.

"Do we understand each other?" he asks.

"Yes," I mumble.

"I didn't hear you."

"Yes."

"Good. In which case, I'll leave you in the company of my associate here, and he'll rubber stamp our understanding, so to speak."

"Eh?"

Grant turns around and strides towards the doorway, nodding at his so-called associate on the way. Seconds later, the front door slams shut, and the shaven-headed bruiser turns to me.

"Get up," he growls.

"I'm fine here, thanks."

"Your choice," he shrugs.

Before I've got a chance to prepare a defence, he pounces. The first punch strikes my jaw, and the second hits my already battered rib cage. The third...

Chapter 30

Standing in the dimly lit bathroom, I examine the blossoming patchwork of bruises in the mirror. At eight o'clock on a Monday morning, thirty-six hours after I sustained them, the aesthetic cues now match the physical. My shaven-headed attacker could have killed me if I'd fought back, but I lost consciousness after the third or fourth punch, and he must have considered his job done at that point.

When I finally regained consciousness in the early hours of Sunday morning, I could barely move; the pain was so bad. Fortunately, my predecessor had a supply of ibuprofen in the bathroom cabinet, and although they took the edge off, I still felt like I'd fallen from a third-floor window. By mid-morning, I had no choice but to seek medical attention. An excruciating taxi ride to Elderton General Hospital then ensued, and a two-hour wait in A&E.

After a bit of prodding and poking, a few awkward questions, and an X-ray, the doctor confirmed my injuries were not as bad as I feared: no broken bones but extensive bruising. Whilst the diagnosis was a relief, the only form of treatment wasn't. The doctor asked what I did for a living, and as much as it killed me to say it, I confirmed I worked in a packing department. I left the hospital with strict instructions to rest for seven days, and under no circumstances should I go to work.

When I woke up this morning, I immediately gulped down two of the heavy-duty painkillers I picked up from the hospital pharmacy. If I sit still or walk slowly and gingerly, they keep the worst of the pain at bay, but even reaching up to get a glass from the cupboard hurts. I'm definitely in no fit state to pack boxes, but I need to make a call and see if there's anything else I can do. First, I need to get dressed.

It takes ten excruciating minutes to put on a pair of jeans and a sweatshirt. That done, I try to make myself as comfortable as possible on the sofa and call Dave, who I apparently work with.

"Morning, Gary," he says brusquely. "What's up?"

"Err, hi, Dave. I've got a bit of a problem. I was mugged on Saturday night, and I took a bit of a battering."

"Bloody hell," he gasps. "Are you alright, mate?"

"If I sit still, I'm fine, but the doctor said I need to rest."

"That's not great 'cos we're snowed under today, but if the doc signed you off, it is what it is."

"Yeah, I'm really sorry, but I was hoping you might have something else I could do — something that doesn't involve heavy lifting."

"I'm warehouse manager, Gary. Everything I'm in charge of involves heavy lifting unless you can drive a forklift?"

"Err, no."

"Then there's nothing."

"What about in the office?"

"I'm not being funny, mate, and I'm really sorry to hear what happened to you, but I ain't got time to piss around trying to find a job for a sicknote. I need to make a call to an agency and get some bodies in here."

"Um, okay. I understand."

"Give me a call when you're feeling better, alright?"

"Sure. Will do."

Dave hangs up.

"Bugger," I sigh, tossing the phone on the sofa.

Today is the fourth day of this new reality, and I'm no closer to escaping it or finding a way to live it than the day I first arrived. And I've only got ten days left before Edith Stimp slams the door to my reality shut, and I'm not able to work for seven of them.

The mild positivity I enjoyed after my trip to Hayling Island is now just a distant memory. If I had the energy, I'd lay blame for negativity on Clare bloody Wood, but I've already wasted a day being angry, and it's got me nowhere. The same could be said of blaming myself. I've gone over every conceivable way I might have played my hand differently, but even if I had, it wouldn't have made one jot of difference to the outcome. Clare was always going to win because she has the money and, therefore, the power. In hindsight, I'm an idiot for believing she'd hand over half a million quid so willingly.

My biggest fear now is not that Grant and his henchman will hurt my parents — it's that I will. My predecessor has already put them through so much. It was easy being positive, knowing that even if I couldn't escape this reality, I had enough money to make a fist of it. Now it looks like I'm destined to live a life with nothing but regrets.

If that is to be my fate, are the same demons of depression waiting in the wings for me? Will my parents watch helplessly as I suffer and struggle again?

I can't let that happen, but there is a way I can protect my parents and have my revenge on Clare. I've wrestled with the consequences since the idea crossed my mind last night, and now that Dave has just shut down the last remaining chance of finding someone to take a trip back in time for me, it's the only option. It's not really an option per se, but a last resort.

There's one significant hurdle I first have to overcome, and that's getting into town. I delicately manoeuvre my bruised carcass off the sofa and shuffle across the lounge. I can't face putting on a jacket, so I leave the flat with just a set of keys and a mobile phone.

It's a chilly, overcast morning, but I've greater concerns as I waddle slowly to the car. If I'm unable to drive, I'll have to get a cab again, and my bank balance is close to being depleted. I don't know if I'm entitled to sick pay, but even if I am, it won't be much.

I remind myself that it won't matter how much money I have if my plan plays out the way I hope.

Getting into the car is every bit as painful as I imagined, but once I fasten the seat belt, fiddle with the gearstick, and try all three pedals, I'm confident I can drive without crying. What I quickly realise, however, is that I won't be able to complete any kind of reversing manoeuvre as the simple act of twisting in my seat summons a jolt of pain across my lower back. God help me if I have to make an emergency stop.

I have the car of a pensioner, and now I have to drive like one: slowly, cautiously, and oblivious to how my driving might infuriate other road users.

Twenty tortuous minutes later, I reach a junction and groan. I'd forgotten that the High Street is still closed to traffic, so I'll have to find a parking space in one of the nearby streets and walk. As it is, the only space I'm able to drive straight into is fifty yards from where I parked my Mercedes coupé. It's another reminder of what I've lost and the risk I'm prepared to take in order to get it back.

Walking like a man who's spent all morning on the loo with explosive diarrhoea, I make my way along the High Street towards Dent's Passage.

When I reach the sturdy door to Edith Stimp's building, I knock three times. If she's not home — if indeed this is her home as well as her workplace — I don't know what I'll do.

I'm about to knock again when the thunk of a bolt allays my concern. Slowly, the door creaks open.

"Good morning, Gary," Edith Stimp says. "To what do I owe this pleasure?"

Even though it's only been four days, she looks markedly paler than the last time I saw her if that's at all possible.

"I need to talk to you. Can I come in?"

"You may."

She steps aside, and I enter. It's as warm as I remember from my first visit, and the air carries a strong scent of beeswax polish.

"Shall we sit?" Edith Stimp asks.

"Please."

I follow her through the maze of furniture to the two wing-backed armchairs at the back of the room.

"Take a seat, Gary."

As I slowly lower myself into the armchair, Edith notices my pained expression.

"Are you okay?"

I have neither the time nor the will to explain how I sustained my injuries.

"I tripped over and hurt my back. It's nothing."

"My Allan suffered from backache occasionally, and he swore that the best remedy is a long soak in a hot bath. It has to be as hot as you can bear, mind."

"Thanks for the advice, but there's no bathtub in my wonderful new home."

"Oh, that's unfortunate."

"On a scale of issues that are unfortunate, not having a bathtub is pretty low down the list, which is why I'm here."

"You've found someone willing to pop back and alter your past?"

"You make it sound so simple, but no, I haven't. I want to go back."

"I thought I'd made it clear that a second trip isn't an option."

"Surely, that's my decision to make. I can't stay here."

"Why not?"

"Because ... because this life is bloody awful, as well you know."

"I know it's not what you hoped for, but it's within your powers to make the best of it."

"This isn't just about me, Edith. My predecessor put my parents through hell, and I'm not willing to risk dragging them down again."

"Then don't. Make a life for yourself."

"You don't get it, do you? I have nothing ... literally nothing."

"You have your health, and a job, and a roof over your head. You have a lot more than many, Gary."

"And a lot less than I had before. This isn't what I signed up for."

"I'm sorry you feel that way, but a second trip is out of the question."

"So you said, but it's my risk to take, surely?"

Edith puffs a tired sigh and closes her eyes momentarily.

"Well?" I prompt.

"Gary, I wasn't exaggerating the risk, and whilst I understand you're concerned about your parents, think how they'll feel while they're organising their son's funeral."

Edith's words don't so much as strike a chord but hit it with a sledgehammer. I have to shake the vision of my own funeral from my mind.

"Do you understand?" she adds.

I do, kind of, but it does little to douse my frustration.

"This is unfair," I huff. "You should have warned me about the consequences."

"It's time travel, Gary — no one can be sure of the consequences."

"I could sue you for negligence."

The second the words pass my lips, I realise how stupid my threat sounds.

Edith snorts a laugh. "You might have a problem finding a solicitor willing to take your case, and even if you could, I'll be long gone before it ever reaches a court."

"Gone? Where are you going?"

"I told you I couldn't stay here much longer. As it is, I've earmarked next Monday as my final day."

I stare back, slack-jawed. "Next Monday?"

"Yes."

"That gives me one week. How the hell am I supposed to find someone willing to entertain the most insane of propositions, let alone convince them to take part?"

"You're a used-car salesman. If anyone has the gift of the gab, surely it's you."

"I'm not trying to sell a high-mileage Nissan Juke for crying out loud. And there's the minor issue of not having anyone I can convince. In this life, I've got no one."

"Your former wife would have been the ideal candidate, don't you think?"

"Eh?"

"I understand she's a spiritualist and, therefore, more open-minded than most."

"Err, maybe."

"And coupled with the fact you were married for twenty-five years, you understand how her mind works as well as anyone. She would have been relatively easy to convince."

"Yes, um ..."

"I must admit I was curious how Clare Wood fared after you altered your mutual past. I thought she, like most people, would live a fairly ordinary life, but I was shocked to discover that merely by not meeting you, she's now a multi-millionaire and the head of a national charity. That's quite a remarkable change of fortune, wouldn't you say?"

"I, err …"

"So remarkable, in fact, one might question how she's achieved so much."

When I first met Edith, I recall thinking she looked a bit like an old-fashioned schoolmistress. Now, she's has the persona to match; eyebrows arched and a hint of cynicism in her tone.

"Um, I don't know where you're going with this, but can we get back to the matter in hand?"

"I must confess, I am curious how Clare became so wealthy. I don't suppose you know?"

"No," I reply in a low voice.

"I'm not a fool, Gary. Something happened when you went back, didn't it?"

"I, err …"

"How did Clare Wood become so wealthy? You might as well tell me because there's nothing to gain by lying."

"Okay," I groan. "It was an accident."

"What happened?"

I spend five minutes explaining the events in 1996 and the failed attempt to make my younger self rich. Edith listens intently and waits until the very end before delivering her opinion.

"I told you not to interact with your younger self, didn't I? It was the very first rule."

"Yes, and I had no intention of breaking the rule, which is why I wrote a letter."

"An interaction is an interaction: phone call, email, letter, carrier pigeon … they all count."

"Maybe you should have been more specific."

"And maybe you shouldn't have been so greedy. Why did you do it?"

"Because I ... I wanted to be filthy rich, okay. Who doesn't?"

"I don't, but that's beside the point. You broke the rules, and as a consequence, the one person who you might have been able to convince to take a trip to fix your mistake is now the least likely person to help you."

"I know. I tried."

"You've spoken to your former wife?"

"I asked her for money."

"How exactly did you ask her?"

"I might have suggested I'd reveal information about her ... information she wouldn't want in the public domain."

"You blackmailed her?"

"I wouldn't put it quite like that, but it's an irrelevance because Clare called my bluff. She has money which means she has power. I have neither."

Edith shakes her head.

"Deary me, Gary. What a mess you've made."

"I know."

If my ribs didn't ache so much, I'd be inclined to lean forward and put my head in my hands. Instead, I just stare up at the ceiling.

"Perhaps a coffee will make everything better," Edith then says.

"Great," I groan. "As if a mocha latte is going to make all my problems magically disappear."

"I know a place not far from here. I'd recommend you stop feeling sorry for yourself and take a stroll over there."

"Unless they have a time travel-enabled coffee machine, I'm not interested. I'm also skint."

Edith reaches down and picks up her handbag. After clicking open the clasp, she pulls out a purse and opens it.

"Here," she says, holding out a clutch of twenty-pound notes. "Take this."

"Christ, how much do they charge for a coffee? I don't need that much."

"Just take it, Gary. I've more than enough money to last me until ... until it's time for me to leave."

"I couldn't."

"Don't be so obstinate," she says forcibly. "Take the money and go buy yourself a coffee."

"Why are you so obsessed with me buying a coffee?"

"Because it could be your route out of the rut you've landed in."

"I don't understand. How—"

"Take it!"

Her demand is matched by an equally stern glare. I do as I'm told and take the cash.

"Thank you," Edith says, her tone again cordial. "Now, the coffee shop is on Station Road. Do you know it?"

"By the train station, perchance?"

"Yes, it's almost opposite."

"And what's so special about this coffee shop."

"You'll find out," she replies, stifling a yawn.

"Can't you tell me?"

"I need a nap."

"Are you ... okay?"

"I'll be right as rain after forty winks and a cup of herbal tea. Can you see yourself out?"

Without waiting for an answer, Edith settles back in the chair and closes her eyes. Short of shaking her awake, I don't know what to do. I came here in the hope of escaping this nightmare, but all I've got is a handful of cash and a recommendation for a coffee shop.

In lieu of being able to press Edith for help, I take the only option available and shut the door on my way out.

Chapter 31

The walk along Elderton High Street is painful on several levels, the greatest of which is the weight of realisation. I've made many bad decisions in my life, but they were *my* decisions in *my* life. I'm now paying the price for decisions I never made.

Or am I?

It was on this very stretch of pavement that I literally bumped into Edith Stimp. Looking back on that moment, my head was a mess after the meeting with Ian Burke and his suggestion I pay Clare what she wanted.

I should have listened to Ian. If I had, I wouldn't be here now.

Trudging on at a snail's pace, I reach the end of the High Street and cut through a narrow lane towards Station Road. The only reason I'm willing to indulge Edith's recommendation is curiosity — it's certainly not hope because my reserves are close to depleted. That said, I could certainly do with a strong coffee and something to eat. When I retrieved the last two slices of bread from the fridge earlier, both were speckled with mould.

I exit the lane some hundred yards from the train station and check the view in both directions. There's an A-board on the pavement to my right, and I can just about read the chalked list of lattes and mochas, pastries, and paninis. I turn and plod along the pavement until I reach what I presume is the coffee shop Edith Stimp suggested.

I reach the front door and enter.

If the name itself — Maria's — wasn't clue enough to the coffee shop being independent, the interior certainly is. The mustard-coloured walls are adorned with a jumble of framed pictures, and the furniture appears reclaimed. It feels homely rather than corporate, and I immediately prefer it to the cookie-cutter coffee shops that feature on every High Street.

The only other customer is a student-aged girl sitting in the corner staring at a laptop. There's no one behind the counter, but there is an archway to the left where I presume the kitchen is.

I step towards the counter and look up at the menu. With Edith's money in my pocket, the prices shouldn't be an issue, but I'm also conscious that I've no groceries in the flat. After a moment's consideration, I'm torn between two of the cheaper items: egg on toast, or a tuna panini.

"Morning," a female voice says while I'm still looking up at the menu. "Can I help?"

My heart stops beating.

Without shifting my gaze from the menu, I'm ninety-nine per cent certain I recognise the voice because I've heard it every weekday morning for the last four years. However, I'm one-hundred per cent certain I don't know how to react on this occasion.

Swallowing hard, I slowly lower my chin and confirm what I already know — the voice belongs to Janine, or a version of Janine I've never met.

"What can I get you?" she asks.

I can't help but stare at her, open-mouthed. Strangely, there's something about her that, on first impression, is different from the woman who managed my office so efficiently. I can't put my finger on what it is. Maybe it's just the harshness of the lighting.

"Sorry," I blurt. "I, err … large white coffee, please."

"Anything to eat?"

Food is suddenly the last thing on my mind as I fight to regain some level of composure. I then realise I'm staring and quickly avert my gaze.

"Um, I ... I haven't made up my mind yet," I mumble. "I'll just take the coffee for now, please."

"Sure. Grab a seat, and I'll bring it over."

I turn and scurry to the table furthest away from the student. I then pull out the only chair that allows me a view of the counter but doesn't directly face it. I'm sure Janine already thinks I'm a total oddball.

I've no time to think before my coffee is ready, and Janine approaches the table.

"One white coffee."

As she places the cup on the table, I notice an absence of any rings on her fingers. Whatever life she's led, it doesn't currently involve engagement or marriage it seems. Or working for Kirkwood Motors, obviously.

"Um, thank you."

"Can I get you anything else?"

It's the same throwaway question she must ask scores of customers every day, but it also happens to be the same question she's asked me countless times, albeit in a different reality.

"I'm okay, thanks."

I'm a million miles from okay, and when Janine flashes a tired smile, it cuts deep. I felt apprehensive about meeting this reality's version of Clare, but I had time to mentally prepare myself for the lack of recognition in her eyes. With Janine, there was no such chance to prepare.

Why the fuck didn't Edith warn me? More to the point, how did she know that Janine works here or that she should be working in my office?

As the initial shock subsides, I take a sip of coffee and consider both questions. I can only speculate on the question of Edith knowing that Janine works here, but there's an obvious answer to her knowing she was my office manager. The first time I met Edith was at the town hall during the business awards, and I was seated next to Janine at the table all evening. She could have seen us together and then visited the Kirkwood Motors website, where all the staff members have a profile listed.

Another question then drifts into play: why send me here? She said it might get me out of a rut, but how? Does Edith think I can persuade Janine to take a trip back in time? If that was her motive, she's deluded. I might have known the previous version of Janine well, but how do I get to know this version in just seven days? We're complete strangers.

Could there be another motive?

I turn my attention back to the coffee, hoping an injection of caffeine might bring a little clarity to my thoughts.

The coffee goes down a treat, but by the time I swallow the last sip, I'm no closer to working out what I do next. Should I try and instigate a conversation with Janine? If so, to what end? I'm still pondering when the woman in question strides over to the adjacent table and sits down. Janine then takes a sip from her coffee cup and pulls out a mobile phone. I presume she's on a break, and if I want to spark a conversation, this is as good a chance as I'll get.

As I consider a suitable opening line, butterflies begin to swarm in my stomach. I can't believe I'm nervous about chatting to a woman I've had thousands of conversations with in the past. I run through a mental list of possibilities, but they all sound corny or clichéd. I'm not trying to chat Janine up, but I can't think of a conversation starter that doesn't suggest I might be.

"Excuse me," she then says.

It takes a moment, but I eventually realise she's talking to me. I look up from the table and try to appear normal, which is no easy feat considering the circumstances.

"Sorry to interrupt," Janine continues. "But have we met before?"

"No, I don't think so."

"You look familiar."

This is it. I have one chance to be myself and break the ice. Fingers crossed that this version of Janine shares the same quirky sense of humour as the one I know.

"I was in a boy band in the nineties," I reply with a wry smile. "Maybe that's it."

"No way," Janine gushes. "Seriously?"

"We were called Throb. You might have seen us on Top of The Pops."

"Throb? Are you winding me up?"

"Maybe," I chuckle.

To my relief, Janine responds with an enthusiastic giggle. For a moment, we could be sitting in my office back at Kirkwood Motors, laughing at some ridiculous YouTube video or idiotic Facebook post.

"Do you have a name?" she then asks.

"Gary. You?"

"Bunty McClumpton."

"Interesting name," I reply, playing along. "You don't look like a Bunty."

"No? What does a Bunty look like?"

"Well, the only Bunty I've ever known had large green eyes and ginger hair."

"Were you close?"

"We shared a bed every now and then."

"Oh."

"But then she got old, and we had to take her to the vet. She never came back."

The penny drops. "Ahh, she was your pet."

"A cat, and I loved her dearly."

I don't know if this version of Janine has two feline housemates called Joff and Jaffa, but I do know that she's always adored cats.

"So, you'd consider yourself a cat person rather than a dog person?"

"Definitely. Cats are cleaner and self-sufficient."

"I've got two cats, and they're definitely cleaner, but I wouldn't say they're self-sufficient. The lazy shits won't even open their own tins of food."

It's my turn to laugh, and then it strikes me that I can't even remember the last time I had cause to.

"Back to my original question," Janine continues. "Have you been in here before?"

"No, I didn't even know it existed."

"And now you do, are we likely to benefit from your custom in the future?"

"That depends."

"On?"

"Whether or not you tell me your real name."

"How do you know my real name isn't Bunty McClumpton?"

"As I said: you don't look like a Bunty."

"What do I look like then?"

"I'd say you look like a ... like a Jasmine."

"So close," she grins. "It's Janine."

"Much better than Bunty, and it's nice to meet you, Janine."

"Likewise."

"And, now I know your name, I'll definitely be back tomorrow."

She replies with a smile before taking a long sip from her cup. I'd love nothing more than to continue the conversation, but I don't want to push my luck. The ice is nicely broken and that's as good a result as I could have hoped for. What it isn't, though, is progress towards convincing a stranger that my broken life is the result of a misguided trip back in time or persuading that stranger to take a similar trip.

"Are you a writer, by any chance?" Janine then asks.

"God, no," I snort. "What made you think I might be?"

"Process of elimination. You're too old to be a student, too young to be retired, and if you had a normal job, you'd be at work at this time on a Monday morning."

"I can't fault your logic, but I'm ... I'm kind of between jobs at the moment."

"Unemployed, you mean?"

"No, I'm trying to work out my future, so to speak."

"Tell me about it," Janine replies wistfully.

"You don't like working in a coffee shop?"

"I do, but it's not quite where I imagined I'd be at this stage of my life."

"No? Where did you imagine you'd be?"

Just as she's about to answer my question, the front door opens, and an elderly couple enter.

"Sorry, duty calls," Janine says, getting to her feet. "Nice meeting you, Gary."

"You too."

As she serves the couple, I reluctantly get to my feet. I'd much rather stay and continue chatting with Janine, but she's already said she needs to get back to work, and I don't want to come across as a stalker.

I trudge towards the door.

"Bye, Gary."

I stop dead and glance back towards the counter. Janine throws a brief wave in my direction before returning her attention to the couple.

The resulting smile remains on my face all the way back to the High Street.

Chapter 32

As I wander back to Rochford Road, in dire need of more painkillers and a long spell on the sofa, the lyrics of a Craig David song float into my head. The song in question, *7 Days*, tells the story of Mr David's week after he meets a young woman on a Monday. He takes her for a drink the following day, and then they spend three days in bed before finally chilling on Sunday.

I remember thinking that Craig David must have been quite the charmer, convincing a girl he'd only just met to spend almost half the week in bed with him. Even he, though, would baulk at my challenge — seven days to convince someone I've just met that they should take a trip back in time for me.

Alas, Janine is my last hope, and I have to try.

I arrive back at the flat and, after taking a couple of painkillers, sit on the sofa with my predecessor's crappy laptop. I know lots about Janine from my reality, but I know nothing of this version's life over the last four years. How did someone so smart and so good at what they do end up working in a coffee shop?

My plan, if it can be called that, is to snoop around Facebook. Unfortunately, I need to set up a Facebook account first, and before that, a new email account — one I can actually access.

It's just as well I don't have a lot in my diary today as it takes twenty painstaking minutes to complete my task. But, with newly minted email and Facebook accounts, I can start the search for Janine Barker.

I enter her name and tap the search icon. Facebook does its thing and eventually populates the page with a list of profiles matching my search. I scroll down the page, past the first dozen, and another dozen appear, and then another dozen. It seems the name Janine Barker is far more common than I estimated, but hopefully, the one I'm looking for added an easily recognisable profile photo. I return to the top of the page and begin checking.

When I do eventually find the woman I'm looking for, I almost skirt past her profile because the moody black and white photo of Janine standing on a beach, looking out towards the sea, fails to capture her dazzling eyes, her brilliant smile, or any aspect of her effervescent personality.

I click the link to her profile.

"Bollocks."

Because I'm not Janine's Facebook friend, I can't see any of the information on her profile: her posts, her photos, her relationship status, or her career history. Frustrated, I check Instagram and Twitter, more in hope than expectation, and waste half an hour searching profiles that aren't Janine's. As a last resort, I search for Maria's Coffee Shop, but it doesn't even have a website.

At a digital dead end, I rack my brain trying to think of other possible sources of information, but it doesn't take long to conclude I'll have to rely on what I already know. Whatever Janine has been up to for the last four years, I'll have to find out the old-fashioned way — by talking to her.

I'm about to close Facebook when an idea strikes. It has nothing to do with Janine but a lot to do with my predecessor. I search for my own name, hoping that there might be a dormant profile for Gary Kirk. Back in my reality, I can't recall exactly when I first opened a Facebook account, but I'm sure it was before the London Olympics in 2012.

As it turns out, there are almost as many Gary Kirks as there are Janine Barkers, although it's a lot easier to spot my own face amongst the crowd, even though my predecessor's profile photo features two people: me and Tara.

Halfway between moving the cursor from the search bar to my profile, I already know I'm likely to experience the same frustration as I did with Janine's profile. From the early days of using the internet, I've always been paranoid about sharing my private data online, so it's no surprise my predecessor was equally paranoid. I can't view any of the posts or photos, but I am able to view his list of 'friends', although it's a particularly short list. It's not beyond the realms of possibility that this profile hasn't been touched in over a decade, and an awful lot has happened to Gary Kirk during those years — none of it good. Like my friends in the real world, I guess my Facebook friends have also drifted away over time, not wanting to be associated with a criminal.

One person is still listed as a friend, though, and that's Tara Mitchell. I click the link to her profile for no reason other than mild curiosity. I'm interested to know what kind of woman I might have married if I hadn't met Clare.

Unlike my profile, and Janine's, Tara's isn't set to private, and it only takes a few seconds of scrolling to see why. Based solely on photographic evidence, Tara is leading the perfect life, although it seems a little too perfect. Every photo is overly staged, and whenever there's a photo of Tara herself, she's in a pose. If I didn't know better, I could be looking at the life of a celebrity or a successful entrepreneur, but then I spot an explanation in her bio. It appears the woman who was once my fiancée is now an influencer.

"Good grief," I snort.

Maybe it's an age thing, but I've never understood what an influencer does or how you become one. I do know that their importance is linked to how many followers they amass on social media, which would explain why I remain one of Tara's four-thousand Facebook friends. If you judge your self-worth by how many random people follow you, then why cull any, even an ex-con?

A question of greater significance, though, is how I ever ended up with a woman like Tara. From what Mum said, Tara was nice enough, but she clearly has a taste for living a certain lifestyle. In this reality, was I so swept along with this vacuous existence where everything is about a portrayed image?

I scroll further and further back on Tara's profile, hoping to see some evidence of our time together. It'll take a while as she posts so frequently, there are hundreds within the last year alone. Slowly, I work my way through the relentless stream of coastal sunsets and cocktails, designer dresses and haute cuisine menus, high-end hotel rooms and poolside posing. By the time I reach Christmas 2012, I can scarcely believe that I was, in this reality at least, part of Tara's grand charade.

I continue scrolling, but there isn't a single photo that features me, and my name doesn't appear on any of Tara's posts. From the time we apparently met through to the post where she announces her engagement to her current husband, it would be easy to assume Tara Mitchell and Gary Kirk never met. I know they did, because my predecessors profile photo shows them together, but patently Tara decided to delete any record of Gary Kirk on her timeline, likely the moment he went to prison.

I don't know if prisoners are able to view social media, but I can imagine my predecessor looking at Tara's Facebook page from his cell. At what point did he realise that his fiancée was not the type to stand by her man? How must he have felt as he watched Tara continue her life in the same glamourised vein but with another man paying for it?

Sitting back on the sofa, I take a break from the screen. The minutes tick by, and little by little, I begin to understand the significance of marrying Clare. I might have underestimated her influencing one business decision I made, but have I also underestimated the levelling effect of merely being married?

I try to put myself in my predecessor's shoes, which is weird because, to all intents and purposes, they're the same shoes. We shared the same childhood, where we were loved, but money was always tight, and we both ducked and dived our way through our teenage years, trying to make something of ourselves. We both took an enormous gamble, setting up our own business and buying premises, and we both worked tirelessly to build that business. Then, one of us made the wrong call, and our paths diverged from that moment onward.

I can almost understand my predecessor's decision to bring in Darren Slade as a partner because I doubt he had many options in such a difficult financial environment, but what I can't understand is how he became so distracted from the business. Actually, I can, because I've just spent the best part of an hour browsing photos of a life that, on a superficial level at least, appears perfect.

It suddenly all makes sense.

Clare was my anchor, but Tara was as flighty as a hot air balloon. Together, we drifted aimlessly towards an Instagram sunset while sipping champagne. She was the worst kind of distraction. I don't like to admit it, but maybe I've carried a working-class chip on my shoulder, and I've tried a little too hard to portray myself as successful. When I think back to the decision to buy our house, Clare questioned why we needed one so big. She was never interested in material possessions or showing the world how much money we had. Tara, on the other hand, clearly revelled in it. Like my predecessor, I wonder if I, too, might have taken Tara's encouragement to the extreme.

Of course, I would. We're the same man.

It's the harshest possible lesson, but as I stare up at the cracks in the ceiling plaster, I can only conclude that Clare did indeed deserve every penny of the money she asked for. She saved me from myself.

What a pity I learned that lesson too late. Now, my last chance to show the world that I've learned from my mistakes rests with a stranger.

In some way, I deserve to fail. In another, I can't afford to.

I have to fix this.

Chapter 33

It wasn't my alarm that woke me this morning but the sound of an incoming text message. Bleary-eyed, I snatched up the phone and read the message from my boss, Dave. He wanted to know if I was well enough to return to work.

I still ache, and I probably could manage a few hours, but as my fingers hovered over the phone's keypad, I made a decision. I have one job for the next six days, and it isn't packing boxes. It's a gamble, but I messaged Dave back, telling him I wouldn't be in for the rest of the week. He didn't reply, and I don't know if I'll have a job to go back to, but I need to put every ounce of effort into ensuring my employment is a moot point.

Today is day two of Project Janine.

It began with a half-decent breakfast and a mug of strong coffee. After spending too much of yesterday feeling sorry for myself, I eventually got off the sofa and walked to the shop for groceries. By the time I returned, I'd made up my mind that even though the odds of escaping this reality are against me, I'm not giving up without a fight.

Admittedly, there's also the added incentive of spending time with Janine. It hadn't occurred to me before I walked into that coffee shop yesterday, but God, I've missed her.

After a long shower, I try to make myself look as presentable as possible and leave the flat. I've timed my departure so I'll arrive at Maria's Coffee Shop at a similar time as yesterday.

Hopefully, it won't be busy, and Janine will again take her break at a nearby table so we can continue our conversation.

Halfway to my destination, it occurs to me that I can't be certain that Janine will even be there. What if she only works a few days a week, or she's off sick or on holiday? That uncertainty undermines my positivity, and by the time I turn into Station Road, the anxiety has really set in.

"Please be there," I whisper as I approach the front door.

I enter Maria's Coffee Shop with my head down and pause a moment. When I look up, the place is deserted: no one at the tables and no one at the counter. Should I clear my throat? Whistle? Call out? In the end, I amble to the counter and wait.

Seconds pass, and then the lightest of footsteps tap from the other side of the archway. A moment later, a figure appears.

"Hello, again," Janine beams while tying up her apron strings. "Twice in two days, eh?"

"Good morning, and yes, I really like the coffee here."

"Just the coffee?"

"The staff are fairly pleasant ... well, the one member of staff I've met."

"I'll pass on your praise. What can I get you?"

"Just a coffee, thanks."

"Grab a seat."

I return a smile before taking the same seat I occupied yesterday. So far, so good.

As I wait for my coffee, I'm able to draw a couple of deep breaths. I no longer have to worry about Janine not being here, but I do have to worry about my next step. Swapping friendly banter is one thing, but I need to channel my inner Craig David if I've any chance of explaining the truth to her.

"One coffee," Janine announces as she places a cup on the table. "Anything else?"

"I'm good, thanks. I hope I didn't interrupt your break."

"I haven't had my break yet, and as you can see, I'm not exactly rushed off my feet."

"Tuesday a slow day?"

"After the morning rush, it is. You're the first customer I've seen in half an hour."

"Not ideal. You strike me as the type who prefers to be busy."

Janine shoots me a look that I hope is surprise.

"That's very observant of you," she sniggers "Being busy is my superpower."

That much I do know about her.

"Any others?"

"I have a keen nose for detecting bullshit."

"That must be handy."

"Very."

"So, if I asked you to join me for a coffee solely because I could do with the company, would you be able to tell if I was bullshitting?"

There's a subtle shift in Janine's body language as she takes a step back. I've jumped in too soon.

"Um, sorry," I splutter. "I'm sure you get hit on all the time, but I swear I'm not—"

"Like that?"

I've no option but to deploy a few white lies.

"No, I'm not ... like that. Truth is, I'm new to town, and I don't really know anyone. You seem like a friendly soul, and I just fancied a chat. Nothing more."

The furrows across her forehead soften, but the cogs continue to whir silently behind her green eyes.

"I apologise," she eventually replies. "I didn't mean to sound rude."

"No apology required," I say breezily. "But I'm sorry for making you feel uncomfortable."

"You didn't, and yes, I'll sit and have a coffee with you."

"Great."

Janine heads back to the counter as I breathe a sigh of relief. I came within a nanosecond of blowing my one and only chance to escape this hell. Realistically, though, the hardest yards are still ahead.

My fledgling friend returns to the table.

"Tell me then, Gary," she says. "What line of work were you in before you became a man of leisure?"

"I worked in the motor trade. Car sales."

"What made you give it up?"

"Let's just say circumstances conspired against me. I'm hoping to return to it soon, though. What about you?"

"What about me?"

"Have you always wanted to work in a coffee shop?"

"Funnily enough, no," she snorts. "But life doesn't always give you what you want."

"That's very true. What did you do before working here?"

Janine then recounts her career history, and I listen intently, although I already know most of it. She then reaches the part where, in my reality, she applied for a job at Kirkwood Motors. In this reality, Kirkwood Motors, or a version of it, ceased trading several years prior.

"Once my boys started school," she continues, "I struggled to find a job that allowed me to work the hours I wanted. It's not easy being a single parent."

"I can imagine."

"Do you have kids?"

"No, but it wasn't a conscious decision not to. It just never happened."

"Because?"

I really didn't want the conversation to revolve around my back story because I've got two of them. A little creative editing is required.

"I was in a relationship for a long time, but we were both too busy with our careers. We eventually split up, and she went on to get married and have kids, and I ... I didn't."

"There's still time, I'm sure."

I'd rather stay away from the subject of kids and relationships, so I take a sip of coffee to break the conversation. Janine mirrors my action, and I take the opportunity to pose another question.

"So, what would you like to do, job-wise, if you weren't serving coffee and listening to boring, middle-aged men?"

"Do you mean ideally or practically?"

"They're not the same?"

"For most people, probably not. Everyone has a job they do to pay the bills, but I wonder how many would call it their dream job. A minority, I reckon."

"Fair point. Tell me what your dream job would be, then."

"My dream job would be to perform on the West End stage."

This, I didn't know.

"Oh, wow. Have you ever got anywhere close to the West End?"

"Alas, not," Janine replies dolefully. "On account, I can't actually sing, dance, or act."

I'm suddenly sitting with the Janine I know, the same devilish sense of humour and wicked glint in her eye. I can't help but laugh.

"They're so judgemental, those West End casting directors," I remark with mock derision.

"Aren't they just."

"I had the same problem when I asked for a trial at Arsenal. You'd think having two left feet would be a bonus for a left-back, but apparently not."

"The world is so unfair."

"Yep, so did you have a backup dream job?"

"I did, although it's more of a business I'd want to own rather than a job."

"Go on."

"I'd love nothing more than to buy a small guest house on the coast. Ideally, in one of those old fishing villages in Cornwall or Devon."

"That sounds like a nice way to earn a living."

"To be honest, I'm more interested in the quality of life than making profits. As they say, money can't buy you happiness."

"Maybe not, but it can certainly buy you options."

"Are you talking from experience?"

"Bitter experience," I chuckle. "But life goes on."

With the ice broken, the conversation flows freely, and we only stop when the odd customer pops in for a coffee to go. At times, I have to remind myself that I'm not sitting at a table with the same Janine from my reality, and once or twice I almost make reference to elements of her life I shouldn't know about.

Before I know it, an hour has passed. Janine notices.

"Gosh, is that the time?" she says, getting to her feet. "I really should get on."

"Yes, me too," I lie. "But thank you."

"For what?"

"The chat. You're very easy to talk to."

"Weirdly, I was thinking the same thing. If I didn't know better, I'd say we have met before."

"In a different life, perhaps," I reply with a wry smile.

"Do you believe in that kind of thing?"

"Err, I'm not sure, but I used to know someone who definitely believed in it. Maybe they were right."

"I hope so. It's the only thing that helps me sleep at night."

"Really? Why's that?"

Janine frowns and then shakes her head. "Ignore me, Gary ... I'll see you again sometime."

With that, she turns and strides past the counter and through the archway. I wasn't expecting a hug goodbye, but it's the most unceremonious of endings to our chat. Did I say something wrong?

It's a slight blemish on what was otherwise a constructive morning. I should probably feel bad for using what I know about Janine to curry favour but needs must. Besides, she did say she enjoyed our chat, and I'm sure she wouldn't have spent so long at the table if she didn't want my company. I made progress, and there's always tomorrow.

The problem is, there aren't many tomorrows left.

As I walk slowly back to the car, my thoughts turn to another woman, the woman who set the deadline I'm struggling to meet. It'd make my challenge less daunting if Edith Stimp agreed to an extension, maybe by a week or two.

Once I reach the junction with the High Street, I come to a stop. I can turn right and continue to where I parked the car, or I can turn left and head towards Dent's Passage. There can't be any harm in asking Edith Stimp to extend her deadline, but there is another valid reason for paying her a visit. It was she who directed me to Maria's Coffee Shop, and I'd like to know how Edith knew about Janine. Maybe she knows more than I've managed to unearth, and I need to hoover up every crumb of information I can if I'm to persuade Janine to help me.

With nowhere else better to be or anything better to do, it's an easy decision.

I turn left.

Chapter 34

When I reach the end of Dent's Passage, I knock on the door three times and wait. I've still no idea if Edith Stimp lives in this building or if she just drops in every now and then. Come to think of it, that's just one of a hundred questions about Edith Stimp that I can't answer.

With no response, I knock three times again.

As the seconds tick by, a troubling thought takes root. What if Edith Stimp has already gone? She never specified where she had to go, only the urgency. If, for some reason, she changed her mind and brought forward her departure, it's game over.

Propelled by low-level panic, I dispense with the door knocking and grab the handle. Just as I'm about to push down, it moves of its own accord, and the door creaks open.

Edith stands in the doorway, squinting up at me.

"Gary," she says in a croaky voice.

"Err, have I called at a bad time?"

"I was asleep."

"Sorry, I didn't mean to wake you."

"It doesn't matter. Come in."

She stands aside as I enter.

"I need a chat," I say. "If that's okay?"

"Of course," Edith replies while stifling a yawn. "You know where the chairs are."

It's my turn to take the lead as I zigzag to the back of the room. Only when I reach the chairs do I realise Edith is shuffling slowly some way behind. She eventually catches up.

"Are you alright?" I ask.

"I'm far from alright, Gary, but that's of no great concern to you ... other than your task of finding a suitable candidate to clear up your mess."

She slowly lowers herself into the usual armchair while trying to mask her obvious discomfort.

"Yes, about that," I reply, taking a seat. "The reason I dropped by is because I was hoping you might consider extending your stay. I don't think I'll be ready by Monday."

"I'm afraid that's out of the question. As you can likely tell, my health has taken a sudden and dramatic turn for the worse. I can't afford to stay here much longer."

"Where are you going? Hospital?"

"I'm not going any *where*, as such. More a case of any *when*."

"I don't follow."

"Nor do you need to. All you need to know is that there's no way I can stay beyond Monday."

"You're sure?"

"Quite sure, yes."

"Right," I puff. "That's not ideal."

"Have you found someone to take the trip back in time for you?"

"Let's not mess around, Edith. I think you know perfectly well I've now met someone who might be able to help."

"Janine Barker, perchance?" she replies with a glint in her eye.

"How did you know?"

"Know what?"

"That I worked with Janine."

"That's a very good question, Gary, but I can think of a better one."

"Like?"

"You never asked what I was doing at the town hall that evening."

"There are a gazillion other questions I'd rather know the answer to."

"I'm sure there are, but the question of my presence at the town hall that night is the most significant ... considering your circumstances."

"Okay, I'll bite. Why were you at the town hall that night?"

Edith smiles and then emits a dreamy sigh. For a moment, she seems to drift off to a time when her health wasn't a concern, but it's a short-lived journey.

"The event at the town hall happened to coincide with my wedding anniversary. And, as we held our reception in the very same hall, I thought it would be a nice trip down Memory Lane."

"Oh, I see."

"I'm not sure you do see, Gary, but I do."

"See what?"

"There's a balcony at the rear of the hall that is seldom used, but I managed to sneak up there so I could sit alone with my memories. I happened to look out over the tables below, and then I spotted you sitting at the table near the stage."

"There were a lot of people there that night. What made me so interesting?"

"I watched you and your wife for fifteen, maybe twenty minutes, and it warmed my heart, seeing a couple so obviously in love."

"No offence, Edith, but when did you last have your eyesight checked?"

"There's nothing wrong with my eyesight, but I was mistaken. It was only when Clare made her speech at the end of the evening that I realised she was Mrs Kirk."

"So, who did … oh."

"Oh indeed. The woman I thought was your wife turned out to be your colleague, Janine Barker."

The room suddenly feels a few degrees warmer.

"You're right about one thing," I cough. "We're just colleagues."

"But you are in love with her?"

Rather than reply, I fidget with my hands.

"Can we change the subject, please?"

"Why? Love should never be the cause of embarrassment. It should be embraced, celebrated."

"Even if I did have feelings for Janine, and I'm not saying I do, she considers our relationship platonic … in this reality and every other."

"For a seemingly intelligent man, that is quite a dumb observation. I could tell within five minutes of watching you at the table that you were in love with one another. Lord, even a fool could see it."

"Um … could they?"

"Yes, Gary, they could, which is why I was disappointed when you didn't seek out Janine of your own accord. I didn't want to intervene, but you were so distracted by your predicament you overlooked one rather significant benefit of this timeline — both you and Janine are unencumbered."

"Unencumbered?"

"You're not colleagues, and neither of you are married."

"Wait … I thought you orchestrated my visit to the coffee shop so I could convince Janine to take a trip back in time for me."

"That's correct, but don't you realise you're now in a win-win situation?"

"You're kidding," I scoff.

"Not at all. If you are able to convince Janine to assist in your quest, you win. However, if there isn't sufficient time before I leave, you're free to forge the relationship you always wanted. As I said: it's a win-win."

I stop fidgeting and sit back in the chair. For a millisecond, I consider the thought of remaining in this reality and forging a relationship with Janine. The reason I only consider it for a millisecond isn't because of Janine, far from it, but every other aspect of this God-awful life.

"I don't want to stay here," I say flatly.

"Even if you could be with the woman you love?"

"I could be with her back in my own life."

"Then, why didn't you act before? You had ample opportunity."

"Because ... lots of reasons, not least that I was married to another woman."

"Ah, yes," Edith says with a smirk. "From what little I witnessed that evening at the town hall, you were married in name only. Wouldn't you agree?"

"Yes, but ... with the fear of repeating myself, I don't want to be here."

"So you said."

Edith folds her arms and stares back at me. If there's anything more to be said, it seems she won't be the one to say it.

"Are you sure you can't stay beyond next Monday?"

"Positive."

"What time on Monday?"

"Let's say noon, shall we."

"That gives me just five days."

"Now you *are* repeating yourself, Gary. It's noon on Monday, and that's non-negotiable."

"And if by some miracle I'm able to persuade Janine, do I just bring her here?"

"Yes, but not before ten in the morning or after eight in the evening. And I might be asleep, so keep knocking until I answer."

"I meant to ask: do you live here?"

"I don't really live anywhere these days, but I converted the cellar into a habitable space with a bed and a few other home comforts."

"And what will happen to this place when you've gone?"

"I'm not sure."

"You must have a vague idea."

"I've no more idea of this building's future than you had of yours when you changed the past."

"What does that mean?"

"I have neither the words nor the energy to explain. Now, unless there's anything else, it's lunchtime, and I am rather peckish."

It proves an effort, but Edith slowly lifts herself from the chair.

"Why is it that after we talk, I always feel like a schoolboy being dismissed?" I grumble as I get to my feet.

"Maybe it's because this is a lesson for you, although I'm not sure you've quite grasped it yet."

"And what is it exactly I'm supposed to learn?"

"You'll know when you know. Now, can you see yourself out?"

"Fine," I huff. "I'll see you on Monday morning, if not before."

"I look forward to it."

Feeling more confused than when I arrived, I wander back to the door and make my way up Dent's Passage to the High Street.

Edith Stimp's words follow me all the way back to the car.

Not wanting to return to the flat, I sit in the driver's seat with the engine off. I had planned on grabbing something for lunch, but I've lost my appetite. Maybe it's just anxiety because Edith refuses to give me more time. Everyone feels anxious when they've got a deadline looming, and the implications if I fail to meet mine are likely to be catastrophic.

That has to be the reason I feel so discombobulated.

Surely. Got to be. It can't be anything else.

I stare out towards the scene beyond the windscreen. My gaze follows the line of cars parked on the opposite side of the street and stops on the sixth car: a pea-green Citroen 2CV.

The sight of the forty-year-old French classic is worth a smile. Not because I'm a fan, but because I remember when the newly appointed office manager of Kirkwood Motors turned up for work on her first day in a pale-blue variant. Most of her new colleagues were not impressed, but Janine loved that car. Unfortunately, it was so unreliable that I eventually offered her a heavily discounted deal on a Ford Focus just to ensure she got to work on time. There wasn't the same emotional attachment, but Janine was incredibly grateful. It was the first time she gave me a hug.

That was three and a half years ago in my reality. Here, it never happened.

Remembering that day provokes an avalanche of fond memories, all involving Janine. There was the day I surprised her with a huge bouquet of flowers on the first anniversary of her joining the company. She actually cried and said no one had ever bought her flowers. There was the Saturday morning when I'd struggled into work with a stinking cold, and even though it was her day off, Janine came in with a flask of homemade soup and insisted I go home. Then, there was the summer BBQ last year when Clare went off on one of her Shamanic retreats. Despite being annoyed with my wife, I had the best evening, dancing all night to a host of cheesy songs, with Janine never letting me leave the dancefloor.

It occurs to me that I could sit here all afternoon and reminisce about the last four years. It'll do me no good, though, because they're memories of a different life with a different woman. Maybe I do have feelings for Janine, but I have to accept that there's a good chance I'll never see her again, and this version isn't the same woman.

At best, all I can hope for is that I might be able to persuade this version of Janine Barker to help me get back to my version. I don't want to think too deeply about what might occur if that happens because I've already lost so much. Edith was right in saying that at least I'm not married here, but why in God's name would a woman like Janine be interested in a loser like me?

I have to face facts — she wouldn't.

All I can do is try my utmost to convince her of my absurd truth and hope she's as kind-hearted and obliging as the woman I left behind. If she's not ...

Chapter 35

I don't know why I feel so nervous. Nothing has changed since yesterday in that I'm driving to the same street where I'll park up, walk to the same coffee shop, and then chat to the same woman behind the counter.

And, yet, my stomach is in knots, and I blame Edith Stimp for putting ideas in my head. I spent much of yesterday afternoon at my parents' place, hoping they'd provide a distraction. Being a pleasant spring afternoon, we went for a long walk on Elderton Common and then had an early dinner at a pub on the way back. Although Dad insisted on paying the bill for our meal, I did head to the bar at one point to buy a round of drinks. As I waited for the barman, I still had a view of our table across the room, and without them knowing, I watched my parents. They continued talking, and then Dad took hold of Mum's hand and gave it a squeeze. She responded by leaning across, and they shared a kiss.

For a moment, I could so easily have been back in my original reality, where my parents always seemed so blissfully content. I like to think that spending time with me, rather than my predecessor, has helped them rediscover what he took from them.

It might turn out to be inconsequential if I escape this reality, but just before we left the pub, Mum said something that gave me hope. With Dad nipping to the gents, Mum and I walked back to the car, and I asked her if she'd had a pleasant afternoon. She replied in a heartbeat, saying that spending the afternoon with the two people she loved most in the world, followed by a beef casserole and spotted dick, was about as perfect an afternoon as she could imagine.

On the drive home, I compared Mum's simple recipe for happiness to that of my predecessor's ex-fiancée, Tara. I never met her, but I did spend a long time poring over her Facebook profile, and I think it would be fair to say that Tara would never have considered a walk across the common and dinner at a pub worthy of a post on Instagram. It did beg the question: did my predecessor ever stop to consider how contented his parents were when he was living a lifestyle that would prove his undoing? Evidence suggests not, and that same evidence suggests he was spectacularly naive.

I arrive at Maria's Coffee Shop just as a smiley young couple are leaving. They're so engrossed in one another that they barely notice when I hold the door open for them. I get a semi-nod from the guy, but no thanks.

My timing is great, though, as I'm once again the only customer. Janine is at the counter, writing something on a notepad. She looks up as I approach.

"I was just thinking about you," she says with a smile.

"Really? Good or bad thoughts?"

"Neither. I just noticed the time, and you've popped in at almost the same time for the last two days."

"I'm a stickler for routines and timekeeping. Sorry."

"Hey, don't apologise. Take it from a woman who's lived with the flakiest of men, there's a lot to be said for being reliable."

"And on that note, can you guess what my order is?"

"One white coffee, coming up. Anything to eat?"

I manage to shift my gaze from Janine to the menu up on the wall, but just being in the presence of the former has rendered the latter inconsequential — the butterflies are too busy.

"I'm okay, thanks."

"Grab a seat."

I briefly consider sitting at a different table, but so far, the one I've chosen on my two previous visits has proven lucky. There's no sense in tempting bad luck by sitting somewhere else.

Janine brings my coffee over and lingers at the table for a moment.

"Can I ask you a question, Gary?"

"Sure."

"You know you said you had a friend who believed in past lives. Do you think they genuinely believed it?"

What I said yesterday was nothing more than a polite, tongue-in-cheek response to Janine's question, but this follow-up question implies it meant something to her.

"She genuinely believed in it, yes, to the point where she started a past-life regression workshop."

"I don't know what that is."

"Um, past-life regression is a form of hypnosis used to recover memories of past lives or incarnations ... well, that's what they believe."

"And you don't?"

"There was a time, not that long ago, I'd have said no. Without getting into the detail, my views on a lot of things have changed recently, so I'm more open-minded."

Janine continues to linger awkwardly and then poses another question.

"Would you be willing to put me in contact with your friend?"

I should have seen the question coming, but now it has, I've no choice but to continue with the hybrid backstory.

"Oh ... um, that would be kind of awkward. The woman in question is my ex, and we're not exactly on speaking terms."

"I'm sorry. I didn't realise."

"It's fine. The last time I saw her, she made it clear that ... that she no longer wanted me in her life."

Janine appears disappointed, which opens up an opportunity for me.

"Tell you what, though," I continue. "I might be able to help you find someone else local. I know more about the subject than most and the pitfalls to avoid."

"You'd do that for me?"

"Sure, I would," I reply casually. "Anything for a friend."

"Friends now, are we?"

"I'd like to think we're on that path."

"Me too," Janine smiles. "So, would you mind having a natter with your friend while she's on her break?"

"It'd be my pleasure."

"Great. Let me just—"

The sound of a mobile phone ringing from the counter steals Janine's attention.

"That's mine," she groans. "Probably a spam caller, but I'd better check."

She hurries over to the counter, snatches up her phone, and answers it while stepping back through the archway. I can just about hear her voice but not the actual conversation.

A minute later, Janine emerges from the archway, her face a picture of concern.

"I'm so sorry, Gary, but I have to lock up."

"Everything okay?"

"No, it's my son, Louis. That was his school calling to say he hurt his ankle during PE. He's on his way to A&E as we speak, so I need to get down there."

"Oh, dear. I'm sorry to hear that."

It's horrible to think it, but my immediate concern isn't so much for Louis but the abrupt termination of my conversation with his mother. Assuming she only works weekdays, I only had three days to work on Janine, and I've just lost one of them. It's also quite likely Louis will be off school for a few days, and his mum won't be able to work.

This is a disaster. I can't just let her walk away.

"Is there anything I can do?" I ask as I get to my feet.

"Could you book me a cab while I close up?"

Obviously, Janine doesn't have a car at the moment, and that opens up the slimmest of opportunities.

"I've got a better idea. I'll go fetch my car and drive you to the hospital."

"I can't ask you to do that."

"You're not asking — I'm offering. I don't have anywhere to be for the rest of the morning, so it really isn't any trouble."

Janine ponders my offer for what feels like ten minutes but is no more than a moment.

"You're sure?"

"It's no big deal, honestly."

"Thank you. A lift would be much appreciated."

"I'll go fetch the car. Back in a few minutes."

I hurry out the door before she changes her mind.

Despite the pain in my still-tender ribs, I jog back to the car. Only when I'm opening the driver's door does it occur to me that I'm about to expose myself as the owner of a shitty Rover. Too late now.

I have only a couple of minutes to work out what I do when we get there. If I just drop her off, that's likely the end of our cosy chats for the foreseeable, and it'll also spell the end of my already dwindling hopes of escaping this reality. I need a reason to hang around.

"Think, Gary. Think."

I'm still thinking when I pull up outside Maria's Coffee Shop, just as Janine is locking up. I get out of the car and open the passenger's door.

"Thanks again for this, Gary," Janine says as she gets in.

"It's no trouble, and I should probably apologise for my car. It's just temporary."

"What's wrong with it?"

"Um, it's an old Rover."

"Who cares if it gets you from A to B?"

I'm about to argue my point, but I stop just in time. This is Janine, and of all the people I used to employ at Kirkwood Motors, she was the least impressed by the high-end cars we frequently stocked.

We fasten our seatbelts and set off towards the hospital.

"You don't have a car at the moment?" I remark as we turn out of Station Road.

"I ... I don't drive."

"Oh."

Janine doesn't expand on her lie, but I'm not supposed to know it's a lie. Maybe she's serving a ban for speeding and is just too embarrassed to explain. The topic of conversation over before it begun, I move on to safer ground.

"How old is your son?"

"He turns eleven in June."

I wait for her to continue, but she doesn't. I suppose it's only natural for a mother to be guarded about her kids when talking to a man she barely knows. For that reason, I don't ask a follow-up question. I then glance across and catch the look of concern on her face, and if I could, I'd kick myself for being unsympathetic.

"I'm sure your lad will be fine," I say breezily. "At his age, I was always getting into scrapes, particularly on the football field.

Cuts, bruises, sprains, and strains ... even broke my nose when I ran into a goal post."

"You're a football fan?"

"I'm a fan of football, but I don't follow any particular club. I used to play regularly in a five-a-side league but ... but over time, the mates I played with all drifted off. You know how it is with life."

"Yes, I do," she replies with the weariest of sighs.

Again, Janine doesn't follow up on her remark. The silence is awkward enough that I reach for the power button on the stereo so we can at least listen to music. Just my luck, they're playing a modern song I've never heard before.

As we close in on our destination, I still can't think of anything to say. I'm a salesman who is literally lost for words, but there's so much more at stake here than another sale. I'm minutes away from Janine getting out of the car.

The song on the radio ends, and another one begins. Right at the last moment, Lady Luck has intervened. I reach for the volume dial and turn it up a notch.

"Keep it to yourself," I chuckle. "But I bloody love this song."

I don't, but I do know that Janine loves *Year 3000* by Busted because she asked the DJ to play it three times during the evening of our summer barbecue last year.

She turns to me, and for the first time since she got in the car, there's a smile on her face.

"No way," she gasps. "This was number one on my seventeenth birthday, and my parents got me tickets to see Busted the following year."

"Oh, really?" I reply, acting surprised.

"I'd never have taken you as a fan, though."

"Why's that? My age?"

"Err, I don't know how old you are, so no. You just don't strike me as a Busted fan."

"I'm not really, but I do love this song."

"You have great taste."

The song seems to have lifted Janine's mood slightly, but its effect is unlikely to last more than the next three minutes. By that point, we'll be at the hospital. I've got one chance to save the day and very little to work with.

We reach the main road where the hospital is located. I turn down the volume on the stereo. I need to call upon my years of sales experience and pose a question Janine can't say no to.

"While I'm here, I'm going to message my dad and see if he fancies an early lunch."

"Your dad is in the hospital?"

"No, he works here ... in the maintenance department."

"Ahh, right."

"If I give you my number, ping me a message when you're done with your lad, and I'll run you home."

"It's fine, thanks. We can get a cab."

I had a feeling she'd say that, and now is the moment where my blag proves a success or dies a death.

"I'm sure you can, but I don't charge anything. And, besides, I've got to drive back across town anyway, so it's no skin off my nose."

"You don't know where I live."

Shit. No, I don't. I know where the other version of Janine lives, but who's to say this version lives at the same address?

"You said you don't drive, so I presumed you live somewhere within walking distance of the coffee shop. I'll be heading back that way after I've seen Dad."

"That's very kind of you, but I don't know how long I'll be."

I could tell her it doesn't matter, and I'll willingly hang around all day if needs be, but there's no way to spin that offer without it sounding desperate, creepy even.

"Well, I'll be here for a while, so if you're ready to leave within an hour or so, ping me a message. If not, I can recommend a good cab company."

"Okay. Thank you."

I breathe a partial sigh of relief. I've bullshitted my way into contention, but now all I can do is hope that Louis is seen quickly and his injury isn't serious. Fingers crossed, it's nothing more than a sprain, and they quickly send him on his way with a packet of painkillers.

We reach the drop-off point, and I pull over.

"It's a new phone, so I don't remember the number," I say as I tap the screen. "Give me two seconds."

Thankfully, it does only take a few seconds to find the number, and Janine quickly adds it to her contact list.

"What's your surname?" she asks when the phone prompts her for it.

"Kirk."

That done, she thanks me again and opens the passenger's door.

"I'd wish you luck, but I'm sure it'll all be fine."

She replies with a feeble smile and gets out of the car. I sit for a moment until she's out of sight.

All I can do now is find somewhere to park up and wait for a call or text that might never come. This really is it now. By the end of the afternoon, I'll know for certain whether I've got a chance of getting back to my reality or I'm stuck in this one for the rest of my days.

Chapter 36

My dad has never worked in the hospital's maintenance department, and he's now retired, but even if he did, and he wasn't, I couldn't stomach lunch.

If I ever meet someone desperate to lose weight, I'll tell them that screwing up your life via the medium of time travel is a pretty effective appetite suppressant. There might be other factors contributing to my lack of appetite, but I can't think about those right now.

I had to drive for almost a mile before I could find somewhere to park. Most of the streets around the hospital are for permit holders only, no doubt to deter those who don't want to pay the extortionate charges levied in the hospital car park. The distance isn't my concern, though — it's time.

I dropped Janine off just before 11.00 am. It's now 12.03 pm. I've been staring at the dashboard clock almost constantly for the last thirty-eight minutes. The only time my eyes have left the clock was to check my phone screen just in case a message arrived without the phone letting me know.

12.04 pm.

I've yet to decide how long I'll sit here and wait, but it seems unlikely that Janine will call after 12.30 pm because I said I'd only be around for an hour or so.

As another minute passes, the futility of staring at a clock hits me. I lean back in the seat and close my eyes.

"What are you doing, Kirk?" I mutter.

There's absolutely nothing more I can do to nudge fate in the right direction, and maybe it's time to stop pushing back and accept the inevitable. Dad always told me that no problem was ever resolved by adding worry, and I'm currently racked with it.

It's time I started considering the real possibility that this is now my reality.

As I let that thought percolate, it doesn't fill me with quite the same sense of utter dread as it did a few days ago. Granted, I'm an ex-con, living in a poky rented flat, and I'm likely to be unemployed on Monday, but there is the thinnest of silver linings, and I've Edith Stimp to thank for pointing it out.

There is Janine.

I've only spent a few hours in the company of this version, but it's enough to accept what I should have accepted a long time ago. I could use the excuse that I was married in my reality, and there was the complication of being Janine's employer, but I did everything I could to ignore how I felt.

Why?

Very little soul-searching is required to come up with an answer. Some might call it an insecurity complex, but I prefer the simplistic label I've used for most of my life: I'm not good enough.

When the reporter from the Elderton Herald, Kate Palfrey, interviewed me in the days before the award ceremony, she asked me what I considered the secret of my success. Was it fiery ambition or a deep-rooted entrepreneurial streak? I replied that it was a bit of both, plus a determination to deliver an exceptional customer experience. It was what she expected to hear, but it wasn't the truth. What really motivates me to get out of bed every day is fear.

When you have nothing, and you build something, the thought of losing it is truly terrifying. No matter how hard

I worked, no matter how many hours I put in, I could never escape the feeling that I didn't deserve success. As the years rolled by, I put much of what I achieved down to luck or good fortune, and I couldn't get past the fear that one day, the winds would change and my modest empire would crumble. I didn't deserve Kirkwood Motors, and I certainly didn't deserve a woman like Janine.

In hindsight, it's no surprise why I reacted so aggressively to Clare's demands. Like a wild animal cornered, my instincts were based upon fear — not for my life, but for the life I'd built.

That life is no more, and if this is what I'm left with, I cannot make the same mistakes again.

My phone rings, and I almost jump out of my seat in surprise. I snatch the phone from the centre console, praying I don't see the name *Dave from work* on the screen. To my relief, the call is from an unknown number, and I jab the screen to accept it.

"Hello."

"Hi, Gary. It's Janine ... from the coffee shop."

"Hey. How's the wounded soldier?"

"He's fine and thank you for asking. It's just a sprain."

"That's good to hear."

There's a split second of silence on the line. I need to take the initiative.

"I'm just finishing lunch, so if you wanted that lift, I'm only around the corner."

"Are you sure? I don't want to impose."

"I am sure, and you're not. Shall I meet you at the main entrance in five minutes?"

"That would be perfect. Thanks, Gary."

I scramble for my seatbelt, start the engine, and rev the Rover like it's never been revved before. There is no ensuing squeal of tyres, but I do make quick progress back towards the hospital and pull up outside the main entrance with a minute to spare.

Janine is already waiting at the kerb, with Louis looking sorry for himself in a wheelchair. I hop out of the car and join them on the pavement.

Janine thanks me again and then introduces her son. He says hello in a quiet voice, but I know he's a shy lad because I've met him several times before in my reality. That could prove an advantage.

"Bad tackle, was it?" I ask, nodding at his bandaged ankle.

"Yep," he replies.

"Did you win the ball?"

"Not quite. I got a yellow card."

"Referees, eh," I snort. "Idiots!"

To my relief, Louis sniggers at my remark.

"Shall we get you into the car, then?"

I step back and open the rear door, and then ask Janine if she needs a hand.

"I'm sure he can cope on his own," she replies. "It's just a sprain, and I don't want him to think that Mum will wait on him hand and foot for the next week."

"Excuse me," I respond, slapping my hand across my chest in mock indignation. "Are you suggesting that us men are prone to exaggerating our aches and ailments?"

"Two words, Gary — man flu."

"Point taken," I chuckle.

I catch Louis smirking from his wheelchair as his mother rolls her eyes.

"You could do me a favour and take the wheelchair back to reception, though," she then says.

"No problem."

Once Louis is out of the chair and hobbling to the back seat of the car with his mother's aid, I fulfil the requested favour. When I return from the hospital reception, Louis is safely in the back seat and Janine in the front passenger's seat.

I get in and put my seatbelt on.

"Can I ask another favour?" Janine then asks. "Well, it's more of a request."

"Go for it."

"Louis is a nervous passenger, so could you take it easy on the drive back, please?"

I glance over my shoulder to the nervous-looking passenger.

"Which lesson do you hate the most, mate?"

"Um, history."

"Because it's boring?"

"Yeah."

"I will drive you home so carefully, it'll be more boring than the most boring of history lessons, okay?"

His obvious tension eases a fraction, and I flash a reassuring smile before starting the engine.

"Right. Where is home?"

"It's Ashton Place. Do you know it?"

I'm taken aback by Janine's answer for two reasons. Firstly, it's not where she lived in my timeline, and secondly, I know exactly where Ashton Place is.

"Small world," I remark. "Ashton Place is only a few streets away from where my mum and dad live. They're in Denby Place."

"Oh, wow. You won't need directions, then."

"I could drive there with my eyes closed."

I glance at Louis in the rearview mirror. "But I won't."

As I pull away, I consider our destination. I don't know how much Janine earns in the coffee shop, but I wouldn't be surprised if it's half what I paid her at Kirkwood Motors. That would explain why she's not currently living in a spacious two-bedroom house on the other side of town.

"Can I play Xbox when we get home?" Louis asks from the back seat.

"I suppose so, but only until I've spoken to Mrs Pickford. I'm sure she'll have some work you can do at home until your ankle is better."

"But ... but ..."

"No buts, young man. I don't want you to fall behind on your schoolwork. It's important."

Louis then mumbles something that I don't quite catch. It's a good opportunity for me to lighten the atmosphere.

"What do you play on Xbox, Louis?" I ask.

"Fortnite."

This I know because Janine once had to bring the boys to work when the school unexpectedly closed due to half an inch of snow. I let them use the computer in my office for the morning and then treated them to lunch at McDonald's.

"Ah, that's the one where you can play Battle Royale, right? You can play as part of a squad."

"Yes, but I like to play solo."

"I hear you. Sometimes it's best to go it alone."

"Do you play?"

"I'm way too old, mate," I chuckle. "But when I was your age, I used to spend every waking hour at my best mate's house because he had a Sega Mega Drive. We used to play a game called World Championship Soccer."

"Was it like FIFA?"

"Kind of, but game consoles were pretty basic back then. When I was old enough and had a job, I bought myself a PlayStation, and I loved playing that."

"I had a PlayStation," Janine interjects.

Again, I know this.

"You played video games?" Louis asks.

"I did a long time ago."

"But you never play video games with me."

"That's because I'm not very good at them. You'd beat me every time."

"Are you good at video games, Gary?" Louis asks.

"Oh, err, I haven't played one in years, but I reckon I could beat your mum at Crash Bandicoot."

I glance across at Janine, and she's staring back at me, open-mouthed.

"How could you possibly know I was a fan of Crash?" she asks.

"Just a gamer's hunch ... and the fact my best mate's sister and all her friends used to play it."

"Ohh."

"What's Crash Bandicoot, Mum?"

"I'll have to show you one day. Maybe we can play together."

We're still discussing the virtues of retro video games when I turn into Ashton Place.

"It's just up here on the right," Janine says, pointing to a layby next to a small block of flats built in the same style as my parents' home.

I pull into the layby and switch off the engine. I've done all I can, and what happens from this point is in the lap of the gods.

"Do you need a hand getting his Lordship inside?" I ask, more in hope than anticipation.

"I'm sure we'll be fine, thanks."

I reply with a smile, although there's little joy in it.

"But I do owe you a coffee, considering you didn't get to finish yours earlier. That's if you've got time?"

Do I have time? It's an interesting question because, on the one hand, I'm fast running out of time, but on the other, I've got all the time in the world. It's a stark contrast to my reality.

"I'd love a coffee. Thanks."

Chapter 37

Janine's ground-floor flat might not look much from the outside, but the interior truly reflects her personality: bright, cheery, and highly organised. The kitchen is tiny, though, and my host instructs me to sit in the lounge while she makes coffee. Louis disappears to his bedroom, his sprain suddenly less of a concern with the prospect of an afternoon of gaming ahead of him.

"I hope you haven't stolen the silverware," Janine jests as she enters the lounge with two mugs of coffee.

"No, but I did consider stealing your sofa. It's much more comfortable than mine."

"If you can carry it out of here on your own, it's yours."

We share a laugh as Janine hands me one of the mugs and then sits at the other end of the sofa. Being only a small three-seater, there's not a lot of space between us.

"You've got quite the eye for interior design," I remark.

"Thank you, but it was more a case of what I could find on the cheap," she replies, waving away my compliment. "I furnished the whole flat by scouring charity shops and car boot sales."

Janine then proceeds to point out various items of décor, asking me to guess how much she paid. I'm wrong every time, perhaps forgetting that I hired Janine in my reality because of her ability to save money.

"You're wasted in that coffee shop," I chuckle. "You should be Chancellor of The Exchequer with your eye for financial prudence."

"I don't think they'd like me. I swear too much, and I'm none too keen on politicians. My dad used to say that people with the ambition to become a politician are usually the last people you want anywhere near the House of Commons."

"Your dad sounds like a wise man."

"He is, bless him. What about your dad — are you close?"

"At the moment, we're very close. Probably less than five-hundred yards."

Janine reaches across and playfully slaps my arm. For a second, I could be back in my office at Kirkwood Motors.

"I mean, do you have a good relationship with your parents?"

"Pretty good, although I think I've been guilty of neglecting them a bit."

"In what way?"

"Mainly, just not spending enough time with them."

"Tut-tut, Gary," Janine chides.

"I know, and I've vowed to make more of an effort in the future."

"Good for you. Family is important."

I'm about to agree when Louis calls from his bedroom. Janine groans and then gets to her feet.

"Sorry. I'd better see what the patient wants."

Janine is gone for a few minutes but then returns with a frown on her face.

"Something wrong?" I ask.

"He's broken his chair, and he wasn't impressed when I said he'd have to wait for a new one."

"Oh, dear. Do you want me to have a look at it?"

"I'm not sure it can be fixed. It was second-hand to start with."

"Entirely up to you. I'm a dab hand with a screwdriver and a socket set, though."

There's a moment of hesitation before my host beckons me to follow her. She opens a cupboard in the hallway and pulls out a toolkit.

"If you can fix it, I'll cover the cost of your coffee in the shop for a week."

"Deal."

"Take that through to the lounge," she says, handing me the toolkit. "I'll wheel the chair through because my son isn't quite as house proud as I am."

"I was a boy once. I'm immune to mess."

"Trust me, Gary. Not the amount of mess Louis creates."

I take the toolkit through to the lounge. A moment later, Janine wheels through an old office chair that's certainly seen better days. Louis hobbles behind, although I'm not sure he's hobbling on the ankle he allegedly injured.

"What's the problem with it, mate?" I ask.

He takes a seat and then demonstrates how the chair wobbles left and right whenever he moves.

"Okay, hop out, and I'll take a look."

"Do you know how to fix chairs?" Louis then asks as I upend his.

"I'm no expert with chairs, but when I was a teenager, I bought and sold old cars. Because I didn't have much money, my dad taught me basic mechanics so I could fix any minor problems. And, if I can change the timing belt on a 1993 Ford Escort, I reckon I might be able to fix an office chair."

I kneel down and inspect the mechanism that attaches the chair to its base. It only requires a cursory glance to identify the problem.

"You're missing two bolts. They probably worked loose and fell out."

Louis turns to his mum. "Did you hoover them up?"

"I don't think so, but if they're somewhere on your bedroom floor, we'll need a search and rescue party to find them."

Louis responds with a sulky frown.

"It's okay," I interject. "I might have another solution. Do you use the foot stand, Louis?"

"No, it's annoying. It gets in the way."

"Not anymore."

I delve into the toolkit and find a suitable spanner. Then, I remove the foot stand and use the bolts to replace the ones missing from the base. That done, I ensure all the other bolts are tight before returning the chair to its castors.

"Do you want to give it a test, mate?"

Louis returns to the chair and shuffles left and right. Unlike last time, the seat doesn't wobble.

"You fixed it!" he beams.

"What do you say, Louis?"

"Thank you."

"You're more than welcome."

Janine also thanks me, and then she wheels the chair back to her son's bedroom. I return the toolkit to the cupboard and reward myself with a few gulps of coffee on the sofa. My host returns.

"You've no idea what a headache you've saved me from," she says, retaking her seat. "He's been moaning about that chair for weeks."

At this point, anyone who didn't know Janine as well as I do might ask why Louis's dad didn't fix the chair. I, however, already know what an unreliable, feckless waste of space he is because Janine has told me often enough.

"All part of the service, Ma'am."

"What other skills do you have besides chair maintenance?"

"I'm a certified professional dishwasher loader."

"No way," Janine giggles. "But you're a man."

"Bit sexist," I laugh. "I'll have you know that some men take great pride in loading a dishwasher efficiently."

"And you're one of them, eh?"

"I like to think so."

Janine takes a slow sip of coffee and poses a question after a moment's thought.

"What's your story, then, Gary?"

"My story?"

"Yeah, you wander into my place of work one day, just some random, mild-mannered, unassuming man, and a few days later, you're sitting in my lounge sipping coffee. I like to think I'm a good judge of character, but I'm interested to know your story."

"I don't really have one. I'm just plain old Gary Kirk."

"That's the modest answer. What's the real one?"

"I'm not being modest. There's really nothing of interest to tell."

"Hmm, I'm not convinced. I reckon there's more to you than meets the eye."

"Why do you say that?"

"Because you have a certain aura about you. I can't put my finger on it, but you're ... intriguing."

"I might be a lot of things, but intriguing isn't one of them."

"You say that, but what about the way you dress?"

"Um, what about it?"

"Don't take this the wrong way, but you obviously dress for function over fashion."

I try not to squirm at her observation, factual as it is.

"What I mean," she continues, "Is that you seem so confident and comfortable in your own skin, you don't care about being judged by the clothes you wear."

I prefer her assumption over the truth; that I don't have the money for designer clothes.

"People do judge," I reply. "Don't they?"

"I don't."

"No?"

Janine adjusts her position on the sofa.

"Take your car as another example."

"My car?"

"Yes, you said you worked in the motor trade, but you drive an old Rover. Even I know they're not great cars, but that doesn't seem to faze you. I don't know you that well, Gary, but you seem like you've worked out your priorities in life, and the need to portray a certain image isn't one of them."

I take a second to reflect on Janine's analysis. That second is long enough to determine that she isn't as wrong as I first thought.

"It wasn't that long ago that I'd have pushed back on that assumption, Janine, but … but not now."

"Did something happen that changed your outlook?"

It's my turn to adjust my position on the sofa. I place my mug on the coffee table and turn to face my host.

"Can I tell you a little story?"

"Sure. I'm all ears."

"I had this acquaintance — let's call him John — and John grew up in a home where there was plenty of love but very little money. When John left school, he was determined to achieve more than his parents had, so he spent years working himself into the ground so he could afford the kind of lifestyle his parents never could."

"And did he achieve his goal?"

"Financially, for sure, but then he realised his parents still had more than he did because they had each other."

"John didn't marry?"

"Oh, he did, but both he and his wife were so focused on their respective careers that they neglected the marriage. It limped on for years, but I don't think John would say it was a happy marriage."

"That's a shame. I can't imagine wasting my life in a loveless relationship."

"It wasn't all bad, and perhaps being married saved John from himself. In another life, he might have married a woman who encouraged him to work less and spend more."

Janine slowly nods and then asks an obvious question.

"This acquaintance of yours, John," she says, eyebrows arched. "I don't suppose he's you, is he?"

"No, he's not," I sigh. "John is no longer with us."

"Oh, Christ. I'm so sorry for your loss."

"Don't be. We weren't close, and John's passing wasn't in vain. His life was quite the cautionary tale, which brings me back to your question about my outlook on life. It has changed of late, but I'm still unsure I'm where I need to be."

"Do you like it where you are?"

"It's growing on me," I reply with a smile. "Little by little."

"Maybe you should stay a while longer, then."

I wish I could read this version of Janine as well as her counterpart in my reality. Mind you, if there's any shred of truth to Edith Stimp's claim, perhaps I didn't understand Janine as well as I thought.

"Yeah, maybe," I reply with a semi-smile.

I finish my coffee and offer to put the mug in the dishwasher, but Janine doesn't have one. No part of me wants to leave, but I don't want to outstay my welcome. Reluctantly, I confirm I have somewhere else I need to be.

We both get to our feet, and Janine thanks me again for playing taxi driver and fixing Louis's chair.

"You're welcome, but don't forget you promised me a free coffee."

"Yes, I did," she grins. "Although I'm afraid you'll have to wait until next week. I can't send Louis back to school until Monday, so I won't be at work for the next few days."

"That's a shame. I was just getting used to our mid-morning chats."

It's more than a shame — it is, to all intents and purposes, the snuffing out of my final hope. It was always the longest of long shots to consider Janine, and maybe with a few more days of getting to know her, I might have dared broach the subject, but it's game over now.

Strangely, it isn't the disappointment of failure that follows me towards the front door but the disappointment of not seeing Janine for the next five days. If I were brave enough, maybe I could ask if she fancies going out for a drink at the weekend, but if I am stuck in this reality, the last thing I want to do is risk losing the only good thing I have here.

I open the front door, then turn and thank Janine for the coffee.

"I'm beginning to think you're obsessed with coffee," she laughs.

"Getting a decent brew isn't easy, you know."

"Ah, so there's an ulterior motive behind your gallantry. You want your own barista."

"Okay, you got me. That was my intention all along."

"Well, that's a shame," she replies coyly. "Because I was going to ask if you had any plans later."

"Err, no ... I mean, I don't have any plans. Why do you ask?"

"I was thinking you might like to pop back about six and join us for a bite to eat. Nothing fancy, just lasagne and salad."

"Oh, right. Um ..."

"Honestly, if you're … you know … oh, God, have I misread the signals? Are you in a relationship?"

"No, it's not that — I'm one-hundred per cent single. It's just … I'd love to join you for dinner."

"You're sure?"

"Sorry, I didn't mean to sound like a dithering idiot. I was just a bit taken aback, really."

"I can see that. You're blushing."

"Am I? Shit. That's not cool, is it?"

"No, but it's endearing," she chuckles. "And it's nice to see a little of what lurks beneath that cool, calm exterior."

"There's a dithering idiot, for starters."

We share another laugh and then say goodbye at the doorstep. The smile on my face stays in situ all the way back to the car.

Could Edith have been right? Is this what she meant by making the most of this life?

As I drive slowly back up the road, my thoughts are no longer dominated by my awful car, the shitty flat I'm returning to, or my lack of a decent job. And no matter how hard I try, I can't even summon the familiar dread about my financial woes.

I have nothing, so why the hell am I still smiling?

The answer, I swiftly conclude, is the woman I just said goodbye to. Six o'clock can't come quickly enough.

Chapter 38

Within thirty minutes of returning to the flat, I left again. I needed to clear my mind, to think, and Elderton Common seemed as good a place as any to while away the rest of the afternoon.

Before I left, I googled the five stages of grief because although I haven't lost someone I care about, I have lost a life I cared about, and it felt important to understand what I was going through. I then ticked my way through each emotion and found some comfort in knowing that after the denial, anger, bargaining, and depression, the acceptance would eventually follow. Is that where I am now? Have I accepted this reality as my reality now?

As I strolled through a wooded area, I thought about what I'd lost but also what I had to gain. The thought of starting again still fills me with dread, but not so much that I can't find a small space for optimism. My brief conversation with Louis came to mind as I considered what skills I had besides running a used-car business and how I might use those skills. It struck me that maybe I could develop my rudimentary mechanical talents and then set myself up as a mobile mechanic. As a sideline, I could find, fix up, and sell the kind of cars that are set to become modern classics. Renovated Golfs, Ford Escorts, and even MG Metros sell for serious money these days.

When I returned to the flat just before five, my mind was ablaze with possibilities, and in some way, the curse of having nothing had become a blessing. A man who has nothing has literally nothing to lose.

I step out of the shower, dry myself off, and get dressed. Even if I wanted to make a good impression on Janine, there's nothing in the wardrobe that I could consider suitable for a date, if that's even what this evening is, and I doubt my host would care anyway.

On the way back to Ashton Place, I stop at Tesco Express and pick up the best bottle of wine I can afford. Fortunately, I know Janine favours a Chardonnay, so no guesswork is involved. I continue on my way with an upbeat tune playing on the stereo and the kind of excitement I haven't experienced in years. As I pull up outside the flat, I could almost kid myself that I'm a teenager again. Fingers crossed I don't make the same mistakes.

I'm a little early but better than late. I ring the bell and wait for Janine to answer the door. When it finally swings open, I rue not picking up a bunch of flowers from Tesco because the woman in front of me has clearly made an effort.

"Hey," I chirp. "You look … lovely."

"Thank you, but as you've never seen me in anything other than my work clothes, I won't let the compliment go to my head."

She doesn't know it, but I have seen her in plenty of other outfits. Indeed, it wasn't that long ago that Janine breezed into the town hall for the Elderton Business Awards, and she took my breath away.

I hand her the bottle of wine.

"That's amazing," she gushes.

"A wine connoisseur might disagree. It's from Tesco Express."

"I mean, it's amazing that you chose my favourite wine. I love Chardonnay."

"Lucky guess on my part."

Janine beckons me inside, and after asking if I want a glass of wine, she suggests I sit in the lounge while she pours the drinks. There's no sign of Louis, or his younger brother, Felix, so I presume they're both playing video games in the bedroom.

"Dinner will be ready in twenty minutes or so," Janine confirms as she enters the lounge. "I'm a bit behind schedule."

"No problem," I reply, taking a glass of Chardonnay from my host. "And cheers."

"Cheers."

We sit down and, judging by her series of gulps, I can only assume that Janine is either thirsty or desperate for alcohol.

"I needed that," she remarks before placing the glass on the coffee table.

"One of those days, eh?"

"Kind of, but more for Dutch courage. I wanted to apologise for earlier."

"Err, you'll have to remind me what you did that warrants an apology."

"I made a tit of myself."

"You really didn't."

"You're being kind, but I should probably give you an explanation about … well, me."

"Sure, if you want to."

"This is the short version, but I was married to an utter dick for too long, although thankfully, I divorced him five years ago. Because of that experience and … and some pretty awful shit in my life, I haven't had much interest in relationships."

"Right."

"And I honestly don't know if I feel like that anymore. I mean, I … I'm not actively looking for a relationship, but I'm also not *not* looking for a relationship. Does that make sense?"

"Are you saying that you're open-minded to whatever fate brings your way?"

"Yes," she replies emphatically. "That's exactly what I'm trying to say."

"Makes sense."

"I hope so because I think you and I could become really good friends, and if we're really good friends, then … you know … something might blossom from there."

"I like the sound of that."

"You do?"

"Yes."

"I'm so out of practice with the opposite sex, I didn't know how to say that I like you without sounding like a giddy teenager. Then, on the other hand, I don't want to come across like an ice maiden and scare away someone who seems like a really nice guy."

"It's fine, honestly," I chuckle. "You're a mum, and I understand you wouldn't want to rush into anything. I'd love to be friends, and if anything develops from there, I think I'd be very happy about that."

"Great," Janine says with a sigh of relief. "So, we're on the same page?"

"I think so, yes."

"Now that's out of the way, I'll start acting like a normal human … or I'll try to."

"Good, and I won't mention that you're now the one blushing."

Janine grabs a cushion and playfully strikes it against my thigh.

"Don't," she giggles. "You're not supposed to notice."

"Sorry."

Any residual awkwardness soon ebbs away as my host empties her glass. She then heads off for a refill while I continue to sip at mine. I hate Chardonnay, but I'm willing to suck it up if it makes Janine happy.

"I'm just sorting a few things for dinner," she calls from the kitchen. "Won't be a minute."

"No problem," I call back. "Anything I can do?"

"It's all under control, thanks."

I sit back and bask in the momentary glow of our exchange. Over the last decade of my marriage, Clare and I rarely enjoyed a meal together at home. More often than not, we'd eat at different times or in different rooms. I guess it's the difference between eating as a family and eating as a couple — one is communal, and in our case, the other was just two people requiring sustenance at similar times of the day.

Across the room, a large, framed photo on the bookcase catches my eye. It's of Louis and Felix together, and I'd guess they're probably four or five years of age. They both look incredibly happy, although I suspect that's down to their mother rather than their father. There are at least a dozen smaller framed photos scattered across the shelves, each featuring one or both of the boys. I already know what a fiercely proud mum Janine is, but if I didn't, the bookcase of memories would confirm it.

"Sorry about that. I forgot to slice the cucumber earlier."

Janine then crosses the room to a small table and places a handful of cutlery down.

"We usually eat on trays in front of the TV," she remarks. "But seeing as we have a guest, I thought we'd better be civilised."

"Honestly, don't change your routine on my account."

"No, it's good to have a meal at the table. We don't do it often enough."

I notice she's only set three places, which presumably means one of the boys won't be eating with us. Perhaps the missing sibling is having dinner at a friend's house.

"Do you want to grab a seat?" Janine then says.

"Are you sure you don't need a hand? I feel like a spare part."

"I think you've done more than enough for me today, and besides, I quite like having someone to fuss over."

"Don't you get enough of that being a mum?"

"It's different ... unless you intend to scoff your dinner down in five minutes flat and then hurry off to play Fortnite?"

"Wasn't planning to."

"Good. Now, sit yourself down while I go and cut the burnt bits off the lasagne."

Giggling to herself, Janine hurries back to the kitchen while I take a seat at the table. The smile that resided on my face earlier returns. Impossible to imagine only a few days ago, but I wonder if it might become a permanent fixture. I could certainly get used to sitting down for dinner with Janine every evening, and from what she said when I first arrived, there's a chance she might, in time, like that idea too.

Louis enters the lounge, carrying a small stack of plates.

"You okay, mate?" I ask. "That chair behaving itself?"

"Yes, thank you," he replies while laying the plates out. "But it still squeaks."

"That's easily fixed. Do you have any WD40?"

He looks at me blankly. "What's that?"

"It's a magic spray that fixes a multitude of things. When I used to sell cars, I used it a lot, and I mean *a lot*."

"No, we don't have any, I don't think."

"Never mind. Next time I pop over, I'll bring some with me and show you how to use it. Then, whenever you get a squeak, you'll know how to fix it yourself."

"What are you two chatting about?" Janine asks as she approaches the table with a salad bowl.

"Magic spray," Louis replies. "Gary said he'll bring some with him next time he comes."

"Did he now? And what does this magic spray do?"

"It fixes squeaks."

"And stiff joints," I add.

"I could do with some of that," Janine snorts. "What's it called?"

"WD40."

"Oh, maybe not then."

She disappears again and returns a moment later, holding a lasagne dish with oven mitts.

"Grubs up."

After Janine dishes out the lasagne and the salad, she invites me to tuck in. The food is delicious and the conversation flows freely, with Louis particularly chatty. He relays an event at school, allowing me to take advantage of information I know from my previous reality.

"You said history is your least favourite subject at school, Louis. What's your favourite?"

"That's easy. Art."

"Ahh, do you prefer digital art or the old stuff with paint and canvas?"

"Digital."

"Are you hoping to be a graphic designer when you get older?"

I already know the answer, and with a mouthful of food, Louis looks at me and nods enthusiastically.

"How'd you guess?" Janine asks.

"Honestly, it's the only job I know where a digital art qualification comes in handy. I took Art at secondary school, and there was a time I thought about becoming a graphic designer."

"Why didn't you?"

"The thought of spending a few more years in education didn't appeal. I was too keen to get out in the world and make money."

"Are you rich?" Louis then asks.

"Louis!" his mum chides. "You don't ask people about their finances. It's rude."

"It's okay," I chuckle. "Your mum is right, but luckily for you, I'm not easily offended. No, I'm not rich ... not when it comes to money, anyway."

"How else can you be rich?"

"Lots of ways. You can make yourself rich with knowledge, or experiences, or just being with people who love you. Having money is nice, but it's no guarantee you'll be happy."

"Amen to that," Janine says.

All too soon, our plates are empty, and Louis asks if he can take a bowl of ice cream to his room. On the proviso he takes his plate out and washes it up, Janine agrees. He shoots off, only remembering to hobble halfway across the lounge.

"His injury seems to have eased a bit," I remark casually once we're alone.

"Yes, it's almost a miracle. I'm sure it had nothing to do with a double period of history this afternoon."

"In fairness, I did something similar at school when it came to Drama. I hated it."

"No future in the West End for you, then?"

"Only as a taxi driver."

Janine laughs and then takes another gulp of Chardonnay.

"He likes you," she says. "Louis."

"You think?"

"He hasn't said so, but I can tell. He's had a rough few years with one thing and another, and doesn't take easily to new people. You seem to put him at ease."

"I'm just being me."

"That's what I was referring to earlier. You have an easy-going nature that's hard not to like."

"Thank you, but you're pretty good company yourself."

"You wouldn't have said that if you'd met me a year or two ago."

"No? Why not?"

She takes another mouthful of wine and then nods towards the bookcase.

"See the picture at the top?"

"I noticed it earlier. You have two sons?"

"Louis and Felix."

"They have your eyes."

"Thank you," Janine replies in a strangely low voice.

"Is Felix having dinner at a friend's house?" I ask.

"No."

"Oh, right."

A troubling thought then strikes. Janine isn't living in the same spacious house she occupies in my reality, and she obviously isn't working in the same well-paid job. What if both those factors came into play when she was fighting for custody of the boys? God, what if my meddling in the past has inadvertently led to Janine losing custody of one of her sons?

"Err, is he with his dad?" I ask somewhat hesitantly.

Janine shakes her head and stares down at the table for a long moment.

"No," she finally says in barely a whisper. "We lost Felix three years ago in a road accident."

Chapter 39

I've only had two small glasses of wine, but the room is spinning like I've downed six bottles.

"I … Christ … I'm so sorry, Janine."

She nods while fiddling with the stem of her wine glass. I want to fill the silence, but the shock is so profound that I can't unscramble my thoughts.

"In the months after it happened," Janine eventually continues. "I had a dozen sessions with a grief counsellor. He assured me that one day, I'd be able to talk about it without breaking down in tears."

Still stunned, I can barely muster a nod in response.

"I've not had cause to tell anyone since, so perhaps this is as good a time as any to try."

"You … you don't have to."

"I know, but I want to. I need to."

"I … err, okay."

Janine empties her glass and then pulls a deep breath.

"I've always had a good memory for dates, but there's one I wish I could forget: Wednesday 19th February. I had an important appointment at 4.30 pm that day, and although I never made it, it did change my life."

My mouth bone dry, I just about manage to rasp a response. "Right."

"I asked Mum if she could watch the boys for me, but her car was off the road, so I said I'd pick them up from school and drop them over to her place. It's only a ten-minute drive, so I had plenty of time to get to my appointment."

Her right hand is resting on the table, and all I want to do is take it. I daren't.

"The journey involves a short stretch of dual carriageway, maybe a mile or so, and I must have driven along it a thousand times over the years. On the day in question, I was behind a truck travelling at about fifty. I pulled out to overtake, and just as I drew level, I remember glancing across and ... it's funny how you remember the weirdest things. I looked at the size of the truck's tyres, and because I had to buy a new tyre the previous week, I questioned how expensive a truck tyre might be."

She closes her eyes for a heartbeat and then continues.

"This is the bit I knew I'd struggle with because it happened so fast. One of the truck's right-hand tyres burst ... exploded, really ... and the fragments of rubber hit my car like shellfire. Both side windows shattered, and the noise ... it was indescribable."

As little as I want to hear what I fear Janine is about to tell me, I nod to confirm she should continue.

"I lost control of the car and hit the barrier. That's the last thing I remember before waking up in a hospital bed. I suffered a concussion, a broken collarbone, and more cuts and bruises than they could count, but ... I then learned just how subjective the word 'suffer' is when my parents came into the room. They were both crying, and Mum broke down when I asked if the boys were okay."

She bites her bottom lip, closes her eyes for a moment, and then continues.

"My counsellor explained how extreme shock affects the memory, which is why I don't remember much about what happened in the days and weeks after the accident. One minute I was lying in a hospital bed and the next, I'm standing at my six-year-old son's grave on the day of his funeral."

"I … I don't have any words, Janine."

"Trust me," she sighs. "There aren't any, and I know that because I heard every platitude under the sun, and not one of them helped. I was in such a dark place that if it wasn't for the fact I had Louis, I … let's just say we wouldn't be sitting here this evening."

It now makes sense why Louis was such a nervous passenger on the journey home from the hospital. The poor kid must have been traumatised by that final journey with his little brother. It also explains why Janine doesn't drive, and it's not because she doesn't have a licence.

"It took about a year to learn how to manage the grief," Janine continues. "And then the sorrow turned to anger. It was a freak accident with no one to blame, so I blamed myself."

"Why?"

"All part of the process, apparently. I just kept thinking that if I hadn't overtaken the truck, or if I'd been going a little faster, or if I'd just turned the wheel a fraction to the left rather than the right, my baby boy would still be alive."

"That's crazy."

"I know, but you have to understand Gary, that grief makes you crazy. Once I'd stopped trying to unpick all the various ifs and maybes surrounding the accident, I decided there was a more compelling reason to blame myself — being on the road at that specific moment."

"How'd you mean?"

"My appointment was for a job interview. If I hadn't been so keen to restart my career, there wouldn't have been an interview, and we'd never have made that journey. I put it all down to my selfishness."

My mind latches on to the first sentence and repeats it over and over and over. I can't have misheard her, but I need to know for sure.

"You were going to a job interview?"

Three years ago, in my reality, Janine celebrated her first year as an employee of Kirkwood Motors. In that reality, she left work on the 19th of February, picked her boys up from school, and drove home — an uneventful day, no different from any other. At least, that's what happened until I messed with my past and, therefore, Janine's. She isn't responsible for Felix's death — I am.

What have I done?

"Can ... can I use your bathroom?"

"Sure. Second door on the right off the hallway."

I rush through to the hall and almost fall through the bathroom door. Dropping to my knees, I lean over the toilet bowl and wait for the nausea to complete its job. The retching soon follows, but my throat is so tight nothing besides bile escapes.

What have I done?

My eyes begin to burn, and it feels like a hundred white-hot needles are piercing the skin across my back and shoulders. The physical symptoms of whatever it is I'm suffering pale compared to the emotional. That beautiful little boy is dead, not because of a truck tyre blowing out, or because his mother lost control of her car, but because of my greed.

What have I done?

There's a knock at the door.

"Is everything alright, Gary?" Janine asks.

"Err, yeah ... I'm just ... give me a moment."

"You're sure?"

"Yeah."

How can I look her in the eye ever again, knowing I'm responsible for her son's death? For one moment, I really thought I might make something of this life and find true happiness with Janine. That's now impossible.

I get up, stagger to the sink, and splash cold water on my face. It's hard to ignore the man in the mirror behind the sink. I look away, but not before catching the look of disgust on his face. The recriminations will have to wait, though, because right now, I have to explain to Janine why I bolted from the table and dry-heaved into her toilet.

Full of dread, I return to the lounge. Janine is sitting at the table but stands up when I enter.

"God, you look peaky," she says. "Are you sure you're okay?"

Hard as it is to lie to her, I've no choice but to spin another untruth to save her feelings.

"It's my fault. I had some strong painkillers before I came out, and I forgot that I'm not supposed to drink alcohol with them."

"Ahh, I see. For one awful moment, I thought I'd poisoned you with my cooking."

"Entirely self-inflicted, and I'm so sorry."

Saying the word, even out of context, feels so unbelievably hollow.

"You don't have to apologise, silly," she says with a sympathetic smile. "I'm always popping pills and forgetting that I shouldn't drink. Thankfully, I've never had a reaction like you just had, though."

"I'll be fine," I lie. "I'm sorry."

"Stop apologising."

"Err, right ... would you think badly of me if I made my excuses? I'm still not feeling too clever."

She steps forward and places her hand on my upper arm. "Of course not. Will you be okay, though?"

"I'll live."

Unlike Felix.

"You're sure?"

"I think I just need a few pints of water and a lie-down."

"Okay, but will you do me a favour?"

"Of course."

"Can you text me later to let me know you're alright? I probably shouldn't admit it, but I'm a bit of a worrier."

"I'll text you. Promise."

With that, Janine guides me to the front door. If the circumstances were different, I wouldn't be leaving barely an hour after arriving, and maybe we might share a hug, but they're not. I feel wretched, but it has nothing to do with pills and alcohol.

"Make sure you get some rest, you poor thing," Janine says as she opens the door.

"I will, and again, I'm sorry."

"Shush, now. I'm sure there will be plenty of other opportunities for us to have a meal together ... I hope."

"Yes, there will."

I flash her a smile, but it's as strained as it is disingenuous. There won't be any more meals because I can't face the woman whose son I killed.

"Bye, Janine."

"Bye, Gary."

In a semi-comatose state, I traipse back to the car and get in. It occurs to me that I could easily relieve the crushing weight of guilt on the way back to the flat. Get the Rover up to sixty miles an hour and then steer it towards an unforgiving object like a tree or a wall. Without a seatbelt, I'd die in an instant, and my suffering would end.

That would be easy, but it'd also be cowardly. My parents have endured enough pain with my predecessor's criminality and depression. Knowing their son committed suicide would push them over the edge, and they don't deserve that.

I start the engine and put my seatbelt on.

As I make my way across town, my mind continues to circle in on itself. There's no escaping the most obvious of conclusions — I'm responsible for inflicting untold pain upon people who least deserve to suffer. It is equally obvious that the responsibility to fix my mistake rests solely on my shoulders.

And fix it, I must, whatever the consequences for Gary Kirk.

Chapter 40

As I sip coffee and stare out the lounge window, I run through my options for the umpteenth time. Using the plural is ridiculous because there's only one viable option. I spent all yesterday evening and half the night trying to think of alternatives, but to no avail.

My phone is on the window ledge, with the last message from Janine displayed on the screen: *Get an early night, and you'll feel better in the morning. Sleep tight. X*

She sent the message just before ten last night, tipping me over the edge. No one deserves to lose a child, but I can't think of anyone less deserving than Janine — her heart literally brims with kindness, compassion, and love. I don't mind admitting that I shed more than a few tears after reading her message.

I leave the flat and hurry down to the street where I abandoned the Rover last night. It's likely the last time I'll get behind the wheel. Small mercies, I suppose.

Unlike the drive back from Janine's yesterday, I head towards the town centre with caution. It's not that I care about safety for my sake, but for those whose lives I've blighted. If anything happens to me before I reach my destination, those lives will remain unchanged. That can't happen.

If I'm grasping at minor consolations for my predicament, the end of the High Street roadworks is a contender. I find a space and pull into it. A sign next to the ticket machine states that parking costs £1.20 an hour for a maximum of three hours. The cost is irrelevant, and so too are the consequences if I don't buy a ticket, so I don't.

A few minutes after ten o'clock, I reach the end of Dent's Passage and knock hard on the wooden door. Edith said I shouldn't call before ten, and I don't want to risk annoying her before a difficult conversation.

I'm about to knock again when the door eases open.

"Oh, it's you," Edith remarks. "I was expecting a delivery from Sainsbury's."

"Sorry to disappoint. I need to talk to you."

"You'd better come in, then."

She steps aside and doesn't bother telling me where to go. I follow the now familiar path through the furniture to the armchairs and coffee table at the back of the room. Edith, when she finally joins me, appears exhausted.

"Let's hear it then," she says, her tone weary.

"I want to go back."

"Back where?"

"To the past. I want to set things back to the way they were."

"We've had this conversation, Gary. You can't."

"You said I couldn't go back because it was too dangerous. I don't care about the danger."

"I won't be responsible for such an act of self-harm."

"You don't understand. This isn't about me — it's about Janine."

"What about her?"

"Her six-year-old son is dead because when I changed my future, I also changed Janine's. The poor kid died in a car accident that should never have happened."

Edith looks genuinely shocked at my revelation.

"Oh dear," she gulps. "That's terrible."

"Yes, it is, and that's why I have to go back."

"But you do understand what another journey means for you? I wasn't exaggerating when I told you about the risk and the likely outcome."

"I understand, but I've thought long and hard about it. It's the only option."

"It's suicide, Gary, plain and simple. If you travel back again, you'll be lucky to live more than a year or two. How will your parents feel about that?"

"They'll be heartbroken, but if either of them were in my shoes, they'd do exactly the same thing. We're talking about the life of a child."

"I understand, but it would be remiss of me not to warn you of the consequences of another trip."

"You've warned me, and I accept the risk. When can I leave?"

"It'll take me an hour or so to prepare the device. Are you sure you want to do this?"

"I'm sure. I'll come back in an hour."

"Very well."

I'm about to get up, but Edith poses another question.

"Have you thought about what you'll do when you return?"

"Do?"

"Once you return to the life you had, what are your plans for that life?"

"I haven't given it much thought."

"Your time will be limited. You should spend it wisely."

"That much I do know."

"Do you?"

"Yes," I huff. "I'd have to be a complete moron not to have learnt anything from this … experience."

"Does that mean you intend to forge a relationship with Janine Barker?"

"No."

Edith blinks twice, her eyebrows arched. "Really?"

"It wouldn't be fair," I reply.

"But my assumption was correct — you do love her?"

"I ... I care deeply about Janine, which is why we can never be more than colleagues."

"I don't understand."

"The reason I'm willing to take another trip back in time is that I can't stand seeing someone I care about in so much pain ... because of my actions. How can I return to my reality, knowing I won't have long, and then get involved romantically with Janine? What kind of future would that be for her?"

"As I said, there's no telling how long you might have. Surely, it's better to enjoy that time with someone you love rather than alone?"

"You're not getting it, are you, Edith? Janine deserves to be happy. She certainly doesn't deserve to get involved with someone and then watch them slowly fade away."

"You're willing to put her happiness above your own?"

"Yes," I reply without hesitation. "And besides, there are her boys to consider, too. They need stability in their lives."

"Boy," Edith retorts. "In this reality, she only has one son."

"And that, above every other argument, is why I have to go back."

My point appears to land as Edith nods solemnly. "One hour."

"Thank you."

I get up and hurry away before she changes her mind.

When I reach the High Street, I stand at the junction of Dent's Passage and consider how I'll spend my last hour in this reality. What I actually do is irrelevant because I won't be here to face the consequences, and that should be a uniquely liberating prospect. It's not.

For a second, I consider heading to a cafe and gorging on the kind of fried breakfast that would make a cardiologist weep, but

I don't have much of an appetite. The pubs aren't open yet, and even if they were, I'm not sure alcohol would be sensible in my current frame of mind.

If the circumstances weren't so dire, I'd stand in the street and laugh. Here I am, able to do almost anything I want without consequences, and I'm struggling to think of a single thing.

I suppose I could find a traffic warden and tell them to get a proper job, or I could nip into my bank and tell that chatty cashier how annoying it is for customers waiting in line when she's nattering away to some old dear. I could block a cyclist on the road and yell at them for holding up motorists. I could call Clare and gloat about how she's about to lose her empire once I undo my mistake.

I could do all those things, but I won't because it would mean leaving this reality just as naively as I entered it. The consequences of my actions — of everyone's actions — have a nasty habit of reverberating in unforeseen ways. Granted, very few will ever travel back in time and screw up as monumentally as I have, but we all live in our own little bubbles and rarely consider how our everyday actions might adversely affect others.

Why ruin someone else's entire day just for a single moment of satisfaction?

I find a coffee shop and head inside. There's a couple waiting at the counter, more or less the same age as my parents, and I step up behind them. I then catch the tail end of their order. The guy behind the counter taps a screen and then confirms the total price: £15.80.

"Excuse me," I interject. "Does anyone mind if I pay for that order?"

The guy serving shrugs his shoulders, and the couple stare at me like I've got two heads.

"It's my good deed for the day," I confirm with a smile. "If you'll allow me to pay for your order?"

The gentleman looks at his wife and then at me. "What's the catch?"

"There isn't one. I promise."

"In which case, thank you, young man. That's very kind of you."

I order coffee, and the server adds it to the bill before I tap my debit card against the payment terminal. The couple thank me again and step to the end of the counter to await their order. I guess if you can do something without worrying about the consequences of destitution and it makes someone else smile, it's worth it. Fortunately, I won't be around when Gary Kirk's bank statement arrives.

With nothing better to do, I take my coffee to a table by the window and watch the people passing by. I try to imagine what they're up to, where they're going and where they've been. I think about their lives, the regrets of the old and the hopes of the young. What I'm doing, in truth, is merely a form of distraction. The term Edith used to describe what I'm about to do isn't one I'd considered, but suicide is an accurate label. My method, however, will be as unconventional and as prolonged as it gets, but the net result is the same — I'll be gone before my time and of my own volition.

I reach for my cup, but I can't stop my hand from shaking. Here, now, alone, there's nothing to stop the fear from taking hold. I am fucking terrified, and it would be so very easy to talk myself out of what I'm about to do. Then, I imagine Janine in that hospital bed and how she must have felt when her parents told her Felix had died in the accident. I then picture the boy himself on that day we went to McDonald's for lunch: his unruly hair, his prominent dimples, and his cheeky grin. Most of all, though, I remember how he looked at his mum and how she looked at both her boys. Love. Pure and unconditional love.

I take a deep breath, manage to settle my shaking hand long enough to finish my coffee, and then leave. Somehow, I end up in a newsagent where I ask the woman behind the counter for twenty Marlboro. I haven't smoked since I was a teenager but boy, I could do with one now. I'm aware that smoking kills, but that's not really an issue.

"£14.50, please."

I stare back at the woman, slack jawed. "Sorry?"

"£14.50," she repeats.

"I thought that's what you said. Is that really how much a packet of cigarettes now costs?"

"I'm afraid so."

"Dare I ask the price of a box of matches?"

"To you, thirty pence."

Almost fifteen quid later, I emerge from the newsagents and find a bench to sit and enjoy my first cigarette in almost three decades. Only when I'm puffing away and becoming increasingly light-headed, does it occur that I'm acting out the clichéd final minutes of a condemned man. There's no firing squad or gallows in my case, but a barber's chair and a woman who is as peculiar as she is mysterious.

I smoke two cigarettes, one after the other, and begin a slow walk back to Dent's Passage.

The wait after knocking on the door is so long that I'm tempted to light another cigarette. Finally, Edith Stimp lets me in.

"You smell of cigarettes," she says as I enter.

"Sorry. I had a couple for old time's sake."

"Don't apologise. I quite like it."

"You're the only person I've ever met who said they like the smell of cigarettes."

"My husband was a Woodbine man, and I always associate the aroma with him."

"I've got eighteen Marlboro going spare if you want them?"

"No, thank you. I've already done quite enough damage to my body."

She turns and shuffles away, beckoning me to follow. I presumed we'd head straight up to the room where the device is, but Edith leads me back to the armchairs.

"Sit down," she orders.

"Can't we just get on with it before I change my mind?"

"Is that likely?"

"No," I sigh. "But putting it off is just adding to the torture."

"You'll be on your way soon enough, but before you go, I want you to do something for me."

"What?"

She reaches down the side of the chair and picks up a jotter pad.

"I want you to tell me everything that's happened to you in this reality."

"You already know most of it."

"I know a few scant details, but I want to hear it all, chapter and verse."

"Why?"

"Because it's important."

"Fine," I groan before casting my mind back to the day I first arrived in this reality. I don't get very far.

"You're just giving me the basic details," Edith complains. "That's not what I asked for."

"Is this really necessary?"

"Yes, it is. Now, start again, but this time, I want you to tell me every detail about how you felt, particularly what you learned. And I want to know about the time you spent with your parents and Janine Barker."

"No," I snap. "I'm not willing to sit here and spill my guts for no good reason."

"There is a good reason, Gary, and if you don't tell me, you're going nowhere."

"For the love of God. Seriously?"

"Yes, seriously. Think of it as a confessional — the more candid, the better."

I close my eyes and draw a deep breath, more to quell my irritation than to prepare myself.

"Ready? We don't have all day."

"Okay."

I've no clue how much time passes, so when Edith finally shuts her notepad and I check my watch, I'm mildly shocked — almost two hours. As annoyed as I was when I began relaying those first few hours in this reality, once I got into my stride, it felt like a counselling session. Edith furiously scribbled notes and occasionally interjected with a question or a request for me to expand on a point. She wanted to know answers to questions that I couldn't understand and for me to reveal thoughts I've never shared with anyone. The process might have almost been cathartic if not for the fact it'll all be irrelevant once I depart this reality.

"What happens now?" I ask.

"You can head upstairs and make yourself comfortable. I just need to grab something."

"I mean, what happens when I go back? Where will I end up, and what do I do to counteract my previous screw-up?"

"I'll set the device to put you back where you were before we bumped into one another on Elderton High Street. Beyond that, you don't need to worry."

"But how will that stop me from making the same mistake?"

"I'm tired, Gary, and I don't have the energy to explain. You'll just have to trust me."

"I don't—"

"Go," Edith barks. "Please."

My protestations curtailed, it seems I have little choice but to trust Edith. She slowly climbs out of her chair and shoos me away. Like a dismissed pupil at the end of a lecture, I trudge across the room to the staircase and climb the stairs to the room of doom.

When I step through the doorway, it's like walking down the steps of an aeroplane after landing in a hot and humid country. I approach the antique barber's chair and sit down. Across the room, there's a slight hum coming from the bank of electronics, and I can just make out a blinking cursor on the monochrome screen of an old cathode-ray monitor.

Sitting in near silence with only my thoughts for company, my mind only wants to focus on the gravity of what I'm about to do. Every fibre of my being is telling me to jump out of the chair and run. For nothing other than distraction, I pull out the crappy mobile phone I inherited and read the message from Janine one final time.

I never did reply to it, and now it really doesn't matter if I do because, in a few minutes, anything and everything I've done here will become irrelevant. This is the one and only chance I'll get to tell a version of Janine how I feel. I begin typing.

I fell in love with you the moment we first met, and I'll still love you when I draw my last breath. I'm so sorry for what I put you through and for not being brave enough to tell you how I truly feel. Forgive me. xxx

I tap the send icon just as Edith enters, carrying a bottle of water.

"You should drink this," she says, handing it to me.

"I'm fine, thanks," I mumble, still staring at the phone screen.

"It wasn't a request, Gary. You need to drink it to try and counter the symptoms of dehydration. They're always worse on the second trip."

A memory of a pounding headache is all the motivation I need. I take the bottle, unscrew the lid, and gulp it back. Edith then takes the empty bottle from me and places it on the floor near the door.

"How are you feeling?" she asks.

"Terrified, if I'm being honest."

"There's still time to change your mind."

"If it wasn't for Janine ... and Felix ... and my parents. None of them deserved what I've put them through. Not by a long chalk."

"Very well. Close your eyes and try to relax."

"Fat chance of that," I snort.

"Just try, please. I'll begin a countdown, and when I reach ten, I'll leave the room."

"You didn't do a countdown last time."

"As I said, the second trip is always harder than the first. Departing in a calm state of mind will help."

I adjust my position in the chair and close my eyes.

"Fifty, forty-nine, forty-eight, forty-seven, forty-six ..."

The slow, rhythmic timbre of Edith's voice is in itself, calming. It's so calming, in fact, that I begin to feel drowsy.

"Thirty-six, thirty-five, thirty-four ..."

My breathing slows, and with every syllable, Edith's voice seems to fade into the distance.

"Twenty-three, twenty-two, twenty-one ..."

My mind closes in on itself. Silence follows, and then ...

Chapter 41

"Gary? Gary?"

"Eh? Err ..."

"Are you okay?" Ian asks.

"Uh?"

"You zoned out for a moment there. Everything alright?"

"I ... um, I'm fine, I think. I just had a funny turn."

"Can I get you a glass of water?"

I look across the desk at my solicitor.

"No, thanks. Where were we?"

"I was about to say that we could write to your wife's solicitor and put forward a counter-proposal, but it's not without risk. From what you've told me, Clare's sole motivation is to buy that property, and if she doesn't fulfil that ambition, she'll have nothing to lose by going for the business."

"No, just ... I need to think about it."

"Understood."

Having made his position clear, Ian offers a few platitudes and then suggests I call him once I've decided on my next move. With two legal experts telling me I should give up the house and walk away, my options appear limited.

I thank Ian for his time and leave.

As I traipse back along the High Street, my mood is as dark as the clouds overhead. It'd be just my luck if the heavens open before I make it back to the car. I pass a coffee shop and consider nipping in to console myself with a double espresso, but what I really want, in truth, is a double scotch.

Christ, I never thought I'd say it, but I fucking hate my wife.

I trudge on with my hands in my pockets, trying to think of another way to undermine Clare's demand. I'm so lost in my thoughts I almost bump into a woman stepping across my path.

"Sorry," I mumble, even though the minor brushing of shoulders wasn't my fault.

"Hello again, Gary," she replies.

I stop and stare at the woman. She looks familiar, but I've met a lot of people over the years, including thousands of customers, and I can't possibly remember everyone's name.

"Um, hello," I reply. "How are you?"

"You don't want to know how I am, and it's not important. We need to talk."

I'm confused by her request, and I think it shows on my face. The woman tilts her head slightly.

"You don't remember me, do you, Gary?"

"Sorry, no."

"We met at the town hall last week. Edith Stimp."

I've tried hard to forget last Friday, which is probably why I've not given a moment's thought to the woman now standing in front of me.

"Oh, yes. My apologies."

"Apology accepted. Now, can we please talk? I don't have much time."

"Talk about what?"

"Mistakes, regrets, second chances — take your pick."

"If you're recruiting for a religious group, you're wasting your time. I'm not into all that."

"I'm not recruiting for anyone. I'm trying to help you."

"Help me? How?"

"It's complicated, and I'm not willing to stand on a street corner and discuss it."

She turns and points over her shoulder towards the opening of an alleyway.

"My premises are at the end," she says. "If you're willing to sit down and talk to me, I guarantee it'll change your life for the better."

"My life is just fine, thanks, and to be honest, I'm a bit pushed for time."

"You have more time than you know, and unless you come with me, you'll never know how to spend it."

"I'm sure I'll be okay," I reply, glancing at my watch.

"If you're not willing to do it for yourself, do it for Janine."

The mention of Janine's name catches me off guard.

"What's Janine got to do with anything? And, come to think of it, how do you know who she is?"

"Because you admitted to me that you're in love with her."

"What?" I snort. "Firstly, that's a ridiculous assumption, and secondly, we barely spoke that night at the town hall."

"It's not ridiculous, and whether you're willing to admit it or not, you are in love with Janine Barker. Now, the question is: are you going to waste the opportunity I've given you?"

If I listen to the logical part of my brain, I'll walk away. This woman is patently mad, and much of what she's said makes no sense. The only reason I haven't walked away is because Mum is always telling me that sometimes the heart makes better decisions than the head. In this instance, my curiosity just about edges out the cynicism.

"I suppose I can spare ten minutes."

Edith Stimp then guides me towards the cobbled alleyway she appeared from.

"Would you mind if I held on to your arm?" she asks. "I'm a little unsteady on my feet."

Now she's mentioned it, the Edith Stimp I briefly met at the town hall didn't seem anywhere near as frail as the woman standing before me now. Maybe the amount of beer and wine I consumed that evening clouded my memory.

"Sure," I reply, holding out my right arm.

After a slow walk in silence, we reach the end of the alleyway and a solid wooden door. Edith Stimp asks if I'll open it.

"It's a bit stiff," she remarks. "Push the handle down and then give it a good shove."

I do as instructed, and the door creaks open.

"After you, Gary."

Tentatively, I step through the doorway, wondering if maybe I should have popped into the coffee shop after all.

"Welcome to my humble workspace," Edith announces as she follows me in.

Her workspace isn't what I expected. Roughly the size of a double garage, the walls are exposed brick with thick oak beams running left to right above my head and slabs of solid stone beneath my feet. It's also crowded with period furniture, and although I'm no expert, I'd guess each piece is from a different period.

"Come and take a seat," Edith then says.

We zigzag slowly through the maze of furniture to the back of the room, where two wingback armchairs are separated by a coffee table that looks too old to be called a coffee table. She's yet to expand on the statements she made on the High Street, and with every passing second, I'm beginning to suspect Edith Stimp might be slightly mad.

"Sorry, I need your assistance again," she says. "It's not lady-like, falling into an armchair."

I let her use my arm as a counterweight as she slowly lowers herself down. It takes some effort on her part and, judging by the sucking of air over her teeth, a fair amount of discomfort.

"Are you okay?" I ask.

"I'm dying, Gary, and I've only got days left, but that's not important."

The frankness of her statement takes me aback. When she said she didn't have much time, she literally meant it.

"I'm ... I'm so sorry."

"I don't need your pity — I need you to listen to what I'm about to tell you."

I sit down in the other armchair; my curiosity edged with sympathy.

"I'm listening," I say.

"Good, but before I begin, I need to make a request. What I'm about to tell you might sound fanciful, possibly ridiculous, but I need you to sit and listen to every last word. If you do that and heed the lessons, you'll find true happiness."

Edith Stimp hasn't even started, and her promise of happiness is enough to spike my scepticism.

"One question before we begin," she says. "Do you believe it's possible to travel in time?"

"I've never given it much thought, but seeing as you've put me on the spot, no, I don't."

"Fair enough, but for the purposes of this conversation, I need you to imagine that it is possible. Can you do that for me, Gary?"

"You want me to pretend that time travel is possible?"

"Yes. Humour me."

"Alright."

"Now that's settled, I'll begin by telling you that this is not the second time we've met. I first bumped into you at the town hall, but our second meeting occurred some twelve days ago."

"Eh? How could our second meeting have happened before the first? The ceremony at the town hall was only six days ago."

"Yes, that is true, but the last time I bumped into you on the High Street, you came back here and told me all about your marital woes and that you'd do anything to avoid paying your wife a significant sum of money."

"You're saying I've already been here?"

"Yes, and without getting too bogged down in the details, I made it possible for you to take a brief journey back in time to 1996 and the day you first met Clare Wood. If memory serves, that was in a pub called The Black Prince."

"How the hell—"

"Please don't interrupt," Edith Stimp interjects. "Over the course of this conversation, I'll relay information that only you could know, and if I have to stop every time, we'll be here all day."

"At least tell me how you know about The Black Prince."

"You told me."

"No, I never."

"Yes, you did, only a few hours ago in that very chair. In fact, you told me so much about your life that I now understand where you've gone wrong."

"Some would argue I'm wrong sitting here, listening to this. It's insane."

"It's only insane if you don't believe in time travel. I did ask you to suspend belief."

"I know but come on."

"You might not currently believe in time travel, Gary, but I hope to prove that not only is it possible, but that you've experienced it. Once you accept the truth, you'll understand what mistakes you've made and what you need to do to avoid making them again."

The only reason I'm still in the chair is that I want an answer to my question about The Black Prince. To the best of my knowledge, only five or six people know where I first met Clare, and Edith Stimp definitely isn't one of them.

"Let me continue, and hopefully, the picture will become clearer."

"I'm listening ... for now."

"Good, and no interruptions, please."

I reply with a nod, and Edith Stimp settles back in her chair.

Although she doesn't begin with the immortal line, once upon a time, it soon becomes apparent that the soon-to-be deceased woman in the chair opposite me has a knack for storytelling. Her tone of voice is engaging, as is her story, but the key difference between Edith's tale and the audiobook stories I occasionally listen to before bed is that I am the protagonist.

Despite the unbelievable plot, I find myself becoming engrossed in the story, probably because Edith continually throws in twist after twist, and I don't see any of them coming. How did she know about my trips to Hayling Island as a child and my thrifty attitude when playing the coin-pusher machine? How did she know about the conversation I had with Clare during the financial crisis, in which I decided to make staff redundant rather than take out a loan? How did she know that I've always had a deep-seated fear of losing everything?

My answer comes towards the end when Edith Stimp claims my time-travelling counterpart told her every last detail about his life in a supposed alternate reality.

"Why would he do that?" I ask.

"Because I told him there wouldn't be a journey back unless he did."

"Presuming he made that journey, and I'm him, why don't I remember any of it?"

"Because he didn't make the journey back."

"Eh? So, where is he?"

"His timeline ended the moment he passed out. I gave him a bottle of water laced with strong sedatives, and he slipped out of consciousness. I then took one final journey back, and here we are."

"I don't understand. Why didn't you just let him go back and fix his mistake?"

"He wanted to, but because of the radiation involved in each journey, he would have suffered a fate akin to those poor souls in Nagasaki and Hiroshima after the Americans dropped their atom bombs."

I scratch my head and take a moment to unpick what Edith Stimp is suggesting

"But ... but if you took the journey back, that would mean ..."

"Yes, I thought Gary Kirk deserved another chance. I was already sick, so it really made no difference, but I had hoped to take one final trip to a different period in time. Alas, we can't always have what we want in life."

"Why, though? It's not as though we're close."

"I did it for one reason, and one reason only: love."

As I stare back at Edith Stimp, my cheeks redden.

"Err, I'm sure you're a lovely woman, and I'm flattered, but ..."

"Not my love for you," she scoffs. "The love you have for Janine Barker."

The redness in my cheeks grows warmer.

"Janine is a good colleague, and we're close, but our relationship is purely platonic."

"Then why were you willing to sacrifice your own life?"

"I ... that person you're referring to wasn't me."

"He *is* you, Gary, and you need to understand that his mistakes are your mistakes. He learned, and I only saved him because I have confidence that you will too."

"He only offered to go back to save Felix, though. That's reason enough."

"You can believe that all you like, but we both know the truth. You love that woman, and she loves you."

"Err, if you say so, but even if that were true, had you forgotten I'm married?"

"Is that a reason or an excuse? To me, it sounds a lot like the latter."

"It's neither — it's just a fact that I can't easily undo. My wife is currently trying to extract a small fortune from me, and I just don't have the ..."

"Enough!" Edith suddenly barks. "You stupid, stupid man. Have you not listened to a word I've said?"

"I heard every word, and it made for an entertaining story, but that's all it was."

"Even the parts that you know are categorically true, and I couldn't possibly know unless you'd told me?"

"Granted, I don't know how, but if I were to draw up a list of possible ways, time travel wouldn't even make the top fifty."

Edith Stimp sinks into her chair and closes her eyes. As silent seconds pass, it crosses my mind that she might actually be dead. I clear my throat, and that seems to reactivate her.

"Do you have any idea what I gave up in order for you to have this opportunity?" she asks.

"I never asked you for anything."

"No, you never, but I'll tell you anyway. I intended to take one last trip back to see my late husband."

I immediately feel a shot of guilt, but it's short-lived. How can I be guilty of preventing the impossible?

"What period were you hoping to visit?" I ask, just to break the awkward silence.

"It doesn't matter. I only came here in the hope of finding a treatment, but it seems medicine hasn't advanced as far as I hoped. Now, this is where I'll die."

"Um, sorry ... again. Is there anything I can do?"

"You could ensure my instincts were not wrong about you. Give your wife what she wants and tell Janine Barker how you really feel about her. The rest will fall into place."

"I'll think about it."

"Will you?"

"I said I would, so I will."

I won't, but there seems precious little point in arguing otherwise.

"Very well, but take it from a woman with barely any time left, don't leave it too long."

"Noted."

I glance at my watch. "I'd better be going."

"Would you like to see the device before you leave?" Edith then says. "If only to add some weight to what I've told you."

"I'm fine, thanks. As I said, I'll think about what we discussed."

"Are you sure? It'll be gone by tomorrow, so this is your one and only chance."

"Seriously, I need to get going."

I stand up, but Edith remains in her chair, staring blankly into space. Looking down on such a withered husk of a human, it's hard not to feel some sympathy.

"Um, will you be okay on your own, Edith? Do you have a nurse or carer who pops in?"

"I'll be fine, thank you. In some way, I'm fortunate in that I know my fate. Yours, on the other hand, is still to be decided."

"Yes, yes, I know," I reply, trying not to let my agitation show. "Give Clare the money she wants and tell Janine how I feel — I get it."

"I hope you do, Gary. I really do."

With nothing left to be said, I say goodbye to Edith Stimp and wish her well. She looks up at me from the chair and nods, but judging by her sallow complexion and sunken eyes, no amount of wishing is likely to help her now.

When I reach the High Street, the clouds open.

"Fuck's sake," I groan.

Not only have I wasted most of the morning, but my umbrella is in the car.

Can this day get any worse?

Chapter 42

On the final stretch of road, before I turn into the industrial estate, I almost jump a red light, only noticing it at the last second. Fortunately, the Mercedes' carbon fibre brakes justify their cost by bringing the car to a rapid halt.

As my heart rate settles, I wait for the lights to turn green and curse the two women guilty of dragging my attention away from the road: my wife and Edith Stimp.

For most of the journey from the town centre, I've tried to focus on my next move in the Kirk marital battle. I pondered Ian Burke's advice and whether it's worth sending a counteroffer to Clare's solicitor. However, while I tried to think through the various permutations of what that might achieve, thoughts of Edith bloody Stimp kept invading my mind like a series of irritating pop-ups on a website — I closed one down, and then another appeared.

The lights turn green, and I pull away.

A minute later, when I turn into my parking bay at Kirkwood Motors, I finally admit defeat on the Edith Stimp front. My mind won't let me ignore our conversation. Considering what we discussed, is it any wonder I can't brush aside the barrage of unanswered questions? It's a distraction I could do without, but as I hurry up to my office, I strike a deal with myself. I'll devote an hour to the cause and see if I can unearth a rational explanation for the most irrational of women.

I wake my computer up and begin with the obvious starting point of any investigation — I google Edith Stimp's name. The search engine immediately spits back a statement and a question: *No results found. Did you mean Edith Stamp?*

No, I did not, and I'm miffed that the search engine hasn't returned a single result. How does someone prevent their name appearing anywhere online? Even complete technophobes like my parents have Facebook profiles, and Dad's name is also listed on the Elderton Allotment Society's website, being he's the vice-chairman. There are probably scores of other websites where one or both of my parents' names are listed. How has Edith Stimp managed to keep hers from the far-reaching clutches of a search engine?

Already at a dead end with an online search, I turn my attention from the woman in question to the information she shared with me. Although it doesn't account for all of the details Edith Stimp knew, a leak within my inner circle of family and friends would explain the majority of it. The first, and most likely leak, is my mother, being that she loves a good gossip.

I grab my phone from the desk and call my parents' number.

"Hi, Mum."

"Hello, Sweetheart. Everything okay?"

"Um, yes. All good with you and Dad?"

"We're fine, although your Dad's back is giving him gyp."

"He should spend a bit less time at the allotment."

"I keep telling him that, but you know what he's like. Says it's good exercise."

"I'm sure it is, but ... sorry, I'm in a bit of a rush, Mum, and I wanted to pick your brains, if I may."

"Pick away," Mum chuckles. "But I'd warn you the pickings will be slim."

"I know the feeling, but let's try anyway. Does the name Edith Stimp mean anything to you?"

"Edith Stimp?"

"Yep."

Mum hums to herself; a sign that she's dredging her memory.

"No, sorry. Doesn't ring any bells."

"You're certain?"

"Certain as I can be."

"What about Dad? Do you think he might know her?"

"He's certainly never mentioned the name to me, so I doubt it. I'll ask him when he comes home."

"Thanks."

"Who is she, anyway?"

"Err, just someone a customer mentioned. It's not important."

"Righto."

"And just one other thing. Do you remember when I was a kid and we used to go to Hayling Island on holiday? I played those coin-pusher machines."

"Yes, I do."

"Do you recall that I'd always walk away once I had more money than I started with?"

"Good Lord. I haven't thought about that in years but yes, I do remember."

"Did you ever tell anyone?"

"Like whom?"

"Anyone."

"I'm not sure why I'd tell anyone about that, but no, I don't think I did."

"And Dad?"

"Again, you'd have to ask him, but I can't think of any reason he'd tell anyone. It was a cute thing you did, but in the overall scheme of a holiday, it wasn't something we'd reminisce about."

"Okay. Thanks, Mum."

I'm about to end the call but another of Edith Stimp's claims comes to mind.

"When was the last time you went to Hayling Island?"

"Let me think. Probably in October last year, although your dad said we might pop down there next weekend if the weather is nice."

"Has it changed much from when I was a kid?"

"Like you wouldn't believe. I'll dig out some old holiday photos and next time you come over, I'll show you."

"That'd be nice. Maybe I'll come down with you next weekend if that's okay?"

"Really?"

"Don't sound so surprised."

"It's just that you've never shown any interest before."

"I know, but ... it'd be nice to spend the day down there. Maybe we can have fish and chips on the beach."

"Now you're talking. I'd love that, Sweetheart."

"Alright. I'd better get on but don't forget to ask Dad."

"I won't."

I end the call and put my phone back on the desk. I could sit here all afternoon and try to think of anyone who might have told Edith Stimp about my childhood frugality, but it'd be pointless. As far as I know, and Mum remembers, only three people were party to those conversations.

How did Stimp know?

It doesn't take long to determine that there's no logical way she could know, and her explanation is anything but logical.

My stomach grumbles to remind me I haven't had lunch. Perhaps I'll think better once I've eaten.

I'm about to get up when there's a tap on my office door, and Janine breezes in.

"That report you asked for yesterday," she says, placing a folder on my desk. "Sorry it took longer than I anticipated. I was waiting on some figures from Justin."

"Um, sure. No worries."

Janine is about to turn and retrace her steps but she hesitates.

"Are you okay, Gary? You look very pale."

"I'm fine," I reply, gulping hard.

"Are you sure?"

"Yes."

For reasons I cannot explain, I'm unable to look my office manager in the eye.

"Why are you squirming in your chair, then?" she asks.

"Am I? I ... err, how are the boys?"

"Nice change of subject," she laughs. "They're both fine, thanks."

"Good. Good."

"So, are you going to tell me what's up?"

"Nothing's up."

As much as I want her to leave, Janine has an uncanny knack for knowing when I'm not being completely honest with her.

"Okay," she huffs. "You don't want to tell me. Fair enough."

"No, it's not that I don't want to tell you ... it's ... it's ..."

"Not unusual?" she says with a smirk.

I sit up and attempt to regain my composure. Where it went is anyone's guess.

"Can I ask you a question?"

"You can ask me anything, Gary. You know that."

"Right, yes ... um ..."

Pull yourself together, man.

"Apparently, there's a coffee shop by the station. Do you know it?"

"I know it very well because an old school friend runs it. Maria."

"Oh, I didn't know that."

"No reason you should, although I did work there briefly before I started here."

"I don't recall you mentioning it on your CV."

"It was only casual work, the odd few hours here and there. I was helping Maria out more than anything because she was having a few issues at home ... if you know what I mean."

"Yes, I know exactly what you mean."

"Why do you want to know about Maria's?" she then asks.

"Oh ... um, someone suggested it as a meeting point, and I just wondered if you knew it, that's all."

Janine fixes me with a look I can't quite decipher.

"Was there anything else?"

"Err, no. That's all. Thanks."

"You really are behaving oddly."

"I'm fine."

"Hmm, course you are."

She once again turns to leave but another question pops into my mind, and I might as well ask it while my sanity is in the spotlight.

"One more question, if I may."

"Go on."

"You might think it's a bit random, and it's not work-related, so tell me to mind my own business if you like."

"I will. Shoot."

"If you could do any job, irrespective of qualifications, what would you do?"

Janine ponders my question while my heart begins to beat a little faster. According to Edith Stimp, Janine Barker and Gary Kirk have already discussed this question, albeit in a different dimension.

"I wouldn't call it a job, as such, but I do daydream about running a little guest house or a B&B."

"No way," I inadvertently gasp. "That's not possible."

"Not on what I earn here," she laughs. "But a girl can dream."

"No ... I mean, it's ... where would be the ideal location for this guest house or B&B?"

"Ahh, that's easy. One of those quaint little fishing villages in Devon or Cornwall."

It's all I can do to stare up at Janine, open mouthed.

"Don't look so shocked," she responds. "It's not a dream I'm likely to fulfil any time soon, or ever I suspect."

"No, it's not that, it's ... have you ever told anyone else what you've just told me?"

"To be honest, I think you're the first person who's ever asked me what my dream job would be, so no."

"You're absolutely certain?"

She takes two steps towards my desk, her features hardening.

"What's going on, Gary? Am I about to be fired?"

"Hell, no," I cough. "You're ... you're irreplaceable."

"Oh. Right. That's nice to hear, but why the odd questions and, if you don't mind me saying, the even odder behaviour?"

I draw a deep breath in an attempt to silence the noise in my head.

"I'll explain another time, but rest assured, it's nothing for you to worry about."

"I don't suppose it has anything to do with, you know, the situation with Clare?"

I've never lied to Janine and I'm not about to start.

"In a way it is, but only loosely. I promise I will tell you, but for now, I need to eat something."

"Okay, but if you need to talk, you know I'm always happy to listen."

"I know, and I appreciate it."

Our eyes lock for a moment but I have to look away before my cheeks begin to burn,

"I'd better get on," Janine then announces. "I wouldn't want to risk losing my irreplaceable status."

She finally turns and walks back towards the door. I've watched her leave my office a thousand times before, but on this occasion, I'm struck by a savage yearning for her to stay.

"Jesus," I pant once she's left. "What's wrong with you, Kirk?"

It's a valid question, but in the scheme of questions that I simply can't answer, it's not worth the headspace. Something bloody strange is going on, and for the life of me, I can't work out what it is or why it's happening.

There are only three possibilities. One, I'm the subject of a scam so elaborate I can't even work out what the scammers are hoping to achieve. Two, I'm losing my mind. Or three ...

No, three isn't even a possibility.

No way.

Definitely not.

Chapter 43

Mentally exhausted, I fell asleep on the sofa last night. I woke up at 3.00 am, the TV still on and half a can of lager sitting on the floor beside me. I crawled up to bed, but sleep proved hard to find. After three hours of tossing and turning, I gave up and hopped in the shower.

Yesterday afternoon was a write-off in every way imaginable. As much as I tried to focus on my Clare-related problems and the minor task of running a business, the results of my brief but enlightening conversations with Mum and Janine dominated my thoughts.

By the end of the afternoon, I'd come to accept the paradox of my problem. The only way I could explain how Edith Stimp knew what she knew was to accept the impossible. I tested that theory while sipping lager on the sofa last night, and maybe the alcohol helped as I let my imagination run wild.

What if Edith Stimp's claim is true?

It's funny, but I managed to offset my perfectly rational scepticism by concentrating on one aspect of that claim, and it wasn't time-travel related. It was my feelings for Janine.

At one point, I opened a web browser on my phone and googled a question: *how do you tell if you're in love with someone?*

In hindsight, I blame the alcohol for my ill-judged search. And yet, despite feeling like a teenager after their first kiss at a youth club disco, I scoured several websites in search of an answer. Much of what I found was fairly vague, but then, I stumbled upon a website that suggested I imagine the person in question in an intimate scene with someone other than me. I then had to consider how that vision made me feel.

Hard as it was to admit, my overriding emotion was jealousy. And the more I thought about Janine being intimate with another man, the more my heart ached.

This morning, in the cold and sober light of day, my head is back in charge. However, now I've broken the seal, certain elements of Edith Stimp's fantasy are proving difficult to brush aside. In some respects, it's like the feeling I had as a child when I lost a tooth. Looking back, I think the prospect of waking up to find a shiny ten-pence piece beneath my pillow quelled my scepticism surrounding the existence of the Tooth Fairy. With the right incentive, you can convince a child to believe in almost anything, but I'm forty-five, for Christ's sake.

I want to believe that in some alternate reality, I met Janine Barker in a coffee shop, and we connected romantically. I want to believe that I could have next to nothing and still find happiness. I want to believe that, if they were being completely honest, my parents wouldn't wish for a bigger home and a few hundred grand in their savings account.

And yet, I also want to believe that I might secure a contract as a professional footballer or launch a singing career and sell out Wembley Stadium. But all the wanting and wishing and hoping and praying in the world won't change the fact that I'm far too old to play professional football, and I can't sing.

Neither will it change the fact that time travel is impossible.

I finish my cereal and carefully place the bowl in the dishwasher. I'm about to make another coffee when my phone rings. Glancing at the screen, the caller's name puts me in two minds about answering, but she won't go away. I accept the call.

"Morning," I say flatly.

"Can you talk?" Clare asks.

"I've got ten minutes before I need to leave. What's up?"

"I'm wondering why you still haven't instructed the estate agent to put the house on the market."

"Who says I haven't?"

"Well, have you?"

"No, not yet."

"Why not?"

"Because I've got a lot on my plate at the moment."

"Haven't we all, Gary," she snaps. "When are you going to do it?"

"I'll call the agent later today if I have time."

"Make time. I meant what I said about that house — if I lose it, I won't be so accommodating when it comes to splitting our marital assets."

"Yes, you've already made that clear, and I said I'll deal with it."

"Fine. Make sure you do."

"Or what?" I snort. "You'll send a couple of heavies around to beat me up?"

"I beg your pardon. Why on earth would you say that?"

I didn't mean to vocalise my flippant thought, not least because Clare isn't aware of the life she led in Edith Stimp's fairytale.

"Forget it."

"No, I won't forget it. Do you really think I'd be capable of such a horrible thing?"

"Not in this reality, but who knows what you'd do if we'd lived different lives."

"You're not making any sense."

"Just ignore me," I sigh. "I had a weird dream in which you became a multi-millionaire, and I was completely skint. After I asked you for money, you sent a couple of goons over to rough me up."

"That's interesting."

"Is it?"

"You know that dreams have a much deeper meaning than we understand, right?"

Now I really regret my flippancy.

"Yes, you've told me a hundred times."

"It's a shame you never listened, then. I think your dream was a warning."

"About what?"

"To stop fretting over money. You're so obsessed that the thought of me having even a modest amount is akin to a physical assault."

"That's an interesting take, but considering you're demanding almost six-hundred grand from me, that adds a layer of impartiality to your theory, wouldn't you say?"

"Perhaps, but that doesn't mean I'm wrong. And for the record, do you know why we've drifted apart over the years?"

"Different ambitions, different values."

"No, it's much deeper than that. For the last fifteen years, maybe more, you've plotted out your life with only three thoughts in your head: how do I make money, how do I protect that money, and when can I retire to spend some of that money? For you, life is about plotting and planning."

"One of us had to be financially responsible."

"I'm not having a dig, Gary. I'll be forever grateful for the years we had, and the creature comforts we enjoyed, but I do worry about you. At some point, you have to stop the planning and plotting, and start living. I want you to be happy ... more than anything."

Clare's sermon sounds suspiciously like one I heard yesterday, and she also happens to be one of the people featured in Edith Stimp's alleged evidence of time travel.

"Does the name Edith Stimp ring any bells with you?"

"No. Should it?"

"You tell me. You're one-hundred per cent certain you've never met her?"

"As certain as I can be."

"You wouldn't lie to me, would you, Clare?"

"I've never lied to you. I swear on my life I don't know who Edith Smith is."

"Stimp. Edith Stimp."

"Or Edith Stimp. Who is she, anyway?"

"Doesn't matter."

I notice the time and bring the conversation to an end, but not before Clare reminds me to call the estate agent later.

After downing a cup of coffee, I leave the house. The journey to work gives me time to reflect on the conversation with Clare and the emotional turbulence of the last twenty-four hours. Why does it feel like the universe is conspiring against me?

I get to work and head up to my office. What I need is to focus on what really matters, and that's my business. I begin with the report Janine gave me yesterday. I'd much rather focus on spreadsheets and pie charts than feelings and emotions.

Over the ensuing half hour, my team drift in one by one. There's a thrum of conversation coming from the main office, and I get up to close my office door. Only then do I notice that Janine isn't at her desk. It's unlike her to be late, and when she is running behind schedule, she usually calls or texts. I wander through to the main office.

"Has anyone seen Janine?" I ask.

"She's probably stuck in traffic," Alice replies. "There's something going on near the town centre."

"Something?"

"Not sure, but they've closed off several roads in that part of town, and there are police cars and fire engines everywhere. My other half just messaged me to say he was almost run off the road by an ambulance ten minutes ago, so whatever it is, it must be serious."

An icy chill runs across my shoulders. The school Felix and Louis both attend isn't far from the town centre.

"Does anyone have any more details?" I ask.

My question is met by much head shaking and shoulder shrugging. I hurry back to my office and call Janine's number. It goes straight to voicemail.

I sit down and ease the panic by reminding myself that Janine is only five minutes late. If the traffic is bad, that's almost certainly the reason. I return my attention to the report, hoping it'll be a distraction, but being that Janine created it, I can hear her voice in every word and every digit.

Minutes tick by until I give up and toss the report back on my desk. I then check the time again: 9.14 am.

"Where are you?" I whisper, getting to my feet and stepping over to the window.

I don't consider myself a pessimist, so it comes as a surprise when my mind decides it wants to conjure up all manner of awful scenarios. The worst is a twisted reversal of Janine's fate in Edith Stimp's supposed alternate reality. In that, Felix died in a road accident, but what if Janine dropped the kids at school, and then the unthinkable happened to her? The thought of those boys losing their mum is almost too painful to consider.

"God, I'm so sorry, Gary."

I spin around.

"Where the hell have you been?" I blast. "You should have called me."

Janine stands silently in front of my desk, the shock of being confronted by my outburst etched across her face.

"Sorry ... I'm sorry," I splutter. "I didn't mean to snap. I was ... I was worried, that's all."

I step slowly towards my desk and flop down in the chair.

"Are you okay, Gary?"

"I'm fine, now that I know you're safe."

"I'm so sorry, I didn't mean to worry you. I would have called, but I forgot to turn my phone on before I left the house and ..."

"It's fine," I interject calmly, which is no mean feat considering my nerves are shredded. "As long as you're okay, that's all that matters."

"I appreciate that, and I'll work through my lunch break to make up for being late."

"No, you will not."

"I don't mind."

"I'm sure you don't, but I'm the boss, and I'm telling you to take your full lunch break."

"Yes, Boss," Janine replies with a semi-smile. "As you say."

As the relief takes hold, I sit back and try to move the conversation away from my ridiculous outburst.

"Alice said something happened near the town centre. I presume that's why the traffic was bad?"

"Bad? It's near gridlock."

"Do you know why?"

"A policeman wandered past while I was stuck in traffic, and I managed to ask him what was going on. He said a building caught fire just after four this morning, and they closed the nearby roads as a precaution."

"Will you need to leave early to pick the boys up?"

"I don't want to take liberties."

"You're not. Keep an eye on the situation, and if there's still a problem with traffic, then leave early."

"Okay, thanks, but fingers crossed they have it sorted by then. In the meantime, shall I grab us both a coffee before we go through the morning meeting?"

"Err, you grab one, but I'm okay … and let's skip the meeting today unless there's anything critical I need to know about."

"I don't think so, no."

I let Janine get on with her work, and with the drama over, I try to do mine. I sit and stare at the computer monitor, but my usual levels of motivation are non-existent. I want to blame Clare and our conversation this morning, but for the first time since she made her demand, I can't seem to muster any resentment. What's wrong with me?

I know the answer, and it's not Clare or even Janine. The reason I'm so discombobulated is Edith Stimp. She's the one who filled my head with nonsense, and now those thoughts are in there, I can't seem to shake them loose. It's almost as if I've been brainwashed.

Maybe I need a break. A long weekend away from it all, where I can recharge my batteries and get my head back in the game. It's times like this that I wish I played golf or understood angling. It's a pity I've never owned a fishing rod, and the last time I swung a putter was as a kid, playing crazy golf at the seaside.

Come to think of it, what do I enjoy when I'm not sitting at this desk?

Before I've time to consider that question, the phone rings with an internal call.

"Yes?"

"Boss, it's Mo. Sorry to be a pain, but could you cover the showroom for an hour? I've got a couple here asking to go on a test drive, and Justin is already out with a customer."

As much as we'd prefer customers to book a test drive in advance, there will always be those who drop in without an appointment.

"I'll come straight down."

Glad of the distraction, I hurry downstairs. Mo is already waiting by the exit with his customers and acknowledges me with a wave before ushering them outside. Within seconds, one of the showroom phones starts ringing. I stride over to the desk, sit down, and answer it.

"Good morning, Kirkwood Motors sales department."

The call turns out to be no different to the thousands I've received over the entirety of my career in car sales. I go through the motions, knowing I'm on the phone with a tyre kicker. He says he'll pop down next week to have a look at a VW Golf, but I'd bet my last fiver he won't.

I'm about to grab a coffee from the machine when the showroom door swings open, and a guy in his thirties rushes towards my desk.

"Is Mo around?" he asks, slightly out of breath.

"He's out with a customer at the moment. Can I help?"

"My name is Lewis Cain, and I had a test drive booked for ten o'clock."

Instinctively, I glance at the clock on the wall behind Mr Cain. He's forty minutes late.

"My apologies, but Mo probably thought you'd forgotten. Unfortunately, one-fifth of all customers who make an appointment fail to show up."

"Yeah, I get it, but I'm not a time waster. I got held up at work, and we're not allowed to make calls when we're on duty otherwise I'd have called."

"It's not a problem. What car did you want to test drive?"

"A 2018 BMW 3-Series. The metallic-grey one."

"Let me just check the stock list. Grab a seat, Mr Cain."

I turn to Mo's monitor and filter the stock by the manufacturer. We've got four BMW 3-Series in stock, but only one of them is metallic-grey. I pull up the details and confirm with the customer it's the car he wants to test drive.

"That's the one."

"We can still arrange a test drive, but would you mind waiting around for ten minutes as both the sales staff are out with other customers?"

"Sure."

"I was about to grab a coffee. Can I get you one?"

"I'd kill for a coffee," Mr Cain replies. "I've just come off a long night shift."

"I'll make it a large one. Milk and sugar?"

"Two sugars and milk, please."

I step over to the coffee machine and grab a couple of mugs.

"What is it you do for a living?" I ask, just to make small talk.

"I'm a firefighter."

"Oh, wow. No wonder you need caffeine, I heard about the fire in the town centre."

"Not the usual quiet night I was hoping for."

"Was it a bad one?"

"Suspected gas explosion. The building was half gone by the time we got there."

"Nasty," I grimace. "I suppose the only saving grace was that it happened in the early hours of the morning when everyone was safely tucked up in bed."

"True, and the fact it was an old warehouse. If it had been a block of flats ... doesn't bear thinking about."

I take the coffee mugs to the desk and place one down in front of the weary firefighter.

"Thanks."

"I think you've earned it," I reply with a smile. "And probably a few pints, too."

"The beers will have to wait until tomorrow. I'm back on shift at ten, and as soon as I'm done here, I'm off home to bed. I'm absolutely knackered."

"Listen, I wouldn't normally do this, but if you want to come back at the weekend, I'll hold the car for you. No obligation."

"That's kind of you, but I need to sort out a car sooner rather than later. It's just my luck we had to tend a fire in Elderton's most inaccessible building. I must have walked ten miles last night ... over bloody cobbles, too."

I'm about to take a sip of coffee, but the mug doesn't reach my lips.

"Cobbles?"

"The building was right at the end of this cobbled alleyway. No other way in or out."

"It wasn't Dent's Passage?"

"It was, actually. I've lived in Elderton for a decade, and I didn't even know it existed."

My blood runs cold. I walked up and down that alleyway only yesterday, and I'm almost certain it only provided access to one building — Edith Stimp's.

"Were there ... do you know if there were any casualties?"

"Even if there were casualties, we're not allowed to discuss that until there's an official public announcement. I'm sure you can appreciate why."

"How can I find out?"

"Same as everyone else. Listen to local radio or keep an eye on the Elderton Herald website. They both had reporters there, getting in the way and hassling the crew."

I'm still trying to process Lewis Cain's revelation when Justin saunters back into the showroom. As he's alone, it's obvious the test drive didn't result in a sale, as the customer would be trailing behind.

"Justin," I call over. "Here, please."

I turn to the firefighter.

"I need to pass you over to Justin. He'll look after you."

After confirming with my colleague that I'll be back shortly, and apologising to Mr Cain, I race up to my office and frantically search my desk drawer for a business card. I only dropped it in the drawer last week, so it can't have gone far.

Finally, I unearth the card. It belongs to the Elderton Herald reporter, Kate Palfrey, who interviewed me last week.

I call her mobile.

Chapter 44

As I wait for Kate Palfrey to answer my call, I consider the chances of the building Lewis Cain and his colleagues tended this morning belonging to anyone other than Edith Stimp. It seems unlikely, but what's more troubling is that Edith seemed so certain she didn't have long to live. That much was obvious just by looking at her, but she also said that she knew her own fate, and yesterday was my one and only opportunity to view her alleged time travel device.

Did she orchestrate the explosion to end her own life? If so, why go to such lengths when she could have swallowed a bottle of sleeping pills?

Kate Palfrey finally answers my call by announcing her name.

"Hi, Kate. This is Gary Kirk from Kirkwood Motors. We met last week when you interviewed me for the Elderton Business Awards."

"Oh, yes. Hi Gary."

"I'm actually calling on an unrelated matter — the explosion and fire near the High Street this morning. I presume you're aware of it?"

"It's the talk of the office this morning, not least because half the team were late for work due to the traffic."

"Were you one of the reporters at the scene? I spoke to a firefighter and he said someone from the Elderton Herald was there."

"No, it was my colleague, Andrew."

"I don't suppose I could have a word with him, could I?"

"I'll see if he's around, but can I ask: what's your angle?"

"My angle?"

"I'm curious why you're interested in the fire."

"Um, I met with someone in that very building yesterday, assuming it was the same building."

"Right. And?"

"I just want to know if she's okay. The firefighter wouldn't say if there were any casualties, but he did say that the local press and radio would be the first to know once the authorities release the information."

"I see. I'll check where Andrew is and ask him to call you."

"Can you stress the urgency, please?"

"I understand. Leave it with me, Gary."

I give Kate both my direct office line and mobile number, and she assures me Andrew will call as soon as possible.

With no concept of what as soon as possible means, I end the call and try to keep busy by browsing potential stock on a supplier's website. As I scroll down the screen, I can't stop thinking about Edith Stimp and what it means if she did indeed take her own life. It would be incredibly sad, but why should it matter if a woman I barely know decides to blow up her own building while she's still in it?

Perhaps it's because I can't sate my curiosity.

Why would a woman at the tail end of her life bother concocting such a ludicrous story? Did she have psychological problems? Her method of suicide, if indeed that's what happened, would suggest so, but why the charade with me? I don't believe her preposterous story for one second, but now there's a chance the author of that story is no more, I'll never know her motivation for telling it. That now irks, perhaps more than it should.

My mobile phone rings. I snatch it up from the desk.

"Gary Kirk."

"Afternoon, Gary. This is Andrew Grant from the Elderton Herald."

"Hi, Andrew. Thanks for getting back to me so promptly."

"No problem. Kate tells me you were enquiring about the incident in the town centre this morning."

"That's right. I was hoping someone at the Herald might be able to tell me if there were any casualties in the fire."

"May I ask why you want to know?"

"I had a brief meeting in that building yesterday, and although I barely knew the woman I met ... in fact, I wouldn't even go as far as to say we're acquaintances, I would like to know if she's okay."

"I honestly can't say for certain, Gary, but shortly after I arrived, so too did a crime scene investigator from Winchester. The only reason the fire service or the police call in an investigator is if they find a body."

"Oh."

"I'm sorry."

"It's, err, fine. As I said, I barely know ... knew her."

Which is why I'm surprised I have to swallow back the lump in my throat.

"We should know for certain within the next day or two," Andrew confirms.

"Understood."

"Can I ask what the nature of your visit was?"

"It was nothing, really. A brief chat about my impending divorce."

"Been there, done that, still got the scars," Andrew scoffs. "I wouldn't wish it on my worst enemy."

"No, but I've got a feeling mine might be resolved sooner than I anticipated."

"Good for you. Was that as a result of your visit?"

"Yes, and no. It's complicated."

"Ironically, so too is the history of the building you visited. I've spent all morning trying to find out who owns it, but I've drawn a blank. I don't suppose you could shed any light on it for me?"

"A woman by the name of Edith Stimp owns it. Or, at least, she did."

"That much I established, but the Land Registry record is woefully out of date, to such an extent that the building isn't even registered with Elderton Council's rates department. My contact there didn't even know it existed."

"How can they not know a building exists?"

"From what little research I've had time to conduct, that warehouse was originally an outbuilding on the grounds of the former Manor House. If you know your Elderton history, the Manor House was destroyed in the early 1900s, and the town centre slowly evolved over the ensuing decades. At some point, the building in question must have been separated from the deeds of the Manor House, which is why there's a Land Registry record, but the council patently didn't update their records. It was a long time ago, obviously before digital records."

"That makes sense, I guess."

"But what doesn't make sense, Gary, is who owns it now. That's what I'm trying to ascertain."

"As I said, Edith Stimp. She happened to mention owning the building when I first walked through the door yesterday."

"I'm sorry? You met Edith Stimp?"

I'm beginning to realise why Andrew is a reporter at the Elderton Herald, rather than one of the national newspapers.

"Yes, I met her," I reply flatly, trying not to let my frustration boil over.

"And how old was this Edith Stimp you met?"

"She never said, and I never asked."

"Can you hazard a guess?"

"Hard to say because she looked so ill, but if I had to, I'd guess she was in her early to mid-fifties."

"Well, whoever you met, Gary, it wasn't Edith Stimp."

"What? How do you know?"

There's a moment's silence before another question comes.

"Have you got an email address? I'd like to send you something quickly."

I quote my email address and then hear a couple of mouse clicks followed by the distinctive sound of an email departing.

"Sent," Andrew confirms. "Can you check your inbox?"

I refresh the page, and almost immediately, a new email arrives. Besides Andrew's full name, job title, and contact details, the email itself is blank, but there is a photo attached. I double-click it.

"The attachment is just loading up," I confirm.

Due to the size, it takes a moment for my computer to open it up. The image is not a digital photo in the literal sense but a scan of a printed photo. That much is obvious because of the resolution, and I can just make out a white border running along the bottom of the image. However, my surprise isn't down to the age of the photo, but the couple the photographer captured.

"Has it loaded?" Andrew asks.

"Uh-huh," I mumble, still preoccupied with the image on my monitor.

"*That* is Edith Stimp," Andrew declares. "And her husband, Allan."

"I wouldn't recognise Allan Stimp if I passed him in the street, but the woman in the photo is definitely Edith Stimp, albeit in much better health than the last time I saw her in person."

"That's the woman you met yesterday?"

"Yes."

"I don't think so, Gary."

"I beg your pardon. Are you calling me a liar?"

"No, I wouldn't go that far because I don't know you. I do know, however, that the photo you're looking at is from the Herald archive, and it was taken in 1968 when Allan and Edith Stimp organised a dance at the Elderton Town Hall to celebrate their thirtieth wedding anniversary. They were both fifty-two in that photo, and four years later, Allan Stimp acquired the building in Dent's Passage. He died in 1974, and if Edith were still alive, which seems highly unlikely, she would be one-hundred-and-seven years of age."

EIGHT WEEKS LATER...

Chapter 45

I like the month of June, particularly the promise of long evenings in the beer garden of my favourite pub, walks on a beach at sunset, and the general air of sunshine-induced positivity.

What I don't like is daybreak occurring at such an ungodly hour. Getting out of bed at 4.00 am is unnatural, but needs must. What I'm about to do is possibly illegal, I think, and therefore I need the cover of darkness.

I set off, safe in the knowledge that the sun won't breach the horizon for another twenty-eight minutes. I'm heading to the rural village of Kingshot, just a couple of miles south of Elderton. It'll be my second visit in the last week, although the first was at a more civilised hour.

If there's any silver lining to my early start, it's the complete lack of traffic. It's just me, the empty roads, and the nondescript cardboard box resting in the passenger's seat next to me. The box, or more specifically, the content of the box, is the reason for my journey.

I take a left turn into the narrow country lane that leads all the way to Kingshot. It's just over a mile long, but I can't see any further ahead than the beam of my headlights as it follows the winding curves of the lane.

As I reach the final hundred yards, the lane widens slightly, and I pass a road sign confirming where I am. There really isn't much in Kingshot: a pub, a small grocery store, a village hall, and St Mark's Church. At this hour, there's not a soul around, which is why I'm here at this hour.

I slow down and pull into the same layby I parked in on my last visit. With my heart beating a little faster than I expected, I turn off the engine and, with it, the car's headlights. It's as dark as it is silent, and I remain in my seat for a few minutes just to be sure I'm not being watched by the odd insomniac at a bedroom window.

Satisfied that the residents of Kingshot are all still tucked up in their beds, I get out of the car and gently shut the door. I specifically wore trainers to avoid the sound of footsteps, and I'm pleased I did as I move silently around the car to the passenger's door and open it.

Besides the cardboard box on the seat, there's a holdall in the foot well. It contains all I need to complete my pre-dawn mission. I quietly unzip it and place the box inside. All set, I close the car door and make my way along the verge towards my ultimate destination.

It could be argued that darkness is darkness, but the reason I chose pre-dawn darkness over the post-dusk alternative is deeply rooted in the human psyche — we fear graveyards at night.

I reach the church lychgate, but I know from my previous visit that they're likely locked. As a security precaution, the padlock is pointless because the flint and stone walls on either side of the lychgate are low enough that I'm able to climb over with minimal effort.

Once I'm within the church grounds, I retrieve a torch from the holdall and switch it on. I purchased it from Amazon specifically for two features. Firstly, I can set the luminosity to a low glow that just about highlights the path, but it's not so bright it'll draw attention should anyone pass by. Secondly, there's a panel on the side that provides the same kind of ambient light as a lamp.

I follow the path down the right-hand flank of the church. As I turn the corner, I look up towards the three huge oak trees standing like sentinels at the far end of the church grounds. If I'd arrived twenty minutes ago, I wouldn't have seen the trees against the ink-black sky, but that sky is now tinged with the slightest smudge of daylight. Any minute now, the first chirps of the dawn chorus will break the silence. Of that, I'm glad.

At the rear of the church, there's a stout wooden door beneath a decorative lintel. I paid particular attention to it on my last visit because it's almost directly in line with a specific gravestone. I turn ninety degrees to my right and take twenty paces forward, coming to a stop by a headstone that's no more than a silhouette until I point the torch at it. The beam highlights a name engraved in the weathered stone: Allan Thomas Stimp.

After glancing over both shoulders to confirm I'm still alone, I place the holdall down on the dewy grass and flick a switch on the torch to turn on the lamp. The change in light illuminates the entire grave, including the cube of stone with an inset rose bowl positioned a couple of feet from the headstone. On my previous visit, I ascertained all that was keeping it in place was its sheer weight and the bed of soft soil beneath it.

I squat down and place both hands on the block of stone. The moss-covered surfaces make handling it difficult, but I eventually relocate it to a temporary home next to the headstone. I then remove two items from the holdall: the cardboard box and a gardening trowel.

Carefully and quietly, I use the trowel to dig a hole in the patch of soil previously occupied by the stone block.

As I'm not planting a rosebush or a geranium, the depth of the hole isn't important. Time is important, though, so I put the trowel down after five minutes of digging. At roughly eight inches across and ten inches deep, the hole looks big enough.

I open the cardboard box and remove a drum-shaped wooden container slightly smaller than the hole I just created. Inside are the ashes of a woman who sacrificed her dying wish to help a stranger, all in the name of love. The least I can do is return the favour and ensure Edith Stimp spends the rest of eternity close to the man she loved.

I gently lower the wooden container into the hole and then use the trowel to tightly pack the excavated soil around it. That done, I manhandle the stone block back to its original position, return the trowel and the empty cardboard box to the holdall, and stand up.

"Godspeed, Edith," I whisper.

With my task complete, I have no need to hurry. Should anyone wander into the church grounds at this early hour, all they'd find is a middle-aged man standing over a grave, head bowed in silent reflection. It's unlikely they'd think twice about the holdall at his feet, and if they were to casually enquire as to the man's motives for being in Kingshot graveyard at daybreak, they certainly wouldn't hear a truthful answer. Even if I felt like telling a stranger the truth, who'd believe me?

Eight weeks ago, I didn't believe me.

After my conversation with Andrew Grant at the Elderton Herald, I spent the rest of the day holed up in my office, staring at the photo of Edith and Allan Stimp. I couldn't say how many hours I spent at my desk or how many times I told myself that there had to be an alternative explanation. All I know is that at some point, I printed off a copy of the photo and left. Fortuitously, I had the weekend to process what I couldn't comprehend during those hours in my office — everything Edith Stimp told me was true.

Despite questioning my own sanity on more than one occasion, acceptance gradually became a comforting place to reside. Everything suddenly made sense, although I still had more questions than answers. I did manage to find some of those answers in subsequent conversations with Andrew Grant, the first of which occurred on Monday afternoon when he confirmed the highlights of the Herald's update on the explosion and fire at a building in Dent's Passage.

The authorities confirmed a body had been found in the charred debris of the property but, due to the intensity of the fire, identifying the victim would take time.

As it transpired, the authorities weren't able to identify the victim via dental records or DNA. All they were able to confirm was the sex and approximate age: a female between fifty and sixty years of age. Not that anyone would have had reason to ask, but she definitely wasn't one hundred and seven years of age.

With no means of identifying the victim and all protocols to locate family members completed, the local authority arranged for Jane Doe to be cremated. At that point, I contacted the crematorium and said that although I had no proof, I suspected that Jane Doe was an old acquaintance by the name of Edith. I could hardly tell them the truth, but I didn't need to. A disinterested administrator said I was welcome to take the ashes away after the cremation.

Two days before my appointment at the crematorium, Andrew Grant called me. By that point, I'd backtracked on my original assertion that the woman in the photo was the same woman I'd met at Dent's Passage. However, being that one of Elderton's oldest buildings had been destroyed by fire, Andrew wanted to write a piece about its history. Some of that history related to Allan and Edith Stimp, and Andrew agreed to share his research with me in return for a discount on a VW Polo for his daughter.

The research was worth every penny of the thousand pounds it cost me.

Allan Stimp and Edith Matthews were both born in 1916. It's impossible to say, but it's likely they first met at the Government's scientific and military research centre at Porton Down, Wiltshire. Both in their early twenties, Allan was employed as a lab assistant and Edith as a secretary. Whilst no one can say for sure how they met, it's on public record that the couple married in April 1938 at St Mark's Church, Kingshot.

After they married, information on Allan's career petered out within five years. It seems likely that he transferred to another of the Government's research centres, but it's also likely that his employment was not made public due to the small matter of the UK being heavily involved in the Second World War.

With no record relating to either Allan or Edith, a significant gap in their history continued up until 1972, when Allan's name appeared on the deeds to a building in Dent's Passage, Elderton. Sadly, he died two years later, aged fifty-eight, and ownership of the building transferred to his widow.

According to Andrew, the last record on any database relating to Edith Stimp stretched back to 1975. A woman by the name of Barbara Hurst filed a missing person's report at Elderton Police Station on the fourteenth of June that year. Edith Stimp was due to meet Barbara Hurst for their weekly afternoon tea, but she failed to show up. Mrs Hurst tried contacting her friend by telephone and eventually letter, but after three weeks without so much as a word, she became worried enough to inform the police.

That missing person's report remains open to this day, although Andrew theorised that Edith Stimp likely emigrated, which is why there's no record of her death on any official UK database.

Although I never shared my thoughts with Andrew, I, too, concluded that Edith went travelling in 1975. I know she never travelled abroad, but beyond her arrival in my time and my life, everything else about Edith Stimp will remain a matter of conjecture. I can, however, make an educated guess about her final act — destroying her husband's creation.

I'll never know, but I think I demonstrated that society is still light-years away from being responsible enough to tinker with time. Edith gave me the ultimate gift — a chance to use my knowledge of the future to influence the past — and I squandered that opportunity. Given that opportunity again and knowing what I know now, I would still write that letter to my younger self, but the instructions would differ. I'd tell the young Gary Kirk that the richest people he will ever know are his parents, because no amount of money will ever buy what they have.

As the first sunbeams break through the lower branches of the oaks, I reach down and pick up the holdall. There's only one thing left to be said before I leave Edith and Allan to rest.

"Thank you," I say quietly. "I won't make the same mistakes again."

Chapter 46

I'm hungry but it's only just gone six. Too early for breakfast?

Who cares?

As it's a Saturday morning, I decide to spoil myself with a bacon sandwich. I line up a row of rashers on the wire rack and slide it under the grill. While I wait for the bacon to cook, I lean up against the worktop and run through the day's to-do list. Close to the top is a task that's been on the list for the last three days and is likely to remain on the list for a few more: packing.

Shortly after the events at Dent's Passage I put the house up for sale. The estate agent said the market was buoyant, and he wasn't exaggerating. Seventeen prospective buyers descended within the first few days, and we received an asking price offer soon after. The conveyancing process then moved at a surprising pace, and we exchanged contracts three days ago, with the completion date set for next Friday.

It is the end of an era, but I don't feel the sense of loss that I feared I might. Maybe it's because this place has never felt like home. In fact, I'll soon be heading back to the only true home I've ever known once the removal men transfer my worldly goods to a storage container on Friday. Mum and Dad were a bit taken aback when I asked if I could stay with them, but when I explained that it would only be temporary, they quickly warmed to the idea — maybe they were hesitant because they'll have to suspend "afternoon delight" for a few weeks. They did enquire about my long-term plans, but at the time, I wasn't sure. I'm still not, but I'll have a better idea by lunchtime today.

The aroma of crisping bacon draws me back to the present, and I flip the rashers over before placing the tray back under the grill.

With a few minutes to kill, I sort through a pile of letters I've not had a chance to file away yet. Even in this age of email and digital communication, selling a property still involves an absurd amount of paperwork. There's also the matter of a divorce, and that, too, has involved no small amount of forms and letters. The most recent of those letters arrived yesterday.

I've never had reason to research the finer details of dissolving a marriage, and naively, I thought the *decree nisi* was the official end of our marriage. It isn't, and we have to wait six weeks before the court issues a *decree absolute*. It's academic, really, as Clare and I have already sorted what needs to be sorted, and she'll be picking up the keys to her new property the same day we hand over the keys to this place.

My nearly ex-wife dropped by yesterday to pack the last of her things, and although we talked about the past and happier times in our marriage, we talked more about the future. Clare was almost beside herself with excitement when the conversation turned to her new venture. While she was sharing her plans for the old building, it struck me that I was married to someone who understood the difference between fulfilment and finance. She's never made much money from her passion, and I doubt she ever will, but to Clare, that's never been important.

We parted with a long hug and a few tears. Most importantly, though, we parted as friends. I even agreed to attend one of her workshops when the new Shamanic centre opens later this year. I think it's fair to say that these days, I'm a bit more open-minded about the unknown mysteries of the universe.

For now, though, I'm more interested in the known deliciousness of a crispy bacon sandwich.

Once breakfast is out of the way, I steel myself for the first packing task of the day and definitely the worst on my list — the garage. For eighteen long years, we've used the garage to store everything we don't really need or want but can't quite force ourselves to throw out. In some way, it's a metaphor for our marriage. I put that off for too long and paid a heavy price, and now I'm about to pay a physical price for the same flawed mindset.

Three hours later, I'm hot, sweaty, and caked in dust, but the reward is a sense of satisfaction. I've whittled down the entire contents of the garage to three piles: a pile of junk I'll take to the tip tomorrow, a collection of boxes and items that a charity would benefit from, and the smallest pile containing a handful of items I want to keep.

Realising I've less time than I estimated, I lock the garage and hurry upstairs to grab a much-needed shower. Sorting the garage was as much about a distraction as it was a necessity before Friday because I'm expecting a visitor at eleven. One way or another, what happens when she arrives will dictate the trajectory of my life from this day onwards. The enormity of it is petrifying, but I can't avoid it. The time for avoidance is over.

Fresh from the shower, I get dressed and glance out of the bedroom window towards the cul-de-sac beyond. It's not quite eleven o'clock yet, but like a kid on Christmas Eve waiting for Santa, I'm full of nervous excitement about my visitor. The excitement, however, doesn't guarantee I'll avoid disappointment, so it's tinged with anxiety.

A Ford Focus comes into view and parks on the driveway next to my car. I pull a deep breath and head down to the hallway.

When I open the front door, my heart skips a beat. Janine has dressed appropriately for the hot weather, and the sight of her in denim shorts and a vest top only doubles the doubts lingering at the back of my mind.

"Hey," she says.

"Morning."

I stand aside and wave her in.

"Go through to the kitchen," I say, forgetting that Janine doesn't know where the kitchen is. "Sorry, this way."

I scuttle across the hallway towards the kitchen door, my nerves jangling with every step.

"Can I get you a drink?" I ask as Janine steps through the doorway.

"A soft drink would be great, thanks."

"Orange juice?"

"Perfect."

"Grab a seat."

Janine hops onto a stool at the breakfast bar while I pour our drinks.

"What are the boys up to this morning?" I ask.

"My parents have taken them to Marwell Zoo."

"Oh, cool. So, you've got the day to yourself, then?"

"I have, although how I spend it depends on why you've summoned me here."

I carry the glasses of juice over to the breakfast bar and take a seat opposite Janine. I can tell by both her body language and a pained smile that she's concerned. Maybe she has every right to be.

"Summoned is a strong word," I remark nervously. "I just wanted a chat away from the office."

"Have you invited anyone else over for a chat?"

"No."

"Just me, then?"

"Yep."

I take a sip of juice purely to lubricate my dry mouth.

"So, Gary. What's the matter?"

"What makes you think anything is the matter?"

"A number of reasons, not least the weird way you've been acting around me for the last month."

"I don't think I've been acting weird."

"Maybe weird isn't the right word. Distant. Standoffish, even."

"Have I?"

"Yes."

"I'm sorry."

"I wasn't after an apology," she replies with a heavy sigh. "I know you've got a lot on your plate at the moment, what with the divorce and the house sale. I'm just disappointed that you obviously felt like you couldn't confide in me."

"I know, and again, I'm sorry. There was a reason I didn't want to confide in you, though."

"Are you going to tell me?"

"That's why I asked you here. It's complicated and not a conversation for the office."

I've planned this part of the conversation a thousand times, and I thought I knew exactly what I wanted to say, but those well-crafted words are now proving elusive.

"I might as well just spit it out — I'm selling Kirkwood Motors."

"Oh."

Not the reaction I expected, but then I didn't deliver the news in quite the way I expected.

"I didn't even realise it was up for sale," Janine adds.

"It's not. I mean, it wasn't."

"I'm confused."

"Long story short, you know I met with Adrian a few months back? Well, I floated the idea that I intended to sell up in two or three years' time, and I needed some ballpark numbers to work with. Anyway, a few weeks later, he happened to hear from a business acquaintance that Honda are actively looking to open a franchise in Elderton, and they were searching for a suitable site. One thing led to another, and I met with their representatives a fortnight ago. We've since agreed a deal in principle."

"Right."

If Janine looked concerned before my revelation, she now looks positively sick.

"You're concerned about your job?" I remark, stating the obvious.

"Yes, unless you're about to tell me I've no reason to be concerned?"

"No, I'm not. They've already confirmed they'll be keeping most of the staff, but they've got an office manager transferring in from another branch. I'm sorry, but I've no option but to make you redundant."

She stares back at me and opens her mouth to say something, but no words follow. In a twisted way, I'm glad because I feared that, at this point, Janine might hurl a few choice expletives my way and storm out.

"That's only part of why I asked you here, though," I quickly add. "The rest of it is more positive ... possibly ... hopefully."

"Go on," she gulps.

Telling Janine she'll be canned from a job she loves was never going to be easy. What I'm about to tell her now, though, is on a whole different level of not easy.

"I have another opportunity I want to discuss with you."

"What opportunity?"

I pull out my phone and, after double-checking that the right photo is displayed on the screen, I place it on the breakfast bar in front of Janine. She takes a glance at the photo and looks up at me with understandable confusion.

"It's a house," she says flatly.

"Technically, yes, but it's actually a business."

She takes a second, longer glance at the photo.

"It's a guest house in Milford on Sea," I continue. "I've got an appointment to view it this afternoon."

"Milford on Sea?"

"I know it's not Cornwall or Devon or even Dorset, but it's a lovely little coastal village less than fifty minutes from Elderton."

"I kind of know where it is, Gary, but I'm struggling to understand why you're showing me the photo of a random guest house or why I need to know you're viewing it this afternoon."

I adjust my position on the stool, so I'm facing Janine.

"Because I want you to manage it."

Her expression immediately shifts from angsty confusion to plain confusion.

"Me?"

"Yes."

"You want me to manage a guest house for you?"

"Not *for* me. *With* me."

For a third time, and without responding to my statement, Janine stares down at the photo. I wonder if it's merely to avoid looking at me, but just in case it isn't, now is the moment to drop the final bombshell.

"I have something I need to tell you, and once I've said it, there's no going back. It's something I should have said to you a long time ago, but ... but I chose to bury my head in the sand and ... and ..."

Janine looks up from the phone.

"Just spit it out, Gary," she says.

I manage a nod, and after another quick sip of orange juice, I go for it.

"I fell in love with you the moment you first breezed into my life, and every day since I've fallen a little bit more in love with you. I have no idea if you feel the same or ever could, but I had to take a chance because ... because I don't want to waste another minute of my life not knowing how wonderful it might be if you ... if we ..."

"Gary. Stop!"

My mouth agape, I stare back at Janine. She, in turn, closes her eyes and bites hard on her bottom lip. This is not a good sign.

"I'm sorry," I mumble. "I should never have said anything."

There's no reaction, and the longest seconds pass. With every one of them, my heart sinks a little lower. I don't know what to do, what to say.

Finally, she opens her eyes and a fat tear rolls down her cheek.

"I didn't mean to upset you," I splutter. "I'm so sorry ... I should have kept my mouth shut."

Still biting her lip, Janine shakes her head.

"I hate you, Gary Kirk," she then cries. "I bloody hate you."

It's my turn to adopt a confused frown.

"Um, okay."

Janine uses the palm of her hand to wipe the tear from her cheek, and then she fixes me with a look I can't decipher.

"Time to go," she says before climbing off the stool.

That's it. I've blown it.

"I'll see you to the door," I reply, unsure what else to say.

Devastated, I clamber off the stool as Janine takes a few steps towards the hallway. She then stops and turns around. There's no longer a tear in her eye — there is, however, a slight glint.

"I meant, it's time for *us* to go," she says, the faintest trace of a smile on her lips.

"Us? Go where?"

"Didn't you book an appointment in Milford on Sea?"

"Err, yes."

"Then what are we waiting for? Let's get going."

"Wait. Does that mean …"

I don't get to finish my question, nor do I receive an answer as Janine bolts forward and flings her arms around me.

"I love you too, Gary Kirk," she whispers in my ear. "But I also hate you for waiting so long to tell me. I'd almost given up hope."

In the same kitchen that hosted so many dishwasher-related arguments with Clare, I get to experience the greatest moment of my life as Janine pulls me into a slow kiss. Time seems to stand still, but if anyone knows that it's just an illusion, it's me.

We eventually come up for air.

"I don't know what to say," Janine says. "I'm … I've been waiting for this moment for the best part of four years."

"Four years?" I cough. "You've had feelings for me that long?"

"Yes, but in fairness, I have tried to keep them to myself."

"Why?"

"Besides the fact you're my boss, you're married."

"I'll be neither for much longer, remember."

"In which case, you're now the right man at the right time."

"You've no idea how happy that makes me."

"And, thank you."

"For?"

"For being brave enough to tell me how you feel, and I do appreciate it was an all-or-nothing gamble. I might have said I didn't feel the same."

"That had crossed my mind, but I had to know."

"And what would you have done if I had said I didn't feel the same?"

"I'd probably have spent the rest of my life a sad and lonely man."

"Really? You wouldn't have tried to find someone else to settle down with?"

"In lieu of you?" I smile. "Never."

THE END

Before You Go...

Thank you so much for reading *In Lieu of You* – if you've got this far, hopefully you enjoyed the story. If you did, I'd be eternally grateful if you could post a (hopefully positive) review on Amazon, or even a nice five-star rating. Positive reviews and ratings are the only way independently published books like mine can compete with those from the big publishing houses.

Acknowledgements

First and foremost, I'd like to thank you for reading this novel. Without my small but loyal band of readers, I wouldn't be able to write full-time, so I owe you all for my career. I'd also like to thank my team of beta readers: Lisa Gresty, Tracy Fisher, Alan Wood, and Adam Eccles. Their input and keen eye for typos helped to create a clean manuscript.

And finally, I'd like to thank my editor, Sian Philips. This is the only part of the book that Sian hasn't edited, so there's bound to be a typo somewhere on this page.

Printed in Great Britain
by Amazon